# THE WORKS OF HONORÉ De BALZAC

‘

# Vautrin

## and
## The Resources of Quinola

### AND OTHER STORIES

UNIVERSITY EDITION

THE
WORKS OF
HONORÉ
De BALZAC

'

# Vautrin

## and

## The Resources of Quinola
### AND OTHER STORIES

With Introductions by
GEORGE SAINTSBURY

UNIVERSITY EDITION

**WILDSIDE PRESS**

# CONTENTS

## PART I

## PART II

# BALZAC AS A DRAMATIST

Honoré de Balzac is known to the world in general as a novel-writer, a producer of romances, in which begin the reign of realism in French fiction. His *Comédie Humaine* is a description of French society, as it existed from the time of the Revolution to that of the Restoration. In this series of stories we find the author engaged in analyzing the manners, motives and external life of the French man and woman in all grades of society. When we open these volumes, we enter a gallery of striking and varied pictures, which glow with all the color, chiaroscuro and life-like detail of a Dutch panel. The power of Balzac is unique as a descriptive writer; his knowledge of the female heart is more profound, and covers a far wider range than anything exhibited by a provincial author, such as Richardson. But he has also the marvelous faculty of suggesting spiritual facts in the life and consciousness of his characters, by the picturesque touches with which he brings before us their external surroundings— the towns, streets and houses in which they dwell; the furniture, ornaments and arrangement of their rooms, and the clothes they wear. He depends upon these details for throwing into relief such a portrait as that of Pons or Madame Hulot. He himself was individualized by his knobbed cane abroad, and his Benedictine habit and statuette of Napoleon at home; but every single one of his creations seems to have in some shape or other a cane, a robe or a decorative attribute, which distinguishes each individual, as if by a badge, from every other member of the company in this Comedy of Life.

(v)

The art of characterization exhibited by the author fasci-
nates us; we gaze and examine as if we were face to face
with real personages, whose passions are laid bare, whose life
is traced, whose countenance is portrayed with miraculousness,
distinctness and verisimilitude. All the phenomena of life in
the camp, the court, the boudoir, the low faubourg, or the
country château are ranged in order, and catalogued. This is
done with relentless audacity, often with a touch of grotesque
exaggeration, but always with almost wearying minuteness.
Sometimes this great writer finds that a description of ac-
tuality fails to give the true spiritual key to a situation, and
he overflows into allegory, or Swedenborgian mysticism, just
as Bastien-Lepage resorts to a coating of actual gilt, in de-
picting that radiant light in his Jeanne d'Arc which flat pig-
ment could not adequately represent.

But this very effort of Balzac to attain realistic characterization has resulted in producing what the ordinary reader
will look upon as a defect in his stories. When we compared
above the stories of this writer to a painting, we had been as
near the truth, if we had likened them to a reflection or photo-
graph of a scene. For in a painting, the artist at his own
will arranges the light and shade and groups, and combines
according to his own fancy the figures and objects which he
finds in nature. He represents not what is, but what might
be, an actual scene. He aims at a specific effect. To this
effect everything is sacrificed, for his work is a synthesis, not
a mere analysis. Balzac does not aim at an effect, above and
independent of his analysis. His sole effort is to emphasize
the facts which his analysis brings to light, and when he has
succeeded in this, the sole end he aims at is attained. Thus
action is less important in his estimation than impression.
His stories are therefore often quite unsymmetrical, even

anecdotic, in construction; some of them are mere episodes, in which the action is irrelevant, and sometimes he boldly ends an elaborate romance without any dramatic dénouement at all. We believe that Honoré de Balzac was the first of European writers to inaugurate the novel without dénouement, and to give to the world examples of the literary torso whose beauty and charm consist not in its completeness, but in the vigor and life-like animation of the lines, features, and contours of a detached trunk.

It is not surprising, therefore, that when we come to study the dramas of Balzac we find that the very qualities that give effectiveness to a stage representation are wanting in them. For the qualities which make a realistic tale impressive render a play intolerable. Thus Balzac's stage pieces are interesting, exciting and vivid in many passages, but they cannot stand the searching glare of the footlights. Balzac, in the first place, looked upon the drama as a department of literature inferior to that of romance, and somewhat cavalierly condescended to the stage without reckoning on either its possibilities or its limitations. He did not take to play-writing because he had exhausted his vein of fiction, but because he was in need of money. This was during the last years of his life. In this period he wrote the five plays which are included in the authorized edition of his works.

Balzac's first play was *Vautrin,* and Vautrin appears as the name of the most astonishing and most original character which Balzac has created and introduced in the five or six greatest novels of the Comedy. So transcendent, superhuman and satanic is Vautrin, Herrera, or Jacques Collin, as he is indifferently called, that a French critic has interpreted this personage as a mere allegorical embodiment of the seductions of Parisian life, as they exist side by side with the potency and resourcefulness of crime in the French metropolis.

Vautrin is described in the *Comédie Humaine* as the tempter and benefactor of Lucien de Rubempré, whom he loves with an intense devotion, and would exploit as a power and influence in the social, literary and political world. The deep-dyed criminal seems to live a life of pleasure, fashion and social rank in the person of this protégé. The abnormal, and in some degree quixotic, nature of this attachment is a purely Balzacian conception, and the contradictions involved in this character, with all the intellectual and physical endowments which pertain to it, are sometimes such as to bring the sublime in perilous proximity to the ridiculous. How such a fantastic creation can be so treated as to do less violence to the laws of artistic harmony and reserve may be seen in Hugo's Valjean, which was undoubtedly suggested by Balzac's Vautrin. In the play of *Vautrin*, the main character, instead of appearing sublime, becomes absurd, and the action is utterly destitute of that plausibility and coherence which should make the most improbable incidents of a play hang together with logical sequence.

Balzac in the *Resources of Quinola* merely reproduces David Séchard, though he places him in the reign of Philip the Second of Spain. He went far out of his way to make Fontanares the first inventor of the steamboat; the improbability of such a supposition quite forfeits the interest of the spectators and, in attempting to effect a love dénouement, he disgusts us by uniting the noble discoverer with the vile Faustine. Even the element of humor is wanting in his portrayal of Quinola—who is a combination of the slave in a Latin comedy and the fool, or Touchstone of Shakespeare.

The play is, however, ingenious, powerful and interesting in many passages.

   *Pamela Giraud* is fantastic and painful in its plot. Balzac's ideal woman, the Pauline of the *Peau de Chagrin,* is here placed in a situation revolting even to a Parisian audience; but the selfish worldliness of the rich and noble is contrasted with the pure disinterestedness of a poor working girl in all of Balzac's strongest, most searching style. The dénouement is well brought about and satisfactory, but scarcely atones for the outrageous nature of the principal situation.

Balzac was especially a novelist of his own period, and the life of his romances is the life he saw going on around him. The principal character in *The Stepmother* is a Napoleonist general typical of many who must have lived in the first half of the nineteenth century. The ruling passion of General de Grandchamp is hatred for those who deserted the cause or forsook the standard of the First Consul. This antipathy is exaggerated by Balzac into murderous hatred, and is the indirect cause of death to the General's daughter, Pauline, and her lover, the son of a soldier of the First Empire. who, by deserting Napoleon, had fallen under the Comte de Grandchamp's ban. The situation is, however, complicated by the guilty passion which Gertrude, the stepmother of Pauline and wife of the General's old age, feels for the lover of Pauline. The main interest of the drama lies in the struggle between these two women, every detail of which is elaborated with true Balzacian gusto and insight. We expect to see virtue triumphant, and Pauline united to the excellent Ferdinand. When they both die of poison, and Gertrude becomes repentant, we feel that the dénoucment is not satisfactory.

The jealousy of the woman and the hatred of the man have
not blended properly.

But there can be no doubt at all that if Balzac had lived,
he might have turned out a successful playwright. When he
began his career as a dramatic writer he was like a musician
taking up an unfamiliar instrument, an organist who was
trying the violin, or a painter working in an unknown me-
dium. His last written play was his best. Fortunately,
the plot did not deal with any of those desperate love passions
which Balzac in his novels has analyzed and described with
such relentless and even brutal frankness. It is filled throughout with a genial humanity, as bright and as expressive as
that which fills the atmosphere of *She Stoops to Conquer* or
*A School for Scandal*. The characters are neither demons,
like Cousin Betty, nor reckless debauchees, like Gertrude in
*The Stepmother*. The whole motif is comic. Molière himself might have lent a touch of his refined and fragrant wit
to the composition; and the situation is one which the author
could realize from experience, but had only learned to regard
from a humorous standpoint in the ripeness of his premature
old age. Balzac makes money rule in his stories, as the most
potent factor of social life. He describes poverty as the
supreme evil, and wealth as the object of universal aspiration.
In line with this attitude comes *Mercadet* with his trials and
schemes. Scenes of ridiculous surprises succeed each other
till by the return of the absconder with a large fortune, the
greedy, usurious creditors are at last paid in full, and poetic
justice is satisfied by the marriage of Julie to the poor man
of her choice.

EPIPHANIUS WILSON.

# INTRODUCTION

The greatest fame of Balzac will rest in the future, as in the past, upon his novels and short stories. These comprise the bulk of his work and his most noteworthy effort—an effort so pronounced as to hide all side-excursions. For this reason his chief side-excursion—into the realms of the drama—has been almost entirely overlooked. Indeed, many of his readers are unaware that he ever wrote plays, while others have passed them by with the idea that they were slight, devoid of interest, and to be classified with the *Works of Youth*. Complete editions—so-called—of Balzac's works have fostered this belief by omitting the dramas; and it has remained for the present edition to include, for the first time, this valuable material, not alone for its own sake, but also in order to show the many-sided author as he was, in all his efficiencies and occasional deficiencies.

For those readers who now make the acquaintance of the dramas, we would say briefly that the Balzac *Théâtre* comprises five plays—*Vautrin, Les Ressources de Quinola, Pamela Giraud, La Marâtre,* and *Mercadet*. These plays are in prose. They do not belong to the apprenticeship period of the *Works of Youth*, but were produced in the heyday of his powers, revealing the mature man and the subtle analyst of character, not at his best, but at a point far above his worst. True, their production aroused condemnation on the part of many contemporary dramatic critics, and were the source of much annoyance and little financial gain to their creator. But this is certainly no criterion for their workmanship. Balzac defied many tenets. He even had the hardihood to dispense with the *claqueurs* at the first night of *Les Ressources de Quinola.* Naturally the play proceeded coldly without the presence of professional applauders. But Balzac declared himself satisfied with the warm praise of such men as Hugo and Lamartine, who recognized the strength of the lines.

The five plays were presented at various times, at the best theatres of Paris, and by the most capable companies. One of them, *Mercadet,* is still revived perennially; and we are of opinion that this play would prove attractive to-day upon an American stage. The action and plots of all these dramas are quite apart from the structure of the *Comédie Humaine.* Vautrin and his "pals" are the only characters borrowed from that series, but his part in the titular play is new beyond the initial situation.

The *Première Édition* of the *Théâtre Complet* was published in a single duodecimo volume from the press of Giraud & Dagneau in 1853. It contained: *Vautrin, Les Ressources de Quinola, Pamela Giraud,* and *La Marâtre.* All prefaces were omitted. *Mercadet* was not given with them in this printing, but appeared in a separate duodecimo, under the title of *Le Faiseur,* from the press of Cadot, in 1853. The next edition of the *Théâtre Complet,* in 1855, reinstated the prefaces. It was not until 1865 that *Mercadet* joined the other four in a single volume published by Mme. Houssiaux.

*Vautrin,* a drama in five acts, was presented for the first time in the Porte-Saint-Martin theatre, March 14, 1840. The preface, dated May 1, 1840, was not ready in time for the printing of the first edition, which was a small octavo volume published by Delloye & Tresse. It appeared in the second

edition, two months later. The dedication was to Laurent-
Jan.[1] The play was a distinct popular failure, but its construction and temper combine to explain this. At the same
time it makes interesting reading; and it will prove especially
entertaining to readers of the *Comédie Humaine* who have
dreaded and half-admired the redoubtable law-breaker, who
makes his initial entrance in *Le Père Goriot* and plays so important a part in *Illusions Perdues,* and *Splendeurs et Misères des Courtisanes.* Here we find Vautrin in a favorite
situation. He becomes the powerful protector of an unknown
young man—much as he picked up Lucien de Rubempré
in *Illusions Perdues,* and attempted to aid Rastignac
in *Le Père Goriot*—and devotes all his sinister craft to
his protégé's material interests. The playwright is careful to
preserve some degree of the young man's self-respect. Chance
favors the two by providing the unknown hero with worthy
parents; and Vautrin's schemes unexpectedly work out for
good. As in the story of *Père Goriot* again, Vautrin, after
furthering matrimonial deals and other quasi-benevolent projects, ends in the clutches of the law. Of Raoul little need be
said. He is the foil for his dread protector and he is saved
from dishonor by a narrow margin. The scene is laid at
Paris, just after the second accession of the House of Bour-
bon, in 1816. Titles and families are in some confusion on
account of the change of dynasties. It is therefore an oppor-
tune time for Vautrin to manufacture scutcheons as occasion
may demand. Since this story of Vautrin is not included in
the *Comédie,* it will not be found among the biographical
facts recorded in the *Repertory.*

*Les Ressources de Quinola,* a comedy in a prologue and

[1] *See* "Jan" in Repertory.

five acts, was presented at the Théâtre de l'Odéon, Paris,
March 19, 1842. Souverain published it in an octavo volume.
Balzac was disposed to complain bitterly of the treatment
this play received (note his preface), but of it may be said,
as in the case of its predecessor, that it makes better reading
than it must have made acting, for the scenes are loosely
constructed and often illogical. Our playwright yet betrays
the amateur touch. It is regrettable, too, for he chose an excellent theme and setting. The time is near the close of the
sixteenth century, under the rule of Philip II. of Spain and
the much-dreaded Inquisition. An inventor, a pupil of
Galileo, barely escapes the Holy Office because of having discovered the secret of the steamboat. Referring to the preface
again, we find Balzac maintaining, in apparent candor, that
he had historic authority for the statement that a boat propelled by steam-machinery had been in existence for a short
time in those days. Be that as it may, one can accept the
statement for dramatic purposes; and the story of the early
inventor's struggles and his servant's "resources" is promising
enough to leave but one regret—that the master-romancer did
not make a novel instead of a play out of the material.
Though this is called a comedy, it contains more than one
element of tragedy in it, and the tone is moody and satirical.
The climax, with its abortive love episode, is anything but satisfactory.

*Pamela Giraud,* a drama in five acts, was first presented in
the Gaîté Théâtre, Paris, September 26, 1843. It was published by Marchand in a single octavo volume, in the same
year. The action takes place at Paris in 1815-24, during the
Napoleonic conspiracies, under Louis XVIII. The Restoration has brought its strong undertow of subdued loyalty for

the Corsican—an undertow of plots, among the old soldiers particularly, which for several years were of concern to more than one throne outside of France. The hero of this play becomes involved in one of the conspiracies, and it is only by the public sacrifice of the young girl Pamela's honor, that he is rescued. Then ensues a clash between policy and duty— a theme so congenial to Balzac, and here handled with characteristic deftness. We notice, also, a distinct improvement in workmanship. Scenes move more easily; dramatic values become coherent; characters stand out from the "chorus" on the stage. Pamela is a flesh-and-blood girl; Jules is real; Joseph is comically individual; Dupré is almost a strong creation, and nearly every one of the other principals is individual.

The discussion of the other two plays is reserved for the succeeding volume, in which they appear. We shall there notice still greater evidences of the evolution of the playwright.

J. WALKER McSPADDEN.

# VAUTRIN

## A DRAMA IN FIVE ACTS

Presented for the First Time at the Porte-Saint-Martin Théâtre,
Paris, March 14, 1840

## AUTHOR'S PREFACE

It is difficult for the playwright to put himself, five days after the first presentation of his piece, in the situation in which he felt himself on the morning after the event; but it is still more difficult to write a preface to *Vautrin*, to which every one has written his own. The single utterance of the author will infallibly prove inferior to so vast a number of divergent expressions. The report of a cannon is never so effective as a display of fireworks.

Must the author explain his work? Its only possible commentator is M. Frédérick Lemaître.

Must he complain of the injunction which delayed the presentation of his play? That would be to betray ignorance of his time and country. Petty tyranny is the besetting sin of constitutional governments; it is thus they are disloyal to themselves, and on the other hand, who are so cruel as the weak? The present government is a spoilt child, and does what it likes, excepting that it fails to secure the public weal or the public vote.

Must he proceed to prove that *Vautrin* is as innocent a work as a drama of Berquin's? To inquire into the morality or immorality of the stage would imply servile submission to the stupid Prudhommes who bring the matter in question.

Shall he attack the newspapers? He could do no more than declare that they have verified by their conduct all he ever said about them.

Yet in the midst of the disaster which the energy of government has caused, but which the slightest sagacity in the world might have prevented, the author has found some compensation in the testimony of public sympathy which has been given him. M. Victor Hugo, among others, has shown himself as steadfast in friendship as he is pre-eminent in poetry; and the present writer has the greater happiness in publishing the good will of M. Hugo, inasmuch as the enemies of that distinguished man have no hesitation in blackening his character.

Let me conclude by saying that *Vautrin* is two months old, and in the rush of Parisian life a novelty of two months has survived a couple of centuries. The real preface to *Vautrin* will be found in the play, *Richard-Cœur-d'Eponge,*[1] which the administration permits to be acted in order to save the prolific stage of Porte-Saint-Martin from being overrun by children.

PARIS, *May* 1, 1840.

[1] A play never enacted or printed.

# PERSONS OF THE PLAY

JACQUES COLLIN, known as Vautrin.

THE DUC DE MONTSOREL.

THE MARQUIS ALBERT DE MONTSOREL, son to Montsorel.

RAOUL DE FRESCAS.

CHARLES BLONDET, known as the Chevalier de Saint-Charles.

FRANÇOIS CADET, known as the Philosopher.

FIL-DE-SOIE.

BUTEUX.

PHILIPPE BOULARD, known as Lafouraille.

A POLICE OFFICER.

JOSEPH BONNET, footman to the Duchess de Montsorel.

THE DUCHESSE DE MONTSOREL (LOUISE DE VAUDREY).

MADEMOISELLE DE VAUDREY, aunt to the Duchesse de Montsorel.

THE DUCHESSE DE CHRISTOVAL.

INEZ DE CHRISTOVAL, PRINCESSE D'ARJOS.

FÉLICITÉ, maid to the Duchesse de Montsorel.

SERVANTS, GENDARMES, DETECTIVES, AND OTHERS.

SCENE: *Paris.* TIME: 1816, *after the second return of the Bourbons.*

Vautrin.

# VAUTRIN

## ACT I.

### SCENE FIRST.

*(A room in the house of the Duc de Montsorel.)*

THE DUCHESSE DE MONTSOREL AND MADEMOISELLE DE
VAUDREY.

##### THE DUCHESS

Ah! So you have been waiting for me! How very good
of you!

##### MLLE. DE VAUDREY

What is the matter, Louise? This is the first time in the
twelve years of our mutual mourning, that I have seen you
cheerful. Knowing you as I do, it makes me alarmed.

##### THE DUCHESS

I cannot help showing my happiness, and you, who have
shared all my sorrows, alone can understand my rapture at
the faintest gleam of hope.

##### MLLE. DE VAUDREY

Have you come upon any traces of your lost son?

##### THE DUCHESS

He is found!

MLLE. DE VAUDREY

Impossible! When you find out your error it will add to your anguish.

THE DUCHESS

A child who is dead has but a tomb in the heart of his mother; but the child who has been stolen, is still living in that heart, dear aunt.

MLLE. DE VAUDREY

Suppose you were overheard!

THE DUCHESS

I should not care. I am setting out on a new life, and I feel strong enough to resist even the tyranny of De Montsorel.

MLLE. DE VAUDREY

After twenty-two years of mourning, what possible occurrence can give you ground for hope?

THE DUCHESS

I have much more than hope! After the king's reception I went to the Spanish ambassador's, where I was introduced to Madame de Christoval. There I saw a young man who resembled me, and had my voice. Do you see what I mean? If I came home late it was because I remained spellbound in the room, and could not leave until he had gone.

MLLE. DE VAUDREY

Yet what slight warrant you had for your elation!

THE DUCHESS

Is not a revelation such as that more than sufficient warrant for the rapture of a mother's heart? At the sight of that young stranger a flame seemed to dart before my eyes;

his glance gave me new life; I felt happy once more. If he were not my son, my feelings would be quite unaccountable.

### MLLE. DE VAUDREY

You must have betrayed yourself!

### THE DUCHESS

Yes, perhaps I did! People doubtless noticed us; but I was carried away by an uncontrollable impulse; I saw no one but him, I wished to hear him talk, and he talked with me, and told me his age. He is twenty-three, the same age as Fernand!

### MLLE. DE VAUDREY

And was the duke present?

### THE DUCHESS

Could I give a thought to my husband? I listened only to this young man, who was talking with Inez. I believe they are in love with each other.

### MLLE. DE VAUDREY

Inez, who is engaged to your son, the marquis? And do you think the warm reception given by her to his son's rival could escape the duke's notice?

### THE DUCHESS

Of course not, and I quite see the dangers to which Fernand is exposed. But I must not detain you longer; I could talk to you about him till morning. You shall see him. I have told him to come at the hour the duke goes to the king's, and then we will question him about his childhood.

### MLLE. DE VAUDREY

For goodness' sake, calm yourself; you will never be able to sleep this night. And send Félicité to bed, she is not accustomed to these late hours. (*She rings the bell.*)

FÉLICITÉ (*entering the room*)

His grace the duke has come in with his lordship the marquis.

THE DUCHESS

I have already told you, Félicité, never to inform me of his grace's movements. (*Exit Félicité.*)

MLLE. DE VAUDREY

I should hate to rob you of an illusion which causes you such happiness; but when I see the height of expectation to which you have soared, I fear a terrible fall for you. The soul, like the body, is bruised by a fall from an excessive height, and you must excuse my saying that I tremble for you.

THE DUCHESS

While you fear the effect of despair for me, I fear that of overwhelming joy.

MLLE. DE VAUDREY (*watching the duchess go out*)

If she should be deceived, she might lose her senses.

THE DUCHESS (*re-entering the room*)

Fernand, dear aunt, calls himself Raoul de Frescas. (*Exit.*)

---

*SCENE SECOND.*

MLLE. DE VAUDREY (*alone*)

She does not see that the recovery of her son would be a miracle. All mothers believe in miracles. We must keep watch over her. A look, a word might ruin her, for if she is right, if God restores her son to her, she is on the brink of a catastrophe more frightful even than the deception she has been practicing. Does she think she can dissemble under the eyes of women?

---

## SCENE THIRD.

### MLLE. DE VAUDREY AND FÉLICITÉ.

#### MLLE. DE VAUDREY
Already here?

#### FÉLICITÉ
Her grace the duchess dismissed me early.

#### MLLE. DE VAUDREY
Has my niece given you no orders for the morning?

#### FÉLICITÉ
None, madame.

#### MLLE. DE VAUDREY
A young man, named M. Raoul de Frescas, is coming to call upon me towards noon; he may possibly ask for the duchess, but you must instruct Joseph to bring him to my apartment. (*Exit.*)

---

## SCENE FOURTH.

### FÉLICITÉ (*alone*)

A young man for her? Not a bit of it. I always said that there was some motive in my lady's retired way of living; she is rich, she is handsome, yet the duke does not love her; and now the first time she goes out, a young man comes next day to see her, and her aunt wishes to receive him. They keep me in the dark; I am neither trusted nor tipped. If this is the way chambermaids are to be treated under the new government, I don't know what will become of us. (*A sidedoor opens, two men are seen, and the door is immediately closed again.*) At any rate we shall have a look at the young man. (*Exit.*)

---

## SCENE FIFTH.

### JOSEPH AND VAUTRIN.

(*Vautrin wears a tan-colored overcoat, trimmed with fur, over the black evening dress of a foreign diplomatic minister.*)

#### JOSEPH

That blasted girl! We would have been down in our luck if she had seen us.

#### VAUTRIN

You mean *you* would have been down in your luck; you take pretty good care not to be caught again, don't you? I suppose then that you enjoy peace of mind in this house?

#### JOSEPH

That I do, for honesty I find to be the best policy.

#### VAUTRIN

And do you quite approve of honesty?

#### JOSEPH

Oh, yes, so long as the place and the wages suit me.

#### VAUTRIN

I see you are doing well, my boy. You take little and often, you save, you even have the honesty to lend a trifle at interest. That's all right, but you cannot imagine what pleasure it gives me to see one of my old acquaintances filling an honorable

position. You have succeeded in doing so; your faults are
but negative and therefore half virtues. I myself once had
vices; I regret them as things of the past; I have nothing but
dangers and struggles to interest me. Mine is the life of an
Indian hemmed in by enemies, and I am fighting in defence
of my own scalp.

JOSEPH

And what of mine?

VAUTRIN

Yours? Ah! you are right to ask that. Well, whatever
happens to me, you have the word of Jacques Collin that he
will never compromise you. But you must obey me in everything!

JOSEPH

In everything? But—

VAUTRIN

There are no buts with me. If there is any dark business
to be done I have my "trusties" and old allies. Have you been
long in this place?

JOSEPH

The duchess took me for her footman when she went with
the court to Ghent, last year, and I am trusted by both the
ladies of the house.

VAUTRIN

That's the ticket! I need a few points with regard to these
Montsorels. What do you know about them?

JOSEPH

Nothing.

VAUTRIN (aside)

He is getting a little too honest. Does he think he knows
nothing about them? Well, you cannot talk for five minutes
with a man without drawing something out of him. (Aloud)
Whose room is this?

JOSEPH

The salon of her grace the duchess, and these are her apartments; those of the duke are on the floor above. The suite
of the marquis, their only son, is below, and looks on the
court.

VAUTRIN

I asked you for impressions of all the keys of the duke's
study. Where are they?

JOSEPH (*hesitatingly*)

Here they are.

VAUTRIN

Every time I purpose coming here you will find a cross in
chalk on the garden gate; every night you must examine the
place. Virtue reigns here, and the hinges of that gate are very
rusty; but a Louis XVIII. can never be a Louis XV! Good-
bye—I'll come back to-morrow night. (*Aside*) I must rejoin
my people at the Christoval house.

JOSEPH (*aside*)

Since this devil of a fellow has found me out, I have been
on tenter-hooks—

VAUTRIN (*coming back from the door*)

The duke then does not live with his wife?

JOSEPH

They quarreled twenty years ago.

VAUTRIN

What about?

JOSEPH

Not even their own son can say.

VAUTRIN

And why was your predecessor dismissed?

JOSEPH

I cannot say. I was not acquainted with him. They did
not set up an establishment here until after the king's second
return.

VAUTRIN (*aside*)

Such are the advantages of the new social order; masters
and servants are bound together by no ties; they feel no
mutual attachment, exchange no secrets, and so give no
ground for betrayal. (*To Joseph*) Any spicy stories at
meal-times?

JOSEPH

Never before the servants.

VAUTRIN

What is thought of them in the servants' hall?

JOSEPH

The duchess is considered a saint.

VAUTRIN

Poor woman! And the duke?

JOSEPH

He is an egotist.

VAUTRIN

Yes, a statesman. (*Aside*) The duke must have secrets, and
we must look into that. Every great aristocrat has some paltry
passion by which he can be led; and if I once get control of
him, his son, necessarily—(*To Joseph*) What is said about
the marriage of the Marquis de Montsorel and Inez de Christoval?

JOSEPH

I haven't heard a word. The duchess seems to take very
little interest in it.

VAUTRIN

And she has only one son! That seems hardly natural.

JOSEPH

Between ourselves, I believe she doesn't love her son.

VAUTRIN

I am obliged to draw this word from your throat, as if it were the cork in a bottle of Bordeaux. There is, I perceive, some mystery in this house. Here is a mother, a Duchesse de Montsorel, who does not love her son, her only son! Who is her confessor?

JOSEPH

She keeps her religious observances a profound secret.

VAUTRIN

Good—I shall soon know everything. Secrets are like young girls, the more you conceal them, the sooner they are discovered. I will send two of my rascals to the Church of St. Thomas Aquinas. They won't work out their salvation in that way, but they'll work out something else.—Good-bye.

---

## SCENE SIXTH.

JOSEPH (*alone*)

He is an old friend—and that is the worst nuisance in the world. He will make me lose my place. Ah, if I were not afraid of being poisoned like a dog by Jacques Collin, who is quite capable of the act, I would tell all to the duke; but in this vile world, every man for himself, and I am not going to pay another man's debt. Let the duke settle with Jacques; I am going to bed. What noise is that? The duchess is getting up. What does she want? I must listen. (*He goes out, leaving the door slightly ajar.*)

## *SCENE SEVENTH.*

THE DUCHESS DE MONTSOREL (*alone*)

Where can I hide the certificate of my son's birth? (*She reads*) "Valencia.... July, 1793." An unlucky town for me! Fernand was actually born seven months after my marriage, by one of those fatalities that give ground for shameful accusations! I shall ask my aunt to carry this certificate in her pocket, until I can deposit it in some place of safety. The duke would ransack my rooms for it, and the whole police are at his service. Government refuses nothing to a man high in favor. If Joseph saw me going to Mlle. de Vaudrey's apartments at this hour, the whole house would hear of it. Ah— I am alone in the world, alone with all against me, a prisoner in my own house!

---

## *SCENE EIGHTH.*

THE DUCHESSE DE MONTSOREL AND MLLE. DE VAUDREY.

### THE DUCHESS

I see that you find it as impossible to sleep as I do.

### MLLE. DE VAUDREY

Louise, my child, I only rose to rid you of a dream, the awakening from which will be deplorable. I consider it my duty to distract you from your insane fancies. The more I think of what you told me the more is my sympathy aroused. But I am compelled to tell you the truth, cruel as it is; beyond doubt the duke has placed Fernand in some compromising situation, so as to make it impossible for him to retrieve his position in the world to which you belong. The young man you saw cannot be your son.

THE DUCHESS

Ah, you never knew Fernand! but I knew him, and in whatever place he is, his life has an influence on mine. I have seen him a thousand times—

MLLE. DE VAUDREY

In your dreams!

THE DUCHESS

Fernand has the blood of the Montsorels and the Vaudreys in his veins. The place to which he was born he is able to take; everything gives way before him wherever he appears. If he became a soldier, he is to-day a colonel. My son is proud, he is handsome, people like him! I am sure he is beloved. Do not contradict me, dear aunt; Fernand still lives; if not, then the duke has broken faith, and I know he values too highly the virtues of his race to disgrace them.

MLLE. DE VAUDREY

But are not honor and a husband's vengeance dearer to him than his faith as a gentleman?

THE DUCHESS

Ah! You make me shudder.

MLLE. DE VAUDREY

You know very well, Louise, that pride of race is hereditary with the Montsorels, as it is with the Mortemarts.

THE DUCHESS

I know it too well! The doubt cast upon his child's legitimacy has almost crazed him.

MLLE. DE VAUDREY

You are wrong there. The duke has a warm heart, and a cool head; in all matters that concern the sentiments on which

they live, men of that temper act promptly in carrying out
their ideas.

### THE DUCHESS

But, dear aunt, do you know at what price he has granted
me the life of Fernand? Haven't I paid dearly for the assurance that his days were not to be shortened? If I had persisted in maintaining my innocence I should have brought
certain death upon him; I have sacrificed my good name to
save my son. Any mother would have done as much. You
were taking care of my property here; I was alone in a foreign
land, and was the prey of ill-health, fever, and with none to
counsel me, and I lost my head; for, since that time it has
constantly occurred to me that the duke would never have
carried out his threats. In making the sacrifice I did, I knew
that Fernand would be poor and destitute, without a name,
and dwelling in an unknown land; but I knew also that his
life would be safe, and that some day I should recover him,
even if I had to search the whole world over! I felt so cheerful as I came in that I forgot to give you the certificate of
Fernand's birth, which the Spanish ambassador's wife has at
last obtained for me; carry it about with you until you can
place it in the hands of your confessor.

### MLLE. DE VAUDREY

The duke must certainly have learnt the measures you
have taken in this matter, and woe be to your son! Since
his return he has been very busy, and is still busy about
something.

### THE DUCHESS

If I shake off the disgrace with which he has tried to cover
me, if I give up shedding tears in silence, be assured that
nothing can bend me from my purpose. I am no longer in
Spain or England, at the mercy of a diplomat crafty as a
tiger, who during the whole time of our emigration was reading the thoughts of the heart's inmost recesses, and with invisi-
ble spies surrounding my life as by a network of steel; turning

my servants into jailers, and keeping me prisoner in the
most horrible of prisons, an open house! I am in France, I
have found you once more, I hold my place at court, I can
speak my mind there; I shall learn what has become of the
Vicomte de Langeac, I shall prove that since the Tenth of
August[1] we have never met, I shall inform the king of the
crime committed by a father against a son who is the heir of
two noble houses. I am a woman, I am Duchesse de Montsorel, I am a mother! We are rich, we have a virtuous priest
for an adviser; right is on our side, and if I have demanded
the certificate of my son's birth—

---

## SCENE NINTH.

THE SAME PERSONS, AND THE DUC DE MONTSOREL (*who
enters as the duchess pronounces the last sentence*).

### THE DUKE

It is only for the purpose of handing it to me.

### THE DUCHESS

Since when have you ventured to enter my apartment without previously sending me word and asking my leave?

### THE DUKE

Since you broke the agreement we made. You swore to
take no steps to find this—your son. This was the sole condition on which I promised to let him live.

### THE DUCHESS

And is it not much more honorable to violate such an oath,
than to remain faithful to all others?

[1] A noteworthy date in French history, August 10, 1792; the day of the storming
of the Tuileries.—J. W. M.

THE DUKE

We are henceforth both of us released from our engagements.

THE DUCHESS

Have you, up to the present day, respected yours?

THE DUKE

I have, madame.

THE DUCHESS

Listen to him, aunt, and bear witness to this declaration.

MLLE. DE VAUDREY

But has it never occurred to you, my dear sir, that Louise
is innocent?

THE DUKE

Of course you think so, Mlle. de Vaudrey. And what would
not I give to share your opinion! The duchess has had twenty
years in which to prove to me her innocence.

THE DUCHESS

For twenty years you have wrung my heart without pity
and without intermission.

THE DUKE

Madame, unless you hand me this certificate, your Fernand
will have serious cause for alarm. As soon as you returned
to France you secured the document, and are trying to employ
it as a weapon against me. You desire to obtain for your son
a fortune and a name which do not belong to him; to secure
his admission into a family, whose race has up to my time
been kept pure by wives of stainless reputation, a family
which has never formed a single mesalliance—

THE DUCHESS

And which will be worthily represented by your son Albert.

### The Duke

Be careful what you say, for you waken in me terrible memories. And your last word shows me that you will not shrink from causing a scandal that will overwhelm all of us with shame. Shall we air in the public courts past occurrences which will show that I am not free from reproach, while you are infamous? (*He turns to Mlle. de Vaudrey*) She cannot have told you everything, dear aunt? She was in love with Viscount Langeac; I knew it, and respected her love; I was so young! The viscount came to me; being without hope of inheriting a fortune, and the last representative of his house, he unselfishly offered to give up Louise de Vaudrey. I trusted in their mutual generosity, and accepted her as a pure woman from his hands. Ah! I would have given my life for her, and I have proved it! The wretched man performed prodigies of valor on the Tenth of August, and called down upon himself the rage of the mob; I put him under the protection of some of my people; he was, however, discovered and taken to the Abbaye. As soon as I learned his predicament, I gave into the hands of a certain Boulard all the money I had collected for our flight! I induced Boulard to join the Septembrists in order to save the viscount from death; I procured his escape! (*To the duchess*) He paid me back well, did he not? I was young, madly in love, impetuous, yet I never crushed the boy! You have to-day made me the same requital for my pity, as your lover made for my trust in him. Well—things remain just as they were twenty years ago excepting that the time for pity is past. And I will repeat what I said to you then: Forget your son, and he shall live.

### Mlle. de Vaudrey

And shall her sufferings during those twenty years count for nothing?

### The Duke

A great crime calls for a great atonement.

### THE DUCHESS

Ah—if you take my grief for a sign of remorse, I will again protest to you, I am innocent! No! Langeac never betrayed your confidence; it was not for his king alone he went to his death, and from the fatal day on which he bade me farewell and surrendered me to you, I have never seen him again.

### THE DUKE

You purchased the life of your son by making an exactly contrary declaration.

### THE DUCHESS

Can a compact dictated by terror be looked upon as an avowal of guilt?

### THE DUKE

Do you intend to give that certificate of birth?

### THE DUCHESS

It is no longer in my possession.

### THE DUKE

I will no longer answer then for your son's safety.

### THE DUCHESS

Have you weighed well the consequences of this threat?

### THE DUKE

You ought to know me by this time.

### THE DUCHESS

The trouble is that you do not know me. You will no longer answer for my son's safety? Indeed—but you had better look after that of your own son. Albert is a guarantee for the life of Fernand. If you keep watch on my proceedings, I shall set a watch on yours; if you rely upon the police of the realm, I have resources of my own, and the assistance of God. If you deal a blow at Fernand, beware of what may happen to Albert. A blow for a blow!—That is final.

### THE DUKE

You are in your own house, madame. I forgot myself. Pray pardon me. I was wrong.

### THE DUCHESS

You are more a gentleman than your son; when he flies into a rage he begs no one's pardon, not he!

### THE DUKE (*aside*)

Has her resignation up to this time been nothing but a pretence? Has she been waiting for the present opportunity to speak? Women who are guided by the advice of bigots travel underground, like volcanic fires, and only reveal themselves when they break out. She knows my secret, I have *lost sight of her son, and my defeat is imminent.* (*Exit.*)

---

## SCENE TENTH.

### MLLE. DE VAUDREY AND THE DUCHESS

### MLLE. DE VAUDREY

Louise, you love the child you have never seen, and hate him who is before your eyes. Ah! you must tell the reason of your hatred for Albert, if you would retain my esteem and my affection.

### THE DUCHESS

Not a word on that subject.

### MLLE. DE VAUDREY

The calm way in which your husband remarks your aver- sion for your son is astonishing.

THE DUCHESS

He is accustomed to it.

MLLE. DE VAUDREY

Yet you could never show yourself a bad mother, could
you?

THE DUCHESS

A bad mother? No. (*She reflects.*) I cannot make up
my mind to forfeit your affection. (*She draws her aunt to
her side.*) Albert is not my son.

MLLE. DE VAUDREY

Can a stranger have usurped the place, the name, the title,
the property of the real child?

THE DUCHESS

No, not a stranger, but his son. After the fatal night on
which Fernand was carried off from me, an eternal separation
between the duke and myself took place. The wife in me was
as cruelly outraged as the mother. But still I purchased
from him peace of mind.

MLLE. DE VAUDREY

I do not understand your meaning.

THE DUCHESS

I allowed the duke to present this Albert, child of a Spanish courtesan, as if he were mine. The duke desired an heir.
Amid the confusion wrought in Spain by the French Revolution the trick escaped notice. Are you surprised that my
blood boils at the sight of this strange woman's child occupying the place of the lawful heir?

MLLE. DE VAUDREY

Now I can deeply sympathize with your hopes; ah! how

glad I should be if you were right in your suspicions and this young man were indeed your son. But what is the matter with you?

### THE DUCHESS

He is, I fear, ruined; for I have brought him under the notice of his father, who will— But stay, something must be done! I must find out where he lives, and warn him not to come here to-morrow morning.

### MLLE. DE VAUDREY

Leave the house at this hour! Louise, you are mad!

### THE DUCHESS

Come, we must save him at any price.

### MLLE. DE VAUDREY

What do you propose doing?

### THE DUCHESS

Neither of us can leave the house to-morrow without being noticed. We must forestall the duke by bribing my chambermaid.

### MLLE. DE VAUDREY

Louise, would you resort to such means as this?

### THE DUCHESS

If Raoul is the son disclaimed by his father, the child over whom I have mourned for the last twenty years, I must show them what a wife, a mother, who has been wrongly accused, can do!

*Curtain to the First Act.*

# ACT II.

## SCENE FIRST.

*(Scene the same as in preceding act.)*

---

THE DUC DE MONTSOREL AND JOSEPH.

JOSEPH (*who is just finishing tidying the room, aside*)

So late to bed, so early to rise, and already in madame's apartment. Something is up. Can that devil of a Jacques have been right?

### THE DUKE

Joseph, I am not at home excepting to one person. If he comes, you will show him up. I refer to Monsieur de Saint-Charles. Find out whether your mistress will see me. (*Exit Joseph.*) The awakening of a maternal instinct, which I thought had been utterly extinguished in her heart, amazes me beyond measure. The secret struggle in which she is engaged must at once be put a stop to. So long as Louise was resigned our life was not intolerable; but disputes like this would render it extremely disagreeable. I was able to control my wife so long as we were abroad, but in this country my only power over her lies in skillful handling, and a display of authority. I shall tell everything to the king. I shall submit myself to his dictation, and Madame de Montsorel must be compelled to submit. I must however bide my time. The detective, whom I am to employ, if he is clever, will soon find out the cause of this revolt; I shall see whether the duchess is merely deceived by a resemblance, or whether she has seen her son. For myself I must confess to having lost sight of him since my agents reported his disappearance twelve years ago. I was very much excited last night. I must be more discreet. If I keep quiet she will be put off her guard and reveal her secrets.

JOSEPH (*re-entering the room*)

Her grace the duchess has not yet rung for her maid.

THE DUKE

Very well.

---

## SCENE SECOND.

### THE PRECEDING AND FÉLICITÉ.

(*To explain his presence in his wife's room, the duke looks over articles lying on the table, and discovers a letter in a book.*)

THE DUKE (*reading*)

"To Mlle. Inez de Christoval." (*Aside*) Why should my wife have concealed a letter of such slight importance? She no doubt wrote it after our quarrel. Is it concerning Raoul? This letter must not go to the Christoval house.

FÉLICITÉ (*looking for the letter in the book*)

Now, where is that letter of madame's? Can she have forgotten it?

THE DUKE

Aren't you looking for a letter?

FÉLICITÉ

Yes, your grace.

THE DUKE

Isn't this it?

FÉLICITÉ

The very one, your grace,

### THE DUKE

It is astonishing that you should leave the very hour your mistress must need your services; she is getting up.

### FÉLICITÉ

Her grace the duchess has Thérèse; and besides I am going out by her orders.

### THE DUKE

Very good. I did not wish to interfere with you.

---

## SCENE THIRD.

THE PRECEDING, AND BLONDET, ALIAS THE CHEVALIER DE SAINT-CHARLES.

(*Joseph and Saint-Charles walk together from the centre door, and eye each other attentively.*)

### JOSEPH (*aside*)

The look of that man is very distasteful to me. (*To the duke*) The Chevalier de Saint-Charles. (*The duke signs to Saint-Charles to approach, and examines his appearance.*)

### SAINT-CHARLES (*giving him a letter, aside*)

Does he know my antecedents, or will he simply recognize me as Saint-Charles?

### THE DUKE

My dear sir—

### SAINT-CHARLES

I am to be merely Saint-Charles.

### THE DUKE

You are recommended to me as a man whose ability, if it had fair scope, would be called genius.

### SAINT-CHARLES

If his grace the duke will give me an opportunity, I will prove myself worthy of that flattering opinion.

### THE DUKE

You shall have one at once.

### SAINT-CHARLES

What are your commands?

### THE DUKE

You see that maid. She is going to leave the house. I do not wish to hinder her doing so; yet she must not cross the threshold, until she receives a fresh order. (*Calls her*) Félicité!

### FÉLICITÉ

What is it, your grace? (*The duke gives her the letter. Exit Félicité.*)

### SAINT-CHARLES (*to Joseph*)

I recognize you, I know all about you: See that this maid remains in the house with the letter, and I will not recognize you, and will know nothing of you, and will let you stay here so long as you behave yourself.

### JOSEPH (*aside*)

This fellow on one side, and Jacques Collin on the other! Well, I must try to serve them both honestly. (*Exit Joseph, in pursuit of Félicité.*)

---

## SCENE FOURTH.

### THE DUKE AND SAINT-CHARLES.

### SAINT-CHARLES

Your grace's commands are obeyed. Do you wish to know the contents of the letter?

### THE DUKE

Why, my dear sir, the power you seem to exercise is something terrible and wonderful.

### SAINT-CHARLES

You gave me absolute authority in the matter, and I used it well.

### THE DUKE

And what if you had abused it?

### SAINT-CHARLES

That would have been impossible, for such a course would ruin me.

### THE DUKE

How is it that men endowed with such faculties are found employing them in so lowly a sphere?

### SAINT-CHARLES

Everything is against our rising above it; we protect our protectors, we learn too many honorable secrets, and are kept in ignorance of too many shameful ones to be liked by people, and render such important services to others that they can only shake off the obligation by speaking ill of us. People think that things are only words with us; refinement is thus mere silliness, honor a sham, and acts of treachery mere diplomacy. We are the confidants of many who yet leave us much to guess at. Our programme consists in thinking and acting, finding out the past from the present, ordering and arranging the future in the pettiest details, as I am about to do—and, in short, in doing a hundred things that might strike dismay to a man of no mean ability. When once our end is gained, words become things once more, and people begin to suspect that possibly we are infamous scoundrels.

THE DUKE

There may be some justice in all this, but I do not suppose you expect to change the opinion of the world, or even mine?

SAINT-CHARLES

I should be a great fool if I did. I don't care about changing another man's opinion; what I do want to change is my own position.

THE DUKE

According to you that would be very easy, wouldn't it?

SAINT-CHARLES

Why not, your grace? Let some one set me to play the spy over cabinets, instead of raking up the secrets of private families. Instead of dogging the footsteps of shady characters, let them put me in charge of the craftiest diplomats. Instead of pandering to the vilest passions, let me serve the government. I should be delighted to play a modest part in a great movement. And what a devoted servant your grace would have in me!

THE DUKE

I am really sorry to employ such great talents as yours in so petty an affair, my friend, but it will give me an opportunity of testing, and then we'll see.

SAINT-CHARLES (*aside*)

Ah—We shall see? That means, all has already been seen.

THE DUKE

I wish to see my son married—

SAINT-CHARLES

To Mlle. Inez de Christoval, Princesse d'Arjos—a good match! Her father made the mistake of entering Joseph Bonaparte's service, and was banished by King Ferdinand. He probably took part in the Mexican revolution.

THE DUKE

Madame de Christoval and her daughter have made the acquaintance of a certain adventurer, named—

SAINT-CHARLES

Raoul de Frescas.

THE DUKE

Is there nothing I can tell you that you do not know?

SAINT-CHARLES

If your grace desires it, I will know nothing.

THE DUKE

On the contrary, I should like you to speak out, so that I may know what secrets you will permit us to keep.

SAINT-CHARLES

Let us make one stipulation; whenever my frankness displeases your grace, call me chevalier, and I will sink once more into my humble rôle of paid detective.

THE DUKE

Go on, my friend. (*Aside*) These people are very amusing.

SAINT-CHARLES

M. de Frescas will not be an adventurer so long as he lives in the style of a man who has an income of a hundred thousand francs.

THE DUKE

Whoever he is you must pierce through the mystery which surrounds him.

SAINT-CHARLES

Your grace requires a very difficult thing. We are obliged to use circumspection in dealing with foreigners. They are our masters; they have turned Paris upside down.

THE DUKE

That's the trouble!

SAINT-CHARLES

Does your grace belong to the opposition?

THE DUKE

I should like to have brought back the king without his fol-
owing—that is my position.

SAINT-CHARLES

The departure of the king resulted from the disorganiza-
tion of the magnificent Asiatic police created by Bonaparte.
An effort is being made nowadays to form a police of respectable people, a procedure which disbands the old police.
Hemmed in by the military police of the invasion, we dare not
arrest any one, for fear we might lay hands on some prince on
his way to keep an assignation, or some margrave who had
dined too well. But for your grace a man will attempt the
impossible. Has this young man any vices? Does he play?

THE DUKE

Yes, in a social way.

SAINT-CHARLES

Does he cheat?

THE DUKE

Chevalier!

SAINT-CHARLES

This young man must be very rich.

THE DUKE

Inquire for yourself.

SAINT-CHARLES

I ask pardon of your grace; but people without passions

cannot know much. Would you have the goodness to tell me whether this young man is sincerely attached to Mlle. de Christoval?

THE DUKE

What! that princess! that heiress! You alarm me, my friend.

SAINT-CHARLES

Has not your grace told me that he is a young man? Now, pretended love is more perfect than genuine love; that is the reason why so many women are deceived! Undoubtedly he has thrown over many mistresses, and heart-free, tongue-free, you know—

THE DUKE

Take care! Your mission is peculiar, and you had best not meddle with the women; an indiscretion on your part may forfeit my good will, for all that relates to M. Frescas must go no further than you and myself. I demand absolute secrecy, both from those you employ, and those who employ you. In fact, you will be a ruined man, if Madame de Montsorel has any suspicion of your designs.

SAINT-CHARLES

Is Madame de Montsorel then interested in this young man? I must keep an eye on her, for this girl is her chambermaid.

THE DUKE

Chevalier de Saint-Charles, to order you to do this would be unworthy of me, and to ask for such an order is quite unworthy of you.

SAINT-CHARLES

Your grace and I perfectly understand each other. But what is to be the main object of my investigations?

THE DUKE

You must find out whether Raoul de Frescas is the real

name of this young man; find out where he was born, ransack his whole life, and consider all you learn about him a secret of state.

### SAINT-CHARLES

You must wait until to-morrow for this information, my lord.

### THE DUKE

That is a short time.

### SAINT-CHARLES

But it involves a good deal of money.

### THE DUKE

Do not suppose that I wish to hear of evil things; it is the method of you people to pander to depraved passions. Instead of showing them up, you prefer to invent rather than to reveal occurrences. I should be delighted to learn that this young man has a family—(*The marquis enters, sees his father engaged, and turns to go out; the duke asks him to remain.*)

---

### SCENE FIFTH.

#### THE PRECEDING AND THE MARQUIS DE MONTSOREL.

### THE DUKE (*continuing*)

If M. de Frescas is a gentleman, and the Princesse d'Arjos decidedly prefers him to my son, the marquis must withdraw his suit.

### THE MARQUIS

But, father, I am in love with Inez.

### THE DUKE (*to Saint-Charles*)

You may go, sir.

SAINT-CHARLES (*aside*)

He takes no interest in the proposed marriage of his son.
He is incapable of feeling jealous of his wife. There is something very serious in these circumstances; I am either a ruined
man or my fortune is made. (*Exit.*)

---

## SCENE SIXTH.

### THE DUKE AND THE MARQUIS.

#### THE DUKE

To marry a woman who does not love you is a mistake which
I shall never allow you to commit, Albert.

#### THE MARQUIS

But there is nothing that indicates that Inez will reject me;
and, in any case, once she is my wife, it will be my object to
win her love, and I believe, without vanity, that I shall succeed.

#### THE DUKE

Allow me to tell you, my son, that your barrack-room ideas
are quite out of place here.

#### THE MARQUIS

On any other subject your words would be law to me; but
every era has a different art of love—I beg of you to hasten
my marriage. Inez has all the pliability of an only daughter,
and the readiness with which she accepts the advances of a
mere adventurer ought to rouse your anxiety. Really, the
coldness with which you receive me this morning amazes me.
Putting aside my love for Inez, could I do better? I shall
be, like you, a Spanish grandee, and, more than that, a prince.
Would that annoy you, father?

### The Duke (*aside*)

The blood of his mother shows itself all the time! Oh! Louise has known well my tender spot! (*Aloud*) Recollect, sir, that there is no rank higher than the glorious title, Duc de Montsorel.

### The Marquis

How have I offended you?

### The Duke

Enough! You forget that I arranged this marriage after my residence in Spain. You are moreover aware that Inez cannot be married without her father's consent. Mexico has recently declared its independence, and the occurrence of this revolution explains the delay of his answer.

### The Marquis

But, my dear father, your plans are in danger of being defeated. You surely did not see what happened yesterday at the Spanish ambassador's? My mother took particular notice there of this Raoul de Frescas, and Inez was immensely pleased with him. Do you know that I have long felt, and now at last admit to myself, that my mother hates me? And that I myself feel, what I would only say to you father, whom I love, that I have little love for her?

### The Duke (*aside*)

I am reaping all that I have sown; hate as well as love is instinctively divined. (*To the marquis*) My son, you should not judge, for you can never understand your mother. She has seen my blind affection for you, and she wishes to correct it by severity. Do not let me hear any more such remarks from you, and let us drop the subject! You are on duty at the palace to-day; repair thither at once: I will obtain leave for you this evening, when you can go to the ball and rejoin the Princesse d'Arjos.

## THE MARQUIS

Before leaving, I should like to see my mother, and beg for her kind offices in my favor, with Inez, who calls upon her this morning.

## THE DUKE

Ask whether she is to be seen, for I am waiting for her myself. (*Exit the marquis.*) Everything overwhelms me at the same time; yesterday the ambassador inquired of me the place of my son's death; last night, my son's mother thought she had found him again; this morning the son of Juana Mendes harrows my feelings! The princess recognizes him instinctively. No law can be broken without a nemesis; nature is as pitiless as the world of men. Shall I be strong enough, even with the backing of the king, to overcome this complication of circumstances?

## SCENE SEVENTH.

### THE DUKE, THE DUCHESS AND THE MARQUIS.

## THE DUCHESS

Excuses? Nonsense! Albert, I am only too happy to see you here; it is a pleasant surprise; you are come to kiss your mother before going to the palace—that is all. Ah! if ever a mother found it in her heart to doubt her son, this eager affection, which I have not been accustomed to, would dispel all such fear, and I thank you for it, Albert. At last we understand each other.

## THE MARQUIS

I am glad to hear you say that, mother; if I have seemed lacking in my duty to you, it is not that I forget, but that I feared to annoy you.

THE DUCHESS (*seeing the duke*)

What! your grace here also!—you really seem to share your son's cordiality,—my rising this morning is actually a fête.

THE DUKE

And you will find it so every day.

THE DUCHESS (*to the duke*)

Ah! I understand— (*To the marquis*) Good-bye! the king is strict about the punctuality of his red-coated guards, and I should be sorry to cause you to be reprimanded.

THE DUKE

Why do you send him off? Inez will soon be here.

THE DUCHESS

I do not think so, I have just written to her.

---

*SCENE EIGHTH.*

THE SAME PERSONS AND JOSEPH.

JOSEPH (*announcing a visitor*)

Their graces the Duchesse de Christoval and the Princesse d'Arjos.

THE DUCHESS (*aside*)

How excessively awkward!

THE DUKE (*to his son*)

Do not go; leave all to me. They are trifling with us.

## *SCENE NINTH.*

THE SAME PERSONS, THE DUCHESSE DE CHRISTOVAL AND
THE PRINCESSE D'ARJOS.

THE DUCHESSE DE MONTSOREL

Ah! madame, it is extremely kind of you thus to anticipate
my visit to you.

THE DUCHESSE DE CHRISTOVAL

I come in this way that there may be no formality between
us.

THE DUCHESSE DE MONTSOREL (*to Inez*)

Have you read my letter?

INEZ

One of your maids has just handed it to me.

THE DUCHESSE DE MONTSOREL (*aside*)

It is evident that Raoul is also coming.

THE DUKE (*to the Duchesse de Christoval, whom he leads to
a seat*)

I hope we see in this informal visit the beginning of a family intimacy?

THE DUCHESSE DE CHRISTOVAL

Pray do not exaggerate the importance of a civility, which
I look upon as a pleasure.

THE MARQUIS

You are seriously afraid, madame, I perceive, of encourag-
ing my hopes? Did I not suffer sufficiently yesterday? The
princess did not notice me, even by a look.

## INEZ

I didn't expect the pleasure of meeting you again so soon, sir. I thought you were on duty; I am glad to have an opportunity of explaining that I never saw you till the moment I left the ball-room, and this lady (*pointing to the Duchesse de Montsorel*) must be the excuse of my inattention.

## THE MARQUIS

You have two excuses, mademoiselle, and I thank you for mentioning only one—my mother.

## THE DUKE

His reproaches spring only from his modesty, mademoiselle. Albert is under the impression that M. de Frescas can give him ground for anxiety! At his age passion is a fairy that makes trifles appear vast. But neither yourself nor your mother, mademoiselle, can attach any serious importance to the claims of a young man, whose title is problematical and who is so studiously silent about his family.

## THE DUCHESSE DE MONTSOREL (*to the Duchesse de Christoval*)

And are you also ignorant of the place where he was born?

## THE DUCHESSE DE CHRISTOVAL

I am not intimate enough with him to ask for such information.

## THE DUKE

There are three of us here who would be well pleased to have it. You alone, ladies, would be discreet, for discretion is a virtue the possession of which profits only those who require it in others.

## THE DUCHESSE DE MONTSOREL

As for me, I do not believe that curiosity is always blameless.

### The Marquis

Is mine then ill-timed? And may I not inquire of madame whether the Frescas of Aragon are extinct or not?

### The Duchesse de Christoval (*to the duke*)

Both of us have known at Madrid the old commander, who was last of his line.

### The Duke

He died, of course, without issue.

### Inez

But there exists a branch of the family at Naples.

### The Marquis

Surely you are aware, mademoiselle, that your cousins, the house of Medina-Cœli, have succeeded to it?

### The Duchesse de Christoval

You are right; there are no De Frescas in existence.

### The Duchesse de Montsorel

Well! well! If this young man has neither title nor family, he can be no dangerous rival to Albert. I do not know why you should be interested in him.

### The Duke

But there are a great many ladies interested in him.

### Inez

I begin to see your meaning—

### The Marquis

Indeed!

INEZ

Yes, this young man is not, perhaps, all he wishes to appear;
but he is intelligent, well educated, his sentiments are noble,
he shows us the most chivalric respect, he speaks ill of no
one; evidently, he is acting the gentleman, and exaggerates
his rôle.

THE DUKE

I believe he also exaggerates the amount of his fortune;
but it is difficult at Paris to maintain that pretension for any
length of time.

THE DUCHESSE DE MONTSOREL (*to the Duchesse de Christoval*)

I am told that you mean to give a series of brilliant enter-
tainments?

THE MARQUIS

Does M. de Frescas speak Spanish?

INEZ

Just as well as we do.

THE DUKE

Say no more, Albert; did you not hear that M. de Frescas
is a highly accomplished young man?

THE DUCHESSE DE CHRISTOVAL

He is really a very agreeable man, but if your doubts were
well founded, I confess, my dear duke, I should be very sorry
to receive any further visits from him.

THE DUCHESSE DE MONTSOREL (*to the Duchesse de Christoval*)

You look as fresh to-day as you did yesterday; I really
admire the way you stand the dissipations of society.

THE DUCHESSE DE CHRISTOVAL (*aside to Inez*)

My child, do not mention M. de Frescas again. The subject annoys Madame de Montsorel.

INEZ (*also aside*)

It did not annoy her yesterday.

---

## SCENE TENTH.

THE SAME PERSONS, JOSEPH AND RAOUL DE FRESCAS.

JOSEPH (*to the Duchesse de Montsorel*)

As Mlle. de Vaudrey is not in, and M. de Frescas is here, will your grace see him?

THE DUCHESSE DE CHRISTOVAL

Is Raoul here?

THE DUKE

So he has already found her out!

THE MARQUIS (*to his father*)

My mother is deceiving us.

THE DUCHESSE DE MONTSOREL (*to Joseph*)

I am not at home.

THE DUKE

If you have asked M. de Frescas to come why do you begin by treating so great a personage with discourtesy? (*To Joseph, despite a gesture of protest from the Duchesse de Montsorel*) Show him in! (*To the marquis*) Try to be calm and sensible.

THE DUCHESSE DE MONTSOREL (*aside*)

In trying to help, I have hurt him, I fear.

JOSEPH

M. Raoul de Frescas.

### RAOUL (*entering*)

My eagerness to obey your commands will prove to you, Madame la Duchesse, how proud I am of your notice, and how anxious to deserve it.

### THE DUCHESSE DE MONTSOREL

I thank you, sir, for your promptitude. (*Aside*) But it may prove fatal to you.

### RAOUL (*bowing to the Duchesse de Christoval and her daughter, aside*)

How is this? Inez here? (*Raoul exchanges bows with the duke; but the marquis takes up a newspaper from the table, and pretends not to see Raoul.*)

### THE DUKE

I must confess, M. de Frescas, I did not expect to meet you in the apartment of Madame de Montsorel; but I am pleased at the interest she takes in you, for it has procured me the pleasure of meeting a young man whose entrance into Parisian society has been attended with such success and brilliancy. You are one of the rivals whom one is proud to conquer, but to whom one submits without displeasure.

### RAOUL

This exaggerated eulogy, with which I cannot agree, would be ironical unless it had been pronounced by you; but I am compelled to acknowledge the courtesy with which you desire to set me at my ease (*looking at the marquis, who turns his back on him*), in a house where I might well think myself unwelcome.

### THE DUKE

On the contrary, you have come just at the right moment;

we were just speaking of your family and of the aged Commander de Frescas whom madame and myself were once well acquainted with.

### RAOUL

I am highly honored by the interest you take in me; but such an honor is generally enjoyed at the cost of some slight gossip.

### THE DUKE

People can only gossip about those whom they know well.

### THE DUCHESSE DE CHRISTOVAL

And we would like to have the right of gossiping about you.

### RAOUL

It is my interest to keep myself in your good graces.

### THE DUCHESSE DE MONTSOREL

I know one way of doing so.

### RAOUL

What is that?

### THE DUCHESSE DE MONTSOREL

Remain the same mysterious personage you are at present.

### THE MARQUIS (*rejoining them, newspaper in hand*)

Here is a strange thing, ladies; one of those foreigners who claim to be noblemen has been caught cheating at play at the field marshal's house.

### INEZ

Is that the great piece of news in which you have been absorbed?

### RAOUL

In these times, everyone seems to be a foreigner.

### The Marquis

It was not altogether this piece of news that set me thinking, but I was struck by the incredible readiness with which people receive at their houses those about whose antecedents they know positively nothing.

### The Duchesse de Montsorel (*aside*)

Is he to be insulted in my house?

### Raoul

If people distrust those whom they do not know, aren't they sometimes likely, at very short notice, to know rather too much about them?

### The Duke

Albert, how can this news of yours interest us? Do we ever receive any one without first learning what his family is?

### Raoul

His grace the duke knows my family.

### The Duke

It is sufficient for me that you are found at Madame de Montsorel's house. We know what we owe to you too well to forget what you owe to us. The name De Frescas commands respect, and you represent it worthily.

### The Duchesse de Christoval (*to Raoul*)

Will you immediately announce who you are, if not for your own sake, at least out of consideration for your friends?

### Raoul

I shall be extremely distressed if my presence here should occasion the slightest discussion; but as certain hints are as galling as the most direct charges, I suggest that we end this

conversation, which is as unworthy of you, as it is of me.
Her grace the duchess did not, I am sure, invite me here
to be cross-examined. I recognize in no one the right to ask
a reason for the silence which I have decided to maintain.

### THE MARQUIS

And you leave us the right to interpret it?

### RAOUL

If 1 claim liberty of action, it is not for the purpose of
refusing the same to you.

### THE DUKE (*to Raoul*)

You are a noble young man, you show the natural distinc-
tion which marks the gentleman; do not be offended at the
curiosity of the world; it is our only safeguard. Your sword
cannot impose silence upon all idle talkers, and the world,
while it treats becoming modesty with generosity, has no pity
for ungrounded pretensions—

### RAOUL

Sir!

### THE DUCHESSE DE MONTSOREL (*whispering anxiously to Raoul*)

Not a word about your childhood; leave Paris, and let me
alone know where you are—hidden! Your whole future
depends on this.

### THE DUKE

1 really wish to be your friend, in spite of the fact that you
are the rival of my son. Give your confidence to a man who
has that of his king. How can you be descended from the
house of De Frescas, which is extinct?

RAOUL (*to the duke*)

Your grace is too powerful to fail of protégés, and I am not so weak as to need a protector.

THE DUCHESSE DE CHRISTOVAL

Sir, I am sure you will understand a mother's feeling that it would be unwise for her to receive many visits from you at the Christoval house.

INEZ (*to Raoul*)

A word would save us, and you keep silence; I perceive that there is something dearer to you than I am.

RAOUL

Inez, I could bear anything excepting these reproaches. (*Aside*) O Vautrin! why did you impose absolute silence upon me? (*He bows farewell to the ladies. To the Duchesse de Montsorel*) I leave my happiness in your charge.

THE DUCHESSE DE MONTSOREL

Do what I order; I will answer for the rest.

RAOUL (*to the marquis*)

I am at your service, sir.

THE MARQUIS

Good-bye, M. Raoul.

RAOUL

De Frescas, if you please.

THE MARQUIS

De Frescas, then! (*Exit Raoul.*)

## *SCENE ELEVENTH.*

### THE SAME PERSONS, EXCEPT RAOUL.

THE DUCHESSE DE MONTSOREL (*to the Duchesse de Christoval*)
You were very severe.

### THE DUCHESSE DE CHRISTOVAL
You may not be aware, madame, that for the last three months this young man has danced attendance on my daughter wherever she went, and that his admission into society was brought about a little incautiously.

THE DUKE (*to the Duchesse de Christoval*)
He might easily be taken for a prince in disguise.

### THE MARQUIS
Is he not rather a nobody disguised as a prince?

### THE DUCHESSE DE MONTSOREL
Your father will tell you that such disguises are difficult to assume.
INEZ (*to the marquis*)
A nobody sir? We women can be attracted by one who is above us, never by him who is our inferior.

### THE DUCHESSE DE CHRISTOVAL
What are you talking about, Inez?

### INEZ
It is of no consequence, mother! Either this young man is crazed or these people are ungenerous.

MADAME DE CHRISTOVAL (*to the Duchesse de Montsorel*)
I can plainly see, madame, that any explanation is impos-

sible, especially in the presence of the duke; but my honor is at stake, and I shall expect you to explain.

### THE DUCHESSE DE MONTSOREL

To-morrow, then. (*Exit the duke with the Duchesse de Christoval and her daughter, followed by the Duchesse de Montsorel.*)

---

## SCENE TWELFTH.

### THE MARQUIS AND THE DUKE.

### THE MARQUIS

The appearance of this adventurer, father, seems to throw both you and my mother into a state of the most violent excitement; it would almost seem as if not only was the marriage of your son jeopardized, but your very existence menaced. The duchess and her daughter went off in high dudgeon—

### THE DUKE

What could have brought them here in the very midst of our discussion?

### THE MARQUIS

And you also are interested in this fellow Raoul?

### THE DUKE

Are not you? Your fortune, your name, your future and your marriage, all that is more to you than life, is now at stake!

### THE MARQUIS

If all these things are dependent upon this young man, I will immediately demand satisfaction from him.

### The Duke

What! a duel? If you had the wretched luck to kill him, the success of your suit would be hopeless.

### The Marquis

What then is to be done?

### The Duke

Do like the politicians; wait!

### The Marquis

If you are in danger, father, do you think I can remain quiet?

### The Duke

Leave this burden to me; it would crush you.

### The Marquis

Ah! but you will speak, father, you will tell me—

### The Duke

Nothing! for we should both of us have too much to blush for.

---

## SCENE THIRTEENTH.

### The Same Persons and Vautrin.

*(Vautrin is dressed all in black; at the beginning of the scene he puts on an air of compunction and humility.)*

### Vautrin

Excuse me, your grace, for having forced my way in, but *(whispering so as not to be overheard)* we have both of us been victimized by an abuse of confidence—allow me to say a word or two to you alone.

THE DUKE (*with a sign to his son to leave them*)
Say on, sir.

VAUTRIN

In these days success is in the power of those alone who exert themselves to obtain office, and this form of ambition pervades all classes. Every man in France desires to be a colonel, and it is difficult to see where the privates are to come from. As a matter of fact society is threatened by disintegration, which will simply result from this universal desire for high positions, accompanied with a general disgust for the low places. Such is the fruit of revolutionary equality. Religion is the sole remedy for this corruption.

THE DUKE

What are you driving at?

VAUTRIN

I beg pardon, but it is impossible to refrain from explaining to a statesman, with whom I am going to work, the cause of a mistake which annoys me. Has your grace confided any secrets to one of my people who came to you this morning, with the foolish idea of supplanting me, and in the hope of making himself known to you as one who could serve your interests?

THE DUKE

What do you mean? that you are the Chevalier de Saint-Charles?

VAUTRIN

Let me tell your grace, that we are just what we desire to be. Neither he nor I is simple enough to be his real self—it would cost us too much.

THE DUKE

Remember, that you must furnish proofs.


VAUTRIN

If your grace has confided any important secret to him, I
shall have immediately to put him under surveillance.


THE DUKE (*aside*)

This man seems more honest and reliable than the other.


VAUTRIN

We put the secret police on such cases.


THE DUKE

You ought not to have come here, sir, unless you were able
to justify your assertions.


VAUTRIN

I have done my duty. I hope that the ambition of this
man, who is capable of selling himself to the highest bidder,
may be of service to you.


THE DUKE (*aside*)

How can he have learned so promptly the secret of my
morning interview?

VAUTRIN (*aside*)

He hesitates; Joseph is right, some important secret is at
stake.

THE DUKE

Sir!

VAUTRIN

Your grace!

THE DUKE

It is the interest of both of us to defeat this man.

VAUTRIN

That would be dangerous, if he has your secret; for he is tricky.

THE DUKE

Yes, the fellow has wit.

VAUTRIN

Did you give him a commission?

THE DUKE

Nothing of importance; I wish to find out all about a certain M. de Frescas.

VAUTRIN (*aside*)

Merely that! (*Aloud*) I can tell your grace all about him. Raoul de Frescas is a young nobleman whose family is mixed up in an affair of high treason, and he does not like to assume his father's name.

THE DUKE

He has a father, then?

VAUTRIN

He has a father.

THE DUKE

And where does he come from? What is his fortune?

VAUTRIN

We are changing our rôles, and your grace must excuse my not answering until you tell me what special interest your grace has in M. de Frescas.

THE DUKE

You are forgetting yourself, sir!

VAUTRIN (*with assumed humility*)

Yes, I am forgetting the fact that there is an enormous difference between spies and those who set them.

### THE DUKE

Joseph!

### VAUTRIN (*aside*)

This duke has set his spies upon us; I must hurry. (*Vautrin disappears through the side door, by which he entered in the first act.*)

### THE DUKE (*turning back*)

You shall not leave the house. Heavens! where is he? (*He rings and Joseph answers.*) Let all the doors of the house be locked, a man has got into the house. Quick! let all look for him, and let him be apprehended. (*He goes to the room of the duchess.*)

### JOSEPH (*looking through the postern*)

He is far away by this time.

*Curtain to the Second Act.*

# ACT III.

## *SCENE FIRST.*

**(*A room in the house of Raoul de Frescas.*)**

LAFOURAILLE (*alone*)

Would my late excellent father, who advised me to frequent none but the best society, have been satisfied with me yesterday? I spent all night with ministers' valets, attendants of the embassy, princes', dukes', peers' coachmen—none but these, all reliable men, in good luck; they steal only from their masters. My master danced with a fine chit of a girl! whose hair was powdered with a million's worth of diamonds, and he had no eyes for anything but the bouquet she carried in her hand; simple young man, we sympathize with you. Old Jacques Collin—Botheration! there I trip again, I cannot reconcile myself to this common name—I mean M. Vautrin, will arrange all that. In a little time diamonds and dowry will take an airing, and they have need of it; to think of them as always in the same strong boxes! 'Tis against the laws of circulation. What a joker he is!—He sets you up as a young man of means. He is so kind, he talks so finely, the heiress comes in, the trick is done, and we all cry shares! The money will have been well earned. You see we have been here six months. Haven't we put on the look of idiots! Everybody in the neighborhood takes us for good simple folk. And who would refuse to do anything for Vautrin? He said to us: "Be virtuous," and virtuous we became. I fear him as I fear the police, and yet I love him even more than money.

VAUTRIN (*calling from the outside*)

Lafouraille!

LAFOURAILLE

There he is! I haven't seen his face this morning—that means a storm; I prefer it should fall upon some one else, and will get out. (*He starts to the door but encounters Vautrin.*)

---

## SCENE SECOND.

### VAUTRIN AND LAFOURAILLE.

(*Vautrin is dressed in long white duck trousers and a waist-coat of the same material, slippers of red morocco, —the morning dress of a business man.*)

VAUTRIN

Lafouraille.

LAFOURAILLE

Sir?

VAUTRIN

Where are you going?

LAFOURAILLE

To get your letters.

VAUTRIN

I have them. Have you anything else to do?

LAFOURAILLE

Yes, your chamber—

VAUTRIN

In so many words you want to avoid me. I have always found that restless legs never go with a quiet conscience. Stay where you are. I want to talk with you.

### LAFOURAILLE

I am at your service.

### VAUTRIN

I hope you are. Come here. You told us, under the fair sky of Provence, a certain story which was little to your credit. A steward beat you at play; do you recollect?

### LAFOURAILLE

A steward? yes, that fellow Charles Blondet, the only man who ever robbed me! Can a fellow forget that?

### VAUTRIN

Had you not on one occasion sold your master to him? That's common enough.

### LAFOURAILLE

On one occasion? I sold him three times over.

### VAUTRIN

That was better. And what business was the steward then engaged in?

### LAFOURAILLE

I was going to tell you. I was footman at eighteen with the De Langeacs—

### VAUTRIN

I thought it was in the Duc de Montsorel's house.

### LAFOURAILLE

No; the duke, fortunately, has only twice set eyes on me, and has, I hope, forgotten me.

### VAUTRIN

Did you rob him?

### LAFOURAILLE

Well, to some small extent.

VAUTRIN

Why do you want him to forget you?

LAFOURAILLE

Because, after seeing him again, yesterday, at the embassy,
I should then feel safe.

VAUTRIN

And it is the same man?

LAFOURAILLE

We are both older by twenty-five years, and that is the only
difference.

VAUTRIN

Tell me all about him. I knew I had heard you mention
his name. Go on.

LAFOURAILLE

The Vicomte de Langeac, one of my masters, and this Duc
de Montsorel were like peas in the same pod. When I was
forced to choose between the nobles and the people, I did not
hesitate; from a mere footman, I became a citizen, and citizen
Philip Boulard was an earnest worker. I had enthusiasm,
and acquired influence in the faubourg.

VAUTRIN

And so you have been a politician, have you?

LAFOURAILLE

Not for long. I did a pretty thing, and that ruined me.

VAUTRIN

Aha! my boy, pretty things are like pretty women—better
fight shy of them; they often bring trouble. What was this
pretty thing?

### LAFOURAILLE

I'll tell you. In the scrimmage of the Tenth of August, the duke confided to my care the Vicomte de Langeac; I disguised and hid him, I gave him food at the risk of my popularity and my life. The duke had greatly encouraged me by such trifles as a thousand gold pieces, and that Blondet had the infamy to offer me a bigger pile to give up our young master.

### VAUTRIN

Did you give him up?

### LAFOURAILLE

Immediately. He was jugged in the Abbaye, and I became the happy possessor of sixty good thousands of francs in gold, in real gold.

### VAUTRIN

And what has this to do with the Duc de Montsorel?

### LAFOURAILLE

Wait a little. When the days of September came, my conduct seemed to me slightly reprehensible; and to quiet my conscience, I determined to propose to the duke, who was leaving the country, that I should rescue his friend.

### VAUTRIN

Did your remorse prove a good investment?

### LAFOURAILLE

That it did; for it was rare in those days! The duke promised me twenty thousand francs if I delivered the viscount from the hands of my comrades, and I succeeded in doing so.

### VAUTRIN

Twenty thousand francs for a viscount!

### LAFOURAILLE

And he was all the more worth it, because he was the last.
I found that out too late.  The steward had disposed of all the
other Langeacs, even to a poor old grandmother whom he had
sent to the Carmelites.

### VAUTRIN

That was good!

### LAFOURAILLE

But then something else happened.  That Blondet heard
of my devotion, he traced me out and found me in the neighborhood of Mortagne, where my master was at the house of
one of my uncles waiting for a chance to reach the sea.  The
noodle offered me as much money as he had already given me.
I saw before me an honest life for the rest of my days; and I
was weak.  My friend Blondet caused the viscount to be shot
as a spy, and my uncle and myself were imprisoned as his
accomplices.  We were not released until I had disgorged all
my gold.

### VAUTRIN

That is the way a knowledge of the human heart is acquired.
You were dealing with a stronger man than yourself.

### LAFOURAILLE

That remains to be seen; for I am still alive.

### VAUTRIN

Enough of that!  There is nothing of use to me in your tale

### LAFOURAILLE

Can I go now?

### VAUTRIN

Come, come.  You seem to experience a keen longing to be
where I am not.  But you went into society yesterday; did you
do anything?

### LAFOURAILLE.

The servants said such funny things about their masters, that I could not leave the antechamber.

### VAUTRIN

Yet I saw you nibbling at the sideboard; what did you take?

### LAFOURAILLE

Nothing—but stay—I took a wineglass of Madeira.

### VAUTRIN

What did you do with the dozen of gold spoons that went with the glass of Madeira?

### LAFOURAILLE

Gold spoons! I've searched diligently, but find nothing of that kind in my memory.

### VAUTRIN

Possibly; but you will find them in your mattress. And was Philosopher also absent-minded?

### LAFOURAILLE

Poor Philosopher! Since morning he has been a laughing-stock below stairs. He induced a coachman who was very young to strip off his gold lace for him. It was all false on the underside. In these days masters are thieves. You cannot be sure of anything, more's the pity.

### VAUTRIN (*whistles*)

This is no joking matter. You will make me lose the house: this must be put a stop to—Here, father Buteux, ahoy! Philosopher! Come here. Fil-de-Soie! My dear friends, let us have a clearing up. You are a pack of scoundrels.

## SCENE THIRD.

THE SAME PERSONS, BUTEUX, PHILOSOPHER AND FIL-DE-SOIE.

### BUTEUX

Present! Is the house on fire?

### FIL-DE-SOIE

Is it some one burning with curiosity?

### BUTEUX

A fire would be better, for it can be put out.

### PHILOSOPHER

But the other can be choked.

### LAFOURAILLE

Bah! he has had enough of this trifling.

### BUTEUX

So we are to have more moralizing—thank you for that.

### FIL-DE-SOIE

He cannot want me for I have not been out.

### VAUTRIN (to Fil-de-Soie)

You? The evening when I bade you exchange your scullion's cap for a footman's hat—poisoner—

### FIL-DE-SOIE

We will drop the extra names.

### VAUTRIN

And you accompanied me as my footman to the field marshal's; while helping me on with my cloak, you stole the watch of the Cossack prince.

### FIL-DE-SOIE

One of the enemies of France.

### VAUTRIN

You, Buteux, you old malefactor, carried off the opera-glass of the Princesse d'Arjos, the evening she set down your young master at our gate.

### BUTEUX

It dropped on the carriage step.

### VAUTRIN

You should have respectfully handed it back to her; but the gold and the pearls appealed to your tigerish talons.

### LAFOURAILLE

Now, now, surely people can have a little fun? Devil take it! Did not you, Jacques—

### VAUTRIN

What do you mean?

### LAFOURAILLE

Did not you, M. Vautrin, require thirty thousand francs, that this young man might live in princely style? We succeeded in satisfying you in the fashion of foreign governments, by borrowing, and getting credit. All those who come to ask for me leave some with us. And you are not satisfied.

### FIL-DE-SOIE

And if, when I am sent to buy provisions without a sou, I may not be allowed to bring back some cash with me,—I might as well send in my resignation.

### PHILOSOPHER

And didn't I sell our custom to four different coach-builders
—5,000 francs each clip—and the man who got the order
lost all? One evening M. de Frescas starts off from home
with wretched screws, and we bring him back, Lafouraille and
I, with a span worth ten thousand francs, which have cost
him only twenty glasses of brandy.

### LAFOURAILLE

No, it was Kirchenwasser.

### PHILOSOPHER

Yes, and yet you fly into a rage—

### FIL-DE-SOIE

How are you going to keep house now?

### VAUTRIN

Do you expect to do things of this kind for long? What
I have permitted in order to set up our establishment, from
this day forth I forbid. You wish, I suppose, to descend
from robbery to swindling? If you do not understand what
I say I will look out for better servants.

### BUTEUX

And where will you find them?

### LAFOURAILLE

Let him hunt for them!

### VAUTRIN

You forget, I see, that I have pledged myself to save your
necks! Dear, dear, do you think I have sifted you, like seeds
in a colander, through three different places of residence, to
let you hover round a gibbet, like flies round a candle? I
wish you to know that any imprudence that brings you to
such a position, is, to men of my stamp, a crime. You ought

to appear as supremely innocent as you, Philosopher, appeared to him who let you rip off his lace.  Never forget the part you are playing; you are honest fellows, faithful domestics, and adore Raoul de Frescas, your master.

### BUTEUX

Do you take this young man for a god?  You have harnessed us to his car; but we know him no better than he knows us.

### PHILOSOPHER

Tell me, is he one of our kind?

### FIL-DE-SOIE

What is he going to bring us to?

### LAFOURAILLE

We obey on condition that the Society of the Ten Thousand be reconstituted, so that never less than ten thousand francs at a time be assigned to us; at present we have not any funds in common.

### FIL-DE-SOIE

When are we all to be capitalists?

### BUTEUX

If the gang knew that for the last six months I have been disguising myself as an old porter, without any object, I should be disgraced.  If I am willing to risk my neck, it is that I may give bread to my Adèle, whom you have forbidden me to see, and who for six months must have been as dry as a match.

### LAFOURAILLE (*to the other two*)

She is in prison.  Poor man! let us spare his feelings.

### VAUTRIN

Have you finished?  Come now, you have made merry here

for six months, eaten like diplomats, drunk like Poles, and have wanted nothing.

BUTEUX

Yes, we are rusting out!

VAUTRIN

Thanks to me, the police have forgotten you! You owe your good luck to me alone! I have erased the brand from your foreheads. I am the head, whose ideas you, the arms, carry out.

PHILOSOPHER

We are satisfied.

VAUTRIN

You must all obey me blindly.

LAFOURAILLE

Blindly.

VAUTRIN

Without a murmur.

FIL-DE-SOIE

Without a murmur.

VAUTRIN

Or else let us break our compact, and be off with you! If I meet with ingratitude from you, to whom can I venture hereafter to do a service?

PHILOSOPHER

To no one, my emperor.

LAFOURAILLE

I should rather say, our great teacher!

BUTEUX

I love you more than I love Adèle.

### FIL-DE-SOIE

We worship you.

### VAUTRIN

If necessary, I shall even have to beat you.

### PHILOSOPHER

We'll take it without a murmur.

### VAUTRIN

To spit in your face; to bowl over your lives like a row of skittles.

### BUTEUX

But I bowl over with a knife.

### VAUTRIN

Very well—Kill me this instant.

### BUTEUX

It is no use being vexed with this man. Do you wish me to restore the opera-glass? I intended it for Adèle!

### ALL (*surrounding him*)

Would you abandon us, Vautrin?

### LAFOURAILLE

Vautrin! our friend.

### PHILOSOPHER

Mighty Vautrin!

### FIL-DE-SOIE

Our old companion, deal with us as you will.

### VAUTRIN

Yes, and I can deal with you as I will. When I think what trouble you make, in your trinket-stealing, I feel inclined to send you back to the place I took you from. You are either above or below the level of society, dregs or foam; but I desire to make you enter into society. People used to hoot you as you went by. I wish them to bow to you; you were once the basest of mankind, I wish you to be more than honest men.

PHILOSOPHER

Is there such a class?

BUTEUX

There are those who are nothing at all.

VAUTRIN

There are those who decide upon the honesty of others. You will never be honest burgesses, you must belong either to the wretched or the rich; you must therefore master one-half of the world! Take a bath of gold, and you will come forth from it virtuous!

FIL-DE-SOIE

To think, that, when I have need of nothing, I shall be a good prince!

VAUTRIN

Of course. And you, Lafouraille, you can become Count of Saint Helena; and what would you like to be, Buteux?

BUTEUX

I should like to be a philanthropist, for the philanthropist always becomes a millionaire.

PHILOSOPHER

And I, a banker.

FIL-DE-SOIE

He wishes to be a licensed professional.

VAUTRIN

Show yourselves then, according as occasion demands it,

blind and clear-sighted, adroit and clumsy, stupid and clever, like all those who make their fortune. Never judge me, and try to understand my meaning. You ask who Raoul de Frescas is? I will explain to you; he will soon have an income of twelve hundred thousand francs. He will be a prince. And I picked him up when he was begging on the high road, and ready to become a drummer-boy; in his twelfth year he had neither name nor family; he came from Sardinia, where he must have got into some trouble, for he was a fugitive from justice.

#### BUTEUX

Oh, now that we know his antecedents and his social position—

#### VAUTRIN

Be off to your lodge!

#### BUTEUX

Little Nini, daughter of Giroflée is there—

#### VAUTRIN

She may let a spy pass in.

#### BUTEUX

She! She is a little cat to whom it is not necessary to point out the stool-pigeons.

#### VAUTRIN

You may judge my power from what I am in process of doing for Raoul. Ought he not to be preferred before all? Raoul de Frescas is a young man who has remained pure as an angel in the midst of our mire-pit; he is our conscience; moreover, he is my creation; I am at once his father, his mother, and I desire to be his guiding providence. I, who can never know happiness, still delight in making other people happy. I breathe through his lips, I live in his life, his passions are my own; and it is impossible for me to know noble and pure emotions excepting in the heart of this being unsoiled by crime. You have your fancies, here I show you mine. In exchange for the blight which society has brought upon me, I give it a man of honor, and enter upon a struggle with destiny; do you wish to be of my party? Obey me.

ALL

In life, and death—

VAUTRIN (*aside*)

So my savage beasts are once more brought to submission (*Aloud*) Philosopher, try to put on the air, the face, the costume of an employe of the lost goods bureau, and take back to the embassy the plate borrowed by Lafouraille. (*To Fil-de-Soie*) You, Fil-de-Soie, must prepare a sumptuous dinner, as M. de Frescas is to entertain a few friends. You will afterwards dress yourself as a respectable man, and assume the air of a lawyer. You will go to number six, Rue Oblin, ring seven times at the fourth-story door, and ask for Père Giroflée. When they ask where you come from, you will answer from a seaport in Bohemia. They will let you in. I want certain letters and papers of the Duc de Christoval; here are the text and patterns. I want an absolute fac-simile, with the briefest possible delay. Lafouraille, you must go and insert a few lines in the newspapers, notifying the arrival of . . . (*He whispers into his ear.*) This forms part of my plan. Now leave me.

LAFOURAILLE

Well, are you satisfied?

VAUTRIN

Yes.

PHILOSOPHER

You want nothing more of us?

VAUTRIN

Nothing.

FIL-DE-SOIE

There will be no more rebellion; every one will be good.

BUTEUX

Let your mind rest easy; we are going to be not only polite, but honest.

VAUTRIN

That is right, boys; a little integrity, a great deal of address. and you will be respected.

(*Exeunt all except Vautrin.*)

---

## SCENE FOURTH.

### VAUTRIN (*alone*)

In order to lead them it is only necessary to let them think they have an honorable future. They have no future, no prospects! Pshaw! if generals took their soldiers seriously, not a cannon would be fired! In a few days, following upon years of subterranean labors, I shall have won for Raoul a commanding position; it must be made sure to him. Lafouraille and Philosopher will be necessary to me in the country where I am to give him a family. Ah, this love! it has put out of the question the life I had destined him to. I wished to win for him a solitary glory, to see him conquering for me and under my direction, the world which I am forbidden to enter. Raoul is not only the child of my intellect and of my malice, he is also my instrument of revenge. These fellows of mine cannot understand these sentiments; they are happy; they have never fallen, not they! they were born criminals. But I have attempted to raise myself. Yet though a man can raise himself in the eyes of God, he can never do so in the eyes of the world. People tell you to repent, and then refuse to pardon. Men possess in their dealings with each other the instincts of savage animals. Once wounded, one is downtrodden by his fellows. Moreover, to ask the protection of a world whose laws you have trampled under foot is like returning to a house which you have burnt and whose roof would fall and crush you. I have well polished and perfected the magnetic instrument of my domination. Raoul was brave, he would have sacrificed his life, like a fool; I had to make him cold and domineering, and to dispel from his mind, one by one, his exalted ideas of life; to render him suspicious and tricky as—an old bill-broker, while all the while he knew not who I was. And at this moment love has broken down the whole scaffolding. He should have been great; now, he can only be happy. I shall therefore retire to live in a corner at the height of his prosperity; his happiness will have been my work. For two days I have been asking myself whether it would not be better that the Princesse d'Arjos should die of some ailment—say brain fever. It's singular how many plans a woman can upset!

## SCENE FIFTH.

### VAUTRIN AND LAFOURAILLE.

#### VAUTRIN

What is the matter? Cannot I be alone one moment? Did I call?

#### LAFOURAILLE

We are likely to feel the claws of justice scratch our shoulders.

#### VAUTRIN

What new blunder have you committed?

#### LAFOURAILLE

The fact is little Nini has admitted a well-dressed gentleman who asks to see you. Buteux is whistling the air, *There's No Place Like Home,* so it must be a sleuth.

#### VAUTRIN

Nothing of the kind, I know who it is; tell him to wait. Everybody in arms! Vautrin must then vanish; I will be the Baron de Vieux-Chêne. Speak in a German accent, fool him well, until I can play the master stroke. (*Exit.*)

## *SCENE SIXTH.*

### LAFOURAILLE AND SAINT-CHARLES.

#### LAFOURAILLE (*speaking with a German accent*)

M. de Frescas is not at home, sir, and his steward, the Baron de Vieux-Chêne, is engaged with an architect, who is to build a grand house for our master.

#### SAINT-CHARLES

I beg your pardon, my dear sir, you said—

#### LAFOURAILLE

I said Baron de Vieux-Chêne.

#### SAINT-CHARLES

Baron!

#### LAFOURAILLE

Yes! Yes!

#### SAINT-CHARLES

He is a baron?

#### LAFOURAILLE

Baron de Vieux-Chêne.

#### SAINT-CHARLES

You are a German.

#### LAFOURAILLE

Not I! Not I! I am an Alsatian, a very different thing.

#### SAINT-CHARLES (*aside*)

This man has certainly an accent too decidedly German to be a Parisian.

#### LAFOURAILLE (*aside*)

I know this man well. Here's a go!

SAINT-CHARLES

If the baron is busy, I will wait.

LAFOURAILLE (*aside*)

Ah! Blondet, my beauty, you can disguise your face, but not your voice; if you get out of our clutches now, you will be a wonder. (*Aloud*) What shall I tell the baron brings you ere? (*He makes as if to go out.*)

SAINT-CHARLES

Stay a moment, my friend; you speak German, I speak French, we may misunderstand one another. (*Puts a purse into his hand.*) There can be no mistake with this for an interpreter.

LAFOURAILLE

No, sir.

SAINT-CHARLES

That is merely on account.

LAFOURAILLE (*aside*)

Yes, on account of my eighty thousand francs. (*Aloud*) And do you wish me to shadow my master?

SAINT-CHARLES

No, my friend, I merely ask for some information, which cannot compromise you.

LAFOURAILLE

In good German we call that spying.

SAINT-CHARLES

But no—that is not it—it is—

LAFOURAILLE

To shadow him. And what shall I say to his lordship the baron?

SAINT-CHARLES

Announce the Chevalier de Saint-Charles.

LAFOURAILLE

We understand each other. I will induce him to see you. But do not offer money to the steward; he is more honest than the rest of us. (*He gives a sly wink.*)

SAINT-CHARLES

That means he will cost more.

LAFOURAILLE

Yes, sir. (*Exit.*)

---

*SCENE SEVENTH.*

SAINT-CHARLES (*alone*)

A bad beginning! Ten louis thrown away. To shadow him indeed! It is too stupid not to have a spice of wit in it, this habit of calling things by their right name, at the outset. If the pretended steward, for there is no steward here, if the baron is as clever as his footman, I shall have nothing to base my information on, excepting what they conceal from me. This room is very fine. There is neither portrait of the king, nor emblem of royalty here. Well, it is plain they do not frame their opinions. Is the furniture suggestive of any-thing? No. It is too new to have been even paid for. But for the air which the porter whistled, doubtless a signal, I should be inclined to believe in the De Frescas people.

## SCENE EIGHTH.

### SAINT-CHARLES, VAUTRIN AND LAFOURAILLE.

(*Vautrin wears a bright maroon coat, of old-fashioned cut, with large heavy buttons; his breeches are black silk, as are his stockings. His shoes have gold buckles, his waist-coat is flowered, he wears two watchchains, his cravat belongs to the time of the Revolution; his wig is white, his face old, keen, withered, dissipated looking. He speaks low, and his voice is cracked.*)

### VAUTRIN (*to Lafouraille*)

Very good; you may go. (*Exit Lafouraille. Aside*) Now for the tug of war, M. Blondet. (*Aloud*) I am at your service, sir.

### SAINT-CHARLES (*aside*)

A worn out fox is still dangerous. (*Aloud*) Excuse me, baron, for disturbing you, while yet unknown to you.

### VAUTRIN

I can guess what your business is.

### SAINT-CHARLES (*aside*)

Indeed?

### VAUTRIN

You are an architect, and have a proposal to make to me; but I have already received most excellent offers.

### SAINT-CHARLES

Excuse me, your Dutchman must have mispronounced my name. I am the Chevalier de Saint-Charles.

### VAUTRIN (*raising his spectacles*)

Let me see—we are old acquaintances. You were at the

Congress of Vienna, and then bore the name of Count of Gor-
cum—a fine name!

### SAINT-CHARLES (*aside*)

Go choke yourself, old man! (*Aloud*)   So you were there
also?

### VAUTRIN

I should think so! And I am glad to have come upon you
again. You were a deuced clever fellow, you know. How you
fooled them all!

### SAINT-CHARLES (*aside*)

We'll stick to Vienna, then. (*Aloud*)   Ah, baron! I
recall you perfectly now; you also steered your bark pretty
cleverly there.

### VAUTRIN

Of course I did, and what women we had there! yes, indeed!
And have you still your fair Italian?

### SAINT-CHARLES

Did you know her? She was a woman of such tact.

### VAUTRIN

My dear fellow, wasn't she, though? She actually wanted to
find out who I was.

### SAINT-CHARLES

And did she find out?

### VAUTRIN

Well, my dear friend, I know you will be glad to hear it, she
discovered nothing.

### SAINT-CHARLES

Come, baron, since we are speaking freely to each other
to-day, I for my part must confess that your admirable Pole—

VAUTRIN

You also had the pleasure?

SAINT-CHARLES

On my honor, yes!

VAUTRIN (*laughing*)

Ha! Ha! Ha! Ha!

SAINT-CHARLES (*laughing*)

Ha! Ha! Ha! Ha!

VAUTRIN

We can safely laugh now, for I suppose you left her there?

SAINT-CHARLES

Immediately, as you did. I see that we are both come to throw away our money in Paris, and we have done well; but it seems to me, baron, that you have accepted a very secondary position, though one which attracts notice.

VAUTRIN

Ah! thank you, chevalier. I hope, however, we may still be friends for many a day.

SAINT-CHARLES

Forever, I hope.

VAUTRIN

You can be extremely useful to me, I can be of immense service to you, we understand each other! Let me know what your present business is, and I will tell you mine.

SAINT-CHARLES (*aside*)

I should like to know whether he is being set on me, or I on him.

VAUTRIN (*aside*)

It is going to be a somewhat slow business.

SAINT-CHARLES

I will tell you.

VAUTRIN

I am attention!

SAINT-CHARLES

Baron, between ourselves, I admire you immensely.

VAUTRIN

What a compliment from a man like you!

SAINT-CHARLES

Not at all! To create a De Frescas in the face of all Paris shows an inventive genius which transcends by a thousand points that of our countesses at the Congress. You are angling for the dowry with rare nerve.

VAUTRIN

I angling for a dowry?

SAINT-CHARLES

But, my dear friend, you would be found out, unless I your friend had been the man chosen to watch you, for I am appointed your shadower by a very high authority. Permit me also to ask how can you dare to interfere with the family of Montsorel in their pursuit of an heiress?

VAUTRIN

To think that I innocently believed you came to propose we should work in company, and speculate, both of us, with the money of M. de Frescas, of which I have entire control—and here you talk to me of something entirely different! Frescas, my good friend, is one of the legal titles of this young man, who has seven in all. Stringent reasons prevent him from revealing the name of his family, which I know, for the next twenty-four hours. Their property is vast, I have seen their estate, from which I am just returned. I do not mind being taken by you for a rogue, for there is no disgrace in the vast sums at stake; but to be taken for an imbecile, capable of dancing attendance on a sham nobleman, and so silly as to defy the Montsorels on behalf of a counterfeit—Really, my friend, it would seem that you have never been to Vienna! We are not in the same class!

## Saint-Charles

Do not grow angry, worthy steward! Let us leave off entangling ourselves in a web of lies more or less agreeable; you cannot expect to make me swallow any more of them. Our cash-box is better furnished than yours, therefore come over to us. Your young man is as much Frescas as I am chevalier and you baron. You picked him up on the frontier of Italy; he was then a vagabond, to-day he is an adventurer, and that's the whole truth of it.

## Vautrin

You are right. We must leave off entangling ourselves in the web of falsehoods more or less agreeable; we must speak the truth.

## Saint-Charles

I will pay you for it.

## Vautrin

I will give it you for nothing. You are an infamous cur, my friend. Your name is Charles Blondet; you were steward in the household of De Langeac; twice have you bought the betrayal of the viscount, and never have you paid the money—it is shameful! You owe eighty thousand francs to one of my footmen. You caused the viscount to be shot at Mortagne in order that you might appropriate the property entrusted to you by the family. If the Duc de Montsorel, who sent you here, knew who you are, ha! ha! he would make you settle some odd accounts! Take off your moustache, your whiskers, your wig, your sham decorations and your badges of foreign orders. (*He tears off from him his wig, his whiskers and decorations.*) Good day, you rascal! How did you manage to eat up a fortune so cleverly won? It was colossal; how did you lose it?

SAINT-CHARLES

Through ill-luck.

VAUTRIN

I understand. . . . What are you going to do now?

SAINT-CHARLES

Whoever you are, stop there; I surrender, I haven't a chance left! You are either the devil or Jacques Collin!

VAUTRIN

I am and wish to be nothing but the Baron de Vieux-Chêne to you. Listen to my ultimatum. I can cause you to be buried this instant in one of my cellars, and no one will inquire for you.

SAINT-CHARLES

I know it.

VAUTRIN

It would be prudent to do so. But are you willing to do for me in Montsorel's house, what Montsorel sent you to do here?

SAINT-CHARLES

I accept the offer; but what are the profits?

VAUTRIN

All you can take.

SAINT-CHARLES

From either party?

VAUTRIN

Certainly! You will send me by the person who accompanies you back all the deeds that relate to the De Langeac family; they must still be in your possession. In case M. de Frescas marries Mlle. de Christoval, you cannot be their steward, but you shall receive a hundred thousand francs. You are dealing with exacting masters. Walk straight, and they will not betray you.

SAINT-CHARLES

It's a bargain!

VAUTRIN

I will not ratify it until I have the documents in hand. Until then, be careful! (*He rings; all the household come in.*) Attend M. le Chevalier home, with all the respect due his high rank. (*To Saint-Charles, pointing out to him Philosopher*) This man will accompany you. (*To Philosopher*) Do not leave him.

SAINT-CHARLES (*aside*)

Once I get safe and sound out of their clutches, I will come down heavy on this nest of thieves.

VAUTRIN

Monsieur le Chevalier, I am yours to command!

---

## SCENE NINTH.

VAUTRIN AND LAFOURAILLE.

LAFOURAILLE

M. Vautrin!

VAUTRIN

Well?

### LAFOURAILLE

Are you letting him go?

### VAUTRIN

Unless he considers himself at liberty, what can we hope
to learn from him? I have given my instructions; he will be
taught not to put ropes in the way of hangmen. When Philosopher brings for me the documents which this fellow is to
hand him, they will be given to me, wherever I happen to be.

### LAFOURAILLE

But afterwards, will you spare his life?

### VAUTRIN

You are always a little premature, my dear. Have you
forgotten how seriously the dead interfere with the peace of
the living? Hush! I hear Raoul—leave us to ourselves.

---

### SCENE TENTH.

#### VAUTRIN AND RAOUL DE FRESCAS.

#### RAOUL (soliloquizing)

After a glimpse of heaven, still remain on earth—such
is my fate! I am a lost man; Vautrin, an infernal yet a
kindly genius, a man who knows everything, and seems able
to do everything, a man as harsh to others as he is good to
me, a man who is inexplicable except by a supposition of
witchcraft, a maternal providence if I may so call him, is not
after all the providence divine. (*Vautrin enters wearing a
plain black peruke, a blue coat, gray pantaloons, a black
waistcoat, the costume of a stock-broker.*) Oh! I know what
love is; but I did not know what revenge was, until I felt I

could not die before I had wreaked my vengeance on these two Montsorels.

VAUTRIN (*aside*)

He is in trouble. (*Aloud*) Raoul, my son, what ails you?

RAOUL

Nothing ails me. Pray leave me.

VAUTRIN

Do you again repulse me? You abuse the right you have to ill-treat a friend—What are you thinking about?

RAOUL

Nothing.

VAUTRIN

Nothing? Come, sir, do you think that he who has taught you that English coldness, under the veil of which men of worth would conceal their feelings, was not aware of the transparency which belongs to this cuirass of pride? Try concealment with others, but not with me. Dissimulation is more than a blunder, for in friendship a blunder is a crime.

RAOUL

To game no more, to come home tipsy no more, to shun the menagerie of the opera, to become serious, to study, to desire a position in life, this you call dissimulation.

VAUTRIN

You are as yet but a poor diplomatist. You will be a great one, when you can deceive me. Raoul, you have made the mistake which I have taken most pains to save you from. My son, why did you not take women for what they are, creatures of inconsequence, made to enslave without being their slave, like a sentimental shepherd? But instead, my Lovelace has been conquered by a Clarissa. Ah, young people will strike

against these idols a great many times, before they discover
them to be hollow!

### RAOUL

**Is this a sermon?**

### VAUTRIN

What? Do you take me, who have trained your hand to
the pistol, who have shown you how to draw the sword, have
taught you not to dread the strongest laborer of the faubourg, who have done for your brains what I have done for
your body, have set you above all men, and anointed you my
king, do you take me for a dolt? Come, now, let us have a
little more frankness.

### RAOUL

Do you wish me to tell you what I was thinking?—But
no, that would be to accuse my benefactor.

### VAUTRIN

Your benefactor! You insult me. Do you think I have
devoted to you my life, my blood, shown myself ready to
kill, to assassinate your enemy, in order that I may receive
that exorbitant interest called gratitude? Have I become an
usurer of this kind? There are some men who would hang
the weight of a benefit around your heart, like a cannon-ball
attached to the feet of——, but let that pass! Such men I
would crush as I would a worm, without thinking that I had
committed homicide! No! I have asked you to adopt me
as your father, that my heart may be to you what heaven is
to the angels, a space where all is happiness and confidence;
that you may tell me all your thoughts, even those which are
evil. Speak, I shall understand everything, even an act of
cowardice.

### RAOUL

God and Satan must have conspired to cast this man of
bronze.

### VAUTRIN

It is quite possible.

RAOUL

I will tell you all.

VAUTRIN

Very good, my son; let us sit down.

RAOUL

You have been the cause to me of opprobrium and despair.

VAUTRIN

Where? When? Blood of a man! Who has wounded you? Who has proved false to you? Tell me the place, name the people—the wrath of Vautrin shall descend upon them!

RAOUL

You can do nothing.

VAUTRIN

Child, there are two kinds of men who can do anything.

RAOUL

And who are they?

VAUTRIN

Kings, who are, or who ought to be, above the law; and—this will give you pain—criminals, who are below it.

RAOUL

But since you are not king—

VAUTRIN

Well! I reign in the region below.

RAOUL

What horrible mockery is this, Vautrin?

VAUTRIN

Did you not say that God and the devil hobnobbed to cast me?

### RAOUL

Heavens, sir, you make me shudder!

### VAUTRIN

Return to your seat! Calm yourself, my son. You must not be astonished at anything, if you wish to escape being an ordinary man.

### RAOUL

Am I in the hands of a demon, or of an angel? You have brought me up without debauching the generous instincts I feel within me; you have enlightened without dazzling me; you have given me the experience of the old, without depriving me of the graces of youth; but it is not with impunity that you have whetted the edge of my intellect, expanded my view, roused my perspicacity. Tell me, what is the source of your wealth, is it an honorable one? Why do you forbid me to confess to you the sufferings of my childhood? Why have you given me the name of the village where you found me? Why do you prevent me from searching out my father and mother? Why do you bow me down under a load of falsehoods? An orphan may rouse the interest of people; an impostor, never. I live in a style which makes me an equal to the son of a duke or a peer; you have educated me well, without expense to the state; you have launched me into the empyrean of the world, and now they fling into my face the declaration, that there are no longer such people as De Frescas in existence. I have been asked who my family are, and you have forbidden me to answer. I am at once a great nobleman and a pariah. I must swallow insults which would drive me to rend alive marquises and dukes; rage fills my heart; I should like to fight twenty duels, and to die. Do you wish me to suffer any further insults? No more secrets for me! Prometheus of hell, either finish your work, or shatter it to pieces!

### VAUTRIN

Who could fail to respond with a glow of sympathy to

this burst of youthful generosity? What flashes of courage blaze forth! It is inspiring to see sentiment at its full tide! You must be the son of a noble race. But, Raoul, let us come down to what I call plain reason.

### RAOUL

Ah! At last!

### VAUTRIN

You ask me for an account of my guardianship. Here it is.

### RAOUL

But have I any right to ask this? Could I live without you?

### VAUTRIN

Silence, you had nothing, I have made you rich. You knew nothing, I have given you a good education. Oh! I have not yet done all for you. A father—all fathers give their life to their children, and as for me, happiness is a debt which I owe you. But is this really the cause of your gloom? There are here—in this casket (*he points to a casket*) a portrait, and certain letters. Often while reading the letters you sigh as if—

### RAOUL

Then you know all—?

### VAUTRIN

I know all.—Are you not touched to the heart?

### RAOUL

To the heart.

### VAUTRIN

O fool! Love lives by treachery, friendship by confidence. —And you—you must seek happiness in your own way.

### RAOUL

But have I the power? I will become a soldier, and— wherever the cannon roars, I will win a glorious name, or die.

VAUTRIN

Indeed! Why should you? You talk nonsense.

RAOUL

You are too old to possess the power of understanding me, and it is no use trying to explain.

VAUTRIN

Well, I will explain to you. You are in love with Ine? de Christoval, Princesse d'Arjos in her own right, daughter of a duke banished by King Ferdinand—an Andalusian who loves you and pleases me, not as a woman, but as a ravishing money-box, whose eyes are the finest in the world, whose dowry is captivating, and who is the most delightful piece of cash, graceful and elegant as some black corvette with white sails which convoys the long-expected galleons of America, and yields all the joys of life, exactly like the Fortune which is painted over the entrance of the lottery agencies. I approve of you here. You did wrong to fall in love, love will involve you in a thousand follies—but I understand.

RAOUL

Do not score me with such frightful sarcasms.

VAUTRIN

See how quickly he feels his ardor damped, and his hat wreathed in crêpe!

RAOUL

Yes. For it is impossible for the child flung by accident into the bosom of a fisher family at Alghero to become Prince of Arjos, while to lose Inez is for me to die of grief.

VAUTRIN

An income of twelve hundred thousand francs, the title of prince, grandeur, and amassed wealth, old man, are not things to be contemplated with melancholy.

RAOUL

If you love me, why do you mock me thus in the hour of my despair?

VAUTRIN

And what is the cause of your despair?

RAOUL

The duke and the marquis have insulted me, in their own house, in her presence, and I have seen then all my hopes extinguished. The door of the Christoval mansion is closed upon me. I do not know why the Duchesse de Montsorel made me come and see her. For the last few days she has manifested an interest in me which I do not understand.

VAUTRIN

And what brought you to the house of your rival?

RAOUL

It seems you know all about it.

VAUTRIN

Yes, and many other things besides. Is it true you desire Inez de Christoval? Then you can get over this present despondency.

RAOUL

You are trifling with me.

VAUTRIN

Look here, Raoul! The Christovals have shut their doors upon you. Well—to-morrow you shall be the accepted lover of the princess, and the Montsorels shall be turned away, Montsorels though they be.

RAOUL

The sight of my distress has crazed you.

VAUTRIN

What reason have you ever had for doubting my word? Did I not give you an Arabian horse, to drive mad with envy the foreign and native dandies of the Bois de Boulogne? Who paid your gambling debts? Who made provision for your excesses? Who gave you boots, you who once went barefoot?

RAOUL

You, my friend, my father, my family!

VAUTRIN

Many, many thanks. In those words is a recompense for all my sacrifices. But, alas! when once you become rich, a grandee of Spain, a part of the great world, you will forget me; a change of atmosphere brings a change of ideas; you will despise me, and—you will be right in doing so.

RAOUL

Do I see before me a genie, a spirit materialized from the Arabian Nights? I question my own existence. But, my friend, my protector, I have no family.

VAUTRIN

Well, we are making up a family for you at this very moment. The Louvre could not contain the portraits of your ancestors, they would overcrowd the quays.

RAOUL

You rekindle all my hopes.

VAUTRIN

Do you wish to obtain Inez?

RAOUL

By any means possible.

VAUTRIN

You will shrink from nothing?   Magic and hell will not intimidate you?

RAOUL

Hell is nothing, if it yields me paradise.

VAUTRIN

What is hell but the hulks and the convicts decorated by justice and the police with brandings and manacles, and driven on their course by that wretchedness from which they have no escape?   Paradise is a fine house, sumptuous carriages, delightful women, and the prestige of rank.   In this world, there exist two worlds.   I put you in the fairest of them, I remain myself in the foulest, and if you remember me, it is all I ask of you.

RAOUL

While you make me shudder with horror, you fill me with the frenzy of delight.

VAUTRIN (*slapping him on the shoulder*)

You are a child!   (*Aside*) Have I not said too much to him?   (*He rings.*)

RAOUL (*aside*)

There are moments when my inmost nature revolts from the acceptance of his benefits.   When he put his hand on my shoulder it was like a red-hot iron ; and yet he has never done anything but good to me!   He conceals from me the means, but the ends are all for me.

VAUTRIN

What are you saying there?

RAOUL

I am resolved to accept nothing, unless my honor—

### VAUTRIN

We will take care of your honor! Is it not I who have fostered your sense of honor? Have I ever compromised it?

### RAOUL

You must explain to me—

### VAUTRIN

I will explain nothing.

### RAOUL

Nothing?

### VAUTRIN

Did you not say, "By any possible means"? When Inez is once yours, does it matter what I have done, or who I am? You will take Inez away; you will travel. The Christoval family will protect the Prince of Arjos. (*To Lafouraille*) Put some bottles of champagne on ice; your master is to be married, he bids farewell to bachelor life. His friends are invited. Go and seek his mistresses, if there are any left! All shall attend the wedding—a general turn-out in full dress.

### RAOUL (*aside*)

His confidence terrifies me, but he is always right.

### VAUTRIN

Now for the dinner!

### ALL

Now for the dinner!

### VAUTRIN

Do not take your pleasure gloomily; laugh for the last time, while liberty is still yours; I will order none but Spanish wines, for they are in fashion to-day.

*Curtain to the Third Act.*

# ACT IV.

## SCENE FIRST.

(*Drawing-room of the Duchesse de Christoval.*)

THE DUCHESSE DE CHRISTOVAL AND INEZ.

INEZ

If M. de Frescas is of obscure birth, mother, I will at once give him up; but you, on your part, must be good enough not to insist upon my marriage with the Marquis de Montsorel.

THE DUCHESS

If I oppose this unreasonable match, it is certainly not for the purpose of making another with a designing family.

INEZ

Unreasonable? Who knows whether it be so or not? You believe him to be an adventurer, I believe he is a gentleman, and we have nothing to refute either view.

THE DUCHESS

We shall not have to wait long for proofs; the Montsorels are too eager to unmask him.

INEZ

And he, I believe, loves me too much to delay proving himself worthy of us. Was not his behavior yesterday noble in the extreme?

THE DUCHESS

Don't you see, silly child, that your happiness is identical

with mine?  Let Raoul satisfy the world, and I shall be ready
to fight for you not only against the intrigues of the Montsorels, but at the court of Spain, itself.

INEZ

Ah, mother, I perceive that you also love him.

THE DUCHESS

Is he not the man of your choice?

------

### SCENE SECOND.

THE SAME PERSONS, A FOOTMAN AND VAUTRIN.

(*The footman brings the duchess a card, wrapped up and
sealed.*)

THE DUCHESS (*to Inez*)

General Crustamente, the secret envoy of his Majesty Don
Augustine I., Emperor of Mexico.  What can he have to say
to me?

INEZ

Of Mexico!  He doubtless brings news of my father!

THE DUCHESS (*to the footman*)

Let him come in.

(*Vautrin enters dressed like a Mexican general, his height
increased four inches.  His hat has white plumes; his coat
blue, with the rich lace of a Mexican general officer; his
trousers white, his scarf crimson, his hair long and frizzed
like that of Murat; he wears a long sabre, and his com-
plexion is copper-hued.  He stutters like the Spaniards of
Mexico, and his accent resembles Provençal, plus the gut-
tural intonation of the Moors.*)

VAUTRIN

Is it indeed her grace, the Duchesse de Christoval that I have the honor to address?

THE DUCHESS

Yes, sir.

VAUTRIN

And mademoiselle?

THE DUCHESS

My daughter, sir.

VAUTRIN

Mademoiselle is then the Señora Inez, in her own right Princesse d'Arjos. When I see you, I understand perfectly M. de Christoval's idolatry of his daughter. But, ladies, before anything further, let me impose upon you the utmost secrecy. My mission is already a difficult one, but, if it is suspected that there is any communication between you and me, we should all be seriously compromised.

THE DUCHESS

I promise to keep secret both your name and your visit.

INEZ

General, if the matter concerns my father, you will allow me to remain here?

VAUTRIN

You are nobles, and Spaniards, and I rely upon your word.

THE DUCHESS

I shall instruct my servants to keep silence on the subject.

VAUTRIN

Don't say a word to them; to demand silence is often to provoke indiscreet talk. I can answer for my own people.

I pledged myself to bring you news of M. de Christoval, as soon as I reached Paris, and this is my first visit.

### THE DUCHESS

Tell us at once about my husband, general; where is he now?

### VAUTRIN

Mexico has become what was sooner or later inevitable, a state independent of Spain. At the moment I speak there are no more Spaniards, only Mexicans, in Mexico.

### THE DUCHESS

At this moment?

### VAUTRIN

Everything seems to happen in a moment where the causes are not discerned. How could it be otherwise? Mexico felt the need of her independence, she has chosen an emperor! Although nothing could be more natural, it may still surprise us: while principles can wait to be recognized men are always in a hurry.

### THE DUCHESS

What has happened to M. de Christoval?

### VAUTRIN

Do not be alarmed, madame; he is not emperor. His grace the duke has been unsuccessful, in spite of a desperate struggle, in keeping the kingdom loyal to Ferdinand VII

### THE DUCHESS

But, sir, my husband is not a soldier.

### VAUTRIN

Of course he is not; but he is a clever loyalist, and has acquitted himself well. If he does eventually succeed, he will be received back again into royal favor.  Ferdinand cannot help appointing him viceroy.

THE DUCHESS

In what a strange century do we live!

VAUTRIN

Revolutions succeed without resembling each other France sets the example to the world.  But let me beg of you not to talk politics; it is dangerous ground.

INEZ

Has my father received our letters, general?

VAUTRIN

In the confusion of such a conflict letters may go astray, when even crowns are lost.

THE DUCHESS

And what has become of M. de Christoval?

VAUTRIN

The aged Amoagos, who exercises enormous influence in those regions, saved your husband's life at the moment I was going to have him shot—

THE DUCHESS AND HER DAUGHTER.

Ah!

VAUTRIN

It was thus that he and I became acquainted.

THE DUCHESS

You, general?

INEZ

And my father?

### VAUTRIN

Well, ladies, I should have been either hanged by him, as a rebel, or hailed by others as the hero of an emancipated nation, and here I am. The sudden arrival of Amoagos, at the head of his miners, decided the question. The safety of his friend, the Duc de Christoval, was the reward of his interference. Between ourselves, the Emperor Iturbide, my master, is no more than a figurehead; the future of Mexico is entirely in the hands of the aged Amoagos.

### THE DUCHESS

And who, pray, is this Amoagos, the arbiter, as you say, of Mexico's destiny?

### VAUTRIN

Is he not known here? Is it possible? I do not know what can possibly be found to weld the old and new worlds together. I suppose it will be steam. What is the use of exploiting gold mines, of being such a man as Don Inigo Juan Varago Cardaval de los Amoagos, las Frescas y Peral—and not be heard over here? But of course he uses only one of his names, as we all do; thus, I call myself simply Crustamente. Although you may be the future president of the Mexican republic, France will ignore you. The aged Amoagos, ladies, received M. de Christoval just as the ancient gentleman of Aragon that he was would receive a Spanish grandee who had been banished for yielding to the spell of Napoleon's name.

### INEZ

Did you not mention Frescas among other names?

### VAUTRIN

Yes, Frescas is the name of the second mine worked by Don Cardaval; but you will learn all that monsieur the duke owes to his host from the letters I have brought you. They are in my pocket-book. (*Aside*) They are much taken by my aged Amoagos. (*Aloud*) Allow me to send for one of

my people. (*He signs Inez to ring. To the duchess*) Permit
me to say a few words to him. (*To the footman*) Tell my
negro—but no, you won't understand his frightful patois.
Make signs to him to come here.

### THE DUCHESS

My child, leave the room for a moment.
(*Enter Lafouraille, made up as a negro, and carrying a
large portmanteau.*)

### VAUTRIN TO LAFOURAILLE.

Jigi roro flouri.

### LAFOURAILLE

Joro.

### INEZ (*to Vautrin*)

The confidence my father has reposed in you ensures you
a warm welcome; but, general, you have won my gratitude
by your promptness in allaying our anxieties.

### VAUTRIN

Your gratitude! Ah, señora, if we are to reckon accounts
I should consider myself in debt to your illustrious father,
after having the happiness to see you.

### LAFOURAILLE

Jo.

### VAUTRIN

Caracas, y mouli joro, fistas, ip souri.

### LAFOURAILLE

Souri, joro.

### VAUTRIN (*to the ladies*)

Ladies, here are your letters. (*Aside to Lafouraille*) Go
round from the antechamber to the court, close your lips,
open your ears; hands off, eye on the watch.

LAFOURAILLE

Ja, mein herr.

VAUTRIN (*angrily*)

Souri joro, fistas.

LAFOURAILLE

Joro.  (*Whispering*) There are the de Langeac papers.

VAUTRIN

I am not for the emancipation of the negroes! when there are no more of them, we shall have to do with whites.

INEZ (*to her mother*)

Mother, allow me to go and read my father's letter.  (*To Vautrin*) General— (*She bows.*)

VAUTRIN

She is charming, may she be happy!  (*Exit Inez, accompanied to the door by her mother.*)

---

## SCENE THIRD.

### THE DUCHESS AND VAUTRIN.

VAUTRIN (*aside*)

If Mexico saw herself represented in this way, the government would be capable of condemning me to embassades for life.  (*Aloud*) Pray excuse me, madame.  I have so many things to think about.

THE DUCHESS

If absent-mindedness may be excused in any one, it is in a diplomat.

VAUTRIN

Yes, to civil diplomats, but I mean to remain a frank soldier. The success which I derive must be the result of candor. But now that we are alone, let us talk, for I have more than one delicate mission to discharge.

### The Duchess

Have you any news which my daughter should not hear?

### Vautrin

It may be so. Let us come to the point; the señora is young and beautiful, she is rich and noble born; she probably has four times as many suitors as any other lady. Her hand is the object of rivalry. Well, her father has charged me to find whether she has singled out any one in particular.

### The Duchess

With a frank man, general, I will be frank. Your question is so strange that I cannot answer it.

### Vautrin

Take care, for we diplomats, in our fear of being deceived, always put the worst interpretation on silence.

### The Duchess

Sir, you forget that we are talking of Inez de Christoval!

### Vautrin

She is in love with no one. That is good; she will be able then to carry out the wishes of her father.

### The Duchess

How has M. de Christoval disposed of his daughter's hand?

### Vautrin

You see my meaning, and your anxiety tells me that she has made her choice. I tremble to ask further, as much as

you do to answer. Ah! if only the young man whom your
daughter loves were a foreigner, rich, apparently without
family, and bent on concealing the name of his native land!—

### The Duchess

The name, Frescas, which you lately uttered, is that of a
young man who seeks the hand of Inez.

### Vautrin

Does he call himself also Raoul?

### The Duchess

Yes, Raoul de Frescas.

### Vautrin

A young man of refinement, elegance and wit, and twenty-
three years of age?

### The Duchess

Gifted with manners which are never acquired, but innate.

### Vautrin

Romantic to the point of desiring to be loved for his own
sake, in spite of his immense fortune; he wishes that passion
should prevail in marriage—an absurdity! The young
Amoagos, for it is he, madame.

### The Duchess

But the name of Raoul is not—

### Vautrin

Mexican—you are right. It was given to him by his
mother, a Frenchwoman, an émigrée, a De Granville, who
came from St. Domingo. Is the reckless fellow favored by
her?

THE DUCHESS

Preferred to all the rest.

VAUTRIN

Well, open this letter, and read it, madame; and you will
see that I have received full authority from Amoagos and
Christoval to conclude this marriage.

THE DUCHESS

Oh, let me call in Inez, sir. (*Exit.*)

---

## SCENE FOURTH.

VAUTRIN (*alone*)

The major-domo is on my side, the genuine deeds, if he
comes upon them, will be handed to me. Raoul is too proud
to return to this house; besides that, he has promised me to
wait. I am thus master of the situation; Raoul, when once
he is a prince, will not lack ancestors; Mexico and I will see
to that.

---

## SCENE FIFTH.

VAUTRIN, THE DUCHESSE DE CHRISTOVAL AND INEZ.

THE DUCHESS (*to her daughter*)

My child, you have reason to thank the general very warmly.

INEZ

To thank you, sir? My father tells me, that among other
missions you have received is that of marrying me to a certain Signor Amoagos, without any regard to my inclinations.

### VAUTRIN

You need not be alarmed, for his name here is Raoul de Frescas.

### INEZ

What! he, Raoul de Frescas!—why then his persistent silence?

### VAUTRIN

Does it need an old soldier to interpret the heart of a young man? He wished for love, not obedience; he wished—

### INEZ

Ah, general, I will punish him well for his modesty and distrust. Yesterday, he showed himself readier to swallow an affront than to reveal the name of his father.

### VAUTRIN

But, mademoiselle, I am still uncertain as to whether the name of his father is that of a man convicted of high treason, or of a liberator of America.

### INEZ

Ah! mother, do you hear that?

### VAUTRIN (*aside*)

How she loves him! Poor girl, she does not deserve to be imposed upon.

### THE DUCHESS

My husband's letter does in truth give you the full authority, general.

### VAUTRIN

I have the authentic documents, and family deeds.

### A FOOTMAN (*as he enters*)

Will 'ner grace the duchess see M. de Frescas?

VAUTRIN (*aside*)

That! Raoul here?

THE DUCHESS (*to the footman*)

Let him come in.

VAUTRIN (*aside*)

What a mess! The patient is liable to dose his doctor.

THE DUCHESS

Inez, you can see M. de Frescas alone hereafter, since he has been acknowledged by your father. (*Inez kisses her mother's hand formally.*)

---

## SCENE SIXTH.

### THE SAME PERSONS AND RAOUL.

(*Raoul salutes the two ladies. Vautrin approaches him.*)

VAUTRIN (*to Raoul*)

Don Raoul de Cardaval.

RAOUL

Vautrin!

VAUTRIN

No! General Crustamente.

RAOUL

Crustamente!

VAUTRIN

Certainly; Mexican Envoy. Bear well in mind the name of your father,—Amoagos, a gentleman of Aragon, friend of the Duc de Christoval. Your mother is dead; I bring the acknowledged titles, and authentic family papers. Inez is yours.

### RAOUL

And do you think that I will consent to such villainies? Never!

### VAUTRIN (*to the two ladies*)

He is overcome by what I have told him, not anticipating so prompt an explanation.

### RAOUL

If the truth should kill, your falsehoods would dishonor me, and I prefer to die.

### VAUTRIN

You wished to obtain Inez by any means possible, yet you shrink from practicing a harmless stratagem.

### RAOUL (*in exasperation*)

Ladies!

### VAUTRIN

He is beside himself with joy. (*To Raoul*) To speak out would be to lose Inez and deliver me to justice; do as you choose, I am at your disposal.

### RAOUL

O Vautrin! in what an abyss you have plunged me!

### VAUTRIN

I have made you a prince; and don't forget that you are at the summit of happiness. (*Aside*) He will give in. (*Exit.*)

## *SCENE SEVENTH.*

INEZ (*standing at the door through which her mother has passed*) ; RAOUL (*at the other side of the stage*).

### RAOUL (*aside*)

Honor bids me to speak out, gratitude to keep silence; well, I accept my rôle of happy man, until he is out of danger; but I will write this evening, and Inez shall learn who I am. Vautrin, after such a sacrifice, I may cry quits with you; all ties between us are severed. I will seek, I care not where, a soldier's death.

### INEZ (*approaching, after gazing at him*)

My father and yours are friends; they consent to our marriage; we make love to each other as if they were opposed to it, and you seem lost in thought, and almost sad!

### RAOUL

You are right, and I have lost my reason. At the very moment you see no obstacle in our way, it is possible that insurmountable difficulties may arise.

### INEZ

Raoul, what a damper you are throwing on our happiness!

### RAOUL

Our happiness! (*Aside*) It is impossible to dissemble. (*Aloud*) In the name of our common love I implore you to believe in my loyalty.

### INEZ

Has not my confidence in you been boundless? And the general has quite justified it, even during your silence before the Montsorels. I forgive you all the little annoyances you were forced to cause me.

### RAOUL (*aside*)

Ah! Vautrin! I trust myself to you! (*Aloud*) Inez, you do not know how great is the impression your words make upon me; they give me power to bear the overwhelming rapture your presence causes—Come then, let us be happy!

---

### SCENE EIGHTH.

### THE SAME PERSONS AND THE MARQUIS DE MONTSOREL.

### THE FOOTMAN (*announcing a visitor*)

M. le Marquis de Montsorel.

### RAOUL (*aside*)

Ah! That name recalls me to myself. (*To Inez*) Whatever happens, Inez, do not judge my conduct until I have myself given an account of it, and believe at the present moment that I am carried along by an invincible fatality.

### INEZ

Raoul, I cannot understand you; but I shall trust you always.

### THE MARQUIS (*aside*)

Again this little gentleman here! (*He salutes Inez.*) I thought you were with your mother, mademoiselle, and I never dreamed my visit would be so inopportune. Be good enough to excuse me—

### INEZ

I beg that you will not go; there is no one but ourselves here, for M. Raoul has been accepted by my family.

### THE MARQUIS

Will M. Raoul de Frescas, then, accept my congratulations?

RAOUL

Your congratulations? I accept them (*they shake hands*) in the same spirit as that in which they are offered.

THE MARQUIS

We understand each other.

INEZ (*to Raoul*)

Manage that he go away, and do you remain. (*To the Marquis*) My mother requires me for a few moments, and I will return with her.

---

## SCENE NINTH.

THE MARQUIS AND RAOUL; LATER, VAUTRIN.

THE MARQUIS

Will you agree to a meeting without seconds—a fight to the death?

RAOUL

Without seconds?

THE MARQUIS

Do you realize that both of us cannot exist in the same world?

RAOUL

Your family is a powerful one; your proposition exposes me, in case I am victorious, to their vengeance. Allow me to say that I do not want to exchange this house for a prison. (*Vautrin appears.*) I will fight to the death—but not without seconds.

THE MARQUIS

Will those on your side stop the duel?

### RAOUL

Our mutual hatred is sufficient guarantee against that.

### VAUTRIN (*aside*)

Well, now—we always commit some blunder in the moment of success! To the death! This child would gamble away his life as if it belonged to him.

### THE MARQUIS

Very well, monsieur; to-morrow at eight o'clock, we meet at the terrace of Saint-Germain, and drive from there to the forest.

### VAUTRIN (*coming forward*)

You will not go. (*To Raoul*) A duel? Are the principals of equal rank? Is this gentleman, like you, the only son of a noble house? Would your father, Don Inigo Juan Varago de los Amoagos de Cardaval las Frescas y Peral, allow you to do it. Raoul?

### THE MARQUIS

I have consented to fight with an unknown man, but the greatness of the house to which the gentleman belongs cannot nullify the agreement.

### RAOUL (*to the marquis*)

Nevertheless, it seems to me, monsieur, that we can treat each other with courtesy, and act like people who esteem each other too much to take the trouble to hate and to kill.

### THE MARQUIS (*looking at Vautrin*)

May I know the name of your friend?

### VAUTRIN

By whom have I the honor to be referred to?

### The Marquis

By the Marquis de Montsorel, sir.

### VAUTRIN (*eyeing him from head to foot*)

I have the right to refuse you, but I will tell you my name, once for all, in a very short time, and you won't repeat it. I am to be one of the seconds of M. de Frescas. (*Aside*) And Buteux shall be the other.

---

## SCENE TENTH.

RAOUL, VAUTRIN, THE MARQUIS AND THE DUCHESSE DE MONTSOREL; LATER, THE DUCHESSE DE CHRISTOVAL AND INEZ.

### FOOTMAN (*announcing a visitor*)

Her grace the Duchesse de Montsorel.

### VAUTRIN (*to Raoul*)

Let me have no nonsense; be calm and firm! I stand face to face with the enemy.

### THE MARQUIS

Ah, mother dear, and are you come to witness my defeat? All is ended. The De Christoval family has trifled with us. This gentleman (*he points to Vautrin*) represents both families.

### THE DUCHESSE DE MONTSOREL

Then Raoul has a family? (*The Duchesse de Christoval and her daughter enter and salute the speaker. To the Duchesse de Christoval*) Madame, my son has told me what has occurred to frustrate all our hopes.

### The Duchesse de Christoval

The interest which yesterday you manifested in M. de Frescas has, I see, changed to indifference?

### The Duchesse de Montsorel (*scrutinizing Vautrin*)

Is it through this gentleman that all your doubts have been satisfied? Who is he?

### The Duchesse de Christoval

He represents the father of M. de Frescas, don Amoagos, and the father of Inez, M. de Christoval. He has brought us the news we expected, and brought letters from my husband.

### Vautrin (*aside*)

Am I to act this part long?

### The Duchesse de Montsorel (*to Vautrin*)

Doubtless you have known the family of M. de Frescas for some time?

### Vautrin

My acquaintance is limited to a father and an uncle—(*to Raoul*) You have not even the mournful satisfaction of remembering your mother. (*To the Duchess*) She died in Mexico, shortly after her marriage.

### The Duchesse de Montsorel

M. de Frescas, then, was born in Mexico?

### Vautrin

Of course he was.

### The Duchesse de Montsorel (*to the Duchesse de Christoval*)

My dear, we are being imposed upon. (*To Raoul*) Sir, you

did not come from Mexico. Your mother is not dead, is she? And have you not been abandoned since your childhood?

RAOUL

Would that my mother were alive!

VAUTRIN

Pardon me, madame, but I am here to satisfy your curiosity, if you wish to learn the secret history which it is not necessary you should seek from this gentleman. (*To Raoul*) Not a word!

THE DUCHESSE DE MONTSOREL

It is he! And this man is making him the tool in some sinister undertaking. (*She approaches the marquis*) My son—

THE MARQUIS

You have put them out, mother, and I share your impression of this man (*he indicates Vautrin*); but only a woman has the right to express her thoughts in a way to expose this frightful imposture.

THE DUCHESSE DE MONTSOREL

Frightful indeed! But pray leave us.

THE MARQUIS

Ladies, in spite of my ill-fortune, do not blame me if I still have hopes. (*To Vautrin*) Often between the cup and the lip there is—

VAUTRIN

Death! (*Exit the marquis, after exchanging bows with Raoul.*)

THE DUCHESSE DE MONTSOREL (*to Madame de Christoval*)

My dear duchess, I implore you to excuse Inez. We cannot make our explanations before her.

THE DUCHESSE DE CHRISTOVAL (*to her daughter, making signs to her to leave the room*)

I will rejoin you in a moment.

RAOUL (*kissing his hand to Inez*)

This is perhaps good-bye forever! (*Exit Inez.*)

---

## SCENE ELEVENTH.

THE DUCHESSE DE CHRISTOVAL, THE DUCHESSE DE MONTSOREL, RAOUL AND VAUTRIN.

VAUTRIN (*to the Duchesse de Christoval*)

Do you suspect the motive that brings madame here?

THE DUCHESSE DE CHRISTOVAL

After what happened yesterday I prefer not to say.

VAUTRIN

I guessed her love for him immediately.

RAOUL (*to Vautrin*)

This atmosphere of falsehood stifles me.

VAUTRIN (*to Raoul*)

One word more, and the affair will be ended.

THE DUCHESSE DE MONTSOREL

Madame, I know well how strange my present conduct must appear to you, and I won't attempt to justify it. There are solemn duties before which the conventions and even the laws of society must give way. What is the character and what the powers of this man?

THE DUCHESSE DE CHRISTOVAL (*to whom Vautrin makes a signal*)

'I am forbidden to answer this question.

THE DUCHESSE DE MONTSOREL

Well, I will tell you; this man is either the accomplice or the dupe in an imposture of which we are the victims. In spite of the letters and documents which he brings to you, I am convinced that all evidence which gives name and family to Raoul is false.

RAOUL

To tell the truth, madame, I do not know what right you have to interfere in personal matters of mine.

THE DUCHESSE DE CHRISTOVAL

Madame, you were wise to send out of the room my daughter and the marquis.

VAUTRIN (*to Raoul*)

What right? (*To Madame de Montsorel*) You need not avow it, for we divine it. I can well understand, madame, the pain you feel at the prospect of this marriage, and am not therefore offended at your suspicions with regard to me, and the authentic documents which I have brought to Madame de Christoval. (*Aside*) Now for the final stroke. (*He takes her aside*) Before becoming a Mexican I was a Spaniard, and I know the cause of your hatred for Albert. And as to the motive which brings you here, we will talk about that very soon at the house of your confessor.

THE DUCHESSE DE MONTSOREL

You know?—

VAUTRIN

All. (*Aside*) She has some motive. (*Aloud*) Will you examine the documents?

THE DUCHESSE DE CHRISTOVAL

Well, my dear?

THE DUCHESSE DE MONTSOREL

Be quick, and send for Inez. Examine the deeds carefully, I implore you. This is the request of a despairing mother.

THE DUCHESSE DE CHRISTOVAL

A despairing mother!

THE DUCHESSE DE MONTSOREL (*to herself, looking at Raoul and Vautrin*)

How is it possible that this man should know my secret and have this hold upon my son?

THE DUCHESSE DE CHRISTOVAL

Will you come. madame? (*Exeunt the two duchesses.*)

-----

### SCENE TWELFTH.

RAOUL, VAUTRIN AND LATER LAFOURAILLE.

VAUTRIN

I thought our star was setting; but it is still in the ascendant.

RAOUL

Have I not been humbled sufficiently? I had nothing in the world but my honor, and that I gave into your keeping. Your power is infernal, I see that plainly. But from this very moment I withdraw from its influence. You are no longer in danger. Farewell.

LAFOURAILLE (*coming in while Raoul speaks*)

No one caught,—'twas lucky,—we had time! Ah, sir,

Philosopher is below, all is lost! The house has been entered by the police.

### VAUTRIN

Disgusting! And no one has been taken?

### LAFOURAILLE

We were too cute for that.

### VAUTRIN

Philosopher is below, as what?

### LAFOURAILLE

As a footman.

### VAUTRIN

Good; let him get up behind my carriage. I want to give you my orders about locking up the Prince d'Arjos, who thinks he is going to fight a duel to-morrow.

### RAOUL

I see that you are in danger. I will not leave you, and I desire to know—

### VAUTRIN

Nothing. Do not worry about your own security. I will look out for you, in spite of you.

### RAOUL

Oh! I know what my future will be.

### VAUTRIN

I too know.

### LAFOURAILLE

Come, things are getting hot.

### VAUTRIN

Nay, the fat is in the fire.

### LAFOURAILLE

No time for sentiment, or dilly-dallying, they are on our track and are mounted.

### VAUTRIN

Let us be off then. (*He takes Lafouraille aside*) If the government should do us the honor to billet its gendarmes on us, our duty is to let them alone. All are at liberty to scatter; but let all be at Mother Giroflée's at midnight. Get off post haste, for I do not wish us to meet our Waterloo, and the Prussians are upon us. We must run for it.

*Curtain to the Fourth Act.*

# ACT V.

## *SCENE FIRST.*

(*The scene is laid at the Montsorel house, in a room on the ground floor.*)

JOSEPH (*alone*)

The cursed white mark appears this evening on the wicket gate of the garden. Things cannot go on long in this way; the devil only knows how it will end. I prefer seeing him there, however, rather than in the apartments; the garden is at least away from the house, and when the warning comes, one can walk out to meet him.

## *SCENE SECOND.*

JOSEPH, LAFOURAILLE AND BUTEUX; LATER, VAUTRIN.

(*The humming sound of a voice is heard for a moment.*)

JOSEPH

'There it is, our national air, which I never hear without trembling. (*Enter Lafouraille*) And who are you? (*Lafouraille makes a sign*) A new one coming?

LAFOURAILLE

No, an old one.

JOSEPH

Oh, he whose mark is in the garden.

### LAFOURAILLE

Can he be waiting here?  He intended to be here.  (*Buteux appears.*)

### JOSEPH

Why, there will be three of you.

### LAFOURAILLE (*pointing to Joseph*)

There will be four of us.

### JOSEPH

And what do you come to do at this hour?  Do you want to snatch up everything here?

### LAFOURAILLE

He takes us for thieves!

### BUTEUX

We prove that we can be, when we are down in our luck; but we never say so.

### LAFOURAILLE

That is, we make money, like other people.

### JOSEPH

But his grace the duke is going—

### LAFOURAILLE

Your duke cannot return home before two o'clock, and that gives us time enough: do not therefore interlard with anxious thought the professional dish which we have to serve—

### BUTEUX

And serve hot.

VAUTRIN (*he wears a brown coat, blue trousers, and a black waistcoat. His hair is short and he is got up as an imitation of Napoleon in undress. As he enters he abruptly puts out the candle and draws the slide of his dark lantern*)

What! You have lights here! You think yourselves still members of respectable society. I can understand that this fool should ignore the first elements of sane conduct—but you others! (*To Buteux, as he points out Joseph to him*) Put wool in this fellow's ears, and talk with him over there. (*To Lafouraille*) And what of the youngster?

LAFOURAILLE

He is kept well out of sight.

VAUTRIN

In what place?

LAFOURAILLE

In the other rookery of Giroflée's woman, near here, behind the Invalides.

VAUTRIN

And see that he does not escape like that slippery eel of a Saint-Charles, that madman, who came for the purpose of breaking up our establishment—for I—but I never threaten.

LAFOURAILLE

Upon the youngster's safety I will stake my head! Philosopher has put buskins on his hands and frills on his feet, he cannot stir hand or foot, and will be given up only to me. As for the other, who could help it? Poor Giroflée cannot resist strong liquors, and Blondet knew it.

VAUTRIN

What did Raoul say?

### LAFOURAILLE

He made a terrible uproar; and swore he was disgraced. Fortunately Philosopher is insensible to metaphors.

### VAUTRIN

Do you think the boy wishes for a fight to the death? A young man is fearful; he has the courage to conceal his terror and the folly to allow himself to be killed. I hope they prevent him from writing to any one.

### LAFOURAILLE (*aside*)

We are in for it! (*Aloud*) I can conceal nothing from you; before he was fastened up the prince sent little Nini with a letter to the Christoval house.

### VAUTRIN

To Inez?

### LAFOURAILLE

To Inez.

### VAUTRIN

He wrote a lot of rubbish, I'll warrant.

### LAFOURAILLE

A pack of lies and absurdities.

### VAUTRIN (*to Joseph*)

Hello there! You—the honest man.

### BUTEUX (*leading Joseph to Vautrin*)

You had better explain things to the master, as he desires.

### JOSEPH

It seems to me that I am not unreasonable to ask what risk I am to run, and what profit is to accrue to me.

### VAUTRIN

Time is short, speech long, let us employ the former and

drop the latter. There are two lives in peril, that of a man I am interested in, and that of a musketeer which I consider useless: we are going to crush him.

### JOSEPH

What! Do you mean monsieur the marquis? I will have nothing to do with it.

### LAFOURAILLE

You have no say in the matter of your consent.

### BUTEUX

We have captured him. Look you, my friend, when the wine is drawn—

### JOSEPH

If it is bad, it must not be drunk.

### VAUTRIN

And you refuse to pledge me in a glass? He who thinks calculates, and he who calculates betrays.

### JOSEPH

Your calculations lead to the scaffold.

### VAUTRIN

Enough! You tire me. Your master is to fight a duel to-morrow. In this duel one of the combatants will never leave the ground alive; imagine that the duel has taken place, and that your master has had no fair chance.

### BUTEUX

That is just it.

### LAFOURAILLE

The master is as deep as Fate.

JOSEPH

A fine condition to be in.


BUTEUX

The devil to pay and no pitch hot!


VAUTRIN (*to Joseph, pointing out Lafouraille and Buteux*)
You will conceal these two.


JOSEPH

Where?

VAUTRIN

I tell you, you must conceal them.  When all are asleep in
the house, excepting us, you must send them up to the musketeer's room.  (*To Buteux and Lafouraille*)  Try to go there
without him; you must be cautious and adroit; the window of
his room overlooks the court.  (*Whispers in their ear*)  Throw
him down.  It will be a case of despair (*turning to Joseph*),
and suicide will be a ground for averting suspicion from all.


——————


*SCENE THIRD.*


VAUTRIN (*alone*)

All is saved! there is only one suspect among us, and I will
change that state of affairs.  Blondet is the traitor, and in this
case bad debts will make good friends, for I will point him out
to the duke in a friendly manner as the murderer of Vicomte
de Langeac.  I must finally discover the motive of the
duchess's singular behavior.  If what I learn explains the suicide of the marquis, what a master stroke it will be!

## SCENE FOURTH.

### JOSEPH AND VAUTRIN.

#### JOSEPH

Your men are well concealed, but you doubtless intend to leave the house?

#### VAUTRIN

No, I am going to do some reading in the study of the Duc de Montsorel.

#### JOSEPH

But if he comes home, won't you be afraid?

#### VAUTRIN

If I feared anything, would I be the master of you all?

#### JOSEPH

But where are you going?

#### VAUTRIN

You are very curious.

---

## SCENE FIFTH.

#### JOSEPH (*alone*)

There, he is disposed of for the moment, his two fellows likewise; I hold them, and, as I don't want to have anything to do with the affair, I am going—

## *SCENE SIXTH.*

JOSEPH, A FOOTMAN; AND AFTERWARDS SAINT-CHARLES.

THE FOOTMAN

M. Joseph, some one is asking for you.

JOSEPH

At this hour?

SAINT-CHARLES

It is I.

JOSEPH (*to the footman*)

You may go.

SAINT-CHARLES

His grace the duke cannot come home until after the king's retirement for the night.   The duchess is on her way home.   I wish to speak to her privately and wait for her here.

JOSEPH

Here?

SAINT-CHARLES

Here.

JOSEPH (*aside*)

O my God! and Jacques—

SAINT-CHARLES

If it inconveniences you—

JOSEPH

Not in the least.

SAINT-CHARLES

Tell me the truth, you are expecting some one.

JOSEPH

I am expecting the duchess.

SAINT-CHARLES

And not Jacques Collin?

JOSEPH

Oh! don't talk to me about that man, you make me shudder.

SAINT-CHARLES

Collin is mixed up with some business that might bring him
here. You must have seen him lately. I have no time to pump
you, and I have no need to bribe, but you must choose between
him and me, and pretty quickly, too.

JOSEPH

What do you require of me?

SAINT-CHARLES

To tell me everything that takes place here.

JOSEPH

Well, the latest thing is the duel of the marquis; he fights
to-morrow with M. de Frescas.

SAINT-CHARLES

What next?

JOSEPH

I see her grace the duchess has just returned.

---

*SCENE SEVENTH.*

SAINT-CHARLES (*alone*)

What a timid beast he is! This duel is a capital excuse for
speaking with the duchess. The duke did not understand me,
he saw in me nothing but a tool, to be taken up and dropped

at pleasure. Did he not, by imposing silence upon me towards his wife, betray his suspicion that I was dangerous to him? The patrimony of the strong is the faculty of utilizing the faults of a neighbor. I have already devoured several patrimonies, and my appetite is still good.

------

### SCENE EIGHTH.

SAINT-CHARLES, THE DUCHESSE DE MONTSOREL AND MLLE. DE VAUDREY.

*(Saint-Charles disappears till the two ladies have passed, and remains at the back, while they come to the front of the stage.)*

MLLE. DE VAUDREY.

You are quite worn out.

THE DUCHESSE DE MONTSOREL *(sinking into an armchair)*

Yes; I am dead! In despair—

SAINT-CHARLES *(coming forward)*

Madame the duchess.

THE DUCHESS

Ah! I had forgotten! Sir, it is impossible at this moment to grant you the interview you ask. To-morrow—or later in the day.

MLLE. DE VAUDREY *(to Saint-Charles)*

My niece, sir, is not in a condition to listen to you.

SAINT-CHARLES

To-morrow, ladies, it will be too late! The life of your son,

the Marquis de Montsorel, who fights a duel to-morrow with
M. de Frescas, is threatened.

### THE DUCHESS

This duel is indeed a frightful thing.

### MLLE. DE VAUDREY (*in a low tone to the duchess*)

You have already forgotten that Raoul is a stranger to
you.

### THE DUCHESS (*to Saint-Charles*)

Sir, my son will know how to acquit himsel

### SAINT-CHARLES

May I venture to inform you of facts which ordinarily
would be kept from a mother? Your son will be killed without any fighting. His adversary's servants are bravoes,
wretches of whom he is the ringleader.

### THE DUCHESS

And what proof have you of this?

### SAINT-CHARLES

A former steward of M. de Frescas has offered me a vast
sum if I would join in this foul conspiracy against the Christoval family. In order to make time, I pretended to assent;
but just as I was on my way to warn the authorities, I was
dashed to the ground by two men who came by at full speed,
and I lost consciousness; they administered to me in this condition a powerful narcotic, thrust me into a cab, and when
I came to myself, I was in a den of criminals. Recovering
my self-possession, I escaped from my confinement, and set
out to track these dare-devils.

### MLLE. DE VAUDREY

You sometimes come here to see M. de Montsorel, according to what Joseph tells us?

SAINT-CHARLES

Yes, madame.

THE DUCHESS

And who, pray, may you be, sir?

SAINT-CHARLES

I am a private detective, whom his grace the duke distrusts, and I am hired for clearing up mysterious occurrences.

MLLE. DE VAUDREY (*to the duchess*)

O Louise!

THE DUCHESS (*fixing her eyes on Saint-Charles*)
And who has had the impertinence to send you to address me?

SAINT-CHARLES

A sense of your danger brings me here. I am paid to be your enemy. You can keep silence as well as I; prove that your protection is more advantageous to me than the hollow promises of the duke, and I can assure you the victory. But time presses, the duke will soon be here, and if he finds us together, the success of our undertaking would be endangered.

THE DUCHESS (*to Mlle. de Vaudrey*)

Ah! we may still hope! (*To Saint-Charles*) And what were you going to do at the house of M. de Frescas?

SAINT-CHARLES

That which, at present, I am doing at yours.

THE DUCHESS

Silence, sir.

SAINT-CHARLES

Your grace has given me no answer; the duke has my word, and he is very powerful.

### THE DUCHESS

And I, sir, am immensely rich; but do not expect to take advantage of me. (*She rises*) I will never be the dupe of M de Montsorel, I recognize his trickery in this secret interview, which you had asked for. (*With emphasis*) Let me complete your information. M. de Frescas is not a wretch; his servants are not assassins; he belongs to a family as rich as it is noble, and he is about to marry the Princesse d'Arjos.

### SAINT-CHARLES

Yes, madame, a Mexican envoy has produced letters from M. de Christoval, and documents remarkably authentic. You have sent for a secretary of the Spanish legation, who has endorsed them: seals, stamps, authentications—ah! all are flawless.

### THE DUCHESS

Yes, sir, the documents are unassailable.

### SAINT-CHARLES

You are very much interested, madame, in their being proved forgeries, I presume?

### THE DUCHESS (*to Mlle. de Vaudrey*)

Never has such torture as this wrung the heart of a mother!

### SAINT-CHARLES (*aside*)

Whose side shall I take, husband's or wife's?

### THE DUCHESS

Sir, any sum you may ask shall be yours, if you can prove to me that M. Raoul de Frescas—

### SAINT-CHARLES

Is a criminal?

### THE DUCHESS

No, but a child—

SAINT-CHARLES

You mean your child, don't you?

THE DUCHESS (*forgetting herself*)

Yes, yes! Be my deliverer, and I will be your eternal protector. (*To Mlle. de Vaudrey*) Ah me! What have I said? (*To Saint-Charles*) Where is Raoul?

SAINT-CHARLES

He has disappeared, and this steward of his, who procured the forged deeds in Rue Oblin, and doubtless played the part of the Mexican envoy, is one of the most astute of criminals. (*The duchess starts.*) Oh, you need not be alarmed; he is too clever to shed blood; but he is more formidable than those who shed it recklessly; and such a man is the guardian of Raoul.

THE DUCHESS

My whole fortune for his life!

SAINT-CHARLES

I am for you, madame. (*Aside*) I know all, and can choose which side I like.

SCENE NINTH.

THE SAME PERSONS, THE DUC DE MONTSOREL AND A FOOTMAN.

THE DUKE

Ah, well, you are getting your own way; there is talk of nothing else but the fortune and coming marriage of M. de Frescas; but of course he can claim a family. (*Whispers to Madame de Montsorel*) He has a mother. (*Perceiving Saint-Charles*) What! you here, chevalier, and with the duchess?

Saint-Charles (*taking the duke aside*)
Your grace will approve of what I have done. (*Aloud*)
You have been at the palace and I thought it necessary to
warn the duchess of the danger which threatens her only son,
the marquis; he is likely to be murdered.

THE DUKE

Murdered?

SAINT-CHARLES

But your grace will listen to my advice—

THE DUKE

Come into my study, my friend, and let us at once take
steps to avert this catastrophe.

Saint-Charles (*exchanging a look of intelligence with the
duchess*)
I have strange things to tell your grace. (*Aside*) I am
certainly going to take the duke's part.

## SCENE TENTH.

THE DUCHESS, MLLE. DE VAUDREY AND VAUTRIN.

MLLE. DE VAUDREY

If Raoul is your son, how vile is the company he keeps.

THE DUCHESS

An angel would purify hell itself.

Vautrin (*who half opens with caution a French casement
that leads to the garden, where he has been listening to the preceding conversation. (Aside)*)
I know all. Two brothers cannot fight a duel. Ah, here is
my duchess! (*Aloud*) Ladies!

MLLE. DE VAUDREY

A man! Help! Help!

THE DUCHESS

It is he!

VAUTRIN (*to the duchess*)

Silence! Women can do nothing but cry out. (*To Mlle. de Vaudrey*) Mlle. de Vaudrey, run to the chamber of the marquis. Two infamous murderers are there; be quick, before they cut his throat. But let the wretches be seized without making a disturbance. (*To the duchess*) Stay where you are, madame.

THE DUCHESS

Go, dear aunt; have no fear for me.

VAUTRIN (*aside*)

My rascals will be vastly surprised. What will they think? This is the way I bring down judgment upon them. (*A noise is heard.*)

*SCENE ELEVENTH.*

THE DUCHESS AND VAUTRIN.

THE DUCHESS

The whole house is in commotion! What will be said, when it is known that I am here?

VAUTRIN

Let us hope that the foundling will be saved.

THE DUCHESS

But you are known here, and the duke is with—

VAUTRIN

The Chevalier de Saint-Charles. I am imperturbed; you will defend me.

THE DUCHESS

I?

VAUTRIN

Yes, you. Or you will never again see your son, Fernand de Montsorel.

THE DUCHESS

Raoul is undoubtedly my son then?

VAUTRIN

He is—I hold in my possession complete proofs of your innocence, and—your son.

THE DUCHESS

You! You shall not leave me until—

------

## SCENE TWELFTH.

THE SAME PERSONS AND MLLE. DE VAUDREY *on one side of the stage,* SAINT-CHARLES *on the other,* AND DOMESTICS.

MLLE. DE VAUDREY

Here he is! (*To Vautrin*)  Begone! At once!

THE DUCHESS (*to Mlle. de Vaudrey*)
You are ruining everything.

SAINT-CHARLES (*to the servants*)
Behold their ringleader and accomplice! Whatever he may say, seize him!

THE DUCHESS (*to the company*)

ï command you to leave me alone with this man.

VAUTRIN

What is it, chevalier?

SAINT-CHARLES

You are a puzzle to me, baron.

VAUTRIN (*whispering to the duchess*)

You behold in this man the murderer of the viscount whom you loved so well.

THE DUCHESS

He the murderer?

VAUTRIN (*to the duchess*)

Let him be closely watched, or he will slip through your fingers like money.

THE DUCHESS

Joseph!

VAUTRIN (*to Joseph*)

What happened up stairs?

JOSEPH

His lordship the marquis drew his sword, and being attacked from the rear, defended himself, and was twice slightly wounded. His grace the duke is with him now.

THE DUCHESS (*to her aunt*)

Return to Albert's room, I implore you. (*To Joseph, pointing out Saint-Charles*) I shall hold you responsible for this man's detention.

VAUTRIN (*to Joseph*)

So shall I.

SAINT-CHARLES (*to Vautrin*)

I see the situation, you have got ahead of me.

VAUTRIN

I bear no malice towards you, my dear fellow.

SAINT-CHARLES (*to Joseph*)

Take me before the duke. (*Exeunt.*)

---

## SCENE THIRTEENTH.

VAUTRIN AND THE DUCHESS.

VAUTRIN (*aside*)

He has a father, an ancestral family, a mother. What a climax! In whom shall I henceforth find an interest? Whom shall I be able to love? After ten years of paternity, the loss is irreparable.

THE DUCHESS (*approaching Vautrin*)

What is it?

VAUTRIN

What is it? It is, that I can never give back to you your son, madame; it is, that I do not feel brave enough to survive his separation from me, nor his contempt for me. The loss of such as Raoul is irretrievable! My life has been bound up in his.

THE DUCHESS

But could he feel affection for you, you a criminal whom one could at any moment give up—

VAUTRIN

To justice do you mean? I thought you would have been

more tender. But you do not, I perceive, see the abyss in
which I am dragging you, your son and the duke, and which
all descend in company.

### The Duchess

Oh! What have you made of my poor child?

### Vautrin

A man of honor.

### The Duchess

And he loves you?

### Vautrin

He loves me still.

### The Duchess

But has that wretch spoken the truth in revealing what
you are and whence you come?

### Vautrin

Yes, madame.

### The Duchess

And have you taken care of my son?

### Vautrin

Your son, our son—yes—have you not perceived that he is
as pure as an angel?

### The Duchess

Ah, may you receive a blessing for what you have done!
May the world pardon you! O God! (*she kneels*) the voice
of a mother must reach Thee, forgive, forgive this man. (*She
looks at Vautrin.*) My tears shall bathe his hands! Oh!
grant that he may repent! (*Turning to Vautrin*) You belong to me; I will change you! But people are deceived, you
are no criminal, and, whatever you are, all mothers will give
you their absolution!

### VAUTRIN

Come, it is time to restore her son to her.

### THE DUCHESS

Did you still harbor the horrible thought of refusing him 'to his mother? But I have waited for him for two and twenty years.

### VAUTRIN

And I, have I not been for ten years his father? Raoul is my very soul! Let me endure anguish, let men heap shame upon me; if he is happy and crowned with honor, I shall see it and my life will once more be bright.

### THE DUCHESS

I am overwhelmed. He loves like a mother.

### VAUTRIN

The only tie that binds me to the world, to life, is this bright link, purer than gold.

### THE DUCHESS

And—without stain?

### VAUTRIN

Ah! People know themselves only in their virtues, and are austere for others alone. But in myself I see but infamy—in him the heart of honor. And yet was he found by me on the highroad from Toulon to Marseilles, the route of the convict. He was twelve years old, without bread, and in rags.

### THE DUCHESS

Bare-foot, it may be?

### VAUTRIN

Yes. But beautiful, with curly hair—

THE DUCHESS

It was thus you saw him?

VAUTRIN

Poor angel, he was crying.  I took him with me.

THE DUCHESS

And you brought him up?

VAUTRIN

I stole the means to do so.

THE DUCHESS

I should, perhaps, myself have done the like.

VAUTRIN

I did more!

THE DUCHESS

He must have suffered much.

VAUTRIN

Never!  I concealed from him the means I took to make his life happy and easy.  I would not let him even suspect them—it would have blighted him.  You may ennoble him by parchments, I have made him noble in heart.

THE DUCHESS

And he was my son!—

VAUTRIN

Yes, a son full of nobility, of winning grace, of high instincts; he needed but to have the way made clear to him.

THE DUCHESS (*wringing the hand of Vautrin*)

You must needs be great indeed, who have so well performed a mother's task!

### VAUTRIN

And better than you mothers do! Often you love your babes amiss—Ah, you will spoil him for me even now!—He was of reckless courage; he wished to be a soldier, and the Emperor would have accepted him. I showed him the world and mankind under their true light—Yet now he is about to renounce me—

### THE DUCHESS

My son ungrateful?

### VAUTRIN

No, 'tis mine I speak of.

### THE DUCHESS

Oh! give him back to me this very instant!

### VAUTRIN

I and those two men upstairs—are we not all liable to prosecution? And ought not the duke to give us assurance of silence and release?

### THE DUCHESS

Those two men then are your agents? And you came—

### VAUTRIN

But for me, of the two, natural and lawful son, there would not, in a few hours, have survived but one child. And they might perchance both have fallen—each by the other's hand.

### THE DUCHESS

Ah! you are a providence of horror!

### VAUTRIN

What would you have had me do?

## SCENE FOURTEENTH.

THE SAME PERSONS, THE DUKE, LAFOURAILLE, BUTEUX, SAINT-CHARLES, AND ALL THE DOMESTICS.

THE DUKE (*pointing to Vautrin*)

Seize him! (*Pointing to Saint-Charles*)  And obey no one but this gentleman.

THE DUCHESS

But you owe to him the life of your Albert!  It was he who gave the alarm.

THE DUKE

He!

BUTEUX (*to Vautrin*)

Ah! you have betrayed us!  Why did you bring us here?

SAINT-CHARLES (*to the duke*)

Does your grace hear them?

LAFOURAILLE (*to Buteux*)

Cannot you keep silence?  Have we any right to judge him?

BUTEUX

And yet he condemns us!

VAUTRIN (*to the duke*)

I would inform your grace that these two men belong to me, and I claim possession of them.

SAINT-CHARLES

Why, these are the domestics of M. de Frescas!

VAUTRIN (*to Saint-Charles*)

Steward of the Langeacs, hold your tongue!  (*He points to*

*Lafouraille*)  This is Philip Boulard.  (*Lafouraille bows.*)
Will your grace kindly send every one out of the room?

### THE DUKE

What!  Do you dare give your orders in my house?

### THE DUCHESS

Ah!  sir, he is master here.

### THE DUKE

What!  this wretch?

### VAUTRIN

If his grace the duke wishes to have an audience present
we will proceed to talk of the son of Doña Mendes.

### THE DUKE

Silence!

### VAUTRIN

Whom you are passing off as the son **of—**

### THE DUKE

Once more I say, silence!

### VAUTRIN

Your grace perceives, evidently, that there **are** too many
people within hearing.

### THE DUKE

All of you begone!

### VAUTRIN (*to the duke*)

Set a watch on every outlet from your house, and let no one
leave it, excepting these two men.  (*To Saint-Charles*)  Do
you remain here.  (*He draws a dagger and cuts the cords by
which Lafouraille and Buteux are bound.*)  Take yourselves
off by the postern; here is the key, and go to the house of

mother Giroflée. (*To Lafouraille*) You must send Raoul to me.

LAFOURAILLE (*as he leaves the room*)
Oh! our veritable emperor.

VAUTRIN
You shall receive money and passports.

BUTEUX (*as he goes out*)
After all, I shall have something for Adèle!

THE DUKE
But how did you learn all these facts?

VAUTRIN (*handing some documents to the duke*)
These are what I took from your study.

THE DUKE
These comprise my correspondence, and the letters of the duchess to the Viscount de Langeac.

VAUTRIN
Who was shot at Mortagne, October, 1792, through the kind efforts of Charles Blondet, otherwise known as the Chevalier de Saint-Charles.

SAINT-CHARLES
But your grace very well knows—

VAUTRIN
It was he himself who gave me these papers, among which you will notice the death certificate of the viscount, which proves that he and her grace the duchess never met after the Tenth of August, for he had then left the Abbaye for the Vendée, accompanied by Boulard, who seized the moment to betray and murder him.

THE DUKE

And so Fernand—

VAUTRIN

The child sent to Sardinia is undoubtedly your son.


THE DUKE

And her grace the duchess—


VAUTRIN

Is innocent.

THE DUKE

My God! (*He sinks back into an armchair.*)   What have 1 done?

THE DUCHESS

What a terrible proof—his death! And the assassin stands before us.

VAUTRIN.

M. le Duc de Montsorel, I have been a father to Fernand, and I have just saved your two sons, each from the sword of the other; you alone are the author of all this complication.


THE DUCHESS

Stop! I know him better than you do, and he suffers at this moment all that I have suffered during twenty years. In the name of mercy, where is my son?


THE DUKE

What, Raoul de Frescas?


VAUTRIN

Fernand de Montsorel is on his way here. (*To Saint-Charles*)  And what do you say about all this?


SAINT-CHARLES

You are a hero; let me be your servant.

### VAUTRIN

You are ambitious.  Would you follow me?

### SAINT-CHARLES

Anywhere.

### VAUTRIN

I can well believe it.

### SAINT-CHARLES

Ah! what a master mind you obtain in me, and what a loss
to the government!

### VAUTRIN

Go; and wait for me at the bureau of passports.  (*Exit
Saint-Charles.*)

---

## *SCENE FIFTEENTH.*

THE SAME PERSONS, THE DUCHESSE DE CHRISTOVAL, INEZ
AND MLLE. DE VAUDREY.

### MLLE. DE VAUDREY

Here they are!

### THE DUCHESSE DE CHRISTOVAL

My daughter, madame, has received a letter from M. Raoul,
in which this noble young man declares that he would rather
give up Inez, than deceive us; he has related his whole life's
history.  He is to fight a duel with your son to-morrow, and
as Inez is the involuntary cause of this duel we are come to
prevent it; for it is now entirely without ground or reason.

### THE DUCHESSE DE MONTSOREL

There will be no duel, madame.

### INEZ

He will live then!

### THE DUCHESSE DE MONTSOREL

And you shall marry the Marquis de Montsorel, my child.

---

## SCENE SIXTEENTH.

THE SAME PERSONS, RAOUL AND LAFOURAILLE. (*The last-named does not tarry.*)

### RAOUL (*to Vautrin*)

What! would you imprison me to prevent my fighting a duel?

### THE DUKE

With your brother?

### RAOUL

My brother?

### THE DUKE

Yes.

### THE DUCHESSE DE MONTSOREL

You are, then, really my child! (*She embraces Raoul.*) Ladies, this is Fernand de Montsorel, my son, the—

### THE DUKE (*taking Raoul by the hand, and interrupting his wife*)

The eldest son, who was carried off from us in childhood. Albert is now no more than Comte de Montsorel.

### RAOUL

For three days I have been in a dream! You, my mother! you, sir—

### THE DUKE

Your father—yes!

RAOUL

Among the very people who asked me to name my family—

VAUTRIN

Your family has been found.

RAOUL

And—are you still to have a place in my life?

VAUTRIN (*to the Duchesse de Montsorel*)

What shall I say to you? (*To Raoul*) Remember, my lord marquis, that I have, in advance, absolved you from all charge of ingratitude. (*To the duchess*) The child will forget me; will the mother also?

THE DUCHESSE DE MONTSOREL

Never.

THE DUKE

But what are the misfortunes that plunged you into so dark an abyss?

VAUTRIN

Can any one explain misfortune?

THE DUCHESSE DE MONTSOREL

Dear husband, is it not in your power to obtain his pardon?

THE DUKE

The sentences under which he has served are irreversible.

VAUTRIN

That word reconciles me to you, it is a statesman's word. Your grace should explain that transportation is the last expedient to which you can resort in overcoming us.

RAOUL

Monsieur—

VAUTRIN

You are wrong; I am not even monsieur at present.

INEZ

I think I understand that you are an outlaw, that my friend owes you a vast debt, and cannot discharge it. Beyond the sea, I have extensive lands, which require a man's energy for their right administration; you shall go and exercise there your talents, and become—

VAUTRIN

Rich, under a new name? Child, can you not realize that in this world there are pitiless necessities? Yes, I could acquire a fortune, but who will give me the opportunity? (*To the duke*) The king could at your grace's intercession grant me a pardon, but who then would take my hand in his?

RAOUL

I would!

VAUTRIN

Ah! It was this I waited for before taking leave. You now have a mother. Farewell!

---

## SCENE SEVENTEENTH.

THE SAME PERSONS, A POLICE OFFICER, GUARDS AND SERVANTS.

(*The window casements are flung open; and an officer enters; at the back of the stage are gendarmes.*)

THE OFFICER (*to the duke*)

In the name of the king, of the law, I arrest Jacques Collin, convicted of having broken—(*All persons present fling them-*

*selves between the armed force and Jacques, in order to give him opportunity for escaping.)*

## The Duke

Gentlemen, I take upon myself—

## Vautrin

In your grace's house the justice of the king must have free course. The matter lies between these gentlemen and me. (*To the officer*) I will follow you. (*To the duchess*) It was Joseph who brought the police; he is one of us; discharge him.

## Raoul

Are we separated forever?

## Vautrin

You will marry very shortly. Within a year, on a day of christening, scan carefully the faces of the poor at the church door; one will be there who wishes to be certain of your happiness. Till then, adieu. (*To the officer*) It is time for us to be moving.

### *Final Curtain.*

# THE RESOURCES OF QUINOLA

## A COMEDY IN A PROLOGUE AND FIVE ACTS

First Presented at the Theatre de l'Odeon, Paris.
March 19, 1842.

## AUTHOR'S PREFACE

Had the author of the following play written it merely for
the purpose of winning for it the universal praise which the
journals have lavished upon his romances, and which perhaps
transcended their merits, *The Resources of Quinola* would
still have been an excellent literary speculation; but, when
he sees himself the object of so much praise and so much condemnation, he has come to the conclusion that it is much more
difficult to make successfully a first venture on the stage than
in the field of mere literature, and he has armed himself,
accordingly, with courage, both for the present and for the
future.

The day will come when this piece will be employed by
critics as a battering ram to demolish some piece at its first
representation, just as they have employed all his novels,
and even his play entitled *Vautrin,* to demolish *The Resources
of Quinola.*

However tranquil may be his mood of resignation, the
author cannot refrain from making here two suggestive
observations.

Not one among fifty feuilleton writers has failed to treat
as a fable, invented by the author, the historic fact upon
which is founded the present play.

Long before M. Arago mentioned this incident in his history of steam, published in the *Annuaire du Bureau des Lon-
gitudes,* the author, to whom the incident was known, had
guessed in imagination the great drama that must have led

up to that final act of despair, the catastrophe which necessarily ended the career of the unknown inventor, who, in the
middle of the sixteenth century, built a ship that moved by
steam in the harbor of Barcelona, and then scuttled it with
his own hands in the presence of two hundred thousand spectators.

This observation is sufficient answer to the derision which
has been flung upon what was supposed to be the author's
hypothesis as to the invention of steam locomotion before the
time of the Marquis of Worcester, Salomon de Caus and
Papin.

The second observation relates to the strange manner in
which almost all the critics have mistaken the character of
Lavradi, one of the personages in this comedy, which they
have stigmatized as a hideous creation. Any one who reads
the piece, of which no critic has given an exact analysis, will
see that Lavradi, sentenced to be transported for ten years
to the *presides,* comes to ask pardon of the king. Every one
knows how freely the severest penalties were in the sixteenth
century measured out for the lightest offences, and how warmly
valets in a predicament such as Quinola's, were welcomed by
the spectators in the antique theatres.

Many volumes might be filled with the laments of feuille-
tonists, who for nearly twenty years have called for comedies
in the Italian, Spanish or English style. An attempt has
been made to produce one, and the critics would rather eat
their own words than miss the opportunity of choking off the
man who has been bold enough to venture upon a pathway
of such fertile promise, whose very antiquity lends to it in
these days the charm of novelty.

Nor must we forget to mention, to the disgrace of our age,
the howl of disapprobation which greeted the title "Duke

of Neptunado," selected by Philip II. for the inventor, a howl in which educated readers will refuse to join, but which was so overwhelming at the presentation of the piece that after its first utterance the actors omitted the term during the remainder of the evening. This howl was raised by an audience of spectators who read in the newspapers every morning the title of the Duke of Vittoria, given to Espartero, and who must have heard of the title Prince of Paz, given to the last favorite of the last but one of the kings of Spain. How could such ignorance as this have been anticipated? Who does not know that the majority of Spanish titles, especially in the time of Charles V. and Philip II., refer to circumstances under which they were originally granted?

Orendayes assumed the title of *La Pes,* from having signed the treaty of peace in 1725.

An admiral took that of *Transport-Real,* from the fact that the dauphin sailed with him to Italy.

Navarro was given the title *La Vittoria* after the sea-fight off Toulon, though the issue of the conflict was indecisive.

These examples, and as many others, are outdone by that of the famous finance minister, a parvenu broker, who chose to be entitled the Marquis Insignificant (*l'Ensenada*).

In producing a work, constructed with all the dramatic irregularity of the early French and Spanish stage, the author has made an experiment which had been called for by the suffrages of more than one "organ of public opinion," as well as of all the "first-nighters" of Paris. He wished to meet the genuine public and to have his piece represented in a house filled with a paying audience. The unsatisfactory result of this ordeal was so plainly pointed out by the whole press, that the indispensability of *claqueurs* has been now forever established.

The author had been confronted by the following dilemma, as stated by those experienced in such matters. If he introduced into the theatre twelve hundred "dead heads," the success secured by their applause would undoubtedly be questioned. If twelve hundred paying spectators were present, the success of the piece was almost out of the question. The author chose to run the risk of the latter alternative. Such is the history of this first representation, where so many people appeared to be made so uncomfortable by their elevation to the dignity of independent judges.

The author intends therefore to return to the beaten track, base and ignoble though it be, which prejudice has laid out as the only avenue to dramatic success; but it may not be unprofitable to state here, that the first representation of *The Resources of Quinola* actually redounded to the advantage of the *claqueurs,* the only persons who enjoyed any triumph, in an evening entertainment from which their presence was debarred!

Some idea of the criticism uttered on this comedy may be gained from the fact that out of the fifty newspapers, all of which for the last twenty years have uttered over the unsuccessful playwright the hackneyed phrase, "the play is the work of a clever man who will some day take his revenge," not one employed it in speaking of *The Resources of Quinola,* which they were unanimous in consigning to oblivion. This result has settled the ambition of the author.

Certain persons, whose good auguries the author had done nothing to call forth, encouraged from the outset this dramatic venture, and thus showed themselves less critical than unkind; but the author counts such miscalculations as blessings in disguise, for the loss of false friends is the best school of

experience. Nor is it less a pleasure than a duty thus publicly to thank the friends, like M. Léon Gozlan, who have
remained faithful, towards whom the author has contracted
a debt of gratitude; like M. Victor Hugo, who protested, so
to speak, against the public verdict at the first representation, by returning to witness the second; like M. de Lamartine and Madame de Girardin, who stuck to their first opinion, in spite of the general public reprobation of the piece.
The approval of such persons as these would be consoling in
any disaster.

LAGNY, 2 *April*, 1842.

# PERSONS OF THE PROLOGUE

PHILIP II., King of Spain.
CARDINAL CIENFUEGOS, Grand Inquisitor.
THE CAPTAIN OF THE GUARDS.
THE DUKE OF OLMEDO.
THE DUKE OF LERMA.
ALFONSO FONTANARES.
LAVRADI, known as Quinola.
A HALBERDIER.
AN ALCALDE OF THE PALACE.
A FAMILIAR OF THE INQUISITION.

THE QUEEN OF SPAIN.
THE MARCHIONESS OF MONDEJAR.

## PERSONS OF THE PLAY

Don Fregose, Viceroy of Catalonia.
Grand Inquisitor.
Count Sarpi, Secretary to the Viceroy.
Don Ramon, a savant.
Avaloros, a banker.
Mathieu Magis, a Lombard.
Lothundiaz, a burgess.
Alfonso Fontanares, an inventor.
Lavradi, known as Quinola, servant to Fontanares.
Monipodio, a retired bandit.
Coppolus, a metal merchant.
Carpano, a locksmith.
Esteban } workmen.
Girone }
The Host of the "Golden Sun."
A Bailiff.
An Alcalde.

Faustine Brancadori.
Marie Lothundiaz, daughter to Lothundiaz.
Dona Lopez, duenna to Marie Lothundiaz.
Paquita, maid to Faustine.

Scene: *Spain—Valladolid and Barcelona.* Time: 1588-89.

# THE RESOURCES OF QUINOLA

## PROLOGUE.

## *SCENE FIRST.*

(*The scene is laid at Valladolid, in the palace of the King of Spain. The stage represents the gallery which leads to the chapel. The entrance to the chapel is on the spectators' left, that to the royal apartment on the right. The principal entrance is in the centre. On each side of the principal door stand two halberdiers. At the rise of the curtain the Captain of the Guards and two lords are on the stage. An alcalde of the palace stands in the centre of the gallery. Several courtiers are walking up and down in the hall that leads to the gallery.*)

THE CAPTAIN OF THE GUARDS, QUINOLA (*wrapped in his mantle*) AND A HALBERDIER.

THE HALBERDIER (*barring the way to Quinola*)
No one passes this way, unless he has the right to do so. Who are you?

QUINOLA (*lifting up the halberd*)
An ambassador. (*All look at him.*)

HALBERDIER
From what state?

QUINOLA (*passing in*)
From what state? From a state of misery.

### The Captain of the Guards

Go and bring the major-domo of the palace, that he may render to this ambassador the honors that are due him. (*To the halberdier*) Three days' imprisonment.

### Quinola (*to the captain*)

And so this is the way you respect people's rights! Listen, my lord, you are very high, and I am very low, but a couple of words will place us on an equal footing.

### The Captain

You are a very droll rascal.

### Quinola (*taking him aside*)

Are not you the cousin of the Marchioness of Mondejar?

### The Captain

What if I am?

### Quinola

Although she is high in favor, she is on the brink of an abyss, into which she may fall and lose her head in falling.

### The Captain

All people of your class trump up these stories!—Listen, you are the twenty-second person, and we have only reached the tenth of the month, who has made an attempt to be introduced to the favorite, for the purpose of squeezing a few pistoles from her. Take yourself off or else—

### Quinola

My lord, it is better to be misled by twenty-two poor devils, twenty-two times, than once to miss the opportunity of heeding him who is sent by your good angel; and you see, I may also say (*he opens his mantle*) I am wearing her wings

### THE CAPTAIN

Let us end this, and tell me what proof of your errand you can give?

### QUINOLA (*handing him a letter*)

This little message you must return to me so that the secret remains in our possession, and hang me if you do not see the marchioness swoon when she reads it. Believe moreover that I profess, in common with an immense majority of Spaniards, a deep-seated aversion for—the gallows.

### THE CAPTAIN

And suppose that some ambitious woman has paid for your life, that she give it in exchange for another's?

### QUINOLA

Should I be in rags? My life is as good as Cæsar's. Look here, my lord. (*He unseals the letter, smells it, folds it up again, and gives it to him*) Are you satisfied?

### THE CAPTAIN (*aside*)

I have yet time. (*To Quinola*) Remain where you are, I am going to her.

---

## SCENE SECOND.

QUINOLA (*alone, in the front of the stage, looking at the departing captain*)

That is all right! O my dear master, if the torture chamber has not broken your bones, you are likely to get out of the cells of the holy—the thrice holy Inquisition—saved by your poor cur Quinola! Poor?—why should I say poor? My master once free, we will end by cashing our hopes. To live at Valladolid for six months without money, and without being nabbed by the alguazils, argues the possession of cer-

tain small talents, which, if applied to—other ends, might
bring a man to—something different in fact! If we knew
where we were going no one would stir a step—I purpose
speaking to the king, I, Quinola. God of the rapscallions,
give me the eloquence—of—a pretty woman, of the Marchioness of Mondejar—

---

## SCENE THIRD.

### QUINOLA AND THE CAPTAIN.

THE CAPTAIN (*to Quinola*)

Here are fifty doubloons which the marchioness sends you,
that you may be enabled to make your appearance here in
decent guise.

QUINOLA (*pouring the gold from one hand into the other*)

Ah, this burst of sunshine has been long expected! I will
return, my lord, radiant as that amorous valet, whose name
I have assumed; Quinola at your service, Quinola soon to be
lord of wide domains, where I shall administer justice, from
the time—(*aside*) I cease to fear its ministers.

---

## SCENE FOURTH.

### THE COURTIERS AND THE CAPTAIN.

THE CAPTAIN (*alone at the front of the stage*)

What secret has this miserable creature discovered? My
cousin almost fainted away. She told me that it concerned
all my friends. The king must have something to do in the
matter. (*To a lord*) Duke of Lerma, is there anything new
in Valladolid?

THE DUKE OF LERMA (*whispering*)

It is said that the Duke of Olmedo was murdered this morning, at three o'clock, just before dawn. It happened a few paces from the Mondejar palace.

THE CAPTAIN

It is quite likely he should be assassinated for prejudicing the king's mind against my cousin; the king, like all great statesmen, esteems as true everything that appears to be probable.

THE DUKE

It is said that enmity between the duke and the marchioness was only a pretence, and that the assassin is not to be prosecuted.

THE CAPTAIN

Duke, this ought not to be repeated unless it can be proved, and even then could not be written excepting with a sword dipped in my blood.

THE DUKE

You asked me the news. (*The duke retires.*)

## SCENE FIFTH.

THE SAME PERSONS AND THE MARCHIONESS OF MONDEJAR.

THE CAPTAIN

Ah! here is my cousin! (*To the marchioness*) Dear marchioness, you are still very much agitated. In the name of our common salvation, control yourself; you will attract attention.

THE MARCHIONESS

Has that man come back?

### The Captain

Now, how can a man of such base condition as he is throw you into such terror?

### The Marchioness

He holds my life in his hands; more than my life, indeed; for he holds in his power the life also of another, who, in spite of the most scrupulous precautions, cannot avoid exciting the jealousy—

### The Captain

Of the king!—Did he cause the assassination of the Duke of Olmedo, as is rumored?

### The Marchioness

Alas! I do not know what to think.—Here I am alone, helpless—and perhaps soon to be abandoned.

### The Captain

You may rely upon me—I shall constantly be in the midst of all our enemies, like a hunter on the watch.

---

## SCENE SIXTH.

### The Same Persons and Quinola.

### Quinola

I have only thirty doubloons left, but I have had the worth of sixty.—Ah! what a lovely scent! The marchioness can now talk to me without fear.

### The Marchioness (*pointing out Quinola*)

Is this our man?

THE CAPTAIN

Yes.

THE MARCHIONESS

Keep watch, my cousin, so that I may be able to talk without being overheard. (*To Quinola*) Who are you, my friend?

QUINOLA (*aside*)

Her friend! As soon as you have a woman's secret, you are her friend. (*Aloud*) Madame, I am a man superior to all considerations and all circumstances.

THE MARCHIONESS

You have reached a pretty good height, at that rate.

QUINOLA

Is that a threat or a warning?

THE MARCHIONESS

Sir, you are very impertinent.

QUINOLA

Do not mistake farsightedness for impertinence. You must study me, before coming to a decision. I am going to describe my character to you; my real name is Lavradi. At this moment Lavradi ought to be serving a ten years' sentence in Africa, at the presides, owing to an error of the alcaldes of Barcelona. Quinola is the conscience, white as your fair hands, of Lavradi. Quinola does not know Lavradi. Does the soul know the body? You may unite the soul, Quinola, to the body, Lavradi, all the more easily because this morning Quinola was at the postern of your garden, with the friends of the dawn who stopped the Duke of Olmedo—

THE MARCHIONESS

What has happened to him?

### QUINOLA

Lavradi would take advantage of this moment, which is full of promise, to ask a pardon; but Quinola is a gentleman.

### THE MARCHIONESS

You are taken up too much with yourself—

### QUINOLA

And not sufficiently with him—that is just. The duke took us for foul assassins; we were simply asking him, at a rather too advantageous hour, to make us a loan, pledged by our rapiers as collateral. The famous Majoral, who was in command of us, being close pressed by the duke, was forced to disable him by a little thrust, of which he knows the secret.

### THE MARCHIONESS

Oh! My God!—

### QUINOLA

Happiness is cheap at such a cost, madame.

### THE MARCHIONESS (*aside*)

Hush! he knows my secret.

### QUINOLA

When we saw that the duke had not a maravedi about him, we left him where he was. As I was the least culpable of all the gang, I was charged to take him home; in adjusting his pockets, which had been turned inside out, I found the letter which he had written to you, and, learning your position at the court, I understood—

### THE MARCHIONESS

That your fortune was made?

### QUINOLA

Not at all—that my life was in danger.

THE MARCHIONESS

Indeed?

QUINOLA

To whom are you speaking? Quinola or Lavradi?

THE MARCHIONESS

Lavradi shall have his pardon. What does Quinola desire?
To enter my service?

QUINOLA

Foundling children are of gentle birth; Quinola will deliver your letter to you without asking a maravedi, without
obliging you to do anything unworthy of you, and he expects that you will refrain from desiring the services of a
poor devil who carries under his wallet the heart of the Cid.

THE MARCHIONESS

How dear you are going to cost me, fellow!

QUINOLA

You said to me just now, "my friend."

THE MARCHIONESS

Were you not my enemy?

QUINOLA

On account of that word I trust you, madame, and intend
to tell you everything. But here—do not laugh—you must
promise—I wish—

THE MARCHIONESS

You wish?

QUINOLA

I wish—to speak to the king—at the moment when he
passes on his way to the chapel; I desire you to lend favor
to my request.

THE MARCHIONESS

But what are you going to ask him?


QUINOLA

The most simple thing in the world—an audience for my master.

THE MARCHIONESS

Explain yourself, for time presses.


QUINOLA

Madame, I am the servant of a philosopher; and if the mark of genius is poverty, we have a great deal too much genius, madame.

THE MARCHIONESS

To the point.

QUINOLA

Señor Alfonso Fontanares has come here from Catalonia to offer the king our master the sceptre of the sea. At Barcelona he was taken for a madman; here he is considered a sorcerer. When it becomes known what he proposes, he is scoffed at in the antechambers. One wishes to protest for the sake of ruining him; another, a philosopher, throws a doubt on the existence of our secret, with the view of filching it; others again make him a business proposition—capitalists who wish to entangle him in their meshes. As things go at present we do not know how they will turn out. No one certainly can deny the forces of mechanics and geometry, but the finest theorems have very little bodily nourishment in them, and the smallest of ragouts is better for the stomach; but, really, science is not to blame for that. During the past winter my master and myself warmed ourselves over our projects, and chewed the cud of our illusions. . . Well, madame, he is now in prison, for he has been accused of being on too friendly terms with the devil; and, unfortunately, the Holy Office is right, this time, for we have constantly seen him at the bottom of our purse. And now,

madame, I implore you, inspire the king with curiosity to
see a man who will give him a dominion as extended as that
which Columbus gave to Spain.

### THE MARCHIONESS

But since Columbus gave a new world to Spain, new world
are being offered to us once in every fortnight!

### QUINOLA

Ah! madame, every man of genius has one of his own to
offer. By heavens, it is so rare that a man can make honestly
a fortune both for himself and the state that the phenomenon
deserves to be favored.

### THE MARCHIONESS

But what is the project about?

### QUINOLA

I must once more beg you not to laugh, madame. His plan
is to make ships travel without sail or oar, against the wind,
by means of a pot filled with water, which is kept boiling.

### THE MARCHIONESS

What an idea! Where do you come from? What do you
mean? Are you dreaming?

### QUINOLA

That is just what they all say! Ah, common heard, ye are
so constituted that the man of genius, who is right ten years
before everybody else, passes for a madman for twenty-five
years. I am the only one who believes in this man, and it is
on this account I love him; to understand another is to be
his equal.

### THE MARCHIONESS

And you want me to repeat this nonsense to the king?

QUINOLA

Madame, you are the only person in the whole of Spain to whom the king will not say, "Be silent."

THE MARCHIONESS

You do not know the king, and I do. (*Aside*) I must get back my letter. (*Aloud*) There is one recent circumstance whose occurrence seems favorable to your master; news comes to the king that the Armada has been lost; wait for him on his way through to chapel and address him. (*Exit.*)

---

## SCENE SEVENTH.

THE CAPTAIN OF THE GUARDS, THE COURTIERS AND QUINOLA.

QUINOLA (*in the front of the stage*)

It is not sufficient to possess genius and to employ it, for there are plenty of people who make a false show to have it and meet with excellent success. There is need also of opportunity and favoring circumstances; a picked up letter, which puts a favorite in danger, in order to obtain an interceding tongue, and the loss of the mightiest of flotillas, in order to open the ears of a prince. Chance is an infamous wretch! And now, in the duel of Fontanares with his century, the hour has come for his poor second to appear. (*Bells are heard; guard is mounted.*) Is yon sound an omen of success? (*To the Captain of the Guards*) How ought the king to be spoken to?

THE CAPTAIN

Step forward, bow your knee, and say: "Sire"—and pray God to guide your tongue aright—(*The royal procession appears*).

QUINOLA

I shall have no trouble in falling upon my knees; they

are giving way already; for it is not only the fate of a man, but of a world, that is at stake.

### A PAGE.

The queen!

### A PAGE.

The king!

*(Tableau.)*

---

## SCENE EIGHTH.

THE SAME PERSONS, THE KING, THE QUEEN, THE MAR-
CHIONESS OF MONDEJAR, THE GRAND INQUISITOR
AND THE WHOLE COURT.

### PHILIP II.

Gentlemen, we are about to pray God and honor Him who has dealt a deadly blow to Spain. England has escaped us, the Armada is lost, and we desire no more to talk of that flotilla. Admiral *(he turns to the admiral)*, you were not sent to give battle to the storms.

### QUINOLA

Sire! *(He falls on one knee.)*

### PHILIP II.

Who are you?

### QUINOLA

The most insignificant and the most devoted of your subjects; the servant of a man who pines in the prisons of the Holy Office, accused of magic, because he desires to give to your Majesty the power of escaping from similar disasters—

### PHILIP II.

If you are merely a servant, rise to your feet. Only grandees are wont to kneel here, in presence of the king.

### QUINOLA

My master, then, shall kneel at your feet.

### PHILIP II.

Explain yourself in brief; the moments of the king's whole life are not so numerous as are his subjects.

### QUINOLA

You must have, then, but one hour for each of your empires. My master, Señor Alfonso Fontanares, is in the prisons of the Holy Office—

### PHILIP II. (*to the Grand Inquisitor*)

Father (*the Grand Inquisitor approaches*), what can you tell us of a certain Alfonso Fontanares?

### THE GRAND INQUISITOR

He is a pupil of Galileo. He professes the heretical doctrine of his master and boasts the power to do wonders while he refuses to explain the means. He is accused of being rather a Moor than a Spaniard.

### QUINOLA (*aside*)

That sallow face is going to spoil all!—(*To the King*) Sire, my master knows no sorcery, excepting so far as he is madly in love, first with the glory of your Majesty, next with a maid of Barcelona, heiress of Lothundiaz, the richest burgess of the town. As he picked up more science than wealth in studying natural science in Italy, the poor youth has failed in his attempt to marry this maid.—And notice, sire, how great men are calumniated; in his despair he made a pilgrimage to the Virgen del Pilar, to beg her assistance, because Marie was the name of the lady he loved. On leaving the church, he sat down wearied under a tree and fell asleep. In his dreams the Virgin appeared to him and communicated to him an invention by which he could navigate ships without sails, without

oars, against wind and tide. He approached you, sire; but
between the sun and him a cloud intervened, and after a
deadly conflict with the cloud, he is now suffering for his confidence in the Virgen del Pilar and in his king. No one but
his servant has sufficient courage to come and throw at your
feet the news that there exists a means of realizing universal
dominion.

### PHILIP II.

I will see your master when I leave the chapel.

### THE GRAND INQUISITOR

Surely, the king will not expose himself to such peril?

### PHILIP II.

My duty is to inquire.

### THE GRAND INQUISITOR

And mine is to make men respect the privileges of the
Sacred Office.

### PHILIP II.

I know them. Obey me and keep silence. I know that I
owe you a hostage. I know it—(*He looks round*) Tell me,
where is the Duke of Olmedo?

### QUINOLA (*aside*)

Aha!

### THE MARCHIONESS (*aside*)

We are lost.

### THE CAPTAIN OF THE GUARDS

Sire, the duke is not yet—arrived—

### PHILIP II.

Who has given him leave thus boldly to forsake the duties
of his office? (*Aside*) Some one is deceiving me. (*To the
Captain of the Guards*) Tell him, if he comes, that the king

has committed him as a prisoner of the Holy Office. (*To the Grand Inquisitor*)   Issue the order.

### THE GRAND INQUISITOR

Sire, I will go myself.

### THE QUEEN

And what if the duke fails to come?

### PHILIP II.

In that case he must be dead.   (*To the captain*)   You will take his place in the execution of my orders.   (*He enters the chapel.*)

### THE MARCHIONESS (*to Quinola*)

Run to the duke's house, tell him to come and comport himself as if he were not wounded to the death.   The report will then be considered mere calumny—

### QUINOLA

You may reckon upon me, but grant us your protection. (*Alone*)   Great heavens!   The king seemed charmed by my little fable of the Virgen del Pilar; I must make a vow to her —but what shall it be?—we will see after we have succeeded.

(*Scene curtain.*)

---

## SCENE NINTH.

### (*A cell of the Inquisition.*)

### FONTANARES (*alone*)

I understand now why Columbus desired that his fetters should be placed beside him in his coffin.   What a lesson for discoverers! A great discovery is a revelation of truth. And truth destroys so many abuses and errors that all those who live by falsehood rise up to slay the truth; they begin by assailing the man. Let inventors then have patience! I myself desire to have it. Unfortunately, my patience proceeds from my love. In the hope of obtaining Marie, I dream of glory and I pursue it.—I saw a piece of straw fly up above a boiler. All men have had the same experience since boilers and straw existed. But I saw there a force; in order to estimate its violence, I put a lid on the boiler; the lid flew off but did not kill me. Archimedes and I are of the same mind! He wished for a lever and a fulcrum to move the world; I possess this lever and have been fool enough to say so; since then—misfortunes have overwhelmed me. If I should die, you, man of genius who shall discover the secret, act on it, but keep silence. The light which we discover, men take from us, only to set on fire our funeral pile. Galileo, my master, is in prison for having said that the earth moves, and I am here for attempting to apply the forces of the earth. No! I am here because I rebel against the cupidity of those who desire to steal my secret; were it not for my love for Marie, I would claim my liberty to-night, leaving to them the profit, keeping to myself the fame.—Ah! What rage is in my heart! —But rage is only fit for children; let me be calm and then I shall be strong. Would that I might have news of the only man who has faith in me! He is at liberty, he, who begged to win me bread.—But faith is only found among the poor, who have need of it—

---

## SCENE TENTH.

THE GRAND INQUISITOR, A FAMILIAR AND FONTANARES.

THE GRAND INQUISITOR

Well, my son, how are you? You were speaking of faith,

doubtless you have made some sage reflections recently. Come now, spare the Holy Office a resort to severity.

#### FONTANARES

Father, what do you wish me to say?

#### THE GRAND INQUISITOR

Before setting you at liberty, the Holy Office must be sure that the means you employ are natural—

#### FONTANARES

Father, if I had made a compact with the Evil One, would he have let me languish here?

#### THE GRAND INQUISITOR

Your words are impious; the devil has a master whose existence is proved by our burning of heretics.

#### FONTANARES

Have you ever seen a ship on the sea? (*The Grand Inquisitor assents.*)  By what means is it propelled?

#### THE GRAND INQUISITOR

The wind fills the sails.

#### FONTANARES

Did the devil reveal this method of navigation to the first sailor?

#### THE GRAND INQUISITOR

Do you know who he was?

#### FONTANARES

He was, perhaps, the founder of some long forgotten power that ruled the sea—at any rate, the means that I employ are not less natural than his. I have seen a certain force in nature, a force controllable by man. For the wind is God's creature, and man is not its master, but the wind propels the ships of man, while my force is in the ship itself.

THE GRAND INQUISITOR (*aside*)

This man may prove a dangerous fellow. (*Aloud*) And you refuse to tell us what it is?

FONTANARES

I will tell the king, in presence of his court; for, after that, no one will be able to rob me of my glory and the fortune that it brings.

THE GRAND INQUISITOR

You call yourself an inventor, and yet you think of nothing but fortune! You are too ambitious to be a man of genius.

FONTANARES

Father, I am so profoundly disgusted by the jealousy of the vulgar, by the avarice of the great, by the behavior of sham philosophers, that—but for my love for Marie—I would give back to chance that which chance has bestowed upon me.

THE GRAND INQUISITOR

Chance?

FONTANARES

I am wrong. I would give back to God the thought which God has sent to me.

THE GRAND INQUISITOR

God did not send it to you that it might be hidden, and we have the right to force you to divulge it—(*to his Familiar*) Bid them prepare the rack.

FONTANARES

I was expecting it.

## *SCENE ELEVENTH.*

THE GRAND INQUISITOR, FONTANARES, QUINOLA AND THH
DUKE OF OLMEDO.

QUINOLA

It isn't a very healthy thing, this torture.

FONTANARES

Quinola! And in what a livery!

QUINOLA

The livery of success, for you are to be free.

FONTANARES

Free? And to pass from hell to heaven in an instant?

THE DUKE OF OLMEDO

As martyrs do.

THE GRAND INQUISITOR

Sir, do you dare to say such words in this place!

THE DUKE OF OLMEDO

I am charged by the king to take out of your custody this
man, and will answer for him to the Holy Inquisition.

THE GRAND INQUISITOR

What a mistake!

QUINOLA

Ah! you would like to boil him in your cauldrons of oil!
Many thanks! His cauldrons are going to carry us 'round
the world—like this. (*He twirls his hat.*)

FONTANARES

Embrace me, my friend, and tell me how—

THE DUKE OF OLMEDO

Say not a word here—

QUINOLA

Yes (*he points to the Inquisitor*), for here the walls have
ears.  Come.  And you (*speaking to the duke*) take courage
You are pale, and I must give to you a tinge of color; but
I know how to do it.

(*Scene curtain.*)

---

## SCENE TWELFTH.

(*Palace gallery as in first scene.*)

THE DUKE OF OLMEDO, THE DUKE OF LERMA, FONTANARES
AND QUINOLA.

THE DUKE OF OLMEDO

We have come just in time !

THE DUKE OF LERMA

You were not wounded then ?

THE DUKE OF OLMEDO

Who said I was?  Would the favorite of the **king ruin me?**
And should I be here, as you see me, if I were dead?  (*To
Quinola*)  Stand close and hold me up—

QUINOLA (*to Fontanares*)

This is a man worthy of your love—

FONTANARES

Who would not envy such a one?  Yet how seldom is
occasion given to show one's love.

QUINOLA

Spare us, good sir, all this rigmarole about love, in the presence of the king; for the king, hark you—

A PAGE

**The king!**

FONTANARES

Come on, and let all our thoughts be for Marie!

QUINOLA (*noticing that the Duke of Olmedo is fainting*)
How are you? (*He puts a flask to his nostrils.*)

---

## SCENE THIRTEENTH.

THE SAME PERSONS, THE KING, THE QUEEN, THE CAPTAIN OF THE GUARDS, THE GRAND INQUISITOR, THE MARCHIONESS OF MONDEJAR, THE PRESIDENT OF THE COUNCIL OF CASTILE AND THE WHOLE COURT.

PHILIP II. (*to the Captain of the Guards*)
Has our man arrived?

THE CAPTAIN

The Duke of Olmedo, whom I met on the palace steps, has at once obeyed the commands of the king.

THE DUKE OF OLMEDO (*falling on one knee*)
Will the king deign to pardon a delay—unpardonable.

PHILIP II. (*raising him by his wounded arm*)
I was told you were dying—(*he glances at the marchioness*)—of a wound received in a nocturnal attack.

THE DUKE OF OLMEDO

Well, you see me here, sire, a sufficient answer.

THE MARCHIONESS (*aside*)

He is rouged!

PHILIP II. (*to the duke*)

Where is your prisoner?

THE DUKE OF OLMEDO (*pointing to Fontanares*)

Yonder he stands.

FONTANARES (*kneeling*)

And ready, to the great glory of God, to do wonders which shall add splendor to the reign of the king, my master.

PHILIP II.

Rise up and speak to me; what is this force miraculous which shall give to Spain the empire of the world?

FONTANARES

It is a force invincible, sire. It is steam; for, when water has become expanded in steam, it demands a much more extensive area than that which it occupies in its natural form; and in order to take that space it would blow up mountains. By my invention this force is confined; the machine is provided with wheels, which beat the sea and propel a vessel as swiftly as the wind, so that tempests cannot resist its course. Voyages can be made in safety and so swiftly that there is no limit to speed, excepting in the revolution of the wheels. Human life is lengthened every time a moment is economized. Sire, Christopher Columbus gave to you a world three thousand leagues across the ocean; I will bring one to you at the port of Cadiz, and you shall claim, with the assistance of God, the dominion of the sea.

### The Queen

You do not seem to be astonished, sire?

### Philip II.

Astonishment is involuntary flattery, and kings may never flatter. (*To Fontanares*) What do you ask of me?

### Fontanares

That which Columbus asked, a ship and the presence of my king to witness the experiment.

### Philip II.

You shall have all—the king, the realm of Spain—the whole world. They tell me that you love a maid of Barcelona. I am about to cross the Pyrenees, to visit my possessions, Roussillon and Perpignan; you shall receive your vessel at Barcelona.

### Fontanares

In granting me this vessel, sire, you have done me justice; in giving it to me at Barcelona, you have bestowed a favor which, from a subject, makes me your slave.

### Philip II.

Yet be cautious; to lose a vessel of the state will be to risk your life, for so the law provides.

### Fontanares

I know it, and accept the risk.

### Philip II.

Well said, brave man! If you succeed in constructing this sailless, oarless vessel that shall face the wind as swiftly as if the wind were in its favor, I will create you—what is your name?

FONTANARES

Alfonso Fontanares.

PHILIP II.

You shall be Don Alfonso Fontanares, Duke of—— Neptunado, Grandee of Spain—

THE DUKE OF LERMA

Sire--the statutes concerning nobility—

PHILIP II.

Silence! Duke of Lerma. It is the duty of a king to exalt the man of genius above all other men and thus to honor the ray of light which God has given to him.

THE GRAND INQUISITOR

Sire—

PHILIP II.

What would you?

THE GRAND INQUISITOR

We did not imprison this man on the charge that he had commerce with the devil, nor because of his impiety, nor because he springs from a family suspected of heresy; but for the safety of monarchies. Printing has permitted clever men to communicate their thoughts to others and the result has been—Luther, whose word has flown abroad in every direction. But this man is endeavoring to make out of all the nations of the earth a single people, and, before a multitude like this, the Holy Office trembles for the fate of monarchy.

PHILIP II.

All progress moves heavenward.

THE GRAND INQUISITOR

Heaven does not command many things which yet it does not hinder men from doing.

### Philip II.

Our duty consists in bringing good out of evil things and in this work of amelioration gathering all within one circle, whose centre is the throne. Do you not see what is here at stake, even the realization of that universal dominion long-sought for by my glorious father?—(*To Fontanares*) When you have won the rank of duke and Spanish grandee of the first class, I will put upon your breast the Golden Fleece; you shall then be appointed Grand Master of Naval Construction in Spain and the Indies—(*to a minister*)—President, you will issue, this very day, under pain of my displeasure, the order to put at the disposal of this man, in our port of Barcelona, such a vessel as he desires, and—see that no obstacle interferes with his enterprise.

### Quinola

Sire—

### Philip II.

What do you desire?

### Quinola

While you are here, grant, sire, full pardon to a wretch named Lavradi, who was sentenced by a deaf magistrate.

### Philip II.

Because the judge was deaf, must the king be blind?

### Quinola

No, but indulgent, sire, which is almost the same thing.

### Fontanares

Pardon! Grant pardon to the only man who has sustained me in my struggle!

PHILIP II. (*to a minister*)

This man has talked with me, and I gave him my hand to kiss; issue to him letters of my full pardon.

THE QUEEN (*to the king*)

If this man (*she points to Fontanares*) is one of those great discoverers, raised up of God, Don Philip you have done a good day's work this morning.

PHILIP II. (*to the queen*)

It is very difficult to distinguish between a man of genius and a madman; but if he is a madman, my promises are only worth the value of his.

QUINOLA (*to the marchioness*)

Here is your letter, but let me beg you, between ourselves, to write no more.

THE MARCHIONESS

We are saved! (*The court follows the king into the royal apartment.*)

---

## SCENE FOURTEENTH.

FONTANARES AND QUINOLA.

FONTANARES

Surely I am dreaming—Duke! Grandee of Spain! The Golden Fleece!

QUINOLA

And Master of Naval Constructions! We shall have plenty of contractors to patronize. The court is an odd place. I should like to succeed there; how is it to be done? By impudence? I have enough of that to sell! By trickery? Why, the

king believes my tale of the Virgen del Pilar—(*he laughs*).
But what is my master thinking about?

FONTANARES

Let us start at once.

QUINOLA

For what place?

FONTANARES

For Barcelona.

QUINOLA

No—for a tavern.  If the air of the court gives the citizens
a good appetite, it makes me devilish thirsty.  After a drink,
my glorious master, you will see your Quinola a very busy
man; for we must not delude ourselves.  Between the word
of the king and the attainment of success, we shall meet with
as many jealous philosophers, scheming tricksters, malicious
cavillers, crooked, rapacious, greedy beasts of prey, thievish
parasites as have ever beset you in your attempts to see the
king.

FONTANARES

Yet to obtain my Marie I must succeed.

QUINOLA

Yes, and for our own sakes also.

*Curtain to the Prologue.*

# ACT I.

## SCENE FIRST.

*(The scene is Barcelona. The stage represents a public place. On the left of the spectator appear houses, among which that of Lothundiaz stands at the corner of the street. To the right is the palace of Señora Brancadori. The time is night, but the day begins to dawn.)*

MONIPODIO *(wrapped in a mantle, seated under the balcony of the Brancadori palace).* QUINOLA *(who glides forth cautiously like a thief, and brushes against Monipodio).*

MONIPODIO

Who is it dares to tread on my shoes?

QUINOLA *(in ragged array)*

A gentleman, who does not wear any.

MONIPODIO

That sounds like Lavradi.

QUINOLA

Monipodio!—I thought that you had been—hanged!

MONIPODIO

I thought that you had been beaten to death in Africa.

QUINOLA

Alas, we have been beaten enough without going to Africa!

MONIPODIO

And do you dare to show yourself here?


QUINOLA

You seem comfortable enough here. As for me, I have the king's pardon in my pocket, and while I am waiting for my patent of nobility I call myself Quinola.


MONIPODIO

I suppose you stole your pardon?


QUINOLA

Yes, from the king.


MONIPODIO

And have you seen the king? (*He sniffs at him.*) You smell of poverty—


QUINOLA

Like a poet's garret. And what are you doing?


MONIPODIO

Nothing.

QUINOLA

That is soon done; if it gives you any income, I would like to embrace your profession.


MONIPODIO

I have been misunderstood, my friend! Hunted by our political enemies—

QUINOLA

The judges, magistrates and police.


MONIPODIO

It is necessary for a man to have a political party.

QUINOLA

I understand you; from being the game you have become
the hunter.

MONIPODIO

What nonsense! I am always myself. I have merely come
to an understanding with the viceroy. When one of my fellows has reached the end of his tether, I say to him: "Get
off," and if he doesn't go, ah! I hale him to justice—you
understand!—That is not treachery is it?

QUINOLA

It is prevision—

MONIPODIO

And, by the bye, you have just come from court.

QUINOLA

Listen. (*Aside*) Here is a man, the very one I want,
knows everything in Barcelona. (*Aloud*) After what you
have told me we ought to be friends.

MONIPODIO

He who has my secret must be my friend—

QUINOLA

You are as watchful here as if you were jealous. What is
it? Come let us moisten our clay and wet our whistle with a
bottle in some tavern; it is daybreak—

MONIPODIO

Do you see how this palace is lit up for a feast? Don Fregose is dining and gaming at the house of Señora Faustine
Brancadori.

QUINOLA

Quite Venetian, Brancadori. 'Tis a rare name! She must
be the widow of some patrician.

### MONIPODIO

She is twenty-two, subtle as musk, and governs the governor, and, let me tell you between ourselves, has already wheedled out of him all that he picked up under Charles V. in the wars of Italy. What comes from the flute—

### QUINOLA

The air takes. What is the age of our viceroy?

### MONIPODIO

He owns up to sixty years.

### QUINOLA

And yet they speak of first love! I know of nothing so terrible as last love; it strangles a man. I am happy that I have been brought up so far with unsinged wings! I might be a statesman—

### MONIPODIO

This old general is still young enough to employ me as a spy upon the Brancadori, while she pays me for her liberty; and—you can understand the joyous life I lead by making no mischief!

### QUINOLA

Now you want to know all, Old Curiosity, in order to place your thumb upon the throat of opportunity? (*Monipodio nods assent.*) Is Lothundiaz still alive?

### MONIPODIO

Yonder is his house, and this palace belongs to him; always grasping more and more property.

### QUINOLA

I had hoped to find the heiress her own mistress. My master is ruined!

MONIPODIO

You bring back a master with you?

QUINOLA

One who will bring me mines of gold.

MONIPODIO

Could not I enter his service?

QUINOLA

I am counting very much upon your co-operation here.—
Listen, Monipodio; we are going to change the face of the
earth. My master has promised the king to make one of his
finest vessels move through the water, without sails or oars, in
the wind's eye, more swiftly than the wind itself.

MONIPODIO (*examining Quinola as he walks round him*)

Something has changed my friend.

QUINOLA

Monipodio, please to remember that men like us must
not be astonished at anything. Leave that to smaller people.
The king has given us the ship, but without a doubloon to go
and get her. We arrived here, therefore, with those two faithful companions of genius, hunger and thirst. A poor man
who discovers a valuable idea has always seemed to me like a
crumb of bread in a fish-pond; every fish takes a bite at him.
We are likely to reach the goal of glory naked and dying.

MONIPODIO

You are probably right.

QUINOLA

One morning at Valladolid, my master was within an ace
of divulging his secret to a philosopher who knew nothing of

it. I warrant you, I showed that gentleman the door, with a
dose of cudgel given with a good will.

### MONIPODIO
But how is it possible for us to gain a fortune honestly?

### QUINOLA
My master is in love. Now love forces a man to do as
many foolish as wise things. We two have first of all to protect our protector. My master is a philosopher who cannot
keep accounts—

### MONIPODIO
Oh! my dear fellow, in choosing a master, you ought to
have selected one—

### QUINOLA
Devotion and address count more with him than money;
for money and favor to him are mere snares. I know him
well; he will either give us or permit us to take enough to end
our days in respectability.

### MONIPODIO
Ah! that is what I have dreamed of.

### QUINOLA
We must then use all our talents, which have been so far
wasted, in carrying out this grand enterprise. We should
have had a great deal of misfortune if the devil had not
favored us.

### MONIPODIO
It will be almost worth while to make a journey to Compos-
tello. I have the smuggler's faith, and I love wine.

### QUINOLA
Are you not still in touch with the coiners of false money,
and the skeleton key-makers?

MONIPODIO

Yes—but for the good of the country—

QUINOLA

Well, that's the trick! As my master constructs his ma-
,hine, I shall take possession of the models of each part and
we will make a duplicate—

MONIPODIO

Quinola!

QUINOLA

What now? (*Paquita shows herself on the balcony.*)

MONIPODIO

You are the greatest of men!

QUINOLA

I know it. Make a discovery, and you will die persecuted
as a criminal; make a copy, and you will live happy as a fool!
And on the other hand, if Fontanares should die, why should
not I save his invention for the good of humanity?

MONIPODIO

Especially, since we ourselves are humanity, as an old
author says.—Let me embrace you—

.

## SCENE SECOND.

THE SAME PERSONS AND PAQUITA.

QUINOLA (*aside*)

Next to an honest dupe, I know nothing better than the
self-deluding rascal.

PAQUITA (*to herself*)

Two friends embrace each other! they cannot therefore be spies.

QUINOLA

You are already in the secrets of the viceroy, you have the confidence of the Brancadori lady. That is a good beginning! Work a miracle and give us some clothes first of all, and if we two, taking counsel with a flask of liquor, do not discover some way by which my master and Marie Lothundiaz may meet, I will not answer for the consequences. For the last two days his constant talk has been of her, and I am afraid he may some day entirely lose his head.

MONIPODIO

The maiden is guarded like a condemned convict. This is the reason: Lothundiaz has had two wives; the first was poor and gave him a son, the second had a fortune, and when she died left all to her daughter, and left it in such a way that she could never be deprived of it. The old man is a miser whose only object is his son's success. Sarpi, the secretary of the viceroy, in order to win the rich heiress, has promised to obtain a title for Lothundiaz, and takes vast interest in his son—

QUINOLA

There you are—an enemy at the very outset.

MONIPODIO

We must use great prudence. Listen. I am going to give a hint to Mathieu Magis, the most prominent Lombard in the city, and a man entirely under my influence. You will find everything you need at his place, from diamonds down to low shoes. When you return here you shall see our young lady. (*Exeunt.*)

## SCENE THIRD.

### PAQUITA AND FAUSTINE.

#### PAQUITA

Madame is right; two men are on sentry under her balcony and are going away on seeing the day dawn.

#### FAUSTINE

This old viceroy will end by disgusting me! He suspects me, even at my own house, while I am within sight and hearing of him. (*Exit Paquita.*)

---

## SCENE FOURTH.

### FAUSTINE AND DON FREGOSE.

#### DON FREGOSE

Madame, you run the risk of catching cold; it is too chilly here—

#### FAUSTINE

Come here, my lord. You tell me, that you have faith in me; but you put Monipodio to watch under my windows. Your behavior is not to be excused like the excessive prudence of a young man, and necessarily exasperates an honest woman. There are two kinds of jealousy: the first makes a man distrust his mistress; the second leads him to lose faith in himself. Confine yourself, if you please, to the second.

#### DON FREGOSE

Do not end so charming a celebration, señora, by a burst of anger which I do not deserve.

FAUSTINE

Was Monipodio, through whom you learn everything that
goes on in Barcelona, under my windows last night, or was
he not? Answer me on your honor as a gentleman.

DON FREGOSE

He might have been in the neighborhood to prevent our
gamesters from being attacked on their way home.

FAUSTINE

This is the evasive stratagem of an old general! I must
know the truth. If you have deceived me I will never see
you again so long as I live! (*She leaves him.*)

### SCENE FIFTH.

DON FREGOSE (*alone*)

Oh, why cannot I give up the sight, the voice of this woman! She delights me even in her very anger, and I love
to call forth her reproaches, that I may listen to her words.

### SCENE SIXTH.

PAQUITA AND MONIPODIO (*disguised as a begging friar at the
door of the Brancadori Palace*).

PAQUITA

Madame told me to learn why Monipodio stationed himself
below, but I saw no one there.

MONIPODIO

Alms, my dear child, is a treasure which is laid up in
heaven.

PAQUITA

I have nothing to give.

MONIPODIO

Never mind, promise me something.

PAQUITA

This is rather a jovial friar.

MONIPODIO

She does not recognize me and I believe I can run the risk. (*He knocks at the door of Lothundiaz.*)

PAQUITA

Ah! If you count upon the alms of our friend the land-owner, you would be richer with my promise. (*To Faustine Brancadori, who appears on the balcony*) Madame, the men are gone.

---

*SCENE SEVENTH.*

MONIPODIO AND DONA LOPEZ (*at the door of the Lothundiaz Mansion*).

DONA LOPEZ

What is it you desire?

MONIPODIO

The brothers of our order have received tidings of your dear Lopez—

DONA LOPEZ

That he was living?

MONIPODIO

As you conduct the Señorita Marie to the convent of the

Dominicans, take a turn round the square; you will meet there an escaped Algerian captive, who will tell you about Lopez.

### Dona Lopez
Merciful heavens! Would that I could ransom him!

### Monipodio
Be careful, first of all, whom you approach on that subject; suppose that he were a Mussulman?

### Dona Lopez
Dear Lopez! I must go and prepare the señorita for her journey. (*Re-enters the house.*)

------

## SCENE EIGHTH.

### Monipodio, Quinola and Fontanares.

### Fontanares
At last, Quinola, we stand beneath her windows.

### Quinola
Yes, but where is Monipodio? Has he allowed himself to be beaten off? (*He turns to the friar*) Sir Beggar?

### Monipodio
All goes well.

### Quinola
Sangodemy! What perfection of mendicancy! Titian ought to paint you. (*To Fontanares*) She will come. (*To Monipodio*) How do you find things?

### Monipodio
Most favorable.

QUINOLA

He shall be a grandee of Spain.

MONIPODIO

Oh!—That is nothing—There is something still better than that!

QUINOLA (*to Fontanares*)

Now, sir, you must above all things be prudent. Let us have no sighing, which might open the eyes of the duenna.

---

## SCENE NINTH.

THE SAME PERSONS, DONA LOPEZ AND MARIE.

MONIPODIO (*to the duenna, pointing at Quinola*)

This is the Christian who escaped from captivity.

QUINOLA (*speaking to the duenna*)

Ah! madame, I recognize you from the portrait of your charms which Señor Lorenzo drew for me. (*He takes her aside.*)

---

## SCENE TENTH.

MONIPODIO, MARIE AND FONTANARES.

MARIE

Is it really you?

FONTANARES

Yes, Marie, and I have so far succeeded; our happiness is assured.

MARIE

Ah! If you only knew how I have prayed for your success!

### FONTANARES

I have millions of things to say to you; but there is **one** thing which I ought to say a million times, to make up **for** all the weary time of my absence.

### MARIE

If you speak thus to me, I shall believe you do not know the depth of my attachment; for it is fed less upon flattering words than upon the interest I feel in all that interests you.

### FONTANARES

What I am most interested in now, Marie, is to learn before engaging in so important an undertaking, whether you have the courage to resist your father, who is said to contemplate a marriage for you.

### MARIE

Do you think then that I could change?

### FONTANARES

With us men, to love is to be forever jealous! You are so rich, I am so poor. When you thought I was ruined, you had no perturbation for the future, but now that success has come we shall have the whole world between us. And you shall be my star! and shall shine upon me though from so great a distance. If I thought that at the end of my long struggle I should not find you at my side, oh! in the midst of all the triumph I should die for grief!

### MARIE

Do you not know me yet? Though I was lonely, almost a recluse while you were absent, the pure feeling which from our childhood united me with you has grown greater with your destiny! When these eyes, which with such rapture look on you again, shall be closed forever; when this heart which only beats for God, for my father and for you shall be reduced to dust, I believe that on earth will survive a soul of mine to love you still! Do you doubt now my constancy?

### FONTANARES

After listening to such words as these, what martyr would not receive new courage at the stake?

## SCENE ELEVENTH.

### THE SAME PERSONS AND LOTHUNDIAZ.

### LOTHUNDIAZ

That cursed duenna has left my door open.

### MONIPODIO (*aside*)

Alas, those poor children are ruined!—(*To Lothundiaz*) Alms is a treasure which is laid up in heaven.

### LOTHUNDIAZ

Go to work, and you can lay up treasures here on earth. (*He looks round*) I do not see my daughter and her duenna in their usual place.

### MONIPODIO (*to Lothundiaz*)

The Spaniard is by nature generous.

### LOTHUNDIAZ

Oh! get away! I am a Catalonian and suspicious by nature. (*He catches sight of his daughter and Fontanares.*) What do I see?—My daughter with a young señor! (*He runs up to them.*) It is hard enough to pay duennas for guarding children with the heart and eyes of a mother without finding them deceivers. (*To his daughter*) How is it that you, Marie, heiress of ten thousand sequins a year, should speak to—do my eyes deceive me?—It is that blasted machinist who hasn't a maravedi. (*Monipodio makes signs to Quinola.*)

### MARIE

Alfonso Fontanares is not without fortune; he has seen the king.

### LOTHUNDIAZ

So much the worse for the king.

### FONTANARES

Señor Lothundiaz, I am quite in a position to aspire to the hand of you daughter.

### LOTHUNDIAZ

Ah!

### FONTANARES

Will you accept for your son-in-law the Duke of Neptunado, grandee of Spain, and favorite of the king? (*Lothundiaz pretends to look for the Duke of Neptunado.*)

### MARIE

But it is he himself, dear father.

### LOTHUNDIAZ

You, whom I have known since you were two feet high, whose father used to sell cloth—do you take me for a fool?

---

## SCENE TWELFTH.

THE SAME PERSONS, QUINOLA AND DONA LOPEZ.

### QUINOLA

Who said fool?

### FONTANARES

As a present upon our wedding, I will procure for you and for my wife a patent of nobility; we will permit you to settle her fortune by entail upon your son—

### MARIE

How is that, father?

### QUINOLA

How is that, sir?

### LOTHUNDIAZ

Why! this is that brigand of a Lavradi!

### QUINOLA

My master has won from the king an acknowledgment of my innocence.

### LOTHUNDIAZ

To obtain for me a patent of nobility cannot then be a difficult matter.

### QUINOLA

And do you really think that a townsman can be changed into a nobleman by letters-patent of the king! Let us make the experiment. Imagine for a moment that I am the Marquis of Lavradi. My dear duke, lend me a hundred ducats?

### LOTHUNDIAZ

A hundred cuts of the rod! a hundred ducats!—It is the rent of a piece of property worth two thousand gold doubloons

### QUINOLA

There! I told you so—and that fellow wishes to be ennobled! Let us try again. Count Lothundiaz, will you advance two thousand doubloons in gold to your son-in-law that he may fulfill his promises to the King of Spain?

LOTHUNDIAZ (*to Fontanares*)

But you must tell me what you have promised.

### FONTANARES

The king of Spain, learning of my love for your daughter, is coming to Barcelona to see a ship propelled without oars or sails, by a machine of my invention, and will himself honor our marriage by his presence.

### LOTHUNDIAZ (*aside*)

He is laughing at me. (*Aloud*) You are very likely to propel a ship without sails or oars! I hope you will do it; I'll go to see it. It would amuse me, but I don't wish to have for a son-in-law any man of such lofty dreams. Girls brought up in our families need no prodigies for husbands, but men who are content to mind their business at their own homes, and leave the affairs of the sun and moon alone. All that I want is that my son-in-law should be the good father of his family.

### FONTANARES

Your daughter, señor, when she was but twelve years old, smiled on me as Beatrice smiled on Dante. Child as she was, she saw in me at first naught but a brother; since then, as we felt ourselves separated by fortune, she has watched me as I formed that bold enterprise which should bridge with glory the gulf that stood between us. It was for her sake I went to Italy and studied with Galileo. She was the first to applaud my work, the first to understand it. She had wedded herself to my thought before it had occurred to her that one day she might wed herself to me. It is thus she has become the whole world to me. Do you now understand how I adore her?

### LOTHUNDIAZ

It is just for that reason that I refuse to give her to you. In ten years' time she would be deserted, that you might run after some other discovery.

MARIE

Is it possible, father, that a lover could prove false to a love which has spurred him on to work such wonders?

LOTHUNDIAZ

Yes, when he can work them no longer.

MARIE

If he should become a duke, grandee of Spain, and wealthy?—

LOTHUNDIAZ

If! If! If!—Do you take me for an imbecile? These ifs are the horses that drag to the hospital all these sham world-discoverers.

FONTANARES

But here are the letters in which the king grants to me the use of a ship.

QUINOLA

Now open your eyes! My master is at once a man of genius and a handsome youth; genius dulls a man and makes him of no use in a home, I grant you; but the handsome youth is there still; what more is needed by a girl for happiness?

LOTHUNDIAZ

Happiness does not consist in these extremes. A handsome youth and a man of genius,—these, forsooth, are fine reasons for pouring out the treasures of Mexico. My daughter shall be Madame Sarpi.

———

*SCENE THIRTEENTH.*

THE SAME PERSONS, AND SARPI (*on the balcony*).

SARPI (*aside*)

Some one uttered my name. What do I see? It is the

heiress and her father! What can they be doing in the square at this hour?

#### LOTHUNDIAZ

Sarpi has not gone to look for a ship in the harbor of Valladolid, but he gained promotion for my son.

#### FONTANARES

Do not, Lothundiaz, merely for the sake of your son's advancement, dispose of your daughter's hand without my consent; she loves me and I love her in return. In a short time I shall be (*Sarpi appears*) one of the most influential men in Spain, and powerful enough to reap my vengeance—

#### MARIE

Oh! not upon my father!

#### FONTANARES

Tell him then Marie, all that I am doing to deserve you.

#### SARPI (*aside*)

What! a rival?

#### QUINOLA (*to Lothundiaz*)

Sir, if you don't consent, you are in a fair way to be damned.

#### LOTHUNDIAZ

Who told you that?

#### QUINOLA

And worse than that,—you are going to be robbed; this I'll swear to.

#### LOTHUNDIAZ

To prevent my either being robbed or damned I am keeping my daughter for a man who may not have genius, but who has common sense—

FONTANARES

At least you will give me time—

SARPI

Why give him time?

QUINOLA (*to Monipodio*)

Who can that be?

MONIPODIO

Sarpi.

QUINOLA

What a bird of prey he looks!

MONIPODIO

And he is as difficult to kill. He is the real governor of Barcelona.

LOTHUNDIAZ

My respects to you, honorable secretary! (*To Fontanares*) Farewell, my friend, your arrival is an excellent reason why I should hurry on the wedding. (*To Marie*) Come, my daughter, let us go in. (*To the duenna*) And you, old hag, you'll have to pay for this.

SARPI (*to Lothundiaz*)

This hidalgo seems to have pretensions—

FONTANARES (*to Sarpi*)

Nay, I have a right! (*Exeunt Marie, the duenna and Lothundiaz.*)

## SCENE FOURTEENTH.

MONIPODIO, SARPI, FONTANARES AND QUINOLA.

SARPI

A right?—Do you know that the nephew of Fra Paolo

Sarpi, kinsman of the Brancadori, count in the Kingdom of
Naples, secretary to the viceroy of Catalonia, makes pretension to the hand of Marie Lothundiaz? When another man
claims a right in the·matter he insults both her and me.

### FONTANARES

Do you know that I for five years, I, Alfonso Fontanares,
to whom the king our master has promised the title of Duke
of Neptunado and Grandee, as well as the Golden Fleece, have
loved Marie Lothundiaz, and that your pretensions, made in
spite of the oath which she has sworn to me, will be considered, unless you renounce them, an insult both by her and
by me?

### SARPI

I did not know, my lord, that I had so great a personage
for a rival. In any case, future Duke of Neptunado, future
Grandee, future Knight of the Golden Fleece, we love the
same woman; and if you have the promise of Marie, I have
that of her father; you are expecting honors, while I possess
them.

### FONTANARES

Now, listen; let us remain just where we are; let us not
utter another word; do not insult me even by a look. Had I
a hundred quarrels, I would fight with no one until I had completed my enterprise and answered successfully the expectation of my king. When that moment comes, I will fight
single-handed against all. And, when I have ended the con·
flict, you will find me—close to the king.

### SARPI

Oh! we are not going to lose sight of each other.

## SCENE FIFTEENTH.

THE SAME PERSONS, FAUSTINE, DON FREGOSE AND PAQUITA.

FAUSTINE (*on the balcony*)

Tell me what is going on, my lord, between that young man and your secretary? Let us go down.

QUINOLA (*to Monipodio*)

Don't you think that my master has pre-eminently the gift of drawing down the lightning on his own head?

MONIPODIO

He carries his head so high!

SARPI (*to Don Fregose*)

My lord, there has arrived in Catalonia a man upon whom the king our master has heaped future honors. According to my humble opinion, he should be welcomed by your excellency in accordance with his merits.

DON FREGOSE (*to Fontanares*)

Of what house are you?

FONTANARES (*aside*)

How many sneers, such as this, have I not been forced to endure! (*Aloud*) The king, your excellency, never asked me that question. But here is his letter and that of his ministers. (*He hands him a package.*)

FAUSTINE (*to Paquita*)

That man has the air of a king.

PAQUITA

Of a king who will prove a conqueror.

FAUSTINE (*recognizing Monipodio*)

Monipodio! Do you know who that man is?

#### MONIPODIO

He is a man who, according to rumor, is going to turn the world upside down.

#### FAUSTINE

Ah! I see; it is that famous inventor of whom I have heard so much.

#### MONIPODIO

And here is his servant.

#### DON FREGOSE

Sarpi, you may file these ministerial documents; I will keep that of the king. (*To Fontanares*) Well, my fine fellow, the letter of the king seems to me to be positive. You are undertaking, I see, to achieve the impossible! However great you may be, perhaps it would be well for you to take the advice, in this affair, of Don Ramon, a philosopher of Catalonia who, on this subject, has written some famous treatises—

#### FONTANARES

In a matter of this kind, your excellency, the finest dissertations in the world are not worth so much as a practical achievement.

#### DON FREGOSE

That sounds presumptuous. (*To Sarpi*) Sarpi, you must place at the disposal of this gentleman whatever vessel in the harbor he may choose.

#### SARPI (*to the viceroy*)

Are you quite sure that such is the king's wish?

#### DON FREGOSE

We shall see. In Spain it is best to say a *paternoster* between every two steps we take.

SARPI

Other letters on the same subject have reached us from
Valladolid.

FAUSTINE (*to the viceroy*)

What are you talking about?

DON FREGOSE

Oh, it is nothing but a chimera.

FAUSTINE

But don't you know that I am rather fond of chimeras?

DON FREGOSE

This is the chimera of some philosopher which the king
has taken seriously on account of the disaster of the Armada.
If this gentleman succeeds, we shall have the court at Barcelona.

FAUSTINE

We shall be much indebted to him for that.

DON FREGOSE

He has staked his life on a commission to propel a vessel,
swift as the wind, yet straight in the wind's eye, without the
employment of either oars or sails.

FAUSTINE

Staked his life? He must be a child to do so.

SARPI

Alfonso Fontanares reckons that the performance of this
miracle will win for him the hand of Marie Lothundiaz.

FAUSTINE

Ah! He loves her then—

QUINOLA (*whispering to Faustine*)

No, señora, he adores her.

FAUSTINE

The daughter of Lothundiaz!

DON FREGOSE

You seem suddenly to feel a great interest in him.

FAUSTINE

I hope the gentleman may succeed, if it were only for the purpose of bringing the court here.

DON FREGOSE

Señora, will you not come and take luncheon at the villa of Avaloros? A vessel is at your service in the harbor.

FAUSTINE

No, my lord, this night of pleasure has wearied me, and a sail would prove too much. I am not obliged, like you, to be indefatigable; youth loves sleep, give me leave then to retire and take a little rest.

DON FREGOSE

You never say anything to me but that your words contain some innuendo.

FAUSTINE

You ought to be grateful that I do not take you seriously
(*Exeunt Faustine, the Viceroy and Paquita.*)

## *SCENE SIXTEENTH.*

AVALOROS, QUINOLA, MONIPODIO, FONTANARES AND SARPI.

SARPI (*to Avaloros*)

It is too late for a sail.

AVALOROS

I do not care; I have won ten crowns in gold.  (*Sarpi and Avaloros talk together.*)

FONTANARES (*to Monipodio*)

Who is this person?

MONIPODIO

It is Avaloros, the richest banker of Catalonia; he has brought the whole Mediterranean to be his tributary.

QUINOLA

I feel my heart filled with tenderness towards him.

MONIPODIO

Every one of us owns him as our master.

AVALOROS (*to Fontanares*)

Young man, I am a banker; if your business is a good one, next to the protection of God and that of the king, nothing is so good as that of a millionaire.

SARPI (*to the banker*)

Make no engagements at present.—You and I together will easily be able to make ourselves masters of this enterprise.

AVALOROS (*to Fontanares*)

Very well, my friend, you must come to see me.  (*Monipodio secretly robs him of his purse.*)

## *SCENE SEVENTEENTH.*

### Monipodio, Fontanares and Quinola

Quinola (*to Fontenares*)

Are you making a good beginning here?

Monipodio

Don Fregose is jealous of you.

Quinola

Sarpi is bent on defeating your enterprise.

Monipodio

You are posing as a giant before dwarfs who are in power!
Before you put on these airs of pride, succeed! People who
succeed make themselves small, slip into small openings and
glide inward to the treasure.

Quinola

Glory?—But my dear sir, it can only be obtained by theft.

Fontanares

Do you wish me to abase myself?

Monipodio

Yes, in order that you may gain your point.

Fontanares

Pretty good for a Sarpi! I shall make an open struggle
for it. But what obstacle do you see between success and me?
Am I not on my way to the harbor to choose a fine galleon?

Quinola

Ah! I am superstitious on that point. Sir, do not choose
the galley!

### FONTANARES

I see no reason why I shouldn't.

### QUINOLA

You have had no experience! You have had something else to make discoveries about. Ah, sir, we are moneyless, without credit at any inn, and if I had not met this old friend who loves me, for there are friends who hate you, we should have been without clothes—

### FONTANARES

But she loves me! (*Marie waves her handkerchief at the window.*) See, see, my star is shining!

### QUINOLA

Why, sir, it is a handkerchief! Are you sufficiently in your right mind to take a bit of advice?—This is not the sort of madonna for you; you need a Marchioness of Mondejar— one of those slim creatures, clad in steel, who through love are capable of all the expedients which distress makes necessary. Now the Brancadori—

### FONTANARES

If you want to see me throw the whole thing up you will go on talking like that! Bear that in mind; love gives the only strength I have. It is the celestial light that leads me on.

### QUINOLA

There, there, do not excite yourself.

### MONIPODIO

This man makes me anxious! He seems to me rather to be possessed by the machinery of love than by the love of machinery.

## SCENE EIGHTEENTH.

### THE SAME PERSONS AND PAQUITA.

#### PAQUITA (*to Fontanares*)

My mistress bids me tell you, señor, that you must be on your guard. You are the object of implacable hatred to certain persons.

#### MONIPODIO

That is my business. You may go without fear through all the streets of Barcelona; if any one seeks your life, I shall be the first to know it.

#### FONTANARES

Danger! Already?

#### PAQUITA

You have given me no answer for her.

#### QUINOLA

No, my pet, people don't think about two machines at the same time;—tell your divine mistress that my master kisses her feet. I am a bachelor, sweet angel, and wish to make a happy end. (*He kisses her.*)

#### PAQUITA (*slapping him in the face*)

You fool!

#### QUINOLA

Oh, charming! (*Exit Paquita.*)

---

## SCENE NINETEENTH.

### FONTANARES, QUINOLA AND MONIPODIO.

#### MONIPODIO

Come to the Golden Sun. I know the host; you will get credit there.

Quinola.—No, my pet, people don't think about two machines at the same time ;
——tell your divine mistress that my master kisses her feet.   I am a bachelor,
sweet angel, and wish to make a happy end.

(Paquita and Quinola)

QUINOLA

The battle is beginning even earlier than I had expected.

FONTANARES

Where shall I obtain money?

QUINOLA

We can't borrow it, but we can buy it. How much do you need?

FONTANARES

Two thousand doubloons in gold.

QUINOLA

I have been trying to make an estimate of the treasury I intended to draw upon; it is not plump enough for that.

MONIPODIO

Well, now, I have found a purse.

QUINOLA

Forget nothing in your estimate; you will require, sir, iron, copper, steel, wood, all of which the merchants can supply. I have an idea! I will found the house of Quinola and Company; if they don't prosper, you shall.

FONTANARES

Ah! what would have become of me without you?

MONIPODIO

You would have been the prey of Avaloros.

FONTANARES

To work then! The inventor must prove the salvation of the lover. (*Exeunt.*)

*Curtain to the First Act.*

# ACT II.

---

## SCENE FIRST.

*(A room in the palace of Señora Brancadori.)*

AVALOROS, SARPI AND PAQUITA.

### AVALOROS

Is the queen of our lives really ill?

### PAQUITA

She is melancholy.

### AVALOROS

Is thought, then, a malady?

### PAQUITA

Yes, and you therefore can be sure of good health.

### SARPI

Say to my dear cousin that Señor Avaloros and I are awaiting her good pleasure.

### AVALOROS

Stay; here are two ducats if you will say that I am sometimes pensive—

### PAQUITA

I will say that your tastes are expensive.  But I must go
and induce the señora to dress herself.  *(Exit.)*

## SCENE SECOND.

### AVALOROS AND SARPI.

#### SARPI

Poor viceroy! He is the youngster.

#### AVALOROS

While your little cousin is making a fool of him, you are displaying all the activity of a statesman and clearing the way for the king's conquest of French Navarre. If I had a daughter I would give her to you. Old Lothundiaz is no fool.

#### SARPI

How fine it would be to be founder of a mighty house; to win a name in the history of the country; to be a second Cardinal Granville or Duke of Alva!

#### AVALOROS

Yes! It would be a very fine thing. I also think of making a name. The emperor made the Fuggers princes of Babenhausen; the title cost them a million ducats in gold. For my part, I would like to be a nobleman at a cheaper rate.

#### SARPI

You! How could you accomplish it?

#### AVALOROS

This fellow Fontanares holds the future of commerce in his own hands.

#### SARPI

And is it possible that you who cling so persistently to the actual have any faith in him?

AVALOROS

Since the invention of gunpowder, of printing and the discovery of the new world I have become credulous. If any one
were to tell me that a man had discovered the means to receive
the news from Paris in ten minutes, or that water contained
fire, or that there are still new Indies to discover, or that it is
possible to travel through the air, I would not contradict it,
and I would give—

SARPI

Your money?

AVALOROS

No; mv attention to the enterprise.

SARPI

If the vessel is made to move in the manner proposed, you
would like then to be to Fontanares what Amerigo Vespucci
was to Christopher Columbus.

AVALOROS

Have I not here in my pocket enough to pay for six men
of genius?

SARPI

But how would you manage the matter?

AVALOROS

By means of money; money is the great secret. With
money to lose, time is gained; and with time to spend, everything is possible; by this means a good business may be made
a bad one, and while those who control it are in despair the
whole profit may be carried off by you. Money,—that is the
true method. Money furnishes the satisfaction of desire, as
well as of need. In a man of genius, there is always a child
full of unpractical fancies; you deal with the man and you
come sooner or later on the child; the child will become your
debtor, and the man of genius will go to prison.

SARPI

And how do you stand with him now?

AVALOROS

He does not trust my offers; that is, his servant does not. I shall negotiate with the servant.

SARPI

I understand you; I am ordered to send all the ships of Barcelona to the coasts of France; and, through the prudence of the enemies which Fontanares made at Valladolid, this order is absolute and subsequent to the king's letter.

AVALOROS

What do you want to get out of the deal?

SARPI

The functions of the Grand Master of Naval Construction—these I wish to be mine.

AVALOROS

But what is your ultimate object?

SARPI

Glory.

AVALOROS

You rascally trickster!

SARPI

You greedy extortioner!

AVALOROS

Let us hunt together; it will be time enough to quarrel when we come to the division of the prey. Give me your hand. (*Aside*) I am the stronger, and I control the viceroy through the Brancadori.

#### SARPI (*aside*)

We have fattened him sufficiently, let us kill him; I know how to destroy him.

#### AVALOROS

We must gain over this Quinola to our interests, and I have sent for him to hold a conference with the Brancadori.

---

### SCENE THIRD.

#### THE SAME PERSONS AND QUINOLA.

#### QUINOLA

I hang like —— between two thieves. But these thieves are powdered over with virtue and tricked out with fine manners. And they would like to hang the rest of us!

#### SARPI

You rogue, while you are waiting for your master to propel the galleys by new methods, you ought to be rowing in them yourself.

#### QUINOLA

The king, who justly appreciates my merits, well understands that he would lose too much by such an arrangement.

#### SARPI

You shall be watched!

#### QUINOLA

That I can well believe, for I keep watch on myself.

#### AVALOROS

You are rousing his suspicions, for he is an honest lad. (*To Quinola*) Come, my good fellow, have you any idea of what is meant by wealth?

QUINOLA

No, for I have seen it from too great a distance.

AVALOROS

Say, such a sum as two thousand golden doubloons?

QUINOLA

What? I do not know what you mean! You dazzle me. Is there such a sum? Two thousand doubloons! That means to be a land-holder, to own a house, a servant, a horse, a wife, an income; to be protected instead of being chased by the Holy Brotherhood!—What must I do to gain it?

AVALOROS

You must assist me in obtaining a contract for the mutual advantage of your master and myself.

QUINOLA

I understand! To tangle him up. O my conscience, that is very fine! But, dear conscience, be silent for a while; let me forget you for a few days, and we will live comfortably together for the rest of my life.

AVALOROS (*to Sarpi*)

We have him.

SARPI (*to Avaloros*)

He is fooling us! If he were in earnest he would not talk thus.

QUINOLA

I suppose you won't give me the two thousand doubloons in gold until after the treaty has been signed?

SARPI (*with eagerness*)

You can have it before.

QUINOLA

You don't mean it!  (*Holding out his hand*)   Give it me then.

AVALOROS

As soon as you sign notes of hand for the amounts which have already matured.

QUINOLA

The Grand Turk himself never offered the bowstring with greater delicacy.

SARPI

Has your master got his ship?


QUINOLA

Valladolid is at some distance from this, I admit; but we control in that city a pen which has the power of decreeing your disgrace.

SARPI

I will grind you to powder.


QUINOLA

I will make myself so small that you can't do it.


AVALOROS

Ah! you scoundrel, what do you propose to do?


QUINOLA

To talk to you about the gold.

----

*SCENE FOURTH.*


THE SAME PERSONS, FAUSTINE AND PAQUITA.


PAQUITA

Gentlemen, here is the señora.   (*Exit.*)

## SCENE FIFTH.

THE SAME PERSONS, WITH THE EXCEPTION OF PAQUITA.

QUINOLA (*approaching the Brancadori*)

Señora, my master talks of killing himself unless he can obtain the ship which Count Sarpi has refused for thirty days to give him; Señor Avaloros asks for his life while offering him his purse; do you understand? (*Aside*) A woman was our salvation at Vallodolid; the women shall be our salvation at Barcelona. (*Aloud*) He is very despondent.

AVALOROS

The wretched man seems daring enough.

QUINOLA

Daring without money is naturally amazing to you.

SARPI (*to Quinola*)

Will you enter my service?

QUINOLA

I am too set in my ways to take a master.

FAUSTINE (*aside*)

He is despondent! (*Aloud*) Why is it that men like you. Sarpi and Avaloros, for whom I have done so much, should persecute, instead of protecting, the poor man of genius who has so lately arrived among us? (*Avaloros and Sarpi are confused.*) I cry shame upon you! (*To Quinola*) You must explain to me exactly their schemes against you master.

SARPI (*to Faustine*)

My dear cousin, it does need much penetration to divine

what malady it is under which you have labored since the arrival of this Fontanares.

#### AVALOROS (*to Faustine*)

You owe me, señora, two thousand doubloons, and you will ꞓed to draw still further on my purse.

#### FAUSTINE

**I?** What have I ever asked of you?

#### AVALOROS

Nothing, but you never refuse anything which I am generous enough to offer you.

#### FAUSTINE

Your monopoly of the wheat trade is a monstrous abuse.

#### AVALOROS

Señora, I owe you a thousand doubloons.

#### FAUSTINE

Write me at once a receipt for the two thousand doubloons, and a check for the like sum which I do not intend to pay you. (*To Sarpi*) After having put you in the position in which you now flourish, I warn you that your best policy is to keep my secret.

#### SARPI

My obligations to you are too great to admit of my being ungrateful.

#### FAUSTINE (*aside*)

He means just the contrary, and he will make the viceroy furious with me. (*Exit Sarpi.*)

## SCENE SIXTH.

### THE SAME PERSONS, WITH THE EXCEPTION OF SARPI.

AVALOROS

Here they are, señora. (*Handing her the receipt and the check.*)

FAUSTINE

Very good.

AVALOROS

We shall still be friends?

FAUSTINE

Your monopoly of the wheat trade is perfectly legal.

AVALOROS

Ah! señora.

QUINOLA (*aside*)

That is what is called doing business.

AVALOROS

Señora, you are a noble creature, and I am—

QUINOLA (*aside*)

A regular swindler.

FAUSTINE (*offering the check to Quinola*)

Here, Quinola, this is for the expenses of your master's machine.

AVALOROS (*to Faustine*)

Don't give it to him, señora, he may keep it for himself. And for other reasons you should be prudent; you should wait—

QUINOLA (*aside*)

I pass from the torrid to the arctic zone; what a gamble is life!

FAUSTINE

You are right. (*Aside*) Better that I should hold in a balance the fortune of Fontanares. (*To Avaloros*) If you wish to keep your monopoly hold your tongue.

AVALOROS

There is nothing keeps a secret better than capital. (*Aside*) These women are disinterested until the day they fall in love I must try to defeat her; she is beginning to cost me too much (*Exit.*)

## SCENE SEVENTH.

### FAUSTINE AND QUINOLA.

FAUSTINE

Did you not tell me he was despondent?

QUINOLA

Everything is against him.

FAUSTINE

But he knows how to wrestle with difficulties.

QUINOLA

We have been for two years half drowned in difficulties; sometimes we have gone to the bottom and the gravel was pretty hard.

FAUSTINE

But what force of character, what genius he has!

QUINOLA

You see, there, señora, the effects of love.

FAUSTINE

And with whom is he in love now?

QUINOLA

Still the same—Marie Lothundiaz.

FAUSTINE

A doll!

QUINOLA

Yes, nothing but a doll!

FAUSTINE

Men of talent are all like that.

QUINOLA

Colossal creatures with feet of clay!

FAUSTINE

They clothe with their own illusions the creature that entangles them; they love their own creation; they are egotists!

QUINOLA (*aside*)

Just like the women! (*Aloud*) Listen, señora, I wish that by some honest means we could bury this doll in the depths of the—that is—of a convent.

FAUSTINE

You seem to me to be a fine fellow.

QUINOLA

I love my master.

FAUSTINE

Do you think that he has noticed me?

QUIÑOLA

Not yet.

FAUSTINE

Speak to him of me.

QUIÑOLA

But then, he would speak to me by breaking **a stick across** my back. You see, señora, that girl—

FAUSTINE

That girl ought to be forever lost to him.

QUIÑOLA

But he would die, señora.

FAUSTINE

He must be very much in love with her.

QUIÑOLA

Ah! that is not my fault! All the way here from Valladolid I have a thousand times argued the point, that a man like he ought to adore women, but never to love an individual woman! Never—

FAUSTINE

You are a pretty worthless rascal! Go and tell Lothundiaz to come and speak with me and to bring his daughter with him. (*Aside*) She shall be put in a convent.

QUIÑOLA (*aside*)

She is the enemy. She loves us so much that she can't **help** doing us a great deal of harm. (*Exit Quinola.*)

## SCENE EIGHTH.

### FAUSTINE AND FREGOSE.

#### FREGOSE.

While you expect the master, you spend your time in corrupting the servant.

#### FAUSTINE

Can a woman ever lose her habit of seduction?

#### FREGOSE

Señora, you are ungenerous; I should think that a patrician lady of Venice would know how to spare the feelings of an old soldier.

#### FAUSTINE

Come, my lord, you presume more upon your white hair than a young man would presume upon his fairest locks, and you find in them a stronger argument than in—(*She laughs*). Let me have no more of this petulance.

#### FREGOSE

How can I be otherwise than vexed when you compromise yourself thus, you, whom I wish to be my wife? Is it nothing to have a chance of bearing one of the noblest of names?

#### FAUSTINE

Do you think it is too noble for a Brancadori?

#### FREGOSE

Yet, you would prefer stooping to a Fontanares!

#### FAUSTINE

But what if he could raise himself as high as to a Brancadori? That would be a proof of love indeed! Besides, as you know from your own experience, love never reasons.

FREGOSE

Ah!  You acknowledge that!

FAUSTINE

Your friendship to me is so great that you have been the first to learn my secret.

FREGOSE

Señora!  Yes, love is madness!  I have surrendered to you more than myself!  Alas, I wish I had the world to offer you. You evidently are not aware that your picture gallery alone cost me almost all my fortune.

FAUSTINE

Paquita!

FREGOSE

And that I would surrender to you even my honor.

---

## SCENE NINTH.

### THE SAME PERSONS AND PAQUITA.

FAUSTINE (*to Paquita*)

Tell my steward that the pictures of my gallery must immediately be carried to the house of Don Fregose.

FREGOSE

Paquita, do not deliver that order.

FAUSTINE

The other day, they tell me, the Queen Catherine de Medici sent an order to Diana of Poitiers to deliver up what jewels she had received from Henry II.; Diana sent them back melted into an ingot.  Paquita, fetch the jeweler.

FREGOSE

You will do nothing of the kind, but leave the room. (*Exit Paquita.*)

## SCENE TENTH.

THE SAME PERSONS, WITH THE EXCEPTION OF PAQUITA.

FAUSTINE

As I am not yet the Marchioness of Fregose, how dare you give your orders in my house?

FREGOSE

I am quite aware of the fact that here it is my duty to receive them. But is my whole fortune worth one word from you? Forgive an impulse of despair.

FAUSTINE

One ought to be a gentleman, even in despair; and in your despair you treat Faustine as a courtesan. Ah! you wish to be adored, but the vilest Venetian woman would tell you that this costs dear.

FREGOSE

I have deserved this terrible outburst.

FAUSTINE

You say you love me. Love me? Love is self-devotion without the hope of recompense. Love is the wish to live in the light of a sun which the lover trembles to approach. Do not deck out your egotism in the lustre of genuine love. A married woman, Laura de Nova, said to Petrarch, "You are mine, without hope—live on without love." But when Italy crowned the poet she crowned also his sublime love, and centuries to come shall echo with admiration to the names of Laura and Petrarch.

### FREGOSE

There are very many poets whom I dislike, but the man you mention is the object of my abomination. To the end of the world women will throw him in the face of those lovers whom they wish to keep without taking.

### FAUSTINE

You are called general, but you are nothing but a soldier.

### FREGOSE

Indeed, and how then shall I imitate this cursed Petrarch?

### FAUSTINE

If you say you love me, you will ward off from a man of genius—(*Don Fregose starts*)—yes, there are such—the martyrdom which his inferiors are preparing for him. Show yourself great, assist him! I know it will give you pain, but assist him; then I shall believe you love me, and you will become more illustrious, in my sight at least, by this act of generosity than by your capture of Mantua.

### FREGOSE

Here, in your presence, I feel capable of anything, but you cannot dream of the tempest which will fall upon my head, if I obey your word.

### FAUSTINE

Ah! you shrink from obeying me!

### FREGOSE

Protect him, admire him, if you like; but do not love him!

### FAUSTINE

The ship given him by the king has been held back; you can restore it to him, in a moment.

FREGOSE

And I will send him to give you the thanks.


FAUSTINE

Do it! and learn how much I love you. (*Exit Don Fregose.*)

---

## SCENE ELEVENTH.

FAUSTINE (*alone*)

And yet so many women wish that they were men.

---

## SCENE TWELFTH.

FAUSTINE, PAQUITA, LOTHUNDIAZ AND MARIE.

PAQUITA

Señora, here are Señor Lothundiaz and his daughter. (*Exit Paquita.*)

---

## SCENE THIRTEENTH.

THE SAME PERSONS, EXCEPTING PAQUITA.

LOTHUNDIAZ

Ah! señora, you have turned my palace into a kingdom!—

FAUSTINE (*to Marie*)

My child, seat yourself by me. (*To Lothundiaz*) Be seated.

LOTHUNDIAZ

You are very kind, señora; but permit me to go and see

that famous gallery, which is spoken of throughout Catalonia. (*Faustine bows assent and Lothundiaz leaves the room.*)

---

## SCENE FOURTEENTH.

### FAUSTINE AND MARIE.

#### FAUSTINE

My child, I love you and have learned of the position in which you stand. Your father wishes you to marry my cousin Sarpi, while you are in love with Fontanares.

#### MARIE

And have been for five years, señora.

#### FAUSTINE

At sixteen one knows not what it is to love.

#### MARIE

What does that matter, if I love him?

#### FAUSTINE

With us, sweet girl, love is but self-devotion.

#### MARIE

I will devote myself to him, señora.

#### FAUSTINE

What! Would you give him up if that were for his interest?

#### MARIE

That would be to die, but yet my life is wholly his.

FAUSTINE (*aside as she rises from her seat*)

What strength in weakness and innocence! (*Aloud*) You have never left your father's house, you know nothing of the world nor of its hardships, which are terrible! A man often dies from having met with a woman who loves him too much, or one who loves him not at all; Fontanares may find himself in this situation. He has powerful enemies; his glory, which is all he lives for, is in their hands; you may disarm them.

MARIE

What must I do?

FAUSTINE

By marrying Sarpi, you will assure the triumph of your dear Fontanares; but no woman would counsel such a sacrifice; it must come, it will come from you. At first you must dissemble. Leave Barcelona for a time. Retire to a convent.

MARIE

And never see him again? Ah! If you knew—he passes every day at a certain hour under my windows, and that hour is all the day to me.

FAUSTINE (*aside*)

She stabs me to the heart! Oh! She shall be Countess Sarpi.

---

## SCENE FIFTEENTH.

THE SAME PERSONS AND FONTANARES.

FONTANARES (*to Faustine*)

Señora. (*He kisses her hand.*)

MARIE (*aside*)

What a pang I feel!

### FONTANARES

Shall I live long enough to testify my gratitude to you? If I achieve anything, if I make a name, if I attain to happiness, it will be through you.

### FAUSTINE

Why that is nothing! I merely tried to smooth the way for you. I feel such pity for men of talent in misfortune that you may ever count upon my help. Yes, I would go so far as to be the mere stepping-stone over which you might climb to your crown.

### MARIE (*drawing Fontanares by his mantle*)

But I am here, I (*he turns around*), and you never saw me.

### FONTANARES

Marie! I have not spoken to you for ten days! (*To Faustine*) Oh! señora, what an angel you are!

### MARIE (*to Fontanares*)

Rather say a demon. (*Aloud*) The señora was advising me to retire to a convent.

### FONTANARES

She!

### MARIE

Yes.

### FAUSTINE

Children that you are, that course were best.

### FONTANARES

I trip up, it seems, on one snare after another, and kindness ever conceals a pitfall. (*To Marie*) But tell me who brought you here?

### MARIE

My father!

FONTANARES

He! Is he blind? You, Marie, in this house!

FAUSTINE

Sir!—

FONTANARES

To a convent indeed, that she might dominate her spirit, and torture her soul!

---

## SCENE SIXTEENTH.

### THE SAME PERSONS AND LOTHUNDIAZ.

FONTANARES

And it was you who brought this angel of purity to the house of a woman for whom Don Fregose is wasting his fortune and who accepts from him the most extravagant gifts without marrying him?—

FAUSTINE

Sir!—

FONTANARES

You came here, señora, widow of a cadet of the house of Brancadori, to whom you sacrificed the small fortune your father gave you; but here you have utterly changed—

FAUSTINE

What right have you to judge my actions?

LOTHUNDIAZ

Keep silence, sir; the señora is a high born lady, who has doubled the value of my palace.

### FONTANARES

She! why she is a ——

### FAUSTINE

Silence!

### LOTHUNDIAZ

My daughter, this is your man of genius! extreme in everything, but leaning rather to madness than good sense. Señor Mechination, the señora is the cousin and protector of Sarpi.

### FONTANARES

Well, take your daughter away from the house of the Marchioness of Mondejar of Catalonia. (*Exeunt Lothundiaz and Marie.*)

---

## SCENE SEVENTEENTH.

### FAUSTINE AND FONTANARES.

### FONTANARES

So, señora, your generosity was merely a trick to serve the interests of Sarpi! We are quits then! And so farewell. (*Exit.*)

---

## SCENE EIGHTEENTH.

### FAUSTINE AND PAQUITA.

### FAUSTINE

How handsome he looked in his rage, Paquita!

PAQUITA

Ah! señora, what will become of you if you love him in this way?

FAUSTINE

My child, I feel that I have never loved before, and in an instant I have been transformed as by a stroke of lightning. In one moment I have loved for all lost time! Perhaps I have set my foot upon the path which leads to an abyss. Send one of my servants to the house of Mathieu Magis, the Lombard. (*Exit Paquita.*)

## SCENE NINETEENTH.

FAUSTINE (*alone*)

I already love him too much to trust my vengeance to the stiletto of Monipodio, for he has treated me with such contempt that I must bring him to believe that the greatest honor he could win would be to have me for his wife! I wish to see him groveling at my feet, or I will perish in the attempt to bring him there.

## SCENE TWENTIETH.

FAUSTINE AND FREGOSE.

FREGOSE

What is this? I thought to find Fontanares here, happy in the possession of the ship you gained for him.

FAUSTINE

You have given it to him then, and I suppose hate him no longer. I thought the sacrifice would be above your strength, and wished to know if hate were stronger than obedience.

FREGOSE

Ah! señora—

FAUSTINE

Could you take it back again?


FREGOSE

Whether obedient or disobedient, I cannot please you. Good ' :avens! Take back the ship! Why, it is crowded with arti- :ans who are its masters.


FAUSTINE

You never know what I want, and what I do not want.


FREGOSE

His death?

FAUSTINE

No, but his disgrace.

FREGOSE

And in that I shall avenge myself for a whole month of anguish.

FAUSTINE

Take care to keep your hands off what is my prey. And first of all, Don Fregose, take back your pictures from my gallery. (*Don Fregose shows astonishment.*) It is my will.


FREGOSE

You refuse then to be marchioness of—


FAUSTINE

They shall be burned upon the public square or sold, and the price given to the poor.


FREGOSE

Tell me, what is your reason for this?

FAUSTINE

I thirst for honor and you have ruined mine.

FREGOSE

Accept my name and all will be well.

FAUSTINE

Leave me, I pray you.

FREGOSE

The more power you have, the more you abuse it. (*Exit.*)

---

## SCENE TWENTY-FIRST.

FAUSTINE (*alone*)

So, so! I am nothing then but the viceroy's mistress! He might as well have said as much! But with the aid of Avaloros and Sarpi I intend to have a pretty revenge—one worthy of old Venice!

---

## SCENE TWENTY-SECOND.

FAUSTINE AND MATHIEU MAGIS.

MATHIEU MAGIS

I am told the señora has need of my poor services.

FAUSTINE

Pray tell me, who are you?

MATHIEU MAGIS

Mathieu Magis, a poor Lombard of Milan, at your service.

FAUSTINE

You lend money?

MATHIEU MAGIS

I lend it on good security—diamonds or gold—a very poor business. Our losses are overwhelming, señora. And at present money seems actually to be asleep. The raising of maravedis is the hardest of farm-labor. One unfortunate deal carries off the profits of ten lucky strokes, for we risk a thousand doubloons in the hands of a prodigal for three hundred doubloons profit. The world is very unjust to us.

FAUSTINE

Are you a Jew?

MATHIEU MAGIS

In what sense do you mean?

FAUSTINE

In religion.

MATHIEU MAGIS

I am a Lombard and a Catholic, señora.

FAUSTINE

You disappoint me.

MATHIEU MAGIS

Señora would have wished—

FAUSTINE

I would have wished that you were in the clutches of the Inquisition.

MATHIEU MAGIS

Why so?

FAUSTINE

That I might be certain of your fidelity.

MATHIEU MAGIS

I keep many secrets in my strong box, señora.

FAUSTINE

If I had your fortune in my power——

MATHIEU MAGIS

You would have my soul.

FAUSTINE (*aside*)

The only way to gain this man's adherence is by appealing to his self-interest, that is plain. (*Aloud*)  You lend——

MATHIEU MAGIS

At twenty per cent.

FAUSTINE

You don't understand what I mean.  Listen; you are lending the use of your name to Señor Avaloros.

MATHIEU MAGIS

I know Señor Avaloros.  He is a banker; we do some business together, but his name in the city stands too high and his credit in the Mediterranean is too sound for him to need the help of poor Mathieu Magis——

FAUSTINE

I see, Lombard, you are very cautious.  If you wish to lend your name to promote an important business undertaking——

MATHIEU MAGIS

Is it smuggling?

FAUSTINE

What difference does it make?  The question is, what would guarantee your absolute silence?

### Mathieu Magis

High profit.

### Faustine (*aside*)

This is a rare hunting dog. (*Aloud*)  Very well, I am going to entrust you with a secret of life and death, for I purpose giving up to you a great man to devour.

### Mathieu Magis

My small business feeds on the great passions of life; (*aside*) where there is a fine woman, there is fine profit.

*Curtain to the Second Act.*

# ACT III.

## SCENE FIRST.

( *The stage setting is the interior of a stable. Overhead are piles of hay; along the walls are wheels, tubes, shafts, a long copper chimney, a huge boiler. To the left of the spectator the Madonna is sculptured on a pillar. To the right is a table strewn with paper and mathematical instruments. Above the table hangs on the wall a blackboard covered with figures; by the side of the table is a shelf on which are onions, a water crock and a loaf. To the right of the spectator is a wide door, and to the left, a door opening on the fields. A straw bed lies by the side of the pillar at the feet of the Madonna. It is night-time.*)

### FONTANARES AND QUINOLA.

( *Fontanares, in a black robe girded by a leathern belt, works at his table. Quinola is checking off the various parts of the machine.*)

#### QUINOLA

Though you wouldn't think it, señor, I also have been in love! Only when I have once understood the woman, I have always bade her good-bye. A full pot and bottle, ah! these never betray, and moreover, you grow fat on them. ( *He glances at his master.* ) Pshaw! He doesn't even hear me. There are three more pieces ready for the forge. ( *He opens the door.* ) Here is Monipodio!

## SCENE SECOND.

### THE SAME PERSONS AND MONIPODIO.

#### QUINOLA

The last three pieces have come in. Bring the models and make duplicates of them, as a provision against accident. (*Monipodio beckons to him from the passage; two men make their appearance.*)

#### MONIPODIO

Carry these away, boys, and not a sound! Vanish like spectres. This is worse than theft. (*To Quinola*) He is dead and buried in his work

#### QUINOLA

He suspects nothing as yet.

#### MONIPODIO

Neither they nor any one else suspect us. Each piece is wrapped up like a jewel and hidden in a cellar. But we need thirty ducats.

#### QUINOLA

Zounds!

#### MONIPODIO

Thirty rascals built like those fellows eat as much as sixty ordinary men.

#### QUINOLA

Quinola and Company have failed, and I am a fugitive!

#### MONIPODIO

From protests?

#### QUINOLA

Stupid! They want me bodily. Fortunately, I have two or three suits of old clothes which may serve to deliver Quinola from the clutches of the keenest sleuths, until I can make payment.

### MONIPODIO

Payment? That is folly.

### QUINOLA

Yes, I have kept a little nest-egg against our thirst. Put on that ragbag of the begging friar and go to Lothundiaz and have a talk with the duenna.

### MONIPODIO

Alas! Lopez has returned from Algeria so often that our dear duenna begins to suspect us.

### QUINOLA

I merely wish her to carry this letter to Señorita Marie Lothundiaz (*handing a letter*). It is a masterpiece of eloquence, inspired by that which inspires all masterpieces. See! we have been living for ten days on bread and water.

### MONIPODIO

And what could we look for? To eat ortolans? If our men had expected fine fare they would have struck long ago.

### QUINOLA

If love would only cash my note of hand, we might still get but of this hole. (*Exit Monipodio.*)

---

## SCENE THIRD.

### QUINOLA AND FONTANARES.

QUINOLA (*rubbing an onion into his bread*)
This is the way we are told the Egyptian pyramid-builders

were fed, but they must also have had the sauce which gives us an appetite, and that is faith. (*Drinks water.*)  You don't appear to be hungry, señor?  Take care that the machine in your head doesn't go wrong!

### FONTANARES

I am nearing the final solution—

QUINOLA (*whose sleeve splits up as he puts back the crock*)

And I have found one in the continuity of my sleeve.  In this trade my clothes are becoming as uncertain as an unknown quantity in algebra.

### FONTANARES

You are a fine fellow!  Always merry, even in the depths of misfortune.

### QUINOLA

And why not, gadzooks!  Fortune loves the merry almost as much as the merry love her.

---

### SCENE FOURTH.

#### THE SAME PERSONS AND MATHIEU MAGIS.

### QUINOLA

Ah!  Here comes our dear Lombard; he looks at all these pieces of machinery as if they were already his lawful property.

### MATHIEU MAGIS

I am your most humble servant, my dear Señor Fontanares.

### QUINOLA

This is he, polished, dry, cold as marble.

FONTANARES

Good-day, Señor Magis. (*Cuts himself a piece of bread.*)

MATHIEU MAGIS

You are a sublime hero, and as far as I am concerned, I wish you all sorts of good luck.

FONTANARES

And is this the reason why you try to bring upon me all sorts of bad luck?

MATHIEU MAGIS

You snap me up very sharply; you do wrong, you forget that in me there are two men.

FONTANARES

I have never seen the other.

MATHIEU MAGIS

I have a heart, away from my business.

FONTANARES

But you are never away from your business.

MATHIEU MAGIS

I am always filled with admiration at the sight of your struggle.

FONTANARES

Admiration is the passion which is the most easily exhausted. Moreover, you never make any loans on sentiment.

MATHIEU MAGIS

There are some sentiments which bring profit, while others cause ruin. You are animated by faith; that is very fine, but it is ruinous. We made six months ago certain little agreements; you asked of me three thousand ducats for your experiments—

QUINOLA

On the condition, that you were to receive five thousand in return.

FONTANARES

Well?

MATHIEU MAGIS

The payment was due two months ago.

FONTANARES

You demanded it by legal process two months ago, the very next day after it was due.

MATHIEU MAGIS

I did it without thought of annoying you, merely as a formality.

FONTANARES

And what do you want now?

MATHIEU MAGIS

You are to-day my debtor.

FONTANARES

Eight months gone already? It has passed like a dream! And I was proposing to myself this evening the solution of the problem how to introduce cold water, so as to dissolve the steam! Magis, my dear friend, assist me in this matter, be my protector, and give me a few days more?

MATHIEU MAGIS

As many as you desire.

QUINOLA

Do you mean it? This is the first appearance of the other

man. (*To Fontanares*)  Señor, I shall make this gentleman my friend.  (*To Magis*)  I appeal to the two Magises and ask if they will give us the sight of a few doubloons!

### FONTANARES

Ah! I begin to breathe freely.

### MATHIEU MAGIS

That can easily be managed.  I am to-day not merely your money-lender, I am money-lender and co-proprietor, and I wish to draw out my share in the property.

### QUINOLA

Double man, and triple dog!

### MATHIEU MAGIS

Capital has nothing to do with faith—

### QUINOLA

Or with hope and charity; crowns are not Catholics.

### MATHIEU MAGIS

When a man comes and asks us to discount a bill, we cannot say: "Wait a bit; we have a man of genius at work trying to find a gold mine in a garret or a stable!"  No, indeed!  Why in six months I could have doubled those ducats over again. Besides, señor, I have a small family.

### FONTANARES (*to Quinola*)

That creature has a wife!

### QUINOLA

Yes, and if she brings forth young they will eat up Catalonia.

#### Mathieu Magis

I have heavy expenses.

#### Fontanares

You see how I live.

#### Mathieu Magis

Ah! If I were rich, I would lend you (*Quinola holds out his hands*) the wherewith to live better.

#### Fontanares

Wait fifteen days longer.

#### Mathieu Magis (*aside*)

This cuts me to the heart. If the matter concerned only myself I would perhaps let it go; but I must earn what has been promised me, which is to be my daughter's dowry. (*Aloud*) Now really, I have a great regard for you, you please me immensely—

#### Quinola (*aside*)

To think that it would be a crime to strangle him!

#### Fontanares

You are of iron; I shall show myself as hard as steel.

#### Mathieu Magis

What do you mean, señor?

#### Fontanares

You shall help me, whether you would or not.

#### Mathieu Magis

I will not! I want my capital! And would think nothing of seizing and selling all this iron work.

### FONTANARES

You compel me to meet trick with trick.  I was proceeding with my work honestly!—Now, if necessary, following your example, I shall leave the straight path.  I shall be of course accused, as if perfection could be expected of me.  But I do not mind calumny.  But to have this cup to drink is too much.  You made a senseless contract with me, you now shall sign another, or you will see me dash my work to fragments, and keep my secret buried here.  (*He strikes his hand on his heart.*)

### MATHIEU MAGIS

Ah! señor, you will not do that.  That would be theft, a piece of rascality of which a great man is incapable.

### FONTANARES

You seize upon my integrity as a weapon by which you would insure the success of monstrous injustice.

### MATHIEU MAGIS

Listen, I wish to have nothing to do with this matter, and if you will come to an understanding with Don Ramon, a most excellent man, I will yield all my rights to him.

### FONTANARES

Don Ramon?

### QUINOLA

Yes, the philosopher whom all Barcelona sets up in opposition to you.

### FONTANARES

After all, I have solved the last problem, and glory and fortune will attend the future current of my life.

### QUINOLA

Your words seem to indicate that there is still a part to be supplied in the machinery.

### FONTANARES

A trifle—a matter of some hundred ducats.

### MATHIEU MAGIS

Such a sum could not be raised from all that you have here, if it were sold by authority of government, counting the costs.

### QUINOLA

Carrion! Will you get out?

### MATHIEU MAGIS

If you humor Don Ramon, he doubtless will be willing to give you the assistance of his credit. (*Turns to Quinola*) As for you, gallows-bird, if ever you fall into my hands, I will get even with you. (*To Fontanares*) Good-bye, man of genius. (*Exit.*)

---

## SCENE FIFTH.

### FONTANARES AND QUINOLA.

### FONTANARES

His words make me shudder.

### QUINOLA

And me also! The good ideas of genius are always caught in the webs of such spiders as he.

### FONTANARES

Well, if only we can get a hundred ducats more, from that time forth we shall have a golden life filled with the banquets of love. (*He takes a drink of water.*)

QUINOLA

I quite believe you, but confess that blooming hope, that heavenly jade, has led us on pretty deep into the mire.

FONTANARES

Quinola!

QUINOLA

I do not complain for myself, I was born to trouble. The question is, how are we to get the hundred ducats. You are in debt to the workmen, to the master locksmith Carpano, to Coppolus the dealer in iron, steel and copper, and to our landlord, who after taking us in, more from fear of Monipodio than from compassion, will end by turning us out of doors; we owe him for nine months' board and lodging.

FONTANARES

But the work is all but finished.

QUINOLA

But what of the hundred ducats?

FONTANARES

How is it that you, usually so brave and merry, begin now to speak to me in such a dolorous tone?

QUINOLA

It is because, as a means of remaining at your side, I shall be obliged to disappear.

FONTANARES

And why?

QUINOLA

Why? Pray what are we to do about the sheriff? I have incurred, for you and for myself, trade debts to the amount of a hundred doubloons; and lo! these debts take, to my mind, the figure, face and feet of tipstaves!

FONTANARES

How much unhappiness is comprised in the term *glory!*

QUINOLA

Come! Do not be downcast. Did you not tell me that your grandfather went, some fifty years ago, with Cortez, to Mexico; has he ever been heard of?

FONTANARES

Never.

QUINOLA

Don't forget you have a grandfather! You will be enabled to continue your work, until you reach the day of your triumph.

FONTANARES

Do you wish to ruin me?

QUINOLA

Do you wish to see me go to prison and your machine to the devil?

FONTANARES

I do not.

QUINOLA

Permit me then to bring about the return of this grandfather? He will be the first of his company to return from the West Indies.

---

### SCENE SIXTH.

THE SAME PERSONS AND MONIPODIO.

QUINOLA

How goes it?

MONIPODIO

Your princess has received her letter.

FONTANARES

What kind of a man is this Don Ramon?

MONIPODIO

He is an ass.

QUINOLA

Is he envious?

MONIPODIO

As three rejected play-writers. He makes himself out to be a wonderful man.

QUINOLA

But does any one believe him?

MONIPODIO

They look upon him as an oracle. He scribbles off his treatises, explaining that the snow is white because it falls from heaven, and he maintains, in contradiction to Galileo, that the earth does not move.

QUINOLA

Do you not plainly see, señor, that I must rid you of this philosopher? (*To Monipodio*) You come with me; you must be my servant. (*Exeunt.*)

*SCENE SEVENTH.*

FONTANARES (*alone*)

What brain, even though it be encased in bronze, could stand the strain of this search after money, while also making an inquiry into the most jealously guarded secrets of nature? How can the mind, engaged in such quests, have time for distrusting men, fighting them, and combining others against them? It is no easy thing to see at once what course had best be taken, in order to prevent Don Ramon from stealing my glory; and Don Ramons abound on every side.  I at last dare to avow that my endurance is exhausted.

---

### SCENE EIGHTH.

FONTANARES, ESTEBAN, GIRONE AND TWO WORKMEN.

#### ESTEBAN

Can any of you tell me where a person named Fontanares is hiding himself?

#### FONTANARES

He is not hiding himself.  I am he; he is merely meditating in silence.  (*Aside*)  Where is Quinola?  He would know how to send them away satisfied.  (*Aloud*)  What do you want?

#### ESTEBAN

We want our money!  We have been working without wages for three weeks; the laborer lives from day to day.

#### FONTANARES

Alas, my friends, I do not live at all!

#### ESTEBAN

You are alone; you can pinch your belly.  But we have wives and children.  At the present moment we have pawned everything.

#### FONTANARES

Have confidence in me.

#### ESTEBAN

Can we pay the baker with this confidence in you?

### FONTANARES

I am a man of honor.

### GIRONE

Hark you! We also are men of honor.

### ESTEBAN

Take the honor of each of us to the Lombard and you will
see how much he will lend you on it.

### GIRONE

I am not a man of talent, not I, and no one will give me
trust.

### ESTEBAN

I am nothing but a villainous workman, but if my wife
needs an iron pot, I pay for it, by heaven!

### FONTANARES

I would like to know who it is has set you on me in this
way?

### GIRONE

Set us on? Are we dogs?

### ESTEBAN

The magistrates of Barcelona have given judgment in favor
of Masters Coppolus and Carpano, and have granted them a
lien on your inventions; pray tell us, where is our lien?

### GIRONE

shan't go away from this place without my money.

### FONTANARES

Can you find any money by staying here? However, here
you may remain. Good-day. (*He takes up his hat and cloak.*)

### ESTEBAN

No! You won't go out without paying us. (*The workmen prepare to bar the door.*)

### GIRONE

There is a piece which I forged myself; I am going to keep it.

### FONTANARES

What! you wretch! (*He draws his sword.*)

### THE WORKMEN

You will not make us budge.

### FONTANARES (*rushing upon them*)

Here is for you! (*He stops short and throws away his sword*). Perhaps these fellows have been sent by Avaloros and Sarpi to push me to extremes. If they succeeded I might be accused of murder and thrown into prison for years. (*He kneels down before the Madonna.*) Oh, my God! are genius and crime the same thing in Thy sight? What have I done to suffer such defeats, such insults and such outrages? Must I pay for my triumph in advance? (*To the workmen*) Every Spaniard is master in his own house.

### ESTEBAN

You have no house. This place is the Golden Sun; the landlord has told us so.

### GIRONE

You haven't paid for your lodging; you pay for nothing.

### FONTANARES

Remain where you are, my masters, I was wrong; I am in debt.

## *SCENE NINTH.*

### THE SAME PERSONS, COPPOLUS AND CARPANO.

#### COPPOLUS

Señor, I come to tell you that the magistrates of Barcelona have granted me a lien on your machine, and I shall take measures that no part of it leaves this place. My confrère, Carpano, your locksmith, shares my claim.

#### FONTANARES

What devil is blinding you? Without me, this machine is nothing but so much iron, steel, copper and wood; with me, it represents a fortune.

#### COPPOLUS

We are not going to leave you. (*The two merchants make a movement as if to hem in Fontanares.*)

#### FONTANARES

What friend embraces you so closely as a creditor? Well, well, I wish the devil would take back the great thought he gave me.

#### ALL

The devil!

#### FONTANARES

Ah! I must keep watch upon my tongue or one word will throw me into the clutches of the Inquisition!—No glory can recompense me for such sufferings as these!

#### COPPOLUS (*to Carpano*)

Shall we have it sold?

#### FONTANARES

But to be worth anything, the machine must be finished,

and one piece is wanting, of which the model is before you. (*Coppolus and Carpano consult together.*)    Two hundred sequins more would be required for its completion.

---

## SCENE TENTH.

THE SAME PERSONS. QUINOLA (*disguised as a fantastic old man*); MONIPODIO (*fancifully dressed*); THE LANDLORD OF THE GOLDEN SUN.

THE LANDLORD OF THE GOLDEN SUN (*pointing to Fontanares*)

Señor, that is he.

QUINOLA

And so you have lodged the grandson of General Fontanares in a stable!  The republic of Venice will set him in a palace!  My dear boy, let me embrace you.  (*He steps up to Fontanares.*)  The most noble republic has learned of your promises to the king of Spain, and I have left the arsenal at Venice, over which I preside, in order that—(*aside*)  I am Quinola.

FONTANARES

Never was an ancestor restored to life more opportunely—

QUINOLA

In what a miserable condition I find you!—Is this then the antechamber of glory!

FONTANARES

Misery is the crucible in which God tests our strength.

QUINOLA

Who are these people?

FONTANARES

Creditors and workmen, clamoring for their wages.

QUINOLA (*to the landlord*)

Rascal of a landlord, is this the dwelling-place of my grand-son?

THE LANDLORD

Certainly, your excellency.

QUINOLA

I have some knowledge of the laws of Catalonia, and I shall send for the magistrate to put these rogues in prison. You may call down the bailiffs upon my grandson, but keep to your own houses, you blackguards! (*He fumbles in his pocket.*) Stay! Now go and drink my health. (*He throws money among them.*) Come to me later on and you shall be paid.

THE WORKMEN

Long live his excellency! (*Exeunt.*)

QUINOLA (*to Fontanares*)

Our last doubloon! But it was a good bluff.

---

*SCENE ELEVENTH.*

THE SAME PERSONS, WITHOUT THE HOST AND THE
WORKMEN.

QUINOLA (*to the two tradesmen*)

As for you, my good fellows, you seem to be of better stuff, and by the intervention of a little money we can come to a settlement.

COPPOLUS

Yes, we shall then, your excellency, be at your service.

QUINOLA

Do I see here, my son, that famous invention about which Venice is so excited? Where is the plan, the elevation, the section, the working drawings of the machine?

COPPOLUS (*to Carpano*)

He knows all about it, but we must get further information before advancing anything.

QUINOLA

You are an amazing man, my son! Like Columbus, you will yet have your day. (*He kneels.*) I thank God for the honor He has done our family. (*To the merchants*) Two hours from this I will pay you. (*Exeunt Coppolus and Carpano.*)

---

### SCENE TWELFTH.

QUINOLA, FONTANARES AND MONIPODIO.

FONTANARES

What will be the result of this imposture?

QUINOLA

You were tottering on the brink of an abyss, and I rescued you.

MONIPODIO

It was well impersonated! But the Venetians have abundance of money, and in order to obtain three months' credit, we must throw dust into the eyes of the creditors, and this is the most expensive kind of dust.

QUINOLA

Didn't I tell you that there was a treasure coming? Well it's here now.

MONIPODIO

Coming of its own accord.  (*Quinola assents with a nod.*)

FONTANARES

His effrontery terrifies me.

---

## SCENE THIRTEENTH.

THE SAME PERSONS, MATHIEU MAGIS AND DON RAMON.

MATHIEU MAGIS

I have brought Don Ramon to you, for I wish to do nothing without his sanction.

DON RAMON (*to Fontanares*)

Señor, I am delighted at this opportunity of sharing the work of so eminent a man of science.  We two will be enabled to bring your invention to the highest perfection.

QUINOLA

Señor knows mechanics, balistics, mathematics, dioptrics, catoptrics, statistics?

DON RAMON

Indeed I do.  I have produced many valuable treatises.

QUINOLA

In Latin?

DON RAMON

No, in Spanish.

QUINOLA

No true philosopher, señor, writes in anything but Latin.
There is a danger that science may be vulgarized.  Do you know Latin?

### Don Ramon

Yes, señor.

### Quinola

So much the better for you.

### Fontanares

Señor, I respect the name which you have made; but 1 cannot accept your offer, because of the dangers attendant on my enterprise; I am risking my head in this work and yours is too precious to be exposed.

### Don Ramon

Do you think, señor, that you can afford to slight Don Ramon, the great scientific authority?

### Quinola

Don Ramon! the famous Don Ramon, who has expounded the causes of so many natural phenomena, which hitherto had been thought to happen without cause?

### Don Ramon

The very man.

### Quinola

I am Fontanaresi, director of the arsenal of the Venetian Republic, and grandfather of our inventor. My son, you may have full confidence in Don Ramon; a man of his position can have no designs upon you; let us tell him everything.

### Don Ramon (*aside*)

Ah! I am going to learn everything about the machine.

### Fontanares (*aside to Quinola*)

What is all this about?

### Quinola (*aside to Fontanares*)

Let me give him a lesson in mathematics; it will do him

no good, and us no harm. (*To Don Ramon*)  Will you come here? (*He points out the parts of the machine*)  All this is meaningless; for philosophers, the great thing—

DON RAMON

The great thing?

QUINOLA

Is the problem itself!  You know the reason why clouds mount upwards?

DON RAMON

I believe it is because they are lighter than the air.

QUINOLA

Not at all!  They are heavy as well as light, for the water that is in them ends by falling as flat as a fool.  I don't like water, do you?

DON RAMON

I have a great respect for it.

QUINOLA

I see that we are made for each other.  The clouds rise to such a height, because they are vapor, and are also attracted by the force of the cold upper air.

DON RAMON

That may be true.  I will write a treatise on the subject.

QUINOLA

My grandson states this in the formula R plus O.  And as there is much water in the air, we simply say, O plus O, which is a new binomial.

DON RAMON

A new binomial!

QUINOLA

Yes, an X, if you like it better.

### Don Ramon

X, ah yes, I understand!

### Fontanares (*aside*)

What a donkey!

### Quinola

The rest is a mere trifle. The tube receives the water which, by some means or other, has been changed to cloud. This cloud is bound to rise and the resulting force is immense.

### Don Ramon

Immense, why immense!

### Quinola

Immense—in that it is natural, since man—pay particular attention to this—does not create force—

### Don Ramon

Very good, then how?—

### Quinola

He borrows it from nature; to invent, is to borrow.—Then —by means of certain pistons,—for in mechanics—you know—

### Don Ramon

Yes, señor, I know mechanics.

### Quinola

Very good! The method of applying a force is child's play, a trifle, a matter of detail, as in the turnspit—

### Don Ramon

Ah! He employs the turnspit then?

QUINOLA

There are two here, and the force is such that it raises the mountains, which skip like rams—as was predicted by King David.

DON RAMON

Señor, you are perfectly right, the clouds, that is, the water—

QUINOLA

Water, señor?—Why! It is the world. Without water, you could not—That is plain. Well now! This is the point on which my grandson's invention is based; water will subdue water. X equals O plus O, that is the complete formula.

DON RAMON (aside)

The terms he employs are incomprehensible.

QUINOLA

Do you understand me?

DON RAMON

Perfectly.

QUINOLA (aside)

This man is a driveling dotard. (Aloud) I have spoken to you in the language of genuine philosophy—

MATHIEU MAGIS (to Monipodio)

Can you tell me who this remarkably learned man is?

MONIPODIO

He is a very great man, to whom I am indebted for my knowledge of balistics; he is the director of the Venetian arsenal, and purposes this evening making us a contribution on behalf of the republic.

MATHIEU MAGIS

I must go and tell Señora Brancadori, she comes from Venice. (*Exit.*)

---

## SCENE FOURTEENTH.

THE SAME PERSONS, WITH THE EXCEPTION OF MATHIEU MAGIS. LOTHUNDIAZ AND MARIE.

MARIE

Am I in time?

QUINOLA (*aside*)

Hurrah! Here comes our treasure. (*Lothundiaz and Don Ramon exchange greetings and examine the pieces of machinery in the centre of the stage.*)

FONTANARES

What! Is Marie here?

MARIE

My father brought me. Ah! my dear friend, your servant told me of your distress—

FONTANARES (*to Quinola*)

You scoundrel!

QUINOLA

What, grandson!

MARIE

And he brought all my agonies to an end.

FONTANARES

Tell me, pray, what was it troubled you?

MARIE

You cannot imagine the persecutions I have endured since

your arrival, and especially since your quarrel with Madame Brancadori. What could I do against the authority of my father? It is absolute. While I remained at home, I doubted my power to help you; my heart was yours in spite of every-thing, but my bodily presence—

### FONTANARES

And so you are another martyr!

### MARIE

By delaying the day of your triumph, you have made my position intolerable. Alas! when I see you here, I perceive that you yourself at the same time have been enduring incredible hardships. In order that I might be with you for a moment, I have feigned an intention of vowing myself to God; this evening I enter a convent.

### FONTANARES

A convent? Is that the way they would separate us? These tortures make one curse the day of his birth. And you, Marie, you, who are the mainspring and the glory of my discovery, the star that protected my destiny, I have forced you to seek ref-uge in heaven! I cannot stand up against that. (*He weeps.*)

### MARIE

But by promising to enter a convent, I obtained my father's permission to come here. I wish in bidding you farewell to bring you hope. Here are the savings of a young girl, of your sister, which I have kept against the day when all would for-sake you.

### FONTANARES

And what care I for glory, for fortune, for life itself, with-out you?

### MARIE

Accept the gift which is all that the woman who intends to be your wife can and ought to offer. If I feel that you are unhappy and in distress, hope will forsake me in my retirement, and I shall die, uttering a last prayer for you!

### QUINOLA (*to Marie*)

Let him play the proud man, we may save him in spite of himself. Do you know it is for this purpose that I am passing myself off as his grandfather? (*Marie gives her purse to Quinola.*)

### LOTHUNDIAZ (*to Don Ramon*)

So you do not think much of him?

### DON RAMON

Oh, no, he is an artisan, who knows nothing and who doubtless stole his secret in Italy.

### LOTHUNDIAZ

I have always doubted him, and it seems I was right in refusing him my daughter in marriage.

### DON RAMON

He would bring her to beggary. He has squandered five thousand sequins, and has gone into debt three thousand, in eight months, without attaining any result! Ah! He is a contrast with his grandfather. There's a philosopher of the first rank for you! Fontanares will have to work hard to catch up with him. (*He points to Quinola.*)

### LOTHUNDIAZ

His grandfather?

### QUINOLA

Yes, señor, my name of Fontanares was changed to that of Fontanaresi.

### LOTHUNDIAZ

And you are Pablo Fontanaresi?

QUINOLA

Yes, Pablo himself.

LOTHUNDIAZ

And are you rich?

QUINOLA

Opulent.

LOTHUNDIAZ

That delights me, señor. I suppose that now you will pay me the two thousand sequins which you borrowed from my father?

QUINOLA

Certainly, if you can show me my signature, I am ready to pay the bond.

MARIE (*after a conversation with Fontanares*)

You will accept this—will you not—as a means of securing your triumph, for is not our happiness staked on that?

FONTANARES

To think that I am dragging down this pearl into the gulf which is yawning to receive me! (*Quinola and Monipodio depart.*)

---

## SCENE FIFTEENTH.

THE SAME PERSONS AND SARPI.

SARPI (*to Lothundiaz*)

You here, Señor Lothundiaz? And your daughter too?

LOTHUNDIAZ

I promised that she should come here to say farewell on condition that she would not refuse to retire to a convent afterwards.

### SARPI

The assembly here is so numerous that I am not surprised, nor in the least offended, by your complaisance towards her.

### FONTANARES

Ah! Here comes the fiercest of my persecutors. How are you, señor; are you come to put my constancy to a fresh test?

### SARPI

I represent the viceroy of Catalonia, señor, and I have a right to your respectful treatment. (*To Don Ramon*) Are you satisfied with him?

### DON RAMON.

If he takes my advice, we are sure of success.

### SARPI

The viceroy has great hopes from your learned co-operation.

### FONTANARES

Surely I am dreaming! Is it possible they are raising up a rival to me?

### SARPI

No! señor; but a guide who is able to save you from failure.

### FONTANARES

Who told you I needed one?

### MARIE

O Alfonso! But suppose that Don Ramon could insure your success?

### FONTANARES

Ah! Even she has lost confidence in me!

### MARIE

They say he is so learned!

### LOTHUNDIAZ

Presumptuous man! He thinks that he knows more than all the learned in the world.

### SARPI

I was induced to come here on account of a question which has been raised and has filled the viceroy with anxiety; you have had in your possession for nearly ten months a ship belonging to the state, and you must now render an account of the loan.

### FONTANARES

The king fixed no term for the time of my experiments.

### SARPI

The administration of Catalonia has the right to demand an account, and we have received a decree of the ministers to this effect. (*Fontanares appears thunderstruck.*) Oh! you can take your time; we do not wish to embarrass a man like you. Nor are we inclined to think that you wish to elude the stipulation with regard to your life by keeping the ship for an indefinite period.

### MARIE

His life?

### FONTANARES

Yes, I am staking my life in these experiments.

### MARIE

And yet, you refuse my help?

### FONTANARES

In three months, Count Sarpi, I shall have completed, with-

out the counsel of another, the work I am engaged upon. **You**
will then see one of the grandest spectacles that a man can
produce for his age to witness.

### SARPI

Here, then, is a bond to that effect; sign it. (*Fontanares
signs it.*)

### MARIE

Farewell, my friend! If you are vanquished in this strug
gle I believe that I shall love you more than ever!

### LOTHUNDIAZ

**Come, my daughter;** the man is mad.

### DON RAMON.

Young man! be sure to read my treatises.

### SARPI

Farewell, future grandee of Spain. (*Exeunt all except
Fontanares.*)

---

### SCENE SIXTEENTH.

### FONTANARES (*alone in the front of the stage*)

While Marie is in a convent the sunlight cannot warm me.
I am bearing up a world, yet fear I am no Titan.—No, I shall
never succeed; all is against me. And this work which cost
me three years of thought and ten months of toil will never
cleave the ocean! But now, I am heavy with sleep. (*He
lies down on the straw.*)

## SCENE SEVENTEENTH.

FONTANARES (*asleep*), QUINOLA AND MONIPODIO (*entering*
*by the Postern*).

#### QUINOLA

Diamonds! Pearls and gold! We are saved.

#### MONIPODIO

Don't forget. The Brancadori is from Venice.

#### QUINOLA

Then I'd better be getting back there. Send me the landlord; I wish to re-establish our credit.

#### MONIPODIO

He is here.

## SCENE EIGHTEENTH.

THE SAME PERSONS AND THE LANDLORD OF THE GOLDEN SUN.

#### QUINOLA

What is this, señor, Landlord of the Golden Sun? You
don't seem to have much confidence in the star of my grandson?

#### THE LANDLORD

A hostelry, señor, is not a banking house.

#### QUINOLA

No, but you should not, for charity's sake, have refused
him bread. The most noble republic of Venice sent me to
bring him to that city, but he is too fond of Spain! I return,
as I arrived, secretly. I have nothing with me that I can
dispose of excepting this diamond. A month from this time

I will remit to you through the bank. Will you arrange with my grandson's servant for the sale of this jewel?

### THE LANDLORD

Your people here, señor, shall be treated like princes of wealth.

### QUINOLA

You may go. (*Exit landlord.*)

---

## SCENE NINETEENTH.

THE SAME PERSONS, EXCEPTING THE LANDLORD.

### QUINOLA

I must go and change my dress. (*He looks at Fontanares.*) He sleeps; that noble heart has at last succumbed to its emotions; it is only we who know how to yield before misfortunes; our carelessness he cannot share. Have I not done well, in always obtaining a duplicate of that which he required? (*To Monipodio*) Here is the plan of the last piece; do you take charge of it. (*Exeunt.*)

---

## SCENE TWENTIETH.

FONTANARES (*sleeping*), FAUSTINE AND MATHIEU MAGIS.

### MATHIEU MAGIS

There he is!

### FAUSTINE

To what a plight have I reduced him! From the depth of the wounds which I have thus inflicted upon myself, I realize the depth of my love! Oh! how much happiness do I owe him in compensation for so much suffering!—

*Curtain to the Third Act*

# ACT IV.

## *SCENE FIRST.*

*(The stage setting represents a public square. In the centre stands a sheriff's officer on an auctioneer's block, around the base of which are the various pieces for the machine. A crowd is gathered on each side of the platform. To the left of the spectator are grouped together Coppolus, Carpano, the Landlord of the Golden Sun, Esteban, Girone, Mathieu Magis. Don Ramon and Lothundiaz. To the right are Fontanares and Monipodio; Quinola conceals himself in a cloak behind Monipodio.)*

FONTANARES, MONIPODIO, QUINOLA, COPPOLUS, THE LAND-LORD OF THE GOLDEN SUN, ESTEBAN, GIRONE, MATHIEU MAGIS, DON RAMON, LOTHUNDIAZ, SHERIFF'S OFFICER, A CROWD OF PEOPLE.

SHERIFF'S OFFICER

Gentlemen, show a little more warmth. Here we have a boiler, big enough to cook a dinner for a regiment of the guards.

THE LANDLORD

Four maravedis.

SHERIFF'S OFFICER

Do I hear more? Come and look at it, examine it!

MATHIEU MAGIS

Six maravedis.

QUINOLA (*to Fontanares*)

Señor, they will not fetch a hundred ducats.

### FONTANARES

We must try to be resigned.

### QUINOLA

Resignation seems to me to be the fourth theological virtu omitted from the list out of consideration for women!

### MONIPODIO

Hold your tongue! Justice is on your track and you would have been arrested before this if they had not taken you for one of my people.

### SHERIFF'S OFFICER

This is the last lot, gentlemen. Going, going—no further bid? Gone! It is knocked down to Señor Mathieu Magis, for ten ducats, six maravedis.

### LOTHUNDIAZ (*to Don Ramon*)

What do you think of that? Thus ends the sublime invention of our great man! He was right, by heaven, when he promised us a rare spectacle!

### COPPOLUS

You can laugh; he does not owe you anything.

### ESTEBAN

It is we poor devils who have to pay for his folly.

### LOTHUNDIAZ

Did you get nothing, Master Coppolus? And what of my daughter's diamonds, which the great man's servant put into the machine?

MATHIEU MAGIS

Why, they were seized in my house.

LOTHUNDIAZ

And are not the thieves in the hand of justice? I would like best of all to see Quinola, that cursed pilferer of jewels, in durance.

QUINOLA (*aside*)

Oh, my young life, what lessons are you receiving! My antecedents have ruined me.

LOTHUNDIAZ

But if they catch him, his goose will soon be cooked, and I shall have the pleasure of seeing him dangling from the gallows, and giving the benediction with his feet.

FONTANARES (*to Quinola*)

Our calamity stirs this dullard's wit.

QUINOLA

You mean his brutality.

DON RAMON

I sincerely regret this disaster. This young artisan had at last listened to my advice, and we were on the point of realizing the promises made by him to the king; but he blindly forfeited his opportunity; I mean to ask pardon for him at the court, for I shall tell the king how useful he will be to me.

COPPOLUS

Here is an example of generosity extremely rare in the conduct of one learned man towards another.

LOTHUNDIAZ

You are an honor to Catalonia!

### FONTANARES (*coming forward*)

I have endured with tranquillity the agony of seeing a piece of workmanship, which entitles me to eternal glory, sold as so much old junk—(*murmurs among the people*). But this passes all endurance. Don Ramon, if you have, I do not say understood, but even guessed, at the use of all these fragments of machinery, displaced and scattered as they are, you ought to have bought them even at the sacrifice of your whole fortune.

### DON RAMON

Young man, I respect your misfortunes; but you know that your apparatus could not possibly go, and that my experience had become necessary to you.

### FONTANARES

The most terrible among all the horrors of destitution is that it gives ground for calumny and the triumph of fools!

### LOTHUNDIAZ

Is it not disgraceful for a man in your position thus to undertake to insult a philosopher whose reputation is established? Where would I be if I had given you my daughter? You would have led me a fine dance down to beggary; for you have already wasted, for absolutely no purpose, ten thousand sequins! Really this grandee of Spain seems particularly small in his grandeur to-day.

### FONTANARES

You make me pity you.

### LOTHUNDIAZ

That is possible, but you do not make me envy you; your life is at the mercy of the tribunal.

DON RAMON

Let him alone; don't you see that he is crazy?

FONTANARES

Not quite crazy enough, señor, to believe that O plus O is a binomial.

---

## SCENE SECOND.

THE SAME PERSONS, DON FREGOSE, FAUSTINE, AVALOROS AND SARPI.

SARPI.

We have come too late; the sale is over—

DON FREGOSE

The king will regret the confidence he placed in a charlatan.

FONTANARES

A charlatan, my lord? In a few days, you may be able to cut my head off; kill me, but don't calumniate me; your position in the state is too high for you to descend so low.

DON FREGOSE

Your audacity equals the extent of your downfall. Are you unaware that the magistrates of Barcelona look upon you as an accomplice of the thief who robbed Lothundiaz? The flight of your servant proves the crime, and the freedom you now enjoy is due to the intercessions of this lady. (*Points to Faustine.*)

FONTANARES

My servant, your excellency, might have been in early life a criminal, but since he has followed my fortunes he has been an innocent man. I declare, on my honor, that he is guiltless of any such act as theft. The jewels which were seized at the moment he was engaged in selling them were the free gift of Marie Lothundiaz, from whom I had refused to accept them.

### FAUSTINE

What pride he shows, even in adversity! Nothing can bend him.

### SARPI.

And how do you explain the resurrection of your grandfather, the pretended director of the Venetian arsenal? Unfortunately for you, the señora and myself were acquainted with the actual man.

### FONTANARES

I caused my servant to put on this disguise in order that he might talk science and mathematics with Don Ramon. Señor Lothundiaz will tell you that the philosopher of Catalonia and Quinola perfectly understood each other.

### MONIPODIO (*to Quinola*)

He has ruined himself!

### DON RAMON

On this subject I appeal to my writings.

### FAUSTINE

Do not be perturbed, Don Ramon; it is so natural for people of this kind, when they find themselves falling, to drag down other people with them!

### LOTHUNDIAZ

Such a disposition is detestable.

### FONTANARES

Before I die I ought to speak the truth, señora, to those who have flung me into the abyss. (*To Don Fregose*) My

lord, the king promised me the protection of his people at
Barcelona, and here I have met with nothing but hatred!
Oh, you grandees of the land, you rich, and all who have in
your hands power and influence, why is it that you thus throw
obstacles in the way of advancing thought? Is it the law of
God that you should persecute and put to shame that which
eventually you will be compelled to adore? Had I been pliant,
abject and a flatterer, I might have succeeded! In me you
have persecuted that which represents all that is noblest in
man—His consciousness of his own power, the majesty of his
labor, the heavenly inspiration which urges him to put his
hand to enterprise, and—love, that spirit of human trust,
which rekindles courage when it is on the point of expiring
in the storm of mockery. Ah! If the good that you do is
done amiss, you are always successful in the accomplishment
of what is bad! But why should I proceed?—You are not
worthy of my anger.

FAUSTINE (*aside*)
Oh! Another word and I must cry out that I adore him!

DON FREGOSE
Sarpi, tell the police officers to advance and carry off the
accomplice of Quinola. (*Applause and cries of "bravo!"*)

---

## SCENE THIRD.

THE SAME PERSONS AND MARIE LOTHUNDIAZ.

(*At the moment the police officers seize Fontanares, Marie
appears, in the habit of a novice, accompanied
by a monk and two sisters.*)

MARIE LOTHUNDIAZ (*to the viceroy*)
My lord, I have just learned that in my desire to save Fon-

tanares from the rage of his enemies I have caused his ruin.
But now an opportunity is given me to vindicate the truth,
and I beg to declare that I myself put into the hands of
Quinola the precious stones and the money I had treasured
as my own. (*Lothundiaz shows some excitement.*) They belonged to me, father, and God grant that you may not have
cause some day to mourn your own blindness.

QUINOLA (*throwing off his cloak*)

Whew! I breathe freely at last!

FONTANARES (*bending his knee before Marie*)

Thanks, radiant and spotless creature, through whose love
I still am kept close to that heaven from which I draw my
faith and hope; you have saved my honor.

MARIE

And is not your honor also mine? Your glory is yet to
come.

FONTANARES

Alas! my work is dismembered and dispersed, held in a
hundred avaricious hands, who will not give it back excepting
at the price it cost to fabricate. To recover it I should double
the amount of my indebtedness and fail to complete the enterprise in time. All is over!

FAUSTINE (*to Marie*)

Only sacrifice yourself for him and he is saved.

MARIE

What say you, father? and you, Count Sarpi? (*Aside*) It
will be my death! (*Aloud*) Will you consent, on condition
I obey you, to give Fontanares all that is necessary for the
success of his undertaking? (*To Faustine*)    I shall devote
myself to God, señora!

### FAUSTINE

You are sublime, sweet angel! (*Apart*) And thus at last deliverance comes to me!

### FONTANARES

Stay, Marie! I would choose the struggle and all its perils, I would choose death itself, rather than the loss of you from such a cause.

### MARIE

Rather than glory? (*To the viceroy*) My lord, you will cause my gems to be restored to Quinola. I return to my convent with a happy mind; either I am his, or I must live to God alone.

### LOTHUNDIAZ

I believe he is a sorcerer.

### QUINOLA

This young maiden restores to me my love for womankind.

### FAUSTINE (*to Sarpi, the viceroy and Avaloros*)

Can we not conquer him, in spite of all?

### AVALOROS

I shall try it.

### SARPI (*to Faustine*)

All is not lost. (*To Lothundiaz*) Take your daughter home; she will soon be obedient to you.

### LOTHUNDIAZ

God grant it! Come, my daughter. (*Exeunt.*)

## *SCENE FOURTH.*

FAUSTINE, FREGOSE, AVALOROS, FONTANARES. QUINOLA AND
MONIPODIO.

### AVALOROS

I have studied you well, young man, and you have a great
heart—a heart firm as steel. Steel will always be the master
of gold. Let us frankly form a copartnership; I will pay
your debts, buy up all that has been sold, give you and
Quinola five thousand ducats, and, at my instance, the viceroy
will be willing to forget your freedom with him.

### FONTANARES

If, in my distress, I have ever failed in respect towards you,
señor, I beg you will pardon me.

### DON FREGOSE

That is quite sufficient, señor. Don Fregose does not easily
take offence.

### FAUSTINE

You have done well, my lord.

### AVALOROS

Thus you see, young man, that tempest is succeeded by
calm, and at present all things smile upon you. The next
thing for us to do is to unite, you and I, in fulfilling your
promises to the king.

### FONTANARES

I care not for fortune excepting for one reason; shall I
be enabled to wed Marie Lothundiaz?

### DON FREGOSE

Is she the only woman in the world you love?

FONTANARES

The only one.   (*Faustine and Avaloros talk together.*)

DON FREGOSE

You never told me that before.   Henceforth, you may count on me, young man; I am your steadfast ally.   (*Exit.*)

MONIPODIO

They are coming to terms; we are ruined.   I shall take myself off to France with the duplicate machine.   (*Exit.*)

---

## SCENE FIFTH.

QUINOLA, FONTANARES, FAUSTINE AND AVALOROS.

FAUSTINE (*to Fontanares*)

Come, now; I also bear no malice, and you must come to the banquet I am giving.

FONTANARES

Señora, your first kindness concealed treachery.

FAUSTINE

Like all those lofty dreamers, who enrich humanity with their inventions, you know neither women, nor the world.

FONTANARES (*aside*)

I have scarcely eight days left.   (*To Quinola*)   I am going to make use of her.

QUINOLA

Do so, as you make use of me.

FONTANARES

I will come to your house, señora.


FAUSTINE

I must thank Quinola for that. (*She offers a purse to Quinola*) Take this. (*To Fontanares*) Till we meet again! (*Exeunt Faustine and Avaloros.*)

---

## SCENE SIXTH.

FONTANARES AND QUINOLA.

FONTANARES

That woman is treacherous as the sun in winter. Unhappy am I that I sought her, for she has taught me to lose faith. Is it possible that there are virtues which it is for our advantage to discard?

QUINOLA

How is it possible, señor, to distrust a woman who sets in gold her slightest words! She loves you; that's the secret. Is your heart so very small that it cannot harbor two affections?


FONTANARES

Nonsense! Marie has given me hope, her words have fired my soul. Yes, I shall succeed.


QUINOLA (*aside*)

Where is Monipodio? (*Aloud*) A reconciliation, señor, is very easy with a woman who yields so easily as Señora Brancadori.

FONTANARES

Quinola!

QUINOLA

Señor, you make me desperate! Would you oppose the
perfidy of a useful love with the loyalty of a love that is blind?
I need the influence of Señora Brancadori in order to get rid
of Monipodio, whose intentions cause me anxiety. If only I
can obtain this influence I will guarantee you success, and you
shall then marry your Marie.

FONTANARES

By what means?

QUINOLA

My dear señor, by mounting on the shoulders of a man who
sees a long distance, as you do, any one can see farther still.
You are an inventor, very good; but I am inventive. You
saved me from—I needn't say what! I, in turn, will deliver
you from the talons of envy and from the clutches of cupidity. Here is gold for us; come dress yourself, make yourself fine, take courage; you are on the eve of triumph. But
above all things, behave graciously towards Señora Brancadori.

FONTANARES

You must at least tell me, how you are going to effect this?

QUINOLA

No, señor, if you knew my secret, all would be ruined; you
are a man of talent, and a man of talent is always simple as a
child. (*Exeunt.*)

---

*SCENE SEVENTH.*

(*The setting represents the drawing-room in Señora Brancadori's palace.*)

FAUSTINE (*alone*)

The hour is come, to which all my efforts for the last four-

teen months have been looking for fulfillment. In a few
moments Fontanares will see that Marie is forever lost to him.
Avaloros, Sarpi and I have lulled the genius to forgetfulness,
and have brought the man up to the very day when his experiment was to have taken place, so that he stands helpless and
destitute. Oh! how totally is he in my power, just as I had
wished! But does a person ever change from contempt to
love? No, never. Little does he know that for a twelvemonth
I have been his adversary, and the misfortune is, that when he
does know he will hate me! But hatred is not the opposite
of love, it is merely the obverse of the golden coin. I shall
tell him everything; I shall make him hate me.

## SCENE EIGHTH.

#### Faustine and Paquita.

#### Paquita

Señora, your orders have been most exactly carried out by
Monipodio. Señorita Lothundiaz has just been informed by
her duenna, of the peril which threatens Señor Fontanares
this evening.

#### Faustine

Sarpi must be here by this time. Tell him I wish to speak
to him. (*Exit Paquita.*)

## SCENE NINTH.

#### Faustine (*alone*)

We must baffle the plans of Monipodio. Quinola fears he
has received the order to get rid of Fontanares; it is too bad
that there should be ground for such a fear.

## SCENE TENTH.

FAUSTINE AND DON FREGOSE.

FAUSTINE

Your arrival is timely, señor, I wish to ask a favor of you,

DON FREGOSE

Say, rather, that you wish to confer one on me.

FAUSTINE

Monipodio must disappear from Barcelona—yes, and from Catalonia, within two hours; send him to Africa.

DON FREGOSE

What has he done to you?

FAUSTINE

Nothing.

DON FREGOSE

Well, what is your reason?

FAUSTINE

Simply because—You understand?

DON FREGOSE

Your wish shall be obeyed. (*He writes.*)

## SCENE ELEVENTH.

THE SAME PERSONS AND SARPI.

FAUSTINE

Have you made the necessary preparations, cousin, for your immediate marriage with Marie Lothundiaz?

SARPI.

I have, and her good father has taken care that the contract should be ready.


FAUSTINE

That is well! Send word to the convent of the Dominicans. The rich heiress will freely consent to be wedded to
you at midnight; she will accept any condition, when she
sees (*whispering to Sarpi*) Fontanares in the hands of justice.


SARPI.

I quite understand, and the only thing now is to have him
arrested. My good fortune seems invincible! And—I owe it
all to you. (*Aside*) What instrument is there more powerful than the hatred of a woman!—


DON FREGOSE

Sarpi, see that this order is strictly carried out and with no
delay. (*Exit Sarpi.*)

———

*SCENE TWELFTH.*

THE SAME PERSONS EXCEPTING SARPI.


DON FREGOSE

And what of your own marriage?


FAUSTINE

My lord, I can think of nothing at present except the coming banquet; you shall have my answer this evening. (*Fontanares appears.*) (*Aside*) Oh, there he comes! (*To Fregose*) If you love me, leave me a while.


DON FREGOSE

Alone with him?

FAUSTINE

Yes, so I desire.

DON FREGOSE

After all he loves no one but his Marie Lothundiaz.
(*Exit.*)

---

## SCENE THIRTEENTH.

FAUSTINE AND FONTANARES.

FONTANARES

The palace of the king of Spain is not more splendid than
yours, señora, and you here display all the pomp of royalty.

FAUSTINE

Listen to me, dear Fontanares.

FONTANARES

Dear?—Ah! señora, you have taught me to distrust such
words as that!

FAUSTINE

She, whom you have so cruelly insulted, will now reveal herself to you. A terrible disaster threatens you. Sarpi has persistently worked against you and in doing so has carried out
the orders of an irresistible power, and this banquet will be for
you, unless I intervene, the scene of a Judas' kiss. I have
been told, in confidence, that on your departure from this
house, perhaps within these very walls, you will be arrested,
flung into prison, and your trial will begin—never to end. Is
it possible that you can put into proper condition in one night
the vessel which otherwise will be forfeited to you? As
regards your work, you know how impossible it is to begin it
over again. I wish to save you, you and your glory, you and
your fortune.

### FONTANARES

You save me? And how?

### FAUSTINE

Avaloros has placed at my disposal one of his ships, Moni-podio has given me his best smugglers for a cruise; let us start for Venice. The republic will make you a patrician and will give you ten times as much gold as Spain has promised. (*Aside*) Why is it they do not arrive?

### FONTANARES

And what of Marie? If we are to take her with us, I will believe in you.

### FAUSTINE

Your thoughts are of her at the very moment when the choice between life and death is to be made. If you delay, we may be lost.

### FONTANARES

We?—Señora!

---

## SCENE FOURTEENTH.

THE SAME PERSONS. GUARDS RUSH IN AT EVERY DOOR. A MAGISTRATE APPEARS. SARPI.

### SARPI

Do your duty!

### THE MAGISTRATE (*to Fontanares*)

In the name of the king, I arrest you.

### FONTANARES

The hour of death has come at last! Yet happily I carry my secret with me to God, and love shall be my winding sheet.

## SCENE FIFTEENTH.

### The Same Persons, Marie and Lothundiaz.

#### Marie

I was not, then, deceived; you have fallen into the hands of your enemies! And what is left to me, dearest Alfonso, but to die for you—and yet, by what a frightful death! O beloved! heaven is jealous of a perfect love, and thus would teach us by those cruel disasters, which we call the chances of life, that there is no true happiness save in the presence of God. What! you here?

#### Sarpi.

Señorita!

#### Lothundiaz

My daughter!

#### Marie

For one moment you have left me free, for the last time in my life! I shall keep my promise, you must not be unfaithful to yours. O sublime discoverer, you will have to discharge the obligations that belong to greatness, and to fight the battle of your lawful ambition! This struggle will be the great interest of your life; while the Countess Sarpi will die by inches and in obscurity, imprisoned in the four walls of her house.—And now let me remind you, father, and you, count, that it was clearly agreed, as the condition of my obedience, that Señor Fontanares should be granted by the viceroy of Catalonia a further extension of time, for the completion of his experiment.

#### Fontanares

Marie, how can I live without you?

#### Marie

How could you live in the hands of your executioner?

### FONTANARES

Farewell! I am ready to die.

### MARIE

Did you not make a solemn promise to the King of Spain, yes, to all the world? (*Speaks low to Fontanares*) Oh! seize your triumph; after that we can die!

### FONTANARES

I will accept, if only you refuse to be his.

### MARIE

Father, fulfill your promise.

### FAUSTINE

I have triumphed!

### LOTHUNDIAZ (*in a low voice to Fontanares*)

You contemptible seducer! (*Aloud*) Here I give you ten thousand sequins. (*In a low voice*) Atrocious wretch! (*Aloud*) My daughter's income for one year. (*In a low voice*) May the plague choke you! (*Aloud*) Upon the presentation of this check, Señor Avaloros will count out to you ten thousand sequins.

### FONTANARES

But does the viceroy consent to this arrangement?

### SARPI.

You have publicly accused the viceroy of Catalonia of belying the promises of the king; here is his answer: (*he draws forth a document*) By this ordinance, he puts a stay on the lawsuits of all your creditors, and grants you a year to complete your experiment.

FONTANARES

I am ready to do so.

LOTHUNDIAZ

He has made up his mind! Come, my daughter; they are expecting us at the Dominican convent, and the viceroy has promised to honor us with his presence at the ceremony.

MARIE

So soon? (*Exeunt the whole party.*)

FAUSTINE (*to Paquita*)

Run, Paquita, and bring me word when the ceremony is ended, and they are man and wife.

## SCENE SIXTEENTH.

### FAUSTINE AND FONTANARES.

FAUSTINE (*aside*)

There he stands, like a man pausing on the brink of a precipice to which tigers have pursued him. (*Aloud*) Why are not you as great as your creative thought? Is there but one woman in the world?

FONTANARES

What! do you think that a man can pluck from his heart a love like mine, as easily as he draws the sword from its scabbard?

FAUSTINE

I can well conceive that a woman should love you and do you service. But, according to your idea, love is self-abdication. All that the greatest men have ever wished for: glory,

honor, fortune, and more than that, a triumphant dominion
which genius alone can establish—this you have gained, conquering a world as Cæsar, Lucullus and Luther conquered
before you! And yet, you have put between yourself and
this splendid existence an obstacle, which is none other than
a love worthy of some student of Alcala. By birth you are
a giant, and of your own will you are dwindling into a dwarf.
But a man of genius can always find, among women, one
woman especially created for him. And such a woman, while
in the eyes of men she is a queen, for him is but a servant,
adapting herself with marvelous suppleness to the chances of
life, cheerful in suffering and as far-sighted in misfortune as
in prosperity; above all, indulgent to his caprices and knowing well the world and its perilous changes; in a word, capable of occupying a seat in his triumphal car after having
helped it up the steepest grades—

FONTANARES

You have drawn her portrait.

FAUSTINE

Whose?

FONTANARES

Marie's!

FAUSTINE

What! Did that child have skill to protect you? Did she
divine the person and presence of her rival? And was she,
who had suffered you to be overcome, worthy of possessing
you for her own—she—the child who has permitted herself to
be drawn, step by step, to the altar where at this moment she
bestows herself upon another?—If it had been I, ere this I
should have lain dead at your feet! And on whom has she
bestowed herself? On your deadliest enemy, who had accepted
the command to secure the shipwreck of your hopes.

FONTANARES

How could I be false to that inextinguishable love, which has thrice come to my succor, which has eventually saved me, which, having no sacrifice but itself to offer on the altar of misfortune, accomplishes the immolation with one hand, and, with the other, offers to me in this (*he shows the letter*) the restoration of my honor, the esteem of my king, the admiration of the universe. (*Enter Paquita, who makes ɑ sign to Faustine, then goes out.*)

FAUSTINE (*aside*)

Ah! Sarpi has now his countess. (*To Fontanares*) Your life, your glory, your fortune, your honor, are at last in my hands alone! Marie no longer stands between us!

FONTANARES

Us! us!

FAUSTINE

Contradict me not, Alfonso! I have conquered all that is yours; do not refuse me your heart! You will never gain a love more devoted, more submissive, more full of sympathy than mine; for at last you shall become the great man that you deserve to be.

FONTANARES

Your audacity astounds me. (*He shows the letter.*) With a sum of money guaranteed me here I am once more the sole arbiter of my destiny. When the king sees the character and the results of my work, he will cancel that marriage, which has been obtained by violence. And my love for Marie is such that I can wait till then.

FAUSTINE

Fontanares, if I love you distractedly, it is perhaps because of that delightful simplicity, which is the badge of genius—

FONTANARES (*aside*)

Her smile freezes me to the heart.

FAUSTINE

That gold you speak of—is it already in your possession?

FONTANARES

It is here.

FAUSTINE

And would I have let them give that to you, if I thought you would ever receive it? To-morrow you will find all your creditors standing between you and the possession of that sum, which you owe to them. What can you accomplish without gold? Your struggle will begin over again! but your work, O great, but simple man, has not been dispersed in fragments; it is all mine; my instrument, Mathieu Magis, has acquired possession of it. I hold it at my feet, in my palace. I am the only one who would not rob you either of your glory, or of your fortune, for what would this be, but to rob myself?

FONTANARES

It is you, then, cursed Venetian woman!

FAUSTINE

Yes—since the moment you insulted me, upon this spot, I have directed everything; it is at my bidding that Magis, and Sarpi, and your creditors, and the landlord of the Golden Sun, and the workmen have acted! But ah! How great a love underlay this simulated hatred. Tell me, have you never been roused from your slumber by a falling tear-drop, the pearl of my repentance, while I was gazing at you with admiration—you—the martyr that I worshiped?

FONTANARES

No! you are not a woman—

### FAUSTINE

Ah! There is more than woman, in a woman who loves as I do.

### FONTANARES

And, as you are not a woman, I could kill you.

### FAUSTINE

What of that, provided it were your hand that did it' (*Aside*) He hates me!

### FONTANARES

I am seeking for—

### FAUSTINE

Is it anything I can find for you?

### FONTANARES

——A punishment great enough for your crime.

### FAUSTINE

Can there be any punishment which a woman who loves can feel? Come, try me.

### FONTANARES

You love me, Faustine. Am I all of life to you? Do you really make my grief your own?

### FAUSTINE

One pang of yours becomes a thousand pangs to me!

### FONTANARES

If then I die, you will die also. 'Tis plain, therefore, although your life is not worthy to be set against the love that I have lost, my course is taken.

### FAUSTINE

Ah!

### Fontanares

With crossed arms I will await the day of my arrest. At the same stroke the soul of Marie and my soul shall rise to heaven.

### Faustine (*flinging herself at the feet of Fontanares*)

O Alfonso! Here, at your feet, I will remain till you have promised me—

### Fontanares

Leave me, shameless courtesan! (*He spurns her.*)

### Faustine

You have spoken this openly and in public; but remember, men oftentimes insult that which they are destined eventually to adore.

---

## SCENE SEVENTEENTH.

### The Same Persons and Don Fregose.

### Don Fregose.

Silence! wretched journeyman! I refrain from transfixing your heart with my sword, only because I intend you to pay more dearly for this insult.

### Faustine

Don Fregose! I love this man; whether he makes of me his slave or his wife, my love shall be the ægis of his life.

### Fontanares

Am I to be the victim of fresh persecutions, my lord? I am overwhelmed with joy. Deal me a thousand blows; they will be multiplied a thousand fold, she says, in her heart. I am ready!

## *SCENE EIGHTEENTH.*

THE SAME PERSONS AND QUINOLA.

QUINOLA

Sir!

FONTANARES

And you also have betrayed me; you!

QUINOLA

Off goes Monipodio, wafted towards Africa with recommendations on his hands and feet.

FONTANARES

What of that?

QUINOLA

Under the pretext of robbing you, I have concealed in a cellar a second machine, for I took care that two should be made, while we only paid for one.

FONTANARES

Thus it is that a true friend renders despair impossible. (*He embraces Quinoïa.*) (*To Fregose*) My lord, write to the king and build, overlooking the harbor, an amphitheatre for two hundred thousand spectators; in ten days I will fulfill my promise, and Spain shall behold a ship propelled by steam in the face of wind and waves. I will wait until there is ɛ storm that I may show how I can prevail against it.

FAUSTINE (*to Quinola*)

You have manufactured a machine—

QUINOLA

No, I have manufactured two, as a provision against ill-luck.

FAUSTINE

What devils have you called in to assist you?

QUINOLA

The three children of Job: Silence, Patience and Perseverance. (*Exeunt Fontanares and Quinola.*)

---

## SCENE NINETEENTH.

FAUSTINE AND DON FREGOSE.

DON FREGOSE (*aside*)

She is hateful, and yet I do not cease to love her.

FAUSTINE

I must have my revenge. Will you assist me?

DON FREGOSE

Yes, and we will yet succeed in bringing him to ruin.

FAUSTINE

Ah! you love me in spite of all, don't you?

*Curtain to the Fourth Act.*

# ACT V.

## SCENE FIRST.

*(The setting is the terrace of the town-hall of Barcelona, on each side of which are pavilions. The terrace looks on the sea and ends in a balcony in the centre of the stage; the open sea and the masts of vessels form the scenery. At the right of the spectator appear a large arm-chair and seats set before a table. The murmur of an immense crowd is heard. Leaning over the balcony Faustine gazes at the steamship. Lothundiaz stands on the left, in a condition of utter stupefaction; Don Fregose is seated on the right with his secretary, who is drawing up a formal account of the experiment. The Grand Inquisitor is stationed in the middle of the stage.)*

LOTHUNDIAZ, THE GRAND INQUISITOR AND DON FREGOSE.

### DON FREGOSE

I am undone, ruined, disgraced! Even if I were to fall at the feet of the king, I should gain no pity from him.

### LOTHUNDIAZ

At what a price have I purchased my patent of nobility! My son has been killed in an ambuscade in Flanders, and my daughter is dying; her husband, the governor of Roussillon, refused her permission to be present at the triumph of this devil of a Fontanares. How well she spoke when she said that I should repent of my wilful blindness!

THE GRAND INQUISITOR *(to Don Fregose)*

The Holy Office has reminded the king of your past services; you will be sent as viceroy to Peru, where you will be able to repair your fortunes; but first finish your work here; let us crush this discoverer and check the progress of his dangerous innovation.

### DON FREGOSE

But how can we do so? The orders of the king must be obeyed, at least ostensibly.

### THE GRAND INQUISITOR

We have taken such measures that obedience may be rendered both to the Holy Office and to the king. You have only to do as you are bidden. (*To Lothundiaz*) Count Lothundiaz, as the first municipal officer of Barcelona, you must offer to Don Ramon, in the name of the city, a crown of gold in honor of his discovery, whose result will secure to Spain the domination of the sea.

### LOTHUNDIAZ (*in astonishment*)

To Don Ramon!

### THE GRAND INQUISITOR AND DON FREGOSE

To Don Ramon.

### DON FREGOSE

You must address a eulogy to him.

### LOTHUNDIAZ

But—

### THE GRAND INQUISITOR

It is the wish of the Holy Office that you do so.

### LOTHUNDIAZ (*kneeling*)

Pardon!

### DON FREGOSE

What is that the people are calling out? (*A cry is heard, "Long live Don Ramon!"*)

LOTHUNDIAZ

Long live Don Ramon! Yes indeed, and so much the better, for I shall be avenged for the wrong which I have done to myself.

---

## SCENE SECOND.

THE SAME PERSONS, DON RAMON, MATHIEU MAGIS, THE LANDLORD OF THE GOLDEN SUN; COPPOLUS, CARPANO, ESTEBAN, GIRONE, AND ALL THE PEOPLE.

*(All form a semicircle, in the centre of which is Don Ramon.)*

THE GRAND INQUISITOR

In the name of the king of Spain, Castile and the Indies, I must express to you, Don Ramon, the congratulations of all upon the success of your mighty genius. (*He leads him to the arm-chair.*)

DON RAMON

After all, he is but the hand, I am the head. The original idea is superior to the work of realizing it. (*To the crowd*) In such a moment as this, modesty would be an insult to the honors which I have attained through midnight vigils, and a man should openly show himself proud of his achievement.

LOTHUNDIAZ

In the name of the city of Barcelona, Don Ramon, I have the honor to offer you this crown, due to your perseverance, as the author of an invention which will give you immortality.

## SCENE THIRD.

THE SAME PERSONS AND FONTANARES (*his garments soiled with the work of his experiment*).

### DON RAMON

I accept these honors, on condition that they be shared by the courageous artisan who has so well assisted me in my enterprise.

### FAUSTINE

What modesty!

### FONTANARES

Is this meant for a joke?

### ALL

Long live Don Ramon!

### COPPOLUS

In the name of the merchants of Catalonia, Don Ramon, we have come to beg your acceptance of this silver crown, a token of their gratitude for a discovery which is likely to prove a new source of prosperity to them.

### ALL

Long live Don Ramon!

### DON RAMON

It is with the keenest pleasure that I see that commerce recognizes the future developments of steam navigation.

### FONTANARES

Let my laborers come forth! You, the children of the people, whose hands have completed my work, bear witness for me! It was from me only that you received the models. Say now, whether it was Don Ramon or I who originated the new power which the sea has felt to-day?

ESTEBAN

By my faith, you would have been in a pretty fix without Don Ramon!

MATHIEU MAGIS

It was two years ago, in the course of a conversation with Don Ramon, that he begged me to furnish funds for this experiment.

FONTANARES (*to Fregose*)

My lord, what strange delusion has fallen upon the people and burgesses of Barcelona? I arrive here in the midst of the acclamations with which Don Ramon is being greeted. Yes, I arrive bearing the traces of the vigils and sweat of this great enterprise, and I find you contentedly sanctioning the most shameful act of robbery that can be perpetrated in the face of heaven and earth. (*Murmurs.*) Alone and unprotected I have risked my life on this enterprise. I was the first who pledged its accomplishment to the king, and unaided I have kept my pledge, and yet here in my place I find Don Ramon—an ignoramus. (*Murmurs.*)

DON FREGOSE

An old soldier knows very little about scientific matters and must accept plain facts. All Catalonia concedes to Don Ramon the priority in this invention, and everybody here declares that without him you could have accomplished nothing. It is my duty to inform his majesty, the king, of these circumstances.

FONTANARES

The priority! Where are the proofs of this?

THE GRAND INQUISITOR

They are as follows: In his treatise on the casting of cannons Don Ramon speaks of a certain invention called Thunder, made by Leonardo da Vinci, your master, and says that it might be applied to the navigation of a ship.

DON RAMON

Ah! young man, acknowledge that you had read my treatises!

FONTANARES (*aside*)

I would sacrifice all my glory for one hour of vengeance!

---

## SCENE FOURTH.

### THE SAME PERSONS AND QUINOLA.

QUINOLA (*aside to Fontanares*)

Señor, the fruit was too fair, and a worm has been found in it!

FONTANARES

What do you mean?

QUINOLA

Hell has belched back upon us, I know not how—Monipodio, all on fire for revenge; he is on board the ship with a band of devils, and swears to scuttle it, unless you guarantee him ten thousand sequins.

FONTANARES (*kneels*)

Thanks, thanks, for that. O ocean, whom I once longed to subdue, thou art the sole protector that is left to me; thou shalt keep my secret to eternity! (*To Quinola*) See that Monipodio steers for the open sea and there scuttles the ship.

QUINOLA

What is this? Do I understand you aright? Which of us two has lost his head?

FONTANARES

Do as I bid you.

QUINOLA

But, my dear master—

FONTANARES

My life and yours are equally at stake.

QUINOLA

Obey, without understanding why? For the first time I'll risk it. (*Exit.*)

---

## *SCENE FIFTH.*

THE SAME PERSONS, WITH THE EXCEPTION OF QUINOLA.

FONTANARES (*to Don Fregose*)

My lord! putting aside the question of priority, which can easily be decided, may I be permitted to withdraw my name from this debate, begging of you to accept the statement which is here drawn up and contains my justification before the king our master?

DON RAMON

You acknowledge then my claim?

FONTANARES

I will acknowledge anything you like, even to the point that O plus O is a binomial!

DON FREGOSE (*after consulting with the Grand Inquisitor*)

Your demand is perfectly legitimate; we will forward a copy of your statement, preserving here the original.

FONTANARES

I have, then, escaped with my life. Let me ask all of you here present, if you look upon Don Ramon as the real inventor of the vessel which has been propelled by steam before the eyes of two hundred thousand Spaniards?

### All.

We do.  (*Quinola makes his appearance.*)

### Fontanares

Very good. Don Ramon has accomplished this prodigy. Don Ramon can begin his work again. (*A loud explosion is heard.*) The prodigy is no longer in existence. The employment of such a force is not without danger, and the danger which Don Ramon had not foreseen, has manifested itself, at the very moment while Don Ramon was receiving your congratulations! (*Cries in the distance; everybody rushes to the balcony and gazes seaward.*) I am avenged!

### Don Fregose

What will the king say?

### The Grand Inquisitor

France is all ablaze, the low countries in revolt, Calvin is stirring up all Europe; the king has too much business on his hands to worry himself about the loss of a ship. This new invention and the Reformation would have been too much at one time for the world! Now for some years the rapacity of maritime peoples has been checked. (*Exeunt omnes.*).

---

## SCENE SIXTH.

### Quinola, Fontanares and Faustine.

### Faustine

Alfonso, I have done you much wrong.

### FONTANARES

Marie is dead, señora; I do not know the meaning of th words right and wrong, nowadays.

### QUINOLA

There is a man for you.

### FAUSTINE

Forgive me, and I will devote myself to your future

### FONTANARES

Forgiveness! That word also has been erased from my heart. There are situations in which the heart either breaks or turns to bronze. I am scarcely twenty-five years old, but to-day you have changed me into a man of fifty. You have lost to me one world, now you owe me another—

### QUINOLA

Let us turn our attention to politics.

### FAUSTINE

And is not my love, Alfonso, worth a world?

### FONTANARES

Yes, for you are a magnificent instrument of ruin and devastation. Yet it will be by means of you that I shall crush all those who have been an obstacle in my pathway; . I take you, not for my wife, but for my slave, and you shall serve me.

### FAUSTINE

Serve you blindly.

### FONTANARES

But without hope that there will be any return—need I say of what? All here (*he strikes his hand upon his heart*) is of bronze. You have taught me what this world is made of.

O world of self-interest, of trickery, of policy and of perfidy, I defy you to the combat!

### QUINOLA

Señor?

### FONTANARES

What is it?

### QUINOLA

Am I in it with you?

### FONTANARES

You? You are the only one who has still a place in my heart. We three will stand together; we will go—

### FAUSTINE

Where?

### FONTANARES

We will go to France.

### FAUSTINE

Let us start at once; I know these Spaniards, and they are sure to plot your death.

### QUINOLA

The resources of Quinola are at the bottom of the sea. Be kind enough to excuse his faults; he will doubtless do better at Paris. Verily, I believe that hell is paved with good inventions.

*Final Curtain.*

# PAMELA GIRAUD

## A PLAY IN FIVE ACTS

Presented for the First Time at Paris at the Theatre de la Gaite,
September 26, 1843.

# PERSONS OF THE PLAY

GENERAL DE VERBY.
DUPRÉ, a lawyer.
ROUSSEAU, a wealthy merchant.
JULES ROUSSEAU, his son.
JOSEPH BINET.
GIRAUD, a porter.
CHIEF OF SPECIAL POLICE.
ANTOINE, servant to the Rousseaus.

PAMELA GIRAUD.
MADAME DU BROCARD, a widow; aunt of Jules Rousseau.
MADAME ROUSSEAU.
MADAME GIRAUD.
JUSTINE, chambermaid to Mme. Rousseau.

SHERIFF.
MAGISTRATE.
POLICE OFFICERS. ·
GENDARMES.

SCENE: *Paris.* TIME: *during the Napoleonic plots under Louis XVIII.* (1815-1824).

# PAMELA GIRAUD

## ACT I.

### SCENE FIRST.

(*Setting is an attic and workshop of an artificial flower-maker. It is poorly lighted by means of a candle placed on the work-table. The ceiling slopes abruptly at the back allowing space to conceal a man. On the right is a door, on the left a fireplace. Pamela is discovered at work, and Joseph Binet is seated near her.*)

PAMELA, JOSEPH BINET AND LATER JULES ROUSSEAU.

PAMELA

Monsieur Joseph Binet!

JOSEPH

Mademoiselle Pamela Giraud!

PAMELA

I plainly see that you wish me to hate you.

JOSEPH

The idea! What? And this is the beginning of our love—
Hate me!

PAMELA

Oh, come! Let us talk sensibly.

JOSEPH

You do not wish, then, that I should express how much I love you?

PAMELA

Ah! I may as well tell you plainly, since you compel me to do so, that I do not wish to become the wife of an upholsterer's apprentice.

JOSEPH

Is it necessary to become an emperor, or something like that, in order to marry a flower-maker?

PAMELA

No. But it is necessary to be loved, and I don't love you in any way whatever.

JOSEPH

In any way! I thought there was only one way of loving.

PAMELA

So there is, but there are many ways of not loving. You can be my friend, without my loving you.

JOSEPH

Oh!

PAMELA

I can look upon you with indifference—

JOSEPH

Ah!

PAMELA

You can be odious to me!—And at this moment you weary me, which is worse!

JOSEPH

I weary her! I who would cut myself into fine pieces to do all that she wishes!

PAMELA

If you would do what I wish, you would not remain here.


JOSEPH

And if I go away—Will you love me a little?


PAMELA

Yes, for the only time I like you is when you are away!


JOSEPH

And if I never came back?


PAMELA

I should be delighted.


JOSEPH

Zounds! Why should I, senior apprentice with M. Morel,
instead of aiming at setting up business for myself, fall in
love with this young lady? It is folly! It certainly hinders
me in my career; and yet I dream of her—I am infatuated
with her. Suppose my uncle knew it!—But she is not the
only woman in Paris, and, after all, Mlle. Pamela Giraud,
who are you that you should be so high and mighty?


PAMELA

I am the daughter of a poor ruined tailor, now become a
porter. I gain my own living—if working night and day can
be called living—and it is with difficulty that I snatch a little
holiday to gather lilacs in the Pres-Saint-Gervais; and I certainly recognize that the senior apprentice of M. Morel is altogether too good for me. I do not wish to enter a family
which believes that it would thus form a mesalliance. The
Binets indeed!

JOSEPH

But what has happened to you in the last eight or ten days,
my dear little pet of a Pamela? Up to ten days ago I used

to come and cut out your flowers for you, I used to make the
stalks for the roses, and the hearts for the violets; we used to
talk together, we sometimes used to go to the play, and have
a good cry there—and I was "good Joseph," "my little
Joseph"—a Joseph in fact of the right stuff to make your
husband. All of a sudden—Pshaw! I became of no account.

### PAMELA

Now you must really go away. Here you are neither in the
street, nor in your own house.

### JOSEPH

Very well, I'll be off, mademoiselle—yes, I'll go away! I'll
have a talk in the porter's lodge with your mother; she does
not ask anything better than my entrance into the family, not
she; she won't change her mind!

### PAMELA

All right! Instead of entering her family, enter her lodge,
the porter's lodge, M. Joseph! Go and talk with my mother,
go on!—(*Exit Joseph.*) Perhaps he'll keep their attention so
that M. Adolph can get up stairs without being seen. Adolph
Durand! What a pretty name! There is half a romance in
it! And what a handsome young man! For the last fifteen
days he has absolutely persecuted me. I knew that I was
rather pretty; but I never believed I was all he called me. He
must be an artist, or a government official! Whatever he is, I
can't help liking him; he is so aristocratic! But what if his
appearance were deceitful, and there were anything wrong
about him!—For the letter which he has just sent me has an
air of mystery about it—(*She draws a letter from her bosom
and reads it*) "Expect me this evening. I wish to see you
alone, and, if possible, to enter unnoticed by any one; my life
is in danger, and oh! if you only knew what a terrible misfortune threatens me! Adolph Durand." He writes in pencil.
His life is in danger—Ah! How anxious I feel!

JOSEPH (*returning*)

Just as I was going down stairs, I said to myself: "Why should Pamela"—(*Jules' head appears at the window.*)

PAMELA

Ah!

JOSEPH

What's the matter? (*Jules disappears.*)

PAMELA

I thought I saw—I mean—I thought I heard a sound overhead. Just go into the garret. Some one perhaps has hidden there. You are not afraid, are you?

JOSEPH

No.

PAMELA

Very well! Go up and search! Otherwise I shall be frightened for the whole night.

JOSEPH

I will go at once. I will climb over the roof if you like. (*He passes through a narrow door that leads to the garret.*)

PAMELA (*follows him*)

Be quick! (*Jules enters.*) Ah! sir, what trouble you are giving me!

JULES

It is to save my life, and perhaps you will never regret it. You know how much I love you! (*He kisses her hand.*)

PAMELA

I know that you have told me so; but you treat me—

JULES

As my deliverer.

PAMELA

You wrote to me—and your letter has filled me with trouble
—I know neither who you are—

JOSEPH (*from the outer room*)

Mademoiselle, I am in the garret.  I have looked over the
whole roof.

JULES

He is coming back—Where can I hide?

PAMELA

But you must not stay here!

JULES

You wish to ruin me, Pamela!

PAMELA

Look, hide yourself there!  (*She points to the cranny
under the sloping roof.*)

JOSEPH (*returning*)

Are you alone, mademoiselle?

PAMELA

No; for are not you here?

JOSEPH

I heard something like the voice of a man.  The voice came
from below.

PAMELA

Nonsense, more likely it came from above—Look down
the staircase—

JOSEPH

Oh!  But I am sure—

PAMELA

Nonsense, sure. Leave me, sir; I wish to be alone.

JOSEPH

Alone, with a man's voice?

PAMELA

I suppose you don't believe me?

JOSEPH

But I heard it plain enough.

PAMELA

You heard nothing.

JOSEPH

Ah! Pamela!

PAMELA

If you prefer to believe the sounds which you say reached your ears, rather than the words which I speak, you would make a very bad husband. That is quite sufficient for me.

JOSEPH

That doesn't prove that I did not hear—

PAMELA

Since I can't convince you, you can believe what you like. Yes! you did hear a voice, the voice of a young man, who is in love with me, and who does whatever I wish—He disappears when he is asked, and comes when he is wanted. And now what are you waiting for? Do you think that while he is here, your presence can be anything but disagreeable to us? Go and ask my father and mother what his name is. He must have told them when he came up-stairs—he, and the voice you heard.

### Joseph

Mlle. Pamela, forgive a poor youth who is mad with love. It is not only my heart that I have lost, but my head also, when I think of you. I know that you are just as good as you are beautiful, I know that you have in your soul more treasures of sweetness than you ever show, and so I know that you are right, and were I to hear ten voices, were I to see ten men here, I would care nothing about it. But one—

### Pamela

Well, what of it?

### Joseph

A single one—that is what wounds me. But I must be off; it seems funny that I should have said all that to you. I know quite well that there is no one here but you. Till we meet again, Mlle. Pamela; I am going—I trust you.

### Pamela (*aside*)

He evidently does not feel quite sure.

### Joseph (*aside*)

There is some one here! I will run down and tell the whole matter to her father and mother. (*Aloud*) Adieu, Mlle. Pamela. (*Exit.*)

---

## SCENE SECOND.

### Pamela and Jules.

### Pamela

M. Adolph, you see to what you are exposing me. That poor lad is a workman, a most kind-hearted fellow; he has an uncle rich enough to set him up in business; he wishes to

marry me, and in one moment I have lost my prospects—
and for whom? I do not know you, and from the manner
in which you imperil the reputation of a young girl who has
no capital but her good behavior, I conclude that you think
you have the right to do so. You are rich and you make
sport of poor people!

JULES

No, my dear Pamela. I know who you are, and I take you
at your true value. I love you, I am rich, and we will never
leave one another. My traveling carriage is with a friend, at
the gate of St. Denis; we will proceed on foot to catch it;
I intend embarking for England. You must come with me.
I cannot explain my intentions now, for the least delay may
prove fatal to me.

PAMELA

What do you mean?

JULES

You shall see—

PAMELA

Are you in your right senses, M. Adolph? After having
followed me about for a month, seen me twice at a dance,
written me several declarations, such as young men of your
sort write to any and every woman, you point-blank propose
an elopement!

JULES

Oh I beg of you, don't delay an instant! You'll repent of
this for the rest of your life, and you will see too late what
mischief you have done.

PAMELA

But, my dear sir, you can perhaps explain yourself in a
couple of words.

JULES

No,—for the secret is a matter of life and death to several
persons.

### PAMELA

If it were only to save your life, whoever you are, I would do a good deal; but what assistance could I be to you in your flight! Why do you want to take me to England?

### JULES

What a child you are! No one, of course, would suspect anything of two runaway lovers! And, let me tell you, I love you well enough to disregard everything else, and even to brave the anger of my parents—Once we are married at Gretna Green—

### PAMELA

Oh, *mon Dieu!* I am quite non-plussed! Here's a handsome young man urges you—implores you—and talks of marriage—

### JULES

They are mounting the staircase—I am lost!—You have betrayed me!—

### PAMELA

M. Adolph, you alarm me! What is going to happen? Wait a moment, I will go and see.

### JULES

In any case, take and keep this twenty thousand francs. It will be safer with you than in the hands of the police—I have only half an hour longer and all will be over.

### PAMELA

There is nothing to fear—It is only my father and mother.

### JULES

You have the kindness of an angel. I trust my fate with you. But you must know that both of us must leave this house at once; and I swear on my honor, that nothing but good shall result to you. (*He hides again under the roof.*)

## SCENE THIRD.

### PAMELA, M. GIRAUD AND MME. GIRAUD.

PAMELA (*who stands in such way as to prevent her parents from entering fully into the room; aside*)

Evidently here is a man in danger—and a man who loves me—two reasons why I should be interested in him.

### MME. GIRAUD

How is this, Pamela—you the solace of all our misfortunes, the prop of our old age, our only hope!

### GIRAUD

A girl brought up on the strictest principles.

### MME. GIRAUD

Keep quiet, Giraud! You don't know what you are talking about.

### GIRAUD

Certainly, Madame Giraud.

### MME. GIRAUD

And besides all this, Pamela, your example was cited in all the neighborhood as a girl who'd be useful to your parents in their declining years!

### GIRAUD

And worthy to receive the prize of virtue!

### PAMELA

Then what is the meaning of all these reproaches?

MME. GIRAUD

Joseph has just told us that you had a man hidden in your room.

GIRAUD

Yes—he heard the voice.

MME. GIRAUD

Silence, Giraud!—Pamela—pay no attention to your father—

PAMELA

And do you, mother, pay no attention to Joseph.

GIRAUD

What did I tell you on the stairs, Madame Giraud? Pamela knows how we count upon her. She wishes to make a good match as much on our account as on her own; her heart bleeds to see us porters, us, the authors of her life! She is too sensible to blunder in this matter. Is it not so, my child, you would not deceive your father?

MME. GIRAUD

There is nobody here, is there, my love? For a young working-girl to have any one in her room, at ten o'clock at night—well—she runs a risk of losing—

PAMELA

But it seems to me that if I had any one you would have seen him on his way up.

GIRAUD

She is right.

MME. GIRAUD

She does not answer straight out. Please open the door of this room.

PAMELA

Mother, stop! Do not come in here,—you shall not come in

here!—Listen to me; as I love you, mother, and you, father,
I have nothing to reproach myself with!—and I swear to it
before God!—Do not in a moment withdraw from your
daughter the confidence which you have had in her for so
long a time.

### Mme. Giraud

But why not tell us?

### Pamela (*aside*)

Impossible! If they were to see this young man every one
would soon know all about it.

### Giraud (*interrupting her*)

We are your father and mother, and we must see!

### Pamela

For the first time in my life, I refuse to obey you!—But
you force me to it!—These lodgings are rented by me from
the earnings of my work!—I am of age and mistress of my
own actions.

### Mme. Giraud

Ah, Pamela! Can this be you, on whom we have placed
all our hopes!

### Giraud

You will ruin yourself!—and I shall remain a porter to
the end of my days.

### Pamela

You needn't be afraid of that! Well—I admit that there
is some one here; but silence! You must go down-stairs
again to your lodge. You must tell Joseph that he does not
know what he is talking about, that you have searched everywhere, that there is no one in my lodging; you must send
him away—then you shall see this young man; you shall

learn what I purpose doing. But you must keep everything the most profound secret.

### GIRAUD

Unhappy girl! What do you take us for? (*He sees the banknotes on the table.*) Ah! what is this? Banknotes!

### MME. GIRAUD

Banknotes! (*She recoils from Pamela.*) Pamela, where did you get them?

### PAMELA

I will tell you when I write.

### GIRAUD

When you write! She must be going to elope!

---

## SCENE FOURTH.

### THE SAME PERSONS, AND JOSEPH BINET.

### JOSEPH (*entering*)

I was quite sure that there was something wrong about him!—He is a ringleader of theives! The gendarmes, the magistrate, all the excitement she showed mean something— and now the house is surrounded!

### JULES (*appearing*)

I am lost!

### PAMELA

I have done all that I could!

### GIRAUD

And you, sir, who are you?

JOSEPH

Are you a—?

MME. GIRAUD

Speak!

JULES

But for this idiot, I could have escaped! You will now have the ruin of an innocent man on your consciences.

PAMELA

M. Adolph, are you innocent?

JULES

I am!

PAMELA

What shall we do? (*Pointing to the dormer window.*) You can elude their pursuit that way out. (*She opens the dormer window and finds the police agents on the roof outside.*)

JULES

It is too late. All you can do is to confirm my statement. You must declare that I am your daughter's lover; that I have asked you to give her in marriage to me; that I am of age; that my name is Adolph Durand, son of a rich business man of Marseilles.

GIRAUD

He offers her lawful love and wealth!—Young man, 1 willingly take you under my protection.

---

## SCENE FIFTH.

THE SAME PERSONS, A SHERIFF, A POLICE OFFICER AND GENDARMES.

GIRAUD

Sir, what right have you to enter an occupied dwelling the domicile of a peaceable young girl?

JOSEPH

Yes, what right have you—?

THE SHERIFF

Young man, don't you worry about our right!—A few moments ago you were very friendly and showed us where the unknown might be found, but now you have suddenly changed your tune.

PAMELA

But what are you looking for? What do you want?

THE SHERIFF

You seem to be well aware that we are looking for somebody.

GIRAUD

Sir, my daughter has no one with her but her future husband, M.——

THE SHERIFF

Rousseau.

PAMELA

M. Adolph Durand.

GIRAUD

Rousseau I don't know.—The gentleman I refer to is M Adolph Durand.

MME. GIRAUD

Son of a respectable merchant of Marseilles.

JOSEPH

Ah! you have been deceiving me! Ah!—That is the secret of your coldness, and he is—

THE SHERIFF (to the Officer of Police)

This does not seem to be the man?

## The Officer

Oh, yes, I am quite sure of it! (*To the gendarmes*) Carry out my orders.

## Jules

Monsieur, I am the victim of some mistake; my name is not Jules Rousseau.

## The Officer

Ah! but you know his first name, which none of us has as yet mentioned.

## Jules

But I heard some one say it. Here are my papers, which are perfectly correct.

## The Sheriff

Let me see them, please.

## Giraud

Gentlemen, I assure you and declare to you—

## The Officer

If you go on in this way, and wish to make us believe that this gentleman is Adolph Durand, son of a merchant of—

## Mme. Giraud

Of Marseilles—

## The Officer

You may all be arrested as his accomplices, locked up in jail this evening, and implicated in an affair from which you will not easily get off. Have you any regard for the safety of your neck?

## Giraud

A great deal!

## The Officer

Very well! Hold your tongue, then.

### MME. GIRAUD

Do hold your tongue, Giraud!


### PAMELA

Merciful heaven! Why did I not believe him at once!


### THE SHERIFF (*to his agents*)

Search the gentleman! (*The agent takes out Jules' pocket handkerchief.*)

### THE OFFICER

It is marked with a J and an R. My dear sir, you are not very clever!


### JOSEPH

What can he have done? Have you anything to do with it, mademoiselle?


### PAMELA

You are the sole cause of the trouble. Never speak to me again!

### THE OFFICER

Monsieur, here we have the check for your dinner—you dined at the Palais Royal. While you were there you wrote a letter in pencil. One of your friends brought the letter here. His name was M. Adolph Durand, and he lent you his passport. We are certain of your identity; you are M. Jules Rousseau.

### JOSEPH

The son of the rich M. Rousseau, whose house we are furnishing?

### THE SHERIFF

Hold your tongue!

### THE OFFICER

You must come with us.

JULES

Certainly, monsieur. (*To Giraud and his wife*) Forgive the annoyance I have caused you—and you, Pamela, do not forget me! If you do not see me again, you may keep what I gave into your hands, and may it bring you happiness!

GIRAUD

O Lord!

PAMELA

Poor Adolph!

THE SHERIFF (*to his agents*)

Remain here. We are going to search this attic, and question every one of these people.

JOSEPH (*with a gesture of horror*)

Ah!—she prefers a criminal to me! (*Jules is put in charge of the agents.*)

*Curtain to the First Act.*

# ACT II.

---

## SCENE FIRST.

*(The setting is a drawing-room in the Rousseau mansion. Antoine is looking through the newspaper.)*

ANTOINE AND JUSTINE.

### JUSTINE

Well, Antoine, have you read the papers?

### ANTOINE

I am reading them. Isn't it a pity that we servants cannot learn, excepting through the papers, what is going on in the trial of M. Jules?

### JUSTINE

And yet the master and mistress and Mme. du Brocard, their sister, know nothing. M. Jules has been for three months—in—what do they call it?—in close confinement.

### ANTOINE

The arrest of the young man has evidently attracted great attention—

### JUSTINE

It seems absurd to think that a young man who had nothing to do but amuse himself, who would some day inherit his aunt's income of twenty thousand francs, and his father's and mother's fortune, which is quite double that amount, should be mixed up in a conspiracy!

### ANTOINE

I admire him for it, for they were plotting to bring back the emperor! You may cause my throat to be cut if you like. We are alone here—you don't belong to the police; long live the emperor! say I.

### JUSTINE

For mercy's sake, hold your tongue, you old fool!—If any one heard you, you would get us all arrested.

### ANTOINE

I am not afraid of that, thank God! The answers I made to the magistrate were non-committal; I never compromised M. Jules, like the traitors who informed against him.

### JUSTINE

Mme. du Brocard with all her immense savings ought to be able to buy him off.

### ANTOINE

Oh, nonsense! Since the escape of Lavalette such a thing is impossible! They have become extremely particular at the gates of the prison, and they were never particularly accommodating. M. Jules will have to take his dose you see; he will be a martyr. I shall go and see him executed. (*Some one rings. Exit Antoine.*)

### JUSTINE

We will go and see him! When one has known a condemned man I don't see how they can have the heart to— As for me I shall go to the Court of Assizes. I feel, poor boy, I owe him that!

## SCENE SECOND.

### Dupré, Antoine and Justine.

ANTOINE (*aside, as he ushers in Dupré*)

Ah! The lawyer. (*Aloud*) Justine, go and tell madame that Monsieur Dupré is waiting. (*Aside*) The lawyer is a hard nut to crack, I'm thinking. (*Aloud*) Sir, is there any hope of saving our poor M. Jules?

### Dupré

I perceive that you are very fond of your young master?

### Antoine

Naturally enough!

### Dupré

What would you do to save him?

### Antoine

Anything, sir!

### Dupré

That means nothing.

### Antoine

Nothing?—I will give whatever evidence you like.

### Dupré

If you are caught in contradicting yourself and convicted of perjury, do you know what you run the risk of?

### Antoine

No, sir.

### Dupré

The galleys.

ANTOINE

That is rather severe, sir.

DUPRÉ

You would prefer to serve him without compromising yourself.

ANTOINE

Is there any other way?

DUPRÉ

No.

ANTOINE

Well! I'll run the risk of the galleys.

DUPRÉ (*aside*)

What devotion is here!

ANTOINE

My master would be sure to settle a pension on me.

JUSTINE

Here is madame.

---

## SCENE THIRD.

THE SAME PERSONS AND MADAME ROUSSEAU.

MME. ROUSSEAU (*to Dupré*)

Ah! monsieur, we have been impatiently expecting this visit. (*To Antoine*) Antoine! Quick, inform my husband. (*To Dupré*) Sir, I trust in your efforts, alone.

DUPRÉ

You may be sure, madame, that I shall employ every energy—

## Mme. Rousseau

Oh! Thank you! But of course Jules is not guilty. To think of him as a conspirator! Poor child, how could any one suspect him, who trembles before me at the slightest reproach—me, his mother! Ah, monsieur, promise that you will restore him to me!

## Rousseau (*entering the room. To Antoine*)

Yes, carry the letter to General de Verby. I shall wait for him here. (*To Dupré*) I am glad to see you, my dear M. Dupré—

## Dupré

The battle will doubtless begin to-morrow; to-day preparations are being made, and the indictment drawn.

## Rousseau

Has my poor Jules made any admissions?

## Dupré

He has denied everything, and has played to perfection the part of an innocent man; but we are not able to oppose any testimony to that which is being brought against him.

## Rousseau

Ah! monsieur, save my son, and the half of my fortune shall be yours!

## Dupré

If I had every half of a fortune that has been promised to me, I should be too rich for anything.

## Rousseau

Do you question the extent of my gratitude?

## Dupré

We will wait till the result of the trial is known, sir.

MME. ROUSSEAU

Take pity on a poor mother!

DUPRÉ

Madame, I swear to you nothing so much excites my curiosity and my sympathy, as a genuine sentiment. And at Paris sincerity is so rare that I cannot be indifferent to the grief of a family threatened with the loss of an only son. You may therefore rely upon me.

ROUSSEAU

Ah! monsieur!

---

## SCENE FOURTH.

THE SAME PERSONS, GENERAL DE VERBY AND MADAME DU BROCARD.

MME. DU BROCARD (*showing in De Verby*)

Come in, my dear general.

DE VERBY (*bowing to Rousseau*)

Monsieur—I simply came to learn—

ROUSSEAU (*presenting Dupré to De Verby*)

General, M. Dupré. (*Dupré and De Verby exchange bows.*)

DUPRÉ (*aside. While De Verby talks with Rousseau*)

He is general of the antechamber, holding the place merely through the influence of his brother, the lord chamberlain; he doesn't seem to me to have come here without some object.

DE VERBY (*to Dupré*)

I understand, sir, that you are engaged for the defence of M. Jules Rousseau in this deplorable affair—

DUPRÉ

Yes, sir, it is a deplorable affair, for the real culprits are not in prison; thus it is that justice rages fiercely against the rank and file, but the chiefs are always passed by. You are General Vicomte de Verby, I presume?

DE VERBY

Simple General Verby—I do not take the title—my opinions of course.—Doubtless you are acquainted with the evidence in this case?

DUPRÉ

I have been in communication with the accused only for the last three days.

DE VERBY

And what do you think of the affair?

ALL

Yes, tell us.

DUPRÉ

According to my experience of the law courts, I believe it possible to obtain important revelations by offering commutation of sentence to the condemned.

DE VERBY

The accused are all men of honor.

ROUSSEAU

But—

DUPRÉ

Characters sometime change at the prospect of the scaffold, especially when there is much at stake.

DE VERBY (*aside*)

A conspiracy ought not to be entered upon excepting with penniless accomplices.

### Dupré

I shall induce my client to tell everything.

### Rousseau

Of course.

### Mme. du Brocard

Certainly.

### Mme. Rousseau

He ought to do so.

### De Verby (*anxiously*)

I presume there is no other way of escape for him?

### Dupré

None whatever; it can be proved that he was of the number of those who had begun to put in execution the plot.

### De Verby

I would rather loose my head than my honor.

### Dupré

I should consider which of the two was worth more.

### De Verby

You have your views in the matter.

### Rousseau

Those are mine.

### Dupré

And they are the opinions of the majority. I have seen many things done by men to escape the scaffold. There are people who push others to the front, who risk nothing, and yet reap all the fruits of success. Have such men any honor? Can one feel any obligation towards them?

### DE VERBY

No, they are contemptible wretches.


### DUPRÉ (*aside*)

He has well said it.  This is the fellow who has ruined poor Jules!  I must keep my eye on him.

---

## SCENE FIFTH.

THE SAME PERSONS, ANTOINE AND JULES (*the latter led in by police agents*).


### ANTOINE

Sir, a carriage stopped at the door.  Several men got out. M. Jules is with them; they are bringing him in.


### M. AND MME. ROUSSEAU

My son!


### MME. DU BROCARD

My nephew!

### DUPRÉ

Yes, I see what it is—doubtless a search-warrant.  They wish to look over his papers.


### ANTOINE

Here he is. (*Jules appears in the centre, followed by the police and a magistrate; he rushes up to his mother*)


### JULES

O mother! my good mother!  (*He embraces his mother.*) Ah! I see you once more!  (*To Mme. du Brocard*) Dear aunt!


### MME. ROUSSEAU

My poor child!  Come! come—close to me; they will not

dare— (*To the police, who approach her*) Leave him, leave him here!

ROUSSEAU (*rushing towards the police*)

Be kind enough—

DUPRÉ (*to the magistrate*)

Monsieur!

JULES

My dear mother, calm yourself! I shall soon be free; yes, be quite sure of that, and we will not part again.

ANTOINE (*to Rousseau*)

Sir, they wish to visit M. Jules's room.

ROUSSEAU (*to the magistrate*)

In a moment, monsieur. I will go with you myself. (*To Dupré, pointing to Jules*) Do not leave him! (*He goes out conducting the magistrate, who makes a sign to the police to keep guard on Jules.*)

JULES (*seizing the hand of De Verby*)

Ah, general! (*To Dupré*) And how good and generous of you, M. Dupré, to come here and comfort my mother. (*In a low voice*) Ah! conceal from her my danger. (*Aloud, looking at his mother*) Tell her the truth. Tell her that she has nothing to fear.

DUPRÉ

I will tell her that it is in her power to save you.

MME. ROUSSEAU

In my power?

MME. DU BROCARD

How can that be?

DUPRÉ (*to Mme. Rousseau*)

By imploring him to disclose the names of those who **have** led him on.

DE VERBY (*to Dupré*)

Monsieur !

MME. ROUSSEAU

Yes, and you ought to do it. I, your mother, demand it of you.

MME. DU BROCARD

Oh, certainly ! My nephew shall tell everything. He has been led on by people who now abandon him to his fate, and he in his turn ought—

DE VERBY (*in a low voice to Dupré*)

What, sir ! would you advise your client to betray—?

DUPRÉ (*quickly*)

Whom ?

DE VERBY (*in a troubled voice*)

But—can't we find some other method ? M. Jules knows what a man of high spirit owes to himself.

DUPRÉ (*aside*)

He is the man—I felt sure of it !

JULES (*to his mother and aunt*)

Never, though I should die for it—never will I com promise any one else. (*De Verby shows his pleasure at this declaration.*)

MME. ROUSSEAU

Ah ! my God ! (*Looking at the police.*) And there is no chance of our helping him to escape here !

MME. DU BROCARD

No! that is out of the question.

ANTOINE (*coming into the room*)

M. Jules, they are asking for you.

JULES

I am coming!

MME. ROUSSEAU

Ah! I cannot let you go! (*She turns to the police with a supplicating look.*)

MME. DU BROCARD (*to Dupré, who scrutinizes De Verby*)

M. Dupré, I have thought that it would be a good thing—

DUPRÉ (*interrupting her*)

Later, madame, later. (*He leads her to Jules, who goes out with his mother, followed by the agents.*)

## SCENE SIXTH.

DUPRÉ AND DE VERBY.

DE VERBY (*aside*)

These people have hit upon a lawyer who is rich, without ambition—and eccentric.

DUPRÉ (*crossing the stage and gazing at De Verby, aside*)

Now is my time to learn your secret. (*Aloud*) You are very much interested in my client, monsieur?

DE VERBY

Very much indeed.

DUPRÉ

I have yet to understand what motive could have led him, young, rich and devoted to pleasure as he is, to implicate him-self in a conspiracy—

DE VERBY

The passion for glory.

DUPRÉ

Don't talk in that way to a lawyer who for twenty years has practiced in the courts; who has studied men and affairs well enough to know that the finest motives are only assumed as a disguise for trumpery passions, and has never yet met a man whose heart was free from the calculations of self-interest.

DE VERBY

Do you ever take up a case without charging anything?

DUPRÉ

I often do so; but I never act contrary to my convictions.

DE VERBY

I understand that you are rich?

DUPRÉ

I have some fortune. Without it, in the world as at present constituted, I should be on the straight road for the poorhouse.

DE VERBY

It is then from conviction, I suppose, that you have under-taken the defence of young Rousseau.

DUPRÉ

Certainly. I believe him to be the dupe of others in a higher station, and I like those who allow themselves to be duped from generous motives and not from self-interest; for

in these times the dupe is often as greedy after gain as the
man who exploits him.

DE VERBY

You belong, I perceive, to the sect of misanthropes.

DUPRÉ

I do not care enough for mankind to hate them, for I have
never yet met any one I could love. I am contented with studying my fellow-men; for I see that they are all engaged in playing each, with more or less success, his own little comedy. I
have no illusion about anything, it is true, but I smile at it
all like a spectator who sits in a theatre to be amused. One
thing I never do; I hiss nothing; for I have not sufficient
feeling about things for that.

DE VERBY (*aside*)

How is it possible to influence such a man? (*Aloud*)
Nevertheless, monsieur, you must sometimes need the services
of others?

DUPRÉ

Never!

DE VERBY

But you are sometimes sick?

DUPRÉ

Then I like to be alone. Moreover, at Paris, anything can
be bought, even attendance on the sick; believe me I live
because it is my duty to do so. I have tested everything—
charity, friendship, unselfish devotion. Those who have
received benefits have disgusted me with the doing of kind
nesses. Certain philanthropists have made me feel a loath
ing for charity. And of all humbugs that of sentiment is the
most hateful.

DE VERBY

And what of patriotism, monsieur?

DUPRÉ

That is a very trifling matter, since the cry of humanity has been raised.

DE VERBY (*somewhat discouraged*)

And so you take Jules Rousseau for a young enthusiast?

DUPRÉ

No, sir, nothing of the sort. He presents a problem which I have to solve, and with your assistance I shall reach the solution. (*De Verby changes countenance.*) Come, let us speak candidly. I believe that you know something about all this.

DE VERBY

What do you mean, sir?

DUPRÉ

You can save this young man.

DE VERBY

I? What can I do?

DUPRÉ

You can give testimony which Antoine will corroborate—

DE VERBY

I have reasons for not appearing as a witness.

DUPRÉ

Just so. You are one of the conspirators!

DE VERBY

Monsieur!

DUPRÉ

It is you who have led on this poor boy.

DE VERBY

Monsieur, this language—!

DUPRÉ

Don't attempt to deceive me, but tell me how you managed to gain this bad influence over him? He is rich, he is in need of nothing.

DE VERBY

Listen!—If you say another word—

DUPRÉ

Oh! my life is of no consideration with me!

DE VERBY

Sir, you know very well that Jules will get off; and that if he does not behave properly, he will lose, through your fault, his chance of marriage with my niece, and thus the succession to the title of my brother, the Lord Chamberlain.

DUPRÉ

Ah, that's what he was after, then! He's like all the rest of the schemers. Now consider, sir, what I am going to propose to you. You have powerful friends, and it is your duty—

DE VERBY

My duty! I do not understand you, sir.

DUPRÉ

You have been able to effect his ruin, and can you not bring about his release? (*Aside*) I have him there.

DE VERBY

I shall give my best consideration to the matter.

DUPRÉ

Don't consider for a moment that you can escape me.


DE VERBY

A general who fears no danger can have no fear of a lawyer—

DUPRÉ

As you will! (*Exit De Verby, who jostles against Joseph.*)

---

*SCENE SEVENTH.*

DUPRÉ AND JOSEPH BINET.

JOSEPH

I heard only yesterday, monsieur, that you were engaged
for the defence of M. Jules Rousseau; I have been to your
place, and have waited for you until I could wait no later.
This morning I found that you had left your home, and as I
am working for this house, a happy inspiration sent me here.
I thought you would be coming here, and I waited for you—


DUPRÉ

What do you want with me?


JOSEPH

I am Joseph Binet.


DUPRÉ

Well, proceed.


JOSEPH

Let me say without offence, sir, that I have fourteen hundred francs of my own—quite my own!—earned sou by sou.
I am a journeyman upholsterer, and my uncle, Du Mouchel, a
retired wine merchant, has plenty of the metal.

DUPRÉ

Speak out openly! What is the meaning of this mysterious preamble?

JOSEPH

Fourteen hundred francs is of course a mere trifle, and they say that lawyers have to be well paid, and that it is because they are well paid that there are so many of them. I should have done better if I had been a lawyer—then she would have married me!

DUPRÉ

Are you crazy?

JOSEPH

Not at all. I have here my fourteen hundred francs; take them. sir—no humbug! They are yours.

DUPRÉ

And on what condition?

JOSEPH

You must save M. Jules—I mean, of course, from death—and you must have him transported. I don't want him to be put to death; but he must go abroad. He is rich, and he will enjoy himself. But save his life. Procure a sentence of simple transportation, say for fifteen years, and my fourteen hundred francs are yours. I will give them to you gladly, and I will moreover make you an office chair below the market price. There now!

DUPRÉ

What is your object in speaking to me in this way?

JOSEPH

My object? I want to marry Pamela. I want to have my little Pamela.

DUPRÉ

Pamela?

JOSEPH

Pamela Giraud.

DUPRÉ

What connection has Pamela Giraud with Jules Rousseau?

JOSEPH

Well I never! Why! I thought that advocates were paid for learning and knowing everything. But you don't seem to know anything, sir. I am not surprised that there are those who say advocates are know-nothings. But I should like to have back my fourteen hundred francs. Pamela is accused, that is to say, she accuses me of having betrayed his head to the executioner, and you will understand that if after all he escapes, and is transported, I can marry, can wed Pamela; and as the transported man will not be in France, I need fear no disturbance in my home. Get him fifteen years; that is nothing; fifteen years for traveling and I shall have time to see my children grown up, and my wife old enough—you understand—

DUPRÉ (*aside*)

He is candid, at any rate—Those who make their calculations aloud and in such evident excitement are not the worst of people.

JOSEPH

I say! Do you know the proverb—"A lawyer who talks to himself is like a pastry cook who eats his own wares,"—eh, sir?

DUPRÉ

I understand you to say that Pamela is in love with M. Jules?

JOSEPH

Ah! I see, you understand matters.

DUPRÉ

They used frequently to meet I suppose?

JOSEPH

Far too frequently! Oh! if I had only known it, I would soon have put a stop to it!

DUPRÉ

Is she pretty?

JOSEPH

Who?—Pamela?—My eye! My Pamela! She is as pretty as the Apollo Belvidere!

DUPRÉ

· Keep your fourteen hundred francs, my friend, and if you have courage, you and your Pamela, you will be able to help me in effecting his deliverance; for the question is absolutely whether we must let him go to the scaffold, or save him from it.

JOSEPH

I beg you, sir, do not think of saying one word to Pamela; she is in despair.

DUPRÉ

Nevertheless you must bring it about that I see her this morning.

JOSEPH

I will send word to her through her parents.

DUPRÉ

Ah! she has a father and mother living then? (*Aside*) This will cost a lot of money. (*Aloud*) Who are they?

JOSEPH

They are respectable porters.

DUPRÉ

That is good.

JOSEPH

Old Giraud is a ruined tailor.

DUPRÉ

Very well, go and inform them of my intended visit, and above all things preserve the utmost secrecy, or M. Jules will be sacrificed.

JOSEPH

I shall be dumb.

DUPRÉ

And let it be thought that we have never met.

JOSEPH

We have never seen each other.

DUPRÉ

Now go.

JOSEPH

I am going. (*He mistakes the door.*)

DUPRÉ

This is the way.

JOSEPH

This is the way, great advocate—but let me give you a bit of advice—a slight taste of transportation will not do him any harm; in fact, it will teach him to leave the government in peace. (*Exit.*)

---

## SCENE EIGHTH.

ROUSSEAU, MADAME ROUSSEAU, MADAME DU BROCARD (*attended by Justine*) AND DUPRÉ.

MME. ROUSSEAU

Poor child! What courage he shows!

DUPRÉ

I hope to save him for you, madame; but it cannot be done without making great sacrifices.

ROUSSEAU

Sir, the half of our fortune is at your disposal.

MME. DU BROCARD

And the half of mine.

DUPRÉ

It is always the half of some fortune or other. I am going to try to do my duty—afterwards, you must do yours; we shall have to make great efforts. You, madame, must rouse yourself, for I have great hopes.

MME. ROUSSEAU

Ah! sir, what can you mean?

DUPRÉ

A little time ago, your son was a ruined man; at the present moment, I believe he can be saved.

MME. ROUSSEAU

What must we do?

MME. DU BROCARD

What do you ask?

ROUSSEAU

You may be sure we will do as you require.

DUPRÉ

I feel certain you will. This is my plan which will undoubtedly succeed with the jury. Your son had an intrigue with a certain working-girl, Pamela Giraud, the daughter of a porter.

### MME. DU BROCARD

What low people!

### DUPRÉ

Yet you will have to humble yourselves to them. Your son was always with this young girl, and in this point lies the sole hope of his deliverance. The very evening on which the public prosecutor avers that he attended a meeting of the conspirators, he was possibly visiting her. If this is a fact, if she declares that he remained with her that night, if her father and her mother, if the rival of Jules confirm the testimony—we shall then have ground for hope. When the choice has to be made between a sentence of guilty and an alibi, the jury prefers the alibi.

### MME. ROUSSEAU (*aside*)

Ah! sir, you bring back life to me.

### ROUSSEAU

Sir, we owe you a debt of eternal gratitude.

### DUPRÉ (*looking at them*)

What sum of money must I offer to the daughter, to the father and to the mother?

### MME. DU BROCARD

Are they poor?

### DUPRÉ

They are, but the matter concerns their honor.

### MME. DU BROCARD

Oh, she is only a working-girl!

### DUPRÉ (*ironically*)

It ought to be done very cheaply.

ROUSSEAU

What do you think?

DUPRÉ

I think that you are bargaining for the life of your son.

MME. DU BROCARD

Well, M. Dupré, I suppose you may go as high as—

MME. ROUSSEAU

As high as—

DUPRÉ

As high as—

ROUSSEAU

Upon my word, I don't understand why you hesitate—and you must offer, sir, whatever sum you consider suitable.

DUPRÉ

Just so, you leave it to my discretion. But what compensation do you offer her if she restores your son to you at the sacrifice of her honor? For possibly he has made love to her.

MME. ROUSSEAU

He shall marry her. I come from the people myself and I am no marchioness.

MME. DU BROCARD

What do you mean by that? You are forgetting Mlle. de Verby.

MME. ROUSSEAU

Sister, my son's life must be saved.

DUPRÉ (aside)

Here we have the beginning of a comedy and the last which I wish to see; but I must keep them to their word. (Aloud)

Perhaps it would be well if you secretly paid a visit to the young girl.

### MME. ROUSSEAU

Oh, yes, I should like to go to see her—to implore her—(*she rings.*)  Justine! Antoine! quick! order the carriage! at once—

### ANTOINE

Yes, madame.

### MME. ROUSSEAU

Sister, will you go with me?—Ah, Jules, my poor son!

### MME. DU BROCARD

They are bringing him back.

----

## SCENE NINTH.

THE SAME PERSONS, JULES (*brought in by the police*), AND LATER DE VERBY.

### JULES (*kissing his mother*)

O mother!—I will not say good-bye; I shall soon be back, very soon· (*Rousseau and Mme. du Brocard embrace Jules.*)

### DE VERBY (*going up to Dupré*)

I will do, monsieur, what you have asked of me. One of my friends, M. Adolph Durand, who facilitated the flight of our dear Jules, will testify that his friend was altogether taken up with a grisette, whom he loved passionately, and with whom he was taking measures to elope.

### DUPRÉ

That is enough; success now depends upon the way we set about things.

THE MAGISTRATE (*to Jules*)

We must be going, monsieur.

### JULES

I will follow you. Be of good courage, mother! (*He bids farewell to Rousseau and Dupré; De Verby signs to him to be cautious.*)

MME. ROUSSEAU (*to Jules, as he is being led away*)

Jules! Jules! Do not give up hope—we are going to save you! (*The police lead Jules away.*)

**Curtain to the Second Act.**

# ACT III.

## *SCENE FIRST.*

*(The stage represents the room of Pamela.)*

PAMELA, GIRAUD AND MADAME GIRAUD.
*(Pamela is standing near her mother, who is knitting; Giraud is at work at a table on the left.)*

#### MME. GIRAUD

The fact of the matter is this, my poor daughter: I do not mean to reproach you, but you are the cause of all our trouble.

#### GIRAUD

No doubt about it! We came to Paris because in the country tailoring is no sort of a business, and we had some ambition for you, our Pamela, such a sweet, pretty little thing as you were. We said to each other: "We will go into service; I will work at my trade; we will give a good position to our child; and as she will be good, industrious and pretty, we can take care of our own old age by marrying her well."

#### PAMELA

O father!

#### MME. GIRAUD

Half of our plans were already carried out.

#### GIRAUD

Yes, certainly. We had a good position; you made as

fine flowers as any gardener could grow; and Joseph Binet, your neighbor, was to be the husband of our choice.

MME. GIRAUD

Instead of all this, the scandal which has arisen in the house has caused the landlord to dismiss us; the talk of the neighborhood was incessant, for the young man was arrested in your room.

PAMELA

And yet I have been guilty of nothing!

GIRAUD

Come, now, we know that well enough! Do you think if it were otherwise that we would stay near you? And that I would embrace you? After all, Pamela, there is nothing like a father and a mother! And when the whole world is against her, if a girl can look into her parents' face without a blush it is enough.

SCENE SECOND.

THE SAME PERSONS AND JOSEPH BINET.

MME. GIRAUD

Well, well! Here is Joseph Binet.

PAMELA

M. Binet, what are you doing here? But for your want of common-sense, M. Jules would not have been found here.

JOSEPH

I am come to tell you about him.

PAMELA

What! really? Well, let us hear, Joseph.

#### JOSEPH

Ah! you won't send me away now, will you? I have seen his lawyer, and I have offered him all that I possess if he would get him off!

#### PAMELA

Do you mean it?

#### JOSEPH

Yes. Would you be satisfied if he was merely transported?

#### PAMELA

Ah! you are a good fellow, Joseph, and I see that you love me! Let us be friends!

#### JOSEPH (*aside*)

I have good hopes that we shall be. (*A knock at the door is heard.*)

---

### SCENE THIRD.

THE PRECEDING, M. DE VERBY AND MADAME DU BROCARD.

#### MME. GIRAUD (*opening the door*)

There are some people here!

#### GIRAUD

A lady and a gentleman.

#### JOSEPH

What did you say? (*Pamela rises from her seat and takes a step toward M. de Verby, who bows to her.*)

#### MME. DU BROCARD

Is this Mlle. Pamela Giraud?

PAMELA

It is, madame.

DE VERBY

Forgive us, mademoiselle, for presenting ourselves without previous announcement—

PAMELA

There is no harm done. May I know the object of this visit?

MME. DU BROCARD

And you, good people, are her father and mother?

MME. GIRAUD

Yes, madame.

JOSEPH

She calls them good people—she must be one of the swells.

PAMELA

Will you please be seated? (*Mme. Giraud offers them seats.*)

JOSEPH (*to Giraud*)

My eye! The gentleman has on the ribbon of the Legion of Honor! He belongs to high society.

GIRAUD (*looking at De Verby*)

By my faith, that's true!

MME. DU BROCARD

I am the aunt of M. Jules Rousseau.

PAMELA

You, madame? Then this gentleman must be his father?

MME. DU BROCARD

He is merely a friend of the family. We are come, made-

moiselle, to ask a favor of you.  (*Looking at Binet with embarrassment.*)  Your brother?

#### GIRAUD

No, madame, just a neighbor of ours.

#### MME. DU BROCARD (*to Pamela*)

Send him away.

#### JOSEPH (*aside*)

Send him away, indeed!  I'd like to know what right she
has—(*Pamela makes a sign to Joseph.*)

#### GIRAUD (*to Joseph*)

My friend, you had better leave us.  It seems that this is a
private matter.

#### JOSEPH

Very well.  (*Exit.*)

---

### SCENE FOURTH.

#### THE SAME PERSONS EXCEPTING BINET.

#### MME. DU BROCARD (*to Pamela*)

You are acquainted with my nephew.  I do not intend to
reproach you.  Your parents alone have the right.

#### MME. GIRAUD

But, thank God, they have no reason.

#### GIRAUD

It is your nephew who has caused all this talk about her,
but she is blameless!

DE VERBY (*interrupting him*)

But suppose that we wish her to be guilty?

PAMELA

What do you mean, sir?

GIRAUD AND MME. GIRAUD

To think of it!

MME. DU BROCARD (*seizing De Verby's meaning*)

Yes, suppose, to save the life of a poor young man—

DE VERBY

It were necessary to declare that M. Jules Rousseau spent nearly the whole night of the twenty-fourth of August here with you?

PAMELA

Ah! sir!

DE VERBY (*to Giraud and his wife*)

Yes, suppose it were necessary to testify against your daughter, by alleging this?

MME. GIRAUD

I would never say such a thing.

GIRAUD

What! Insult my child! Sir, I have had all possible troubles. I was once a tailor, now I am reduced to nothing. I am a porter! But I have remained a father. My daughter is our sole treasure, the glory of our old age, and you ask us to dishonor her!

MME. DU BROCARD

Pray listen to me, sir.

### GIRAUD

No, madame, I will listen to nothing. My daughter is the hope of my gray hairs.

### PAMELA

Calm yourself, father, I implore you.

### MME. GIRAUD

Keep quiet, Giraud!　Do let this lady and gentleman speak!

### MME. DU BROCARD

A family in deep affliction implores you to save them.

### PAMELA (*aside*)

Poor Jules!

### DE VERBY (*in a low voice to Pamela*)

His fate is in your hands.

### MME. GIRAUD

We are respectable people and know what it is for parents, for a mother, to be in despair.　But what you ask is out of the question.　(*Pamela puts a handkerchief to her eyes.*)

### GIRAUD

We must stop this!　You see the girl is in tears.

### MME. GIRAUD

She has done nothing but weep for several days.

### GIRAUD

I know my daughter; she would be capable of going and making the declaration they ask, in spite of us.

## MME. GIRAUD

Yes,—for you must see, she loves him, she loves your nephew! And to save his life—Well! well! I would have done as much in her place.

## MME. DU BROCARD

Have compassion on us!

## DE VERBY

Grant this request of ours—

## MME. DU BROCARD (*to Pamela*)

If it is true that you love Jules—

## MME. GIRAUD (*leading Giraud up to Pamela*)

Did you hear that? Well! Listen to me. She is in love with this youth. It is quite certain that he also is in love with her. If she should make a sacrifice like that, as a return, he ought to marry her.

## PAMELA (*with vehemence*)

Never! (*Aside*) These people would not wish it, not they.

## DE VERBY (*to Mme. du Brocard*)

They are consulting about it.

## MME. DU BROCARD (*in a low voice to De Verby*)

It will be absolutely necessary for us to make a sacrifice. We must appeal to their interest. It is the only plan!

## DE VERBY

In venturing to ask of you so great a sacrifice, we are quite aware of the claims that you will have on our gratitude. The family of Jules, who might have blamed you on account of your relations with him, are, on the contrary, anxious to discharge the obligations which bind them to you.

### MME. GIRAUD

Ah! Did I not tell you so?

### PAMELA

Can it be possible that Jules—

### DE VERBY

I am authorized to make a promise to you.

### PAMELA (*with emotion*)

Oh!

### DE VERBY

Tell me, how much do you ask for the sacrifice required of you?

### PAMELA (*in consternation*)

What do you mean? How much—I ask—for saving Jules? What do you take me for?

### MME. DU BROCARD

Ah! mademoiselle!

### DE VERBY

You misunderstand me.

### PAMELA

No, it is you who misunderstand us! You are come here, to the house of poor people, and you are quite unaware of what you ask from them. You, madame, ought to know that whatever be the rank or the education of a woman, her honor is her sole treasure! And that which you in your own families guard with so much care, with so much reverence, you actually believe that people here, living in an attic, would be willing to sell! And you have said to yourselves: "Let us offer them money! We need just now the sacrifice of a working-girl's honor!"

### GIRAUD

That is excellent! I recognize my own blood there.

### MME. DU BROCARD

My dear child, do not be offended! Money is money, after all.

### DE VERBY (*addressing Giraud*)

Undoubtedly! And six thousand francs for a solid annual income as the price of—a—

### PAMELA

As the price of a lie! For I must out with it. But thank God I haven't yet lost my self-respect! Good-bye, sir. (*She makes a low bow to Mme. du Brocard, then goes into her bedchamber.*)

### DE VERBY

What is to be done?

### MME. DU BROCARD

I am quite nonplussed.

### GIRAUD

I quite admit that an income of six thousand francs is no trifle, but our daughter has a high spirit, you see; she takes after me—

### MME. GIRAUD

And she will never yield,

## SCENE FIFTH.

THE SAME PERSONS, JOSEPH BINET, DUPRÉ AND MME ROUS-
SEAU.

#### JOSEPH

This way, sir. This way, madame. (*Dupré and Mme.
Rousseau enter.*) These are the father and mother of Pamela
Giraud!

#### DUPRÉ (*to De Verby*)

I am very sorry, sir, that you have got here before me!

#### MME. ROUSSEAU.

My sister has doubtless told you, madame, the sacrifice
which we expect your daughter to make for us. Only an angel
would make it.

#### JOSEPH

What sacrifice?

#### MME. GIRAUD

It is no business of yours.

#### DE VERBY

We have just had an interview with Mlle. Pamela—

#### MME. DU BROCARD

She has refused!

#### MME. ROUSSEAU

Oh, heavens!

#### DUPRÉ

Refused what?

#### MME. DU BROCARD

An income of six thousand francs.

DUPRÉ

I could have wagered on it. To think of offering money!

MME. DU BROCARD

But it was the only way—

DUPRÉ

To spoil everything. (*To Mme. Giraud*) Madame, kindly tell your daughter that the counsel of M. Jules Rousseau is here and desires to see her.

MME. GIRAUD

Oh, as for that you will gain nothing.

GIRAUD

Either from her or from us.

JOSEPH

But what is it they want?

GIRAUD

Hold your tongue.

MME. DU BROCARD (*to Mme. Giraud*)

Madame, offer her—

DUPRÉ

Now, Mme. du Brocard, I must beg you—(*To Mme. Giraud*) It is in the name of the mother of Jules that I ask of you permission to see your daughter.

MME. GIRAUD

It will be of no use, of no use at all, sir! And to think that they point-blank offered her money when the young man a little time before had spoken of marrying her!

MME. ROUSSEAU (*with excitement*)

Well, why not?

MME. GIRAUD (*with vehemence*)

How was that, madame?

DUPRÉ (*seizing the hand of Mme. Giraud*)

Come, come! Bring me your daughter. (*Exit Mme Giraud.*)

DE VERBY AND MME. DU BROCARD.

You have then made up your mind?

DUPRÉ

It is not I, but madame who has made up her mind.

DE VERBY (*questioning Mme. du Brocard*)

What has she promised?

DUPRÉ (*seeing that Joseph is listening*)

Be silent, general; stay for a moment, I beg you, with these ladies. Here she comes. Now leave us alone, if you please. (*Pamela is brought in by her mother. She makes a curtsey to Mme. Rousseau, who gazes at her with emotion; then Dupré leads all but Pamela into the other room; Joseph remains behind.*)

JOSEPH (*aside*)

I wonder what they mean. They all talk of a sacrifice! And old Giraud won't say a word to me! Well, I can bide my time. I promised the advocate that I would give him my fourteen hundred francs, but before I do so, I would like to see how he acts with regard to me.

DUPRÉ (*going up to Joseph*)

Joseph Binet, you must leave the room.

JOSEPH

And not hear what you say about me?

DUPRÉ

You must go away.

JOSEPH (*aside*)

It is evident that they are concealing something from me.
(*To Dupré*) I have prepared her mind; she is much taken
with the idea of transportation.  Stick to that point.

DUPRÉ

All right!  But you must leave the room.

JOSEPH (*aside*)

Leave the room!  Oh, indeed! not I.  (*He makes as if he
had withdrawn, but, quietly returning, hides himself in a
closet.*)

DUPRÉ (*to Pamela*)

You have consented to see me, and I thank you for it.  I
know exactly what has recently taken place here, and I am not
going to address you in the same way as you have been recently addressed.

PAMELA

Your very presence assures me of that, sir.

DUPRÉ

You are in love with this fine young man, this Joseph?

PAMELA

I am aware, sir, that advocates are like confessors!

DUPRÉ

My child, they have to be just as safe confidants.  You may
tell me everything without reserve.

## PAMELA

Well, sir, I did love him; that is to say, I thought I loved
him, and I would very willingly have become his wife. I
thought that with his energy Joseph would have made a good
business, and that we could lead together a life of toil. When
prosperity came, we would have taken with us my father and
my mother; it was all very clear—it would have been a
united family!

## DUPRÉ (*aside*)

The appearance of this young girl is in her favor! Let us
see whether she is sincere or not. (*Aloud*) What are you
thinking about?

## PAMELA

I was thinking about those past days, which seemed to me
so happy in comparison with the present. A fortnight ago my
head was turned by the sight of M. Jules; I fell in love with
him, as young girls do fall in love, as I have seen other young
girls fall in love with young men—with a love which would
endure everything for those they loved! I used to say to myself: shall I ever be like that? Well, at this moment I do
not know anything that I would not endure for M. Jules. A
few moments ago they offered me money,—they, from whom
I expected such nobleness, such greatness; and I was disgusted! Money! I have plenty of it, sir! I have twenty
thousand francs! They are here, they are yours! that is to
say, they are his! I have kept them to use in my efforts to save
him, for I have betrayed him, because I doubted him, while
he was so confident, so sure of me—and I was so distrustful
of him!

## DUPRÉ

And he gave you twenty thousand francs?

## PAMELA

Ah, sir! he entrusted them with me. Here they are. I

shall return them to his family, if he dies; but he shall not
die! Tell me? Is it not so? You ought to know.

### DUPRÉ

My dear child, bear in mind that your whole life, perhaps
your happiness, depend upon the truthfulness of your answers.
Answer me as if you stood in the presence of God.

### PAMELA

I will.

### DUPRÉ

You have never loved any one before?

### PAMELA

Never!

### DUPRÉ

You seem to be afraid! Come, I am terrifying you. You
are not giving me your confidence.

### PAMELA

Oh, yes I am, sir; I swear I am! Since we have been in
Paris, I have never left my mother, and I have thought of
nothing but my work and my duty. I was alarmed and
thrown into confusion a few moments ago, sir, but you inspire
me with confidence, and I can tell you everything. Well, I
acknowledge it,—I am in love with Jules; he is the only one
I love, and I would follow him to the end of the world! You
told me to speak as in the presence of God.

### DUPRÉ

Well, it is to your heart that I am going to appeal. Do for
me what you have refused to do for others. Tell me the
truth! You alone have the power to save him before the face
of justice! You love him, Pamela; I understand what it
would cost you to—

PAMELA

To avow my love for him? Would that be sufficient to save him?

DUPRÉ

I will answer for that!

PAMELA

Well?

DUPRÉ

My child!

PAMELA

Well—he is saved.

DUPRÉ (*earnestly*)

But—you will be compromised—

PAMELA

But after all it is for him.

DUPRÉ (*aside*)

I never expected it, but I shall not die without having seen with my own eyes an example of beautiful and noble candor, destitute alike of self-interest and designing reserve. (*Aloud*) Pamela, you are a good and generous girl.

PAMELA

To act this way consoles me for many little miseries of life

DUPRÉ

My child, that is not everything! You are true as steel, you are high-spirited. But in order to succeed it is necessary to have assurance—determination—

PAMELA

Oh, sir! You shall see!

### DUPRÉ

Do not be over-anxious. Dare to confess everything. Be brave! Imagine that you are before the Court of Assizes, the presiding judge, the public prosecutor, the prisoner at the bar, and me, his advocate; the jury is on one side. The ⸱ig court-room is filled with people. Do not be alarmed.

### PAMELA

You needn't fear for me.

### DUPRÉ

A court officer brings you in; you have given your name and surname! Then the presiding judge asks you "How long have you known the prisoner, Rousseau?"—What would you answer?

### PAMELA

The truth!—I met him about a month before his arrest at the Ile d'Amour, Belleville.

### DUPRÉ

Who were with him?

### PAMELA

I noticed no one but him.

### DUPRÉ

Did you hear them talk politics?

### PAMELA (*in astonishment*)

Oh, sir! The judges must be aware that politics are matters of indifference at the Ile d'Amour.

### DUPRÉ

Very good, my child! But you must tell them all you know about Jules Rousseau.

PAMELA

Of course. I shall still speak the truth, and repeat my testimony before the police justice. I knew nothing of the conspiracy, and was infinitely surprised when he was arrested in my room; the proof of which is that I feared M. Jules was a thief and afterwards apologized for my suspicion.

DUPRÉ

You must acknowledge that from the time of your first acquaintance with this young man, he constantly came to see you. You must declare—

PAMELA

I shall stick to the truth—He never left me alone! He came to see me for love, I received him from friendship, and I resisted him from a sense of duty—

DUPRÉ

And at last?

PAMELA (*anxiously*)

At last?

DUPRÉ

You are trembling! Take care!—Just now you promised me to tell the truth!

PAMELA (*aside*)

The truth! Oh my God!

DUPRÉ

I also am interested in this young man; but I recoil from a possible imposture. If he is guilty, my duty bids me defend him, if he is innocent, his cause shall be mine. Yes, without doubt, Pamela, I am about to demand from you a great sacrifice, but he needs it. The visits which Jules made to you were in the evening, and without the knowledge of your parents.

PAMELA

Why no! never!

DUPRÉ

How is this? for in that case there would be no hope for him.

PAMELA (*aside*)

No hope for him! Then either he or I must be ruined. (*Aloud*) Sir, do not be alarmed; I felt a little fear because the real danger was not before my eyes. But when I shall stand before the judges!—when once I shall see him, see Jules—and feel that his safety depends upon me—

DUPRÉ

That is good, very good. But what is most necessary to be made known is that on the evening of the twenty-fourth, he came here. If that is once understood, I shall be successful in saving him; otherwise, I can answer for nothing. He is lost!

PAMELA (*murmuring, greatly agitated*)

Lost!—Jules lost!—No, no, no!—Better that my own good name be lost! (*Aloud*) Yes, he came here on the twenty-fourth. (*Aside*) God forgive me! (*Aloud*) It was my saint's day—my name is Louise Pamela—and he was kind enough to bring me a bouquet, without the knowledge of my father or my mother; he came in the evening, late. Ah! you need have no fear, sir—you see I shall tell all. (*Aside*) And all is a lie!

DUPRÉ

He will be saved! (*Rousseau appears.*) Ah! sir! (*running to the door of the room*) Come all of you and thank your deliverer!

## SCENE SIXTH.

ROUSSEAU, DE VERBY, MADAME DU BROCARD, GIRAUD, MADAME GIRAUD, DUPRÉ, AND LATER JOSEPH BINET.

ALL

Does she consent?

ROUSSEAU

You have saved my son. I shall never forget it.

MME. DU BROCARD

You have put us under eternal obligations, my child.

ROUSSEAU

My fortune shall be at your disposal.

DUPRÉ

I will not say anything to you, my child! We shall meet again!—

JOSEPH (*coming out of the closet*)

One moment! one moment! I have heard everything— and do you believe that I am going to put up with that? I was here in concealment all the time. And do you·think you are going to let Pamela, whom I have loved and have wished to make my wife, say all that? (*To Dupré*) This is the way you are going to earn my fourteen hundred francs, eh! Well, I shall go to court myself and testify that the whole thing is a lie.

ALL

Great heavens!

DUPRÉ

You miserable wretch!

DE VERBY

If you say a single word—

JOSEPH

Oh, I ain't afraid!

DE VERBY (*to Rousseau and Mme. du Brocard*)

He shall never go to court! If necessary, I will have him shadowed, and I will put men on the watch to prevent him . from entering.

JOSEPH

I'd just like to see you try it! (*Enter a sheriff's officer, who goes up to Dupré.*)

DUPRÉ

What do you want?

THE SHERIFF'S OFFICER

I am the court officer of the assizes—Mlle. Pamela Giraud! (*Pamela comes forward.*) In virtue of discretionary authority of the presiding judge, you are summoned to appear before him to-morrow at ten o'clock.

JOSEPH (*to De Verby*)

I will go also.

THE OFFICER ~

The porter has told me that you have here a gentleman named Joseph Binet.

JOSEPH

Here I am!

THE OFFICER

Please take your summons.

JOSEPH

I told you that I would go! (*The officer withdraws; every one is alarmed at the threats of Binet. Dupré tries to speak to him and reason with him, but he steals away.*)

*Curtain to the Third Act.*

# ACT IV.

---

## SCENE FIRST.

*(The stage represents Madame du Brocard's salon, from which can be seen the Court of Assizes.)*

MADAME DU BROCARD, MADAME ROUSSEAU, ROUSSEAU, JOSEPH BINET, DUPRÉ AND JUSTINE.

*(Dupré is seated reading his note-book.)*

### MME. ROUSSEAU.

M. Dupré!

### DUPRÉ

Yes, madame, the court adjourned after the speech of the prosecuting attorney. And I came over to reassure you personally.

### MME. DU BROCARD

I told you, sister, that some one was sure to come and keep us informed about things. In my house here, which is so close to the court house, we are in a favorable position for learning all that goes on at the trial. Ah, M. Dupré! How can we thank you enough! You spoke superbly! *(To Justine)* Justine, bring in something to drink—Quick!

### ROUSSEAU

Sir, your speech—*(To his wife)* He was magnificent.

### DUPRÉ

Sir,—

JOSEPH (*in tears*)

Yes, you were magnificent, magnificent!

DUPRÉ

I am not the person you ought to thank, but that child, that Pamela, who showed such astonishing courage.

JOSEPH

And didn't I do well?

MME. ROUSSEAU.

And he (*pointing to Binet*) did he carry out the threat he made to us?

DUPRÉ

No, he took your side.

JOSEPH

It was your fault! but for you—Ah!—Well—I reached the court house, having made up my mind to mix up everything; but when I saw all the people, the judge, the jury, the crowd, and the terrible silence, I trembled! Nevertheless I screwed up my courage. When I was questioned, I was just about to answer, when my glance met the eyes of Mlle. Pamela, which were filled with tears—I felt as if my tongue was bound. And on the other side I saw M. Jules—a handsome youth, his fine face conspicuous among them all. His expression was as tranquil as if he had been a mere spectator. That knocked me out! "Don't be afraid," said the judge to me. I was absolutely beside myself! I was afraid of making some mistake; and then I had sworn to keep to the truth; and then M. Dupré fixed his eye on me. I can't tell you what that eye seemed to say to me—My tongue seemed twisted up. I broke out into a sweat—my heart beat hard—and I began to cry, like a fool. You were magnificent. And then in a moment it was all over. He made me do exactly what he wanted. This is the way I lied: I said that on the evening of the twenty-fourth I unexpectedly came to Pamela's room

and found M. Jules there—Yes, at Pamela's, the girl whom
I was going to marry, whom I still love—and our marriage
will be the talk of the whole neighborhood.  Never mind, he's
a great lawyer!  Never mind!  (*To Justine*)  Give me something to drink, will you?

ROUSSEAU, MME. ROUSSEAU, MME. DU BROCARD (*To Joseph*)

Dear friend!  You showed yourself a fine fellow!

### DUPRÉ

The energy shown by Pamela makes me hopeful.  I trembled for a moment while she was giving evidence; the prosecuting attorney pressed her very hard and seemed to doubt
her veracity; she grew pale and I thought she was going to
faint.

### JOSEPH

And what must my feelings have been?

### DUPRÉ

Her self-sacrifice was wonderful.  You don't realize all that
she has undergone for you; I, myself even, was deceived in
her; she was her own accuser, yet all the time was innocent.
Only one moment did she falter; but darting a rapid glance
at Jules, she suddenly rallied, a blush took the place of pallor
on her countenance, and we felt that she had saved her lover;
in spite of the risk she was running, she repeated once more
before all those people the story of her own disgrace, and
then fell weeping into the arms of her mother.

### JOSEPH

Yes, she is a fine girl.

### DUPRÉ

But I must leave you; the summing up of the judge will
come this afternoon.

ROUSSEAU

We must be going then.

DUPRÉ

One moment! Do not forget Pamela! That young girl has compromised her own honor for you and for him.

JOSEPH

As for me, I don't ask anything, but I have been led to expect—

MME. DU BROCARD, MME. ROUSSEAU.

We can never pay our debt of gratitude to you.

DUPRÉ

Very good; come, gentlemen, we must be starting. (*Exeunt Dupré and Rousseau.*)

---

## SCENE SECOND.

THE SAME PERSONS EXCEPTING DUPRÉ AND ROSSEAU.

MME. DU BROCARD (*stopping Joseph on his way out*)
Listen to me!

JOSEPH

What can I do for you?

MME. DU BROCARD

You see in what a state of anxiety we are; don't fail to let us know the least turn in our favor which the trial takes.

MME. ROUSSEAU

Yes, keep us well informed on the whole business.

### JOSEPH

You may rest assured of that—But look here, I needn't leave the court house to do that, I intend to see everything, and to hear everything. But do you see that window there? My seat is just under it; you watch that window, and if he is declared innocent you will see me wave my handkerchief.

### MME. ROUSSEAU

Do not forget to do so.

### JOSEPH

No danger of that; I am a poor chap, but I know what a mother's heart is! I am interested in this case, and for you, and for Pamela, I have said a lot of things! But when you are fond of people you'll do anything, and then I have been promised something—you may count upon me. (*Exit.*)

---

## SCENE THIRD.

THE SAME PERSONS EXCEPTING DUPRÉ AND ROUSSEAU.

### MME. ROUSSEAU

Justine, open this window, and wait for the signal which the young man has promised to give—Ah! but suppose my boy were condemned!

### MME. DU BROCARD

M. Dupré has spoken very hopefully about matters.

### MME. ROUSSEAU

But with regard to this good girl, this admirable Pamela— what must we do for her?

### MME. DU BROCARD

We ought to do something to make her happy! I acknowledge that this young person is a succor sent from heaven! Only a noble heart could make the sacrifice that she has made! She deserves a fortune for it! Thirty thousand francs! that is what she ought to have. Jules owes his life to her. (*Aside*) Poor boy, will his life be saved? (*She looks toward the window.*)

#### MME. ROUSSEAU

Well, Justine, do you see anything?

#### JUSTINE

Nothing, madame.

#### MME. ROUSSEAU

Nothing yet! Yes you are right, sister, it is only the heart that can prompt such noble actions. I do not know what you and my husband would think about it, but if we considered what was right, and had full regard to the happiness of Jules, apart from the brilliant prospect of an alliance with the family of De Verby, if my son loved her and she loved my son— it seems to me reasonable—

#### MME. DU BROCARD AND JUSTINE

No! No!

#### MME. ROUSSEAU

Oh, sister! say yes! Has she not well deserved it? But there is some one coming. (*The two women remain in their seats with clasped hands.*)

---

## SCENE FOURTH.

### THE SAME PERSONS AND DE VERBY.

#### JUSTINE

M. le General de Verby!

MME. ROUSSEAU AND MME. DU BROCARD.

Ah!

### DE VERBY

Everything is going on well! My presence was no longer necessary, so I return to you. There are great hopes of your son's acquittal. The charge of the presiding judge is decidedly in his favor.

### MME. ROUSSEAU *(joyfully)*

Thank God!

### DE VERBY

Jules had behaved admirably! My brother the Comte de Verby is very much interested in his favor. My niece looks upon him as a hero, and I know courage and honorable conduct when I see them. When once this affair has been settled, we will hasten the marriage.

### MME. ROUSSEAU

We ought to tell you, sir, that we have made certain promises to this young girl.

### MME. DU BROCARD

Never mind that, sister.

### DE VERBY

Doubtless the young girl deserves some recompense, and I suppose you will give her fifteen or twenty thousand francs,— that is due her.

### MME. DU BROCARD

You see, sister, that M. de Verby is a noble and generous man, and since he has fixed upon this sum, I think it will be sufficient.

### JUSTINE

M. Rousseau!

MME. DU BROCARD

O brother!

MME. ROUSSEAU

Dear husband!

---

## SCENE FIFTH.

THE SAME PERSONS AND ROUSSEAU.

DE VERBY (*to Rousseau*)

Have you good news?

MME. ROUSSEAU

Is he acquitted?

ROUSSEAU

No, but it is rumored that he is going to be; the jury are in consultation; I couldn't stay there any longer; I couldn't stand the suspense; I told Antoine to hurry here as soon as the verdict is given.

MME. ROUSSEAU

We shall learn what the verdict is from this window; we have agreed upon a signal to be given by that youth, Joseph Binet.

ROUSSEAU

Ah! keep a good look out, Justine.

MME. ROUSSEAU

And how is Jules? What a trying time it must be for him!

ROUSSEAU

Not at all! The unfortunate boy astonishes me by his coolness. Such courage as he has is worthy of a better cause than that of conspiracy. To think of his having put us in such a position! But for this I might have been appointed President of the Chamber of Commerce.

### DE VERBY

You forget that, after all, his marriage with a member of my family will make some amends for his trouble.

### ROUSSEAU (*struck by a sudden thought*)

Ah, general! When I left the court room, Jules stood surrounded by his friends, among whom were M. Dupré and the young girl Pamela. Your niece and Madame de Verby must have noticed it, and I hope that you will try to explain matters to them. (*While Rousseau speaks with the general the ladies are watching for the signal.*)

### DE VERBY

Rest assured of that! I will take care that Jules appears as white as snow! It is of very great importance to explain this affair of the working-girl, otherwise the Comtesse de Verby might oppose the marriage. We must explain away this apparent *amour,* and she must be made to understand that the girl's evidence was a piece of self-sacrifice for which she had been paid.

### ROUSSEAU

I certainly intend to do my duty towards that young girl. I shall give her eight or ten thousand francs. It seems to me that that will be liberal, very liberal!

### MME. ROUSSEAU (*while Mme. du Brocard tries to restrain her*)

Ah! sir, but what of her honor?

### ROUSSEAU

Well, I suppose that some one will marry her.

## SCENE SIXTH.

### The Same Persons and Joseph.

JOSEPH (*dashing in*)

Monsieur! Madame! Give me some cologne or something I beg you!

ALL

Whatever can be the matter?

JOSEPH

M. Antoine, your footman, is bringing Pamela here.

ROUSSEAU

Has anything happened?

JOSEPH

When she saw the jury come in to give their verdict she
was taken ill! Her father and mother, who were in the crowd
at the other end of the court, couldn't stir. I cried out, and
the presiding judge made them put me out of court!

MME. ROUSSEAU

But Jules! my son! What did the jury say!

JOSEPH

I know nothing!—I had no eyes except for Pamela—As for
your son, I suppose he is all right, but first with me comes
Pamela—

DE VERBY

But you must have seen how the jury looked!

JOSEPH

Oh, yes! The foreman of the jury looked so gloomy—so
severe—that I am quite persuaded—(*He shudders.*)

MME. ROUSSEAU

My poor Jules!

JOSEPH

Here comes Antoine and Mlle. Pamela.

---

## SCENE SEVENTH.

THE SAME PERSONS, ANTOINE AND PAMELA.
(*They lead Pamela to a seat and give her smelling salts.*)

MME. DU BROCARD

My dear child!

MME. ROUSSEAU

My daughter!

ROUSSEAU

Mademoiselle!

PAMELA

I couldn't stand it any longer, the excitement was too great—and the suspense was so cruel. I tried to brace up my courage by the calmness of M. Jules while the jury was deliberating; the smile which he wore made me share his presentiment of coming release! But I was chilled to the heart when I looked at the pale, impassive countenance of M. Dupré!—And then, the sound of the bell that announced the return of the jury, and the murmur of anxiety that ran through the court—I was quite overcome!—A cold sweat suffused my cheek and I fainted.

JOSEPH

As for me, I shouted out, and they threw me into the street.

DE VERBY (*to Rousseau*)

If by mischance—

### ROUSSEAU

Sir!

### DE VERBY (*to Rousseau and the women*)

If it should be found necessary to appeal the case (*pointing to Pamela*), could we count upon her?

### MME. ROUSSEAU

On her?—To the end; I am sure of that.

### MME. DU BROCARD

Pamela!

### ROUSSEAU

Tell me, you who have shown yourself so good, so generous,—if we should still have need of your unselfish aid, would you be ready?

### PAMELA

Quite ready, sir! I have but one object, one single thought!—and that is, to save M. Jules!

### JOSEPH (*aside*)

She loves him, she loves him!

### ROUSSEAU

Ah! all that I have is at your disposal. (*A murmur and cries are heard; general alarm.*)

### ALL

What a noise they are making! (*Pamela totters to her feet; Joseph runs to the window, where Justine is watching.*) Listen to their shouts!

### JOSEPH

There's a crowd of people rushing down the steps of the court,—they are coming here!

JUSTINE AND JOSEPH

It is M. Jules!


ROUSSEAU AND MME. ROUSSEAU

My son!

MME. DU BROCARD AND PAMELA

Jules! (*They rush forward to Jules.*)


DE VERBY

He is acquitted!

---

## SCENE EIGHTH.

THE SAME PERSONS AND JULES (*brought in by his mother
and his aunt and followed by his friends*).

JULES (*He flings himself into the arms of his mother; he
does not at first see Pamela, who is seated
in a corner near Joseph*)

O mother! Dear aunt! And my father! Here I am
restored to liberty again! (*To General de Verby and the
friends who have come with him*) Let me thank you, general,
and you, my friends, for your kind sympathy. (*After general
handshaking the friends depart.*)


MME. ROUSSEAU

And so my son has at last come back to me! It seems too
good to be true.

JOSEPH (*to Pamela*)

Well, and what of you? He hasn't said a word to you, an
you are the only one he hasn't seen.


PAMELA

Silence, Joseph, silence! (*She retires to the end of the
stage.*)

## DE VERBY

Not only have you been acquitted, but you have also gained a high place in the esteem of those who are interested in the affair! You have exhibited both courage and discretion, such as have gratified us all.

## ROUSSEAU

Everybody has behaved well. Antoine, you have done nobly; you will end your life in this house.

## MME. ROUSSEAU (*to Jules*)

Let me express my gratitude to M. Adolph Durand? (*Jules presents his friend.*)

## JULES

Yes, but my real deliverer, my guardian angel is poor Pamela! How well she understood my situation and her own also! What self-sacrifice she showed! Can I ever forget her emotion, her terror!—and then she fainted! (*Mme. Rousseau, who has been thinking of nothing else but her son, now looks around for Pamela, sees her, and brings her up to Jules.*) Ah, Pamela! Pamela! My gratitude to you shall be eternal!

## PAMELA

Ah, M. Jules!—How happy I feel!!

## JULES

We will never part again? Will we, mother? She shall be your daughter!

## DE VERBY (*to Rousseau with vehemence*)

My sister and my niece are expecting an answer; you will have to exercise your authority, sir. This young man seems to have a lively and romantic imagination. He is in danger of missing his career through a too scrupulous sense of honor, and a generosity which is tinged with folly!

ROUSSEAU (*in embarrassment*)

The fact is—

DE VERBY

But I have your word.

MME. DU BROCARD

Speak out, brother!

JULES

Mother, do you answer them, and show yourself on my side?

ROUSSEAU (*taking Jules by the hand*)

Jules!—I shall never forget the service which this young girl has done us. I understand the promptings of your gratitude; but as you are aware the Comte de Verby has our promise; it is not right that you should lightly sacrifice your future! You are not wanting in energy, you have given sufficient proof of that! A young conspirator should be quite able to extricate himself from such an affair as this.

DE VERBY (*to Jules*)

Undoubtedly! and our future diplomat will have a splendid chance.

ROUSSEAU

Moreover my wishes in the matter—

JULES

O father!

DUPRÉ (*appearing*)

Jules, I still have to take up your defence.

PAMELA AND JOSEPH.

M. Dupré!

JULES

My friend!

### MME. DU BROCARD

It is the lawyer.

### DUPRÉ

I see! I am no longer "my dear Monsieur Dupré"!

### MME. DU BROCARD

Oh, you are always that! But before paying our debt of gratitude to you, we have to think about this young girl.

### DUPRÉ (*coldly*)

I beg your pardon, madame.

### DE VERBY

This man is going to spoil everything.

### DUPRÉ (*to Rousseau*)

I heard all you said. It transcends all I have ever experienced. I could not have believed that ingratitude could follow so soon on the acceptance of a benefit. Rich as you are, rich as your son will be, what fairer task have you to perform than that of satisfying your conscience? In saving Jules, this girl has brought disgrace upon herself! Can it be possible that the fortune which you have so honorably gained should have killed in your heart every generous sentiment, and that self-interest alone—(*He sees Mme. du Brocard making signs to her brother.*) Ah! that is right, madame! It is you that give the tone in this household! And I forgot while I was pleading with this gentleman, that you would be at his elbow when I was no longer here.

### MME. DU BROCARD

We have pledged our word to the Count and Countess of Verby!—Mlle. Pamela, whose friend I shall be all my life, did not effect the deliverance of my nephew on the understanding that she should blight his prospects,

### Rousseau

There ought to be some basis of equality in a union by marriage. My son will some day have an income of eighty thousand francs.

### Joseph (*aside*)

That suits me to a T. I shall marry her now. But this fellow here, he talks more like a Jewish money-changer than a father.

### De Verby (*to Dupré*)

I think, sir, that your talent and character are such as to claim our highest admiration and esteem. The Rousseau family will always preserve your name in grateful memory; but these private discussions must be carried on without witnesses from the outside. M. Rousseau has given me his word and I keep him to his promise! (*To Jules*) Come, my young friend, come to my brother's house; my niece is expecting you. To-morrow we will sign the marriage contract. (*Pamela falls senseless on her chair.*)

### Joseph

Ah, what have you done! Mlle. Pamela!

### Dupré and Jules (*darting towards her*)

Good heavens!

### De Verby (*taking Jules by the hand*)

Come—-come—

### Dupré

Stop a moment! I should have been glad to think that I was not the only protector that was left her! But listen, the matter is not yet ended! Pamela will certainly be arrested as a false witness! (*Seizes the hand of De Verby.*) And you will all be ruined. (*He leads off Pamela.*)

### Joseph (*hiding behind a sofa*)

Don't tell anybody that I am here!

*Curtain to the Fourth Act.*

# ACT V.

## SCENE FIRST.

(*The stage setting represents the private study in Dupré's house. On one side is a bookcase, on the other a desk. On the left is a window hung with heavy, sweeping silk curtains.*)

DUPRÉ, PAMELA, GIRAUD AND MADAME GIRAUD.

(*Pamela is seated on a chair reading; her mother is standing in front of her; Giraud is examining the pictures on the wall; Dupré is striding up and down the room.*)

DUPRÉ (*stopping, addresses Giraud*)

Did you take your usual precautions in coming here this morning?

GIRAUD

You may rest assured of that, sir; when I come here I walk with my head turned backwards! I know well enough that the least want of caution quickly results in misfortune. Your heart, my daughter, has led you astray this time; perjury is a terrible thing and I am afraid you are in a serious mess.

MME. GIRAUD

I agree with you. You must be very careful, Giraud, for if any one were to follow you and discover that our poor daughter was here in concealment, through the generosity of M. Dupré—

DUPRÉ

Come now, enough of that! (*He continues to stride hastily about the room.*) What ingratitude! The Rousseau family are ignorant of what steps I have taken. They believe that Pamela has been arrested, and none of them trouble their heads about it! They have sent Jules off to Brussels; De Verby is in the country; and Rousseau carries on his business at the Bourse as if nothing else was worth living for. Money, ambition, are their sole objects. The higher feelings count for nothing! They all worship the golden calf. Money makes them dance round their idol; the sight of it blinds them.

PAMELA (*who has been watching him, rises and approaches him*)

M. Dupré, you are agitated, you seem unwell. I fear it is on my account.

#### DUPRÉ

Have you not shared my disgust at the hateful want of feeling manifested by this family, who, as soon as their son is acquitted, throw you aside as a mere tool that has served their purpose?

#### PAMELA

But what can we do about it, sir?

#### DUPRÉ

Dear child, does your heart feel no bitterness against them?

#### PAMELA

No, sir! I am happier than any of them; for I feel that I have done a good deed.

#### MME. GIRAUD (*embracing Pamela*)

My poor dear daughter!

#### GIRAUD

This is the happiest moment of my life.

### DUPRÉ (*addressing Pamela*)

Mademoiselle, you are a noble girl!—No one has better ground for saying it than I, for it was I who came to you imploring you to speak the truth; and pure and honorable as you are, you have compromised your character for the sake of another. And now they repulse you and treat you with contempt; but I look upon you with hearty admiration—you shall yet be happy, for I will make full reparation to you! Pamela, I am forty-eight years old. I have some reputation, and a fortune. I have spent my life as an honest man, and will finish it as such; will you be my wife?

### PAMELA (*much moved*)

I, sir?

### GIRAUD

His wife! Our daughter his wife! What do you say to that, Mme. Giraud?

### MME. GIRAUD

Can it be possible?

### DUPRÉ

Why should you wonder at this? Let us have no idle phrases. Put the question to your own heart—and answer yes or no—Will you be my wife?

### PAMELA

You are a great man, sir, and I owe everything to you. Do you really wish to add to the debt? Ah! my gratitude—!

### DUPRÉ

Don't let me hear you use that word,—it spoils everything! The world is something that I despise! And I render to it no account of my conduct, my hatred or my love. From the moment I saw your courage and your resignation—I loved you. Try to love me in return!—

**PAMELA**

Ah, sir, indeed I will!

**MME. GIRAUD**

Could any one help loving you?

**GIRAUD**

Sir, I am only a poor porter. I repeat it, I am nothing but a porter. You love our daughter, you have told her so. Forgive me—my eyes are full of tears—and that checks my utterance. (*He wipes his eyes.*) Well, well, you do right to love her!—It proves that you have brains!—for Pamela—there are a great many landowners' children who are her inferiors. But it is humiliating for her to have parents such as us.

**PAMELA**

O father!

**GIRAUD**

You are a leader among men!—Well, I and my wife, we will go and hide ourselves somewhere far into the country!— And on Sunday, at the hour of mass, you will say, "They are praying to God for us!" (*Pamela kisses her parents.*)

**DUPRÉ**

You are good people, and to think that such as you have neither title nor fortune! And if you are pining for your country home, you shall return there and live there in happiness and tranquillity, and I will make provision for you.

**GIRAUD AND MME. GIRAUD**

Oh! our gratitude—

**DUPRÉ**

That word again—I should like to cut it out of the dictionary!—Meanwhile I intend to take you both with me into the country, so set about packing up.

GIRAUD

Sir!—

DUPRÉ

Well, what is it?

GIRAUD

Poor Joseph Binet is also in danger. He does not know that we are all here. But three days ago, he came to see your servant and seemed scared almost to death, and he is hidden here, as in a sanctuary, up in the attic.

DUPRÉ

Call him down-stairs.

GIRAUD

He will not come, sir; he is too much afraid of being arrested—they pass him up food through a hole in the ceiling!

DUPRÉ

He will soon be at liberty, I hope. I am expecting a letter which will relieve all your minds.

GIRAUD

At once?

DUPRÉ

I expect the letter this evening.

GIRAUD (*to his wife*)

I am going to make my way cautiously to the house. (*Madame Giraud accompanies him, and gives him advice. Pamela rises to follow her.*)

DUPRÉ (*restraining Pamela*)

You are not in love with this Binet, are you?

PAMELA

Oh, never!

DUPRÉ

And the other?

PAMELA (*struggling with her feelings*)

I shall love none but you! (*She starts to leave the room.* ***A*** *noise is heard in the antechamber. Jules appears.*)

---

## SCENE SECOND.

PAMELA, DUPRÉ AND JULES.

JULES (*to the servants*)

Let me pass in! I tell you—I must speak to him at once! (*Noticing Dupré*) Ah, sir! What has become of Pamela? Is she at liberty? Is she safe?

PAMELA (*stopping at the door*)

Jules!

JULES

Good heavens! you here?—

DUPRÉ

And you, sir, I thought you were at Brussels?

JULES

Yes, they sent me away against my will, and I yielded to them! Reared as I have been in obedience, I still tremble before my family! But I carried away with me the memory of what I had left behind! It has taken me six months to realize the situation, and I now acknowledge that I risked my life in order to obtain the hand of Mlle. de Verby, that I might gratify the ambition of my family, or, if you like, might humor my own vanity. I hoped some day to be a man of title, I, the son of a rich stock-broker!—Then I met Pamela, and I fell in love with her!—The rest you know!—What was a mere sentiment has now become a duty, and every hour that has kept me from her I have felt that obedience to my family was rank cowardice; and while they believe I am far away, I have returned! You told me she had been arrested—and to think that I should run away (*to both of them*) without coming to see you, who had been my deliverer, and will be hers also.

DUPRÉ (*looking at them*)

Good! very good! He is an honorable fellow after all.

PAMELA (*aside, drying her tears*)

Thank God for that!

DUPRÉ

What do you expect to do? What are your plans?

JULES

What are my plans? To unite my fortune with hers. If necessary, to forfeit everything for her, and under God's protection to say to her, "Pamela, will you be mine?"

DUPRÉ

The deuce you say! But there is a slight difficulty in the way—for I am going to marry her myself!

JULES (*in great astonishment*)

You?

DUPRÉ

Yes, I! (*Pamela casts down her eyes.*) I have no family to oppose my wishes.

JULES

I will win over mine.

DUPRÉ

They will send you off to Brussels again.

### JULES

I must run and find my mother; my courage has returned!
Were I to forfeit the favor of my father, were my aunt to cut
me off with a sou, I would stand my ground. If I did otherwise, I should be destitute of self-respect, I should prove myself a soulless coward.—After that, is there any hope for me?

### DUPRÉ

Do you ask such a question of me?

### JULES

Pamela, answer, I implore you!

### PAMELA (*to Dupré*)

I have given you my word, sir.

---

### SCENE THIRD.

THE SAME PERSONS AND A SERVANT. (*The latter hands a card to Dupré.*)

### DUPRÉ (*looking at the card with great surprise*)

How is this? (*To Jules*) Do you know where M. de
Verby is?

### JULES

He is in Normandy, staying with his brother, Comte de
Verby.

### DUPRÉ (*looking at the card*)

Very good. Now you had better go and find your mother.

### JULES

But you promise me?

DUPRÉ

I promise nothing.

JULES

Good-bye, Pamela! (*Aside, as he goes out*)  I will come back soon.

DUPRÉ (*turning towards Pamela, after the departure of Jules*)

Must he come back again?

PAMELA (*with deep emotion, throwing herself into his arms*)
Ah! sir! (*Exit.*)

DUPRÉ (*looking after her and wiping away a tear*)

Gratitude, forsooth! (*Opening a narrow secret door.*)  Come in, general; come in!

---

## SCENE FOURTH.

### DUPRÉ AND DE VERBY.

DUPRÉ

Strange, sir, to find you here, when every one believes that you are fifty leagues away from Paris.

DE VERBY

I arrived this morning.

DUPRÉ

Without doubt some powerful motive brought you here?

DE VERBY

No selfish motive; but I couldn't remain wholly indifferent to the affairs of others! You may prove useful to me.

DUPRÉ

I shall be only too happy to have an opportunity of serving you.

DE VERBY

M. Dupré, the circumstances under which we have become acquainted have put me in a position fully to appreciate your value. You occupy the first place among the men whose talents and character claim my admiration.

DUPRÉ

Ah! sir, you compel me to say that you, a veteran of the Empire, have always seemed to me by your loyalty and your independence to be a fitting representative of that glorious epoch. (*Aside*) I hope I have paid him back in full.

DE VERBY

I suppose I may rely upon you for assistance?

DUPRÉ

Certainly.

DE VERBY

1 would like to ask for some information with regard to young Pamela Giraud.

DUPRÉ

I felt sure that was your object.

DE VERBY

The Rousseau family have behaved abominably.

DUPRÉ

Would you have behaved any better?

DE VERBY

I intend to espouse her cause! Since her arrest as a perjurer, how do things go on?

DUPRÉ

That can have very little interest for you.


DE VERBY

That may be true, but—


DUPRÉ (*aside*)

He is trying to make me talk in order to find out whether
he is likely to be compromised in the case. (*Aloud*) General
de Verby, there are some men who cannot be seen through,
either in their plans or in their thoughts; the actions and
events which they give rise to alone reveal and explain such
men. These are the strong men. I humbly beg that you will
pardon my frankness when I say that I don't look upon you
as being one of them.

DE VERBY

Sir! what language to use to me! You are a singular man!


DUPRÉ

More than that!—I believe that I am an original man!
Listen to me. You throw out hints to me, and you think that
as a future ambassador you can try on me your diplomatic
methods; but you have chosen the wrong man and I am going
to tell you something, which you will take no pleasure in
learning. You are ambitious, but you are also prudent, and
you have taken the lead in a certain conspiracy. The plot
failed, and without worrying yourself about those whom you
had pushed to the front, and who eagerly strove for success,
you have yourself sneaked out of the way. As a political
renegade you have proved your independence by burning
incense to the new dynasty! And you expect as a reward to
be made ambassador to Turin! In a month's time you will
receive your credentials; meanwhile Pamela is arrested, you
have been seen at her house, you may possibly be compromised
by her trial for perjury! Then you rush to me, trembling
with the fear of being unmasked, of losing the promotion

which has caused you so many efforts to attain! You come
to me with an air of obsequiousness, and with the word of
flattery, expecting to make me your dupe, and thus to show
your sincerity! Well, you have sufficient reason for alarm—
Pamela is in the hands of justice, and she has told all.

### DE VERBY

What then is to be done?

### DUPRÉ

I have one suggestion to make: Write to Jules that you
release him from his engagement, and that Mlle. de Verby
withdraws her promise to be his wife.

### DE VERBY

Is that your advice?

### DUPRÉ

You find that the Rousseau family have behaved abominably, and you ought to despise them!

### DE VERBY

But you know—engagements of this sort—

### DUPRÉ

I'll tell you what I know; I know that your private fortune is not equal to the position which you aspire to. Mme.
du Brocard, whose wealth is equal to her pride, ought to come
to your assistance, if this alliance—

### DE VERBY

Sir! How dare you to affront my dignity in this way?

### DUPRÉ

Whether what I say be true or false, do what I tell you!
If you agree, I will endeavor to save you from being com-

promised. But write—or get out of the difficulty the best way you can. But stay, I hear some clients coming.

DE VERBY

I don't want to see anybody! Everybody, even the Rousseau family, believes that I have left the city.

A SERVANT (*announcing a visitor*)

Madame du Brocard!

DE VERBY

Oh, heavens! (*Rushes into an office on the right.*)

---

## SCENE FIFTH.

DUPRÉ AND MADAME DU BROCARD. (*She enters, her face idden by a heavy black veil which she cautiously raises.*)

MME. DU BROCARD

I have been here several times without being lucky enough to find you in. We are quite alone here?

DUPRÉ (*smiling*)

Quite alone!

MME. DU BROCARD

And so this harrowing affair has broken out afresh?

DUPRÉ

It has, unhappily!

MME. DU BROCARD

That wretched young man! If I had not superintended his education, I would disinherit him! My life at present is

not worth living. Is it possible that I, whose conduct and
principles have won the esteem of all, should be involved in
all this trouble? And yet on this occasion the only thing that
gives me any anxiety is my conduct towards the Girauds!

### DUPRÉ

I can well believe it, for it was you who led astray and
who induced Pamela to act as she did!

### MME. DU BROCARD

I feel, sir, that it is always a mistake to associate with
people of a certain class—say, with a Bonapartist—a man
who has neither conscience nor heart. (*Verby, who has been
listening, shrinks back with a gesture of rage.*)

### DUPRÉ

You always seemed to have such a high opinion of him!

### MME. DU BROCARD

His family was highly thought of! And the prospect of
this brilliant marriage!—I always dreamt of a distinguished
future for my nephew.

### DUPRÉ

But you are forgetting the general's affection for you, his
unselfishness.

### MME. DU BROCARD

His affection! His unselfishness! The general does not
possess a sou, and I had promised him a hundred thousand
francs, when once the marriage contract was signed.

DUPRÉ (*coughs loudly, as he turns in the direction of
De Verby*)

Oh! indeed!

### MME. DU BROCARD

I am come to you secretly, and in confidence, in spite of all

that has been said by this M. de Verby, who avers that you are
a half-rate lawyer! He has said the most frightful things
about you, and I come now to beg that you will extricate me
from this difficulty. I will give you whatever money you
demand.

DUPRÉ

What I wish above all is that you promise to let your nephew
marry whom he chooses, and give him the fortune you had
designed for him, in case he married Mlle. de Verby.

MME. DU BROCARD

One moment; you said, whom he pleased?

DUPRÉ

Give me your answer!

MME. DU BROCARD

But I ought to know.

DUPRÉ

Very well then, you must extricate yourself without my
assistance.

MME. DU BROCARD

You are taking advantage of my situation! Ah! some one
is coming!

DUPRÉ (*looking towards the newcomers*)

It is some of your own family!

MME. DU BROCARD (*peering cautiously*)

It is my brother-in-law Rousseau—What is he up to now?
He swore to me that he would keep quiet!

DUPRÉ

You also took an oath. In fact, there has been a great deal
of swearing in your family lately.

MME. DU BROCARD

I hope I shall be able to hear what he has to say! (*Rousseau appears with his wife. Mme. du Brocard conceals herself behind the curtain.*)

DUPRÉ (*looking at her*)

Very good! But if these two want to hide themselves, I don't know where I shall put them!

---

## SCENE SIXTH.

DUPRÉ, ROUSSEAU AND MADAME ROUSSEAU.

ROUSSEAU

Sir, we are at our wits' end—Madame du Brocard, my sister-in-law, came this morning and told us all sorts of stories,

MME. ROUSSEAU

Sir, I am in the most serious alarm.

DUPRÉ (*offering her a seat*)

Pray be seated, madame.

ROUSSEAU

If all she says be true, my son is still in difficulties.

DUPRÉ

I pity you; I do indeed!

ROUSSEAU

It seems as if I should never get free! This unfortunate affair has lasted for six months, and it seems to have cut ten years off my life. I have been forced to neglect the most

magnificent speculations, financial combinations of absolute
certitude, and to let them pass into the hands of others. And
then came the trial! But when I thought the affair was all
over, I have been compelled once more to leave my business,
and to spend my precious time in these interviews and solicita-
tions.

DUPRÉ

I pity you; I do indeed!

MME. ROUSSEAU

Meanwhile it is impossible for me—

ROUSSEAU

It is all your fault, and that of your family. Mme. du Brocard, who at first used always to call me "my dear Rousseau"
—because I had a few hundred thousand crowns—

DUPRÉ

Such a sum is a fine varnish for a man.

ROUSSEAU

From pride and ambition, she threw herself at the head of
M. de Verby. (*De Verby and Mme. du Brocard listen.*)
Pretty couple they are! Two charming characters, one a mili-
tary lobbyist, and the other an old hypocritical devotee!
(*The two withdraw their heads quickly.*)

MME. ROUSSEAU

Sir, she is my sister!

DUPRÉ

Really, you are going too far!

ROUSSEAU

You do not know them! Sir, I address you once again,
there is sure to be a new trial. What has become of that girl?

DUPRÉ

That girl is to be my wife, sir.


ROUSSEAU AND MME. ROUSSEAU

Your wife!


DE VERBY AND MME. DU BROCARD

His wife!

DUPRÉ

Yes, I shall marry her as soon as she regains her liberty—that is, provided she doesn't become the wife of your son!


ROUSSEAU

The wife of my son!—


MME. ROUSSEAU

What did he say?

DUPRÉ

What is the matter? Does that astonish you? You're bound to entertain this proposal—and I demand that you do so.


ROUSSEAU (*ironically*)

Ah! M. Dupré, I don't care a brass button about my son's union with Mlle. de Verby—the niece of a disreputable man! It was that fool of a Madame du Brocard who tried to bring about this grand match. But to come down to a daughter of a porter—

DUPRÉ

Her father is no longer that, sir!


ROUSSEAU

What do you mean?

DUPRÉ

He lost his place through your son, and he intends returning to the country, to live on the money (*Rousseau listens attentively*)—on the money which you have promised to give him.

ROUSSEAU

Ah! you are joking!

DUPRÉ

On the contrary, I am quite serious. Your son will marry their daughter—and you will provide a pension for the old people.

ROUSSEAU

Sir—

---

## SCENE SEVENTH.

THE SAME PERSONS AND JOSEPH (*coming in pale and faint*).

JOSEPH

M. Dupré, M. Dupré, save me!

ALL THREE

What has happened? What is the matter?

JOSEPH

Soldiers! Mounted soldiers are coming to arrest me!

DUPRÉ

Hold your tongue! Hold your tongue! (*Everybody seems alarmed. Dupré looks with anxiety towards the room in which is Pamela. To Joseph*) To arrest you?

JOSEPH

I saw one of them. Don't you hear him? He is coming up-stairs. Hide me! (*He tries to hide himself in the small room, from which De Verby comes out with a cry.*) Ah! (*He gets behind the curtain and Mme. du Brocard rushes forth with a shriek.)* Oh, heavens!—

### MME. ROUSSEAU

My sister!

### ROUSSEAU

M. de Verby! *(The door opens.)*

### JOSEPH *(falling exhausted over a chair)*

We are all nabbed!

### THE SERVANT *(entering, to Dupré)*

A message from the Keeper of the Seals.

### JOSEPH

The Keeper of the Seals! That must be about me!

### DUPRÉ *(advancing with a serious face and addressing the four others)*

I shall now leave you all four face to face—you whose mutual love and esteem is so great. Ponder well all I have said to you; she who sacrificed all for you, has been despised and humiliated, both for you and by you.—It is yours to make full reparation to her—to make it to-day—this very instant—in this very room. And then, we can take measures by which all can obtain deliverance, if indeed you are worth the trouble it will cost me. *(Exit Dupré.)*

## SCENE EIGHTH.

THE SAME PERSONS (*with the exception of Dupré. They stand looking awkwardly at each other for a moment*).

JOSEPH (*going up to them*)

We are a nice lot of people! (*To De Verby*) I should like to know when we are put in prison, whether you are going to look out for me, for my pocket is as light as my heart is heavy. (*De Verby turns his back on him. To Rousseau*) You know well enough that I was promised something for my services. (*Rousseau withdraws from him without answering. To Mme. du Brocard*) Tell me now, wasn't something promised to me?

MME. DU BROCARD

We will see about that later.

MME. ROUSSEAU

But what do you fear? What are you doing in this place? Were you pursued by any one?

JOSEPH

Not at all. I have been four days in this house, hidden like so much vermin in the garret. I came here because the old Giraud people were not to be found in their quarters. They have been carried off somewhere. Pamela has also disappeared—she is doubtless in hiding. I had no particular desire to run any risk; I admit that I lied to the judge. If I am condemned I will obtain my freedom by making a few startling revelations; I will tell on everybody!—

DE VERBY (*with energy*)

It must be done! (*Sits at the table and writes.*)

### MME. DU BROCARD

O Jules, Jules! wretched child, you are the cause of all this!

### MME. ROUSSEAU (*to her husband*)

You see, this lawyer has got you all in his power! You will have to agree to his terms. (*De Verby rises from the table. Mme. du Brocard takes his place and begins to write.*)

### MME. ROUSSEAU (*to her husband*)

My dear, I implore you!

### ROUSSEAU (*with decision*)

By heavens! I shall promise to this devil of a lawyer all that he asks of me; but Jules is at Brussels.

(*The door opens, Joseph cries out in alarm, but it is Dupré who enters.*)

---

## SCENE NINTH.

### THE SAME PERSONS AND DUPRÉ.

### DUPRÉ

How is this? (*Mme. du Brocard hands him the letter she has been writing; De Verby hands him his; and it is passed over to Rousseau who reads it with astonishment; De Verby casts a furious glance at Dupré and the Rousseau family, and dashes out of the room. To Rousseau*) And what decision have you made, sir?

### ROUSSEAU

I shall let my son do exactly what he wants in the matter

### MME. ROUSSEAU

Dear husband!

DUPRÉ (*aside*)

He thinks that Jules is out of town.

ROUSSEAU

At present Jules is at Brussels, and he must return at once.

DUPRÉ

That is perfectly fair! It is quite clear that I can't demand anything at this moment of you, so long as he is away; to do so would be absurd.

ROUSSEAU

Certainly! We can settle matters later.

DUPRÉ

Yes, as soon as he returns.

ROUSSEAU

Oh! as soon as he returns. (*Aside*) I will take pretty good care that he remains where he is.

DUPRÉ (*going towards the door on the left*)

Come in, young man, and thank your family, who have given their full consent to your marriage.

MME. ROUSSEAU

It is Jules!

MME. DU BROCARD

It is my nephew!

JULES

Can it be possible?

DUPRÉ (*darting towards another room*)

And you, Pamela, my child, my daughter!—embrace your husband! (*Jules rushes towards her.*)

MME. DU BROCARD (*to Rousseau*)

How has all this come about?

#### DUPRÉ

Pamela never was arrested. There is no likelihood of her ever being. I haven't a title of nobility. I am not the brother of a peer of France, but still I have some influence. The self-sacrifice of this poor girl has aroused the sympathy of the government—the indictment has been quashed. The Keeper of the Seals has sent me word of this by an orderly on horseback, whom this simpleton took for a regiment of soldiers in pursuit of him.

#### JOSEPH

It is very hard to see plainly through a garret window.

#### MME. DU BROCARD

Sir, you have caught us by surprise; I take back my promise.

#### DUPRÉ

But I still have possession of your letter. Do you wish to have a lawsuit about it? Very well, I will appear against you on the other side.

GIRAUD AND MME. GIRAUD (*entering and approaching Dupré*)

M. Dupré!

#### DUPRÉ

Are you satisfied with me? (*In the meantime Jules and Mme. Rousseau have been imploring Rousseau to yield his consent; he hesitates, but at last kisses Pamela on the forehead. Dupré approaches Rousseau and, seeing him kiss Pamela, wrings his hand.*) You have done well, sir. (*Then turning to Jules*) Will you make her happy?

#### JULES

Ah, my friend, you need not ask! (*Pamela kisses the hand of Dupré.*)

JOSEPH (*to Dupré*)

What a fool I have been! Well, he is going to marry her, and I am actually glad for them! But am I not to get something out of all this?

DUPRÉ

Certainly, you shall have all the fees that come to me from the lawsuit.

JOSEPH

You may count on my gratitude.

DUPRÉ

That will be receipt in full!

*Final Curtain.*

# INTRODUCTION

*La Marâtre* (The Stepmother) is characterized as an "intimate" drama in five acts and eight tableaux. It was first presented at the Théâtre-Historique, Paris, May 25, 1848. Its publication, by Michel Lévy in the same year, was in brochure form. The time is just a little later than that of *Pamela Giraud,* and one similar motif is found in the Napoleonic influence still at work for years after Waterloo. Though this influence is apparently far beneath the surface, and does not here manifest itself in open plottings, it is nevertheless vital enough to destroy the happiness of a home—when mixed in the mortar of a woman's jealousy. The action is confined to a single château in Normandy. A considerable psychological element is introduced. The play is a genuine tragedy, built upon tense, striking lines. It is strong and modern enough to be suitable, with some changes, for our present day stage. The day of the playwright's immaturity (noticed in the three preceding plays) is past. With this, as with all of Balzac's work, he improved by slow, laborious plodding, gaining experience from repeated efforts until success was attained.

In his dramas he was not to succeed at the first trial, nor the second, nor the third. But here at the fourth he has nearly grasped the secret of a successful play. While at the fifth—*Mercadet*—we are quite ready to cry "Bravo!" Who knows, if he had lived longer (these plays were written in the last years of their author's life), to what dramatic heights Balzac might have attained!

To *Mercadet* then we turn for the most striking example of the playwright's powers. This first appeared as *Le Faiseur* (The Speculator), being originally written in 1838-40. Justice compels us to state, however, that another hand is present in the perfected play. In the original it was a comedy in five acts; but this was revamped and reduced to three acts by M. d'Ennery, before its presentation at the Gymnase Théâtre, August 24, 1851. It was then re-christened *Mercadet,* and took its place as a 12mo brochure in the "Theatrical Library" in the same year. The original five-act version was first published as *Mercadet,* in *Le Pays,* August 28, 1851 (probably called forth by the presentation of the play four days earlier), and then appeared in book form, as *Le Faiseur,* from the press of Cadot, in 1853. It is of interest to note that the play was not presented till over a year subsequent to Balzac's death. The presented version in three acts has generally been regarded as the more acceptable, M. de Lovenjoul, the Balzacian commentator, recognizing its superior claims. It is the form now included in current French editions, and the one followed in the present volume.

Although *Mercadet,* like the others, excited the ridicule of supercilious critics, it has proven superior to them and to time. As early as the year 1869, the Comédie Française— the standard French stage—added *Mercadet* to its repertory; and more than one company in other theatres have scored success in its representation. The play contains situations full of bubbling humor and biting satire. Its motif is not sentiment. Instead, it inveighs against that spirit of greed and lust for gain which places a money value even upon affection. But during all the arraignment, Balzac, the born speculator, cannot conceal a sympathy for the wily Mercadet while the promoter's manœuvres to escape his creditors must have been a recollection in part of some of Balzac's own pathetic struggles.  For, like Dumas père, Balzac was never able to square the debit side of his books—be his income never so great.  The author of *César Birotteau* and *Le Maison Nucingen* here allows one more view of the seamy side of business.

Structurally, too, the play is successful.  With so great an element of chance in the schemes of the speculator, it would have been easy to transcend the limits of the probable.  But the author is careful to maintain his balances.  Situation succeeds plot, and catastrophe situation, until the final moment when the absconding partner actually arrives, to the astonishment of Mercadet more than all the rest.  And with Mercadet's joyful exclamation, "I am a creditor!" the play has reached its logical final curtain.

J. WALKER MCSPADDEN.

# THE STEPMOTHER

## A DRAMA IN FIVE ACTS

Presented for the First Time in Paris, at the Théâtre-Historique,
May 25, 1848.

# PERSONS OF THE PLAY

COMTE DE GRANDCHAMP, a Napoleonic General.
EUGÈNE RAMEL, a State's Attorney.
FERDINAND MARCANDAL.
DOCTOR VERNON.
GODARD.
AN INVESTIGATING MAGISTRATE.
FELIX, servant to Général de Grandchamp.
CHAMPAGNE, a foreman.
BAUDRILLON, a druggist.
NAPOLEON, son to Général de Grandchamp by his second wife.
GERTRUDE, second wife to Général de Grandchamp.
PAULINE, daughter to Général de Grandchamp by his first wife.
MARGUERITE, maid to Pauline.
GENDARMES, SHERIFF'S OFFICER, THE CLERGY.

SCENE: *Château of the Général de Grandchamp, near Louviers, Normandy.* TIME: 1829.

# THE STEPMOTHER

## ACT I.

### *SCENE FIRST.*

(*A richly decorated drawing-room; on the walls are portraits
of Napoleon I. and his son. The entry is by a large
double glass door, which opens on a roofed veranda and
leads by a short stairway to a park. The door of Pauline's apartments are on the right; those of the General
and his wife are on the left. On the left side of the
central doorway is a table, and on the right is a cabinet.
A vase full of flowers stands by the entrance to Pauline's
room. A richly carved marble mantel, with a bronze
clock and candelabras, faces these apartments. In the
front of the stage are two sofas, one on the left, the other
on the right. Gertrude enters, carrying the flowers
which she has just plucked, and puts them in the vase.*)

GERTRUDE AND THE GENERAL.

### GERTRUDE

I assure you, my dear, that it would be unwise to defer any
longer giving your daughter in marriage. She is now twenty-
two. Pauline has been very slow in making her choice ; and,
in such a case, it is the duty of parents to see that their children are settled. Moreover, I am very much interested in her.

### THE GENERAL

In what way?

### GERTRUDE

The position of a stepmother is always open to suspicion; and for some time it has been rumored in Louviers that I am the person who throws obstacles in the way of Pauline's marriage.

### THE GENERAL

That is merely the idle gossip of little towns. I should like to cut out some of those silly tongues. And to think that they should attack you of all people, Gertrude, who have been a real mother to Pauline—whom you have educated most excellently!

### GERTRUDE

It is the way of the world! They will never forgive us for living so close to the town, yet never entering it. The society of the place revenges itself upon us for slighting it. Do you think that our happiness can escape envy? Even our doctor—

### THE GENERAL

Do you mean Vernon?—

### GERTRUDE

Yes, Vernon is very envious of you; he is vexed to think that he has never been able to inspire any woman with such affection as I have for you. Moreover, he pretends that I am merely playing a part,—as if I could do it for twelve years! Rather unlikely, I should think.

### THE GENERAL

No woman could keep up the pretence for twelve years without being found out. The idea is absurd! and Vernon also is—

### GERTRUDE

Oh, he is only joking! And so, as I told you before, you had better see Godard. I am astonished that he has not yet arrived. He is so rich that it would be folly to refuse him. He is in love with Pauline, and although he has his faults, and is somewhat provincial, he is quite able to make her happy.

THE GENERAL

I have left Pauline quite free to choose a husband for herself.

GERTRUDE

There is no cause for anxiety. A girl so gentle, so well brought up, so well behaved, is sure to do right.

THE GENERAL

Gentle, did you say? She is headstrong, like her father.

GERTRUDE

She, headstrong? And you, come now, do you not always act as I wish?

THE GENERAL

You are an angel, and always wish what pleases me! By the bye, Vernon takes dinner with us after his autopsy.

GERTRUDE

Was it necessary to tell me that?

THE GENERAL

I only told you, in order that he might have his favorite wines.

FELIX (enters, announcing)

Monsieur de Rimonville!

THE GENERAL

Ask him in.

GERTRUDE (*making a sign to Felix to arrange the vase of flowers*)

I will go to Pauline's room, while you are talking business. I should like to superintend the arrangement of her toilet. Young people do not always understand what is most becoming to them.

### THE GENERAL

She has no expense spared her! During the last eighteen months her dress has cost twice as much as it previously did; after all, poor girl, it is the only amusement she has.

### GERTRUDE

How can you say it is her only amusement while she has the privilege of living with us! If it were not my happy lot to be your wife, I should like to be your daughter. I will never leave you, not I! Did you say for the last eighteen months? That is singular! Well, when I come to think of it, she has begun to care more about laces, jewels, and other pretty things.

### THE GENERAL

She is quite rich enough to indulge her tastes.

### GERTRUDE

And she is now of age. (*Aside*) Her fondness of dress is the smoke. Can there be any fire? (*Exit.*)

---

## SCENE SECOND.

### THE GENERAL (*alone*)

What a pearl among women! Thus I am made happy after twenty-six campaigns, a dozen wounds, and the death of an angel, whose place she has taken in my heart; truly a kind

Providence owed me some such recompense as this, if it were only to console me for the death of the Emperor.

---

## SCENE THIRD.

### GODARD AND THE GENERAL.

#### GODARD (*entering*)

Well, General!

#### THE GENERAL

Ah! good day, Godard! I hope you are come to spend the day with us?

#### GODARD

I thought perhaps I might spend the week, General, if you should regard favorably the request which I shall venture to make of you.

#### THE GENERAL

Go in and win! I know what request you mean—My wife is on your side. Ah, Godard, you have attacked the fortress at its weak point!

#### GODARD

General, you are an old soldier, and have no taste for mere phrases. In all your undertakings you go straight ahead, as you did when under fire.

#### THE GENERAL

Straight and facing the whole battery.

#### GODARD

That suits me well, for I am rather timid.

### The General

You! I owe you, my dear friend, an apology; I took you for a man who was too well aware of his own worth.

### Godard

You took me to be conceited! But General, as a matter of fact, I intend to marry because I don't know how to pay my court to women.

### The General (*aside*)

What a civilian! (*Aloud*) How is this? You talk like an old man, and—that is not the way to win my daughter.

### Godard

Do not misunderstand me. I have a warm heart; I wish only to feel sure that I shall be accepted.

### The General

That means that you don't mind attacking unwalled towns.

### Godard

That is not it at all, General. You quite alarm me with your banter.

### The General

What do you mean then?

### Godard

I understand nothing about the tricks of women. I know no more when their yes means no, than when their no means yes; and when I am in love, I wish to be loved in return.

### The General (*aside*)

With such ideas as those he has precious little chance.

GODARD

There are plenty of men like me, men who are supremely
bored by this little warfare of manners and whims.

THE GENERAL

But there is something also delightful in it,—I mean in the
feminine show of resistance, which gives one the pleasure of
overcoming it.

GODARD

Thank you, nothing of that sort for me! When I am hungry, I do not wish to coquette with my soup. I like to have
things decided, and care very little how the decision is arrived
at, although I do come from Normandy. In the world, I see
coxcombs who creep into the favor of women by saying to
them, "Ah! madame, what a pretty frock you have on. Your
taste is perfect. You are the only person who could wear
that," and starting from such speeches as that they go on
and on—and gain their end. They are wonderful fellows,
upon my honor! I don't see how they reach success by such
idle talk. I should beat about the bush through all eternity
before I could tell a pretty woman the effect she has made
on me.

THE GENERAL

The men of the Empire were not of that sort.

GODARD

It is on account of that, that I put on a bold face! This
boldness when backed by an income of forty thousand francs
is accepted without protest, and wins its way to the front.
That is why you took me for a good match. So long as there
are no mortgages on the rich pasture lands of the Auge Val-
ley, so long as one possesses a fine château, well furnished—for
my wife need bring with her nothing but her trousseau, since
she will find there even the cashmeres and laces of my late
mother—when a man has all that, General, he has got all the

courage he need have.   Besides, I am now Monsieur de Rimonville.

THE GENERAL

No, you're only Godard.

GODARD

Godard de Rimonville.

THE GENERAL

Godard for short.

GODARD

General, you are trying my patience.

THE GENERAL

As for me, it would try my patience to see a man, even if
he were my son-in-law, deny his father; and your father, a
right honest man, used himself to drive his beeves from Caen
to Poissy, and all along the road was known as Godard—
Father Godard.

GODARD

He was highly thought of.

THE GENERAL

He was, in his own class.   But I see what's the matter; as
his cattle provided you with an income of forty thousand
francs, you are counting upon other animals to give you
the name of De Rimonville.

GODARD

Now come, General, you had better consult Mlle. Pauline; she belongs to her own epoch—that she does.   We are
now in the year 1829 and Charles X. is king.   She would
sooner hear the valet call out, as she left a ballroom, "the
carriage of Madame de Rimonville," than, "the carriage of
Madame Godard."

### THE GENERAL

Well, if such silliness as this pleases my daughter, it makes no difference to me. For, after all, you would be the one they'd poke fun at, my dear Godard.

### GODARD

De Rimonville.

### THE GENERAL

Godard, you are a good fellow, you are young, you are rich, you say that you won't pay your court to women, but that your wife shall be the queen of your house. Well, if you gain her consent you can have mine; for bear in mind, Pauline will only marry the man she loves, rich or poor. There may be one exception, but that doesn't concern you. I would prefer to attend her funeral rather than take her to the registry office to marry a man who was a son, grandson, brother, nephew, cousin or connection of one of the four or five wretches who betrayed—you know what my religion is—

### GODARD

Betrayed the Emperor. Yes, everyone knows your creed, General.

### THE GENERAL

God, first of all; then France or the Emperor—It is all the same to me. Lastly, my wife and children! Whoever meddles with my gods becomes my enemy; I would kill him like a hare, remorselessly. My catechism is short, but it is good. Do you know why, in the year 1816, after their cursed disbanding of the army of the Loire, I took my little motherless child and came here, I, colonel of the Young Guard, wounded at Waterloo, and became a cloth manufacturer of Louviers?

### GODARD

I suppose you didn't wish to hold office under them.

### The General

No, because I did not wish to die as a murderer on the scaffold.

### Godard

What do you mean?

### The General

If I had met one of those traitors, I should have finished his business for him. Even to-day, after some fifteen years, my blood boils if I read their names in the newspaper or any one mentions them in my presence. And indeed, if I should meet one of them, nothing would prevent me from springing at his throat, tearing him to pieces, strangling him—

### Godard

You would do right. (*Aside*) I must humor him.

### The General

Yes, sir, I would strangle him! And if my son-in-law were to ill-treat my dear child, I would do the same to him.

### Godard

Ah!

### The General

I shouldn't wish him to be altogether under her thumb. A man ought to be king in his own house, as I am here.

### Godard (*aside*)

Poor man! How he deceives himself!

### The General

Did you speak?

### Godard

I said, General, that your threat had no terrors for me! When one has nothing but a wife to love, he loves her well.

THE GENERAL

Quite right, my dear Godard. And now with regard to the marriage settlement?

GODARD

Oh, yes!

THE GENERAL

My daughter's portion consists of—

GODARD

Consists of—

THE GENERAL

It comprises her mother's fortune and the inheritance of her uncle Boncoeur. It will be undivided, for I give up my rights to it. This will amount to three hundred and fifty thousand francs and a year's interest, for Pauline is twenty-two.

GODARD

This will make up three hundred and sixty-seven thousand five hundred francs.

THE GENERAL

No.

GODARD

Why not?

THE GENERAL

It will be more!

GODARD

More?—

THE GENERAL

Four hundred thousand francs. (*Godard seems astonished.*) I make up the difference! But when I die there will be nothing more coming to her. Do you understand?

GODARD

I do not understand.

THE GENERAL

I am very much attached to little Napoleon.

GODARD

You mean the young Duke of Reichstadt?

THE GENERAL

No, my son whom they would enter in the register only under the name of Leon; but I had inscribed here (*he places his hand upon his heart*) the name of Napoleon! Do you see I must provide for him and his mother.

GODARD (*aside*)

Especially for his mother; she'll take care of that!

THE GENERAL

What are you saying? If you don't agree with me, out with it!

GODARD (*aside*)

If I did so, we should find ourselves in the law courts. (*Aloud*) I agree, and will back you in everything, General.

GENERAL

Good for you! And I'll tell you why, my dear Godard.

GODARD

De Rimonville.

THE GENERAL

Godard, I prefer Godard. I'll tell you why. After having commanded the grenadiers of the Young Guard, I, Général Comte de Grandchamp, now weave the cloth for their uniforms.

GODARD

That is very commendable! You should keep on storing up, General, so that your widow may not be left without a fortune.

THE GENERAL

She is an angel, Godard!

GODARD

De Rimonville.

THE GENERAL

Godard, she is an angel, to whom you are indebted for the education of your intended, whom she has moulded after her own image. Pauline is a pearl, a jewel; she has never left this home; she is as pure and innocent as she was in her cradle.

GODARD

General, let me admit that Mlle. Pauline is beautiful!

THE GENERAL

I am quite sure of that.

GODARD

She is very beautiful; but there are numbers of beautiful girls in Normandy, some of them very rich, much richer than she is. Well now, you'll scarcely believe how the mothers and fathers of these heiresses run after me! It is scarcely decent. But it amuses me immensely; I visit their châteaus; they overwhelm me with attentions—

THE GENERAL

I said he was conceited!

GODARD

Oh, I am quite aware that it is not for my sake! I don't delude myself as to that; it is for my unmortgaged pastures:

for my savings, and for my habit of living within my income.
Do you know what it is that makes me seek an alliance with
you above all others?

### THE GENERAL

No.

### GODARD

There are certain rich would-be fathers-in-law who promise
to obtain from his Majesty a decree, by which I shall be
created Comte de Rimonville and Peer of France.

### THE GENERAL

You?

### GODARD

Yes, I.

### THE GENERAL

Have you won any battles? Have you saved your country?
Have you added to its glory? This is pitiful!

### GODARD

Pitiful? (*Aside*) What shall I say? (*Aloud*) We differ
in our views on this subject, but do you know why I prefer
your adorable Pauline?

### THE GENERAL

I suppose it is because you love her.

### GODARD

That is a matter of course; but it is also on account of the
harmony, the tranquillity, the happiness which reign here!
It is so delightful to enter a family of high honor, of pure,
sincere, patriarchal manners! I am a man of observation.

### THE GENERAL

That is to say, you are inquisitive.

GODARD

Curiosity, General, is the mother of observation. I know the seamy side of the whole department.

THE GENERAL

Really?

GODARD

Yes, really! In all the families of which I have spoken to you, I have seen some shabbiness or other. The public sees the decent exterior of irreproachable mothers of family, of charming young persons, of good fathers, of model uncles; they are admitted to the sacrament without confession, they are entrusted with the investments of others. But just learn their inner side, and it is enough to startle a police magistrate.

THE GENERAL

Ah! That is the way you look at the world, is it? For my part, I try to keep up the illusions in which I have lived. To peer into the inner life of people in that way is the business of priests and magistrates; I have no love for the black robed gentlemen, and I hope to die without ever having seen them! But the sentiment which you express with regard to my house is more pleasing to me than all your fortune. Stick to that point, and you will win my esteem, something which I lightly bestow on no one.

GODARD

Thank you, General. (*Aside*) I have won over the father-in-law at any rate.

_____

## SCENE FOURTH.

THE SAME PERSONS, PAULINE AND GERTRUDE.

THE GENERAL (*catching sight of Pauline*)
Ah! Here you are, darling.

GERTRUDE

Doesn't she look beautiful?

GODARD

Madame.

GERTRUDE

Forgive me, sir. I had no eyes excepting for my handi-work.

GODARD

Mademoiselle is radiant!

GERTRUDE

We have some people to dinner to-day, and I am something more than a stepmother to her; I love to deck her out, for she is to me like my own daughter.

GODARD (*aside*)

They were evidently expecting me!

GERTRUDE (*aside to Godard*)

I am going to leave you alone with her. Now is the time for your declaration. (*To the General*) My dear, let us go out on the veranda and see if our friend the doctor is coming.

THE GENERAL

I am at your service, as usual. (*To Pauline*) Good-bye, my pet. (*To Godard*) I shall see you later. (*Gertrude and the General go to the veranda, but Gertrude keeps her eye on Godard and Pauline. Ferdinand shows his head at the door of Pauline's chamber, but at a quick sign from her, he hurriedly withdraws it unobserved.*)

GODARD (*at the front of the stage*)

Let me see, what fine and dainty speech can I make to her?

Ah, I have it! (*To Pauline*) It is a very fine day, mademoiselle.

PAULINE

It certainly is, sir.

GODARD

Mademoiselle—

PAULINE

Sir?

GODARD

It is in your power to make the day still finer for me.

PAULINE

How can I do that?

GODARD

Don't you understand me? Has not Madame de Grandchamp said anything to you about the subject nearest my heart?

PAULINE

While she was helping me to dress, an instant ago, she said a great many complimentary things about you!

GODARD

And did you agree with her, even in the slightest way?

PAULINE

Oh, sir, I agreed with all she said!

GODARD (*seating himself on a chair, aside*)

So far so good. (*Aloud*) Did she commit a pardonable breach of confidence by telling you that I was so much in love with you that I wished to see you the mistress of Rimonville?

PAULINE

She gave me to understand by her hints that you were coming with the intention of paying me a very great compliment.

GODARD (*falling on his knees*)

I love you madly, mademoiselle; I prefer you to Mlle. de Blondville, to Mlle. de Clairville, to Mlle. de Verville, to Mlle de Pont-de-Ville—to—

PAULINE

Oh, that is sufficient, sir, you throw me into confusion by these proofs of a love which is quite unexpected! Your victims make up almost a hecatomb. (*Godard rises.*) Your father was contented with taking the victims to market! but you immolate them.

GODARD (*aside*)

I really believe she is making fun of me. But wait awhile! wait awhile!

PAULINE

I think at least that we ought to wait awhile; and I must confess—

GODARD

You do not wish to marry yet. You are happy with your parents, and you are unwilling to leave your father.

PAULINE

That is it, exactly.

GODARD

In that case, there are some mothers who would agree that their daughter was too young, but as your father admits that you are twenty-two I thought that you might possibly have a desire to be settled in life.

PAULINE

Sir!

GODARD

You are, I know, quite at liberty to decide both your own destiny and mine; but in accordance with the wishes of your father and of your second mother, who imagine that your heart is free, may I be permitted still to have hope?

PAULINE

Sir, however flattering to me may be your intention in thus seeking me out, that does not give you any right to question me so closely.

GODARD (*aside*)

Is it possible I have a rival? (*Aloud*) No one, mademoiselle, gives up the prospect of happiness without a struggle.

PAULINE

Do you still continue in this strain? I must leave you, sir.

GODARD

Thank you, mademoiselle. (*Aside*) So much for your sarcasm!

PAULINE

Come sir, you are rich, and nature has given you a fine person; you are so well educated and so witty that you will have no difficulty in finding some young person richer and prettier than I am.

GODARD

How can that be when one is in love?

PAULINE

Well sir, that is the very point.

GODARD (*aside*)

She is in love with some one; I must find out who it is. (*Aloud*) Mademoiselle, will you at least permit me to feel that I am not in disgrace and that I may stay here a few days?

### PAULINE

My father will answer you on that score.

### GERTRUDE (*coming forward to Godard*)

Well, how are things going?

### GODARD

A blunt refusal, without even a hope of her relenting; her heart is evidently already occupied.

### GERTRUDE (*to Godard*)

Her heart occupied? This child has been brought up by me, and I know to the contrary; and besides that, no one ever comes here. (*Aside*) This youth has roused in me suspicions which pierce my heart like a dagger. (*To Godard*) Why don't you ask her if such is the case?

### GODARD

How could I ask her anything? At my first word of jealous suspicion, she resented my curiosity.

### GERTRUDE

Well, I shall have no hesitation in questioning her.

### THE GENERAL

Ah, here comes the doctor! We shall now learn the truth concerning the death of Champagne's wife.

---

## SCENE FIFTH.

### THE SAME PERSONS AND DR. VERNON.

### THE GENERAL

Well, how are you?

**VERNON**

I was quite sure of it. Ladies (*he bows to them*), as a general rule when a man beats his wife, he takes care not to poison her; he would lose too much by that. He doesn't want to be without a victim.

**THE GENERAL** (*to Godard*)

He is a charming fellow!

**GODARD**

Charming!

**THE GENERAL** (*to the doctor, presenting Godard to him*)

M. Godard.

**GODARD**

De Rimonville.

**VERNON** (*looking at Godard*)

If he kills her, it is by mistake from having hit her a little too hard; and he is overwhelmed with grief; while Champagne is innocently delighted to have been made a widower by natural causes. As a matter of fact, his wife died of cholera. It was a very rare case, but he who has once seen Asiatic cholera cannot forget it, and I am glad that I had that opportunity; for, since the campaign in Egypt, I have never met with a case. If I had been called in in time I could have saved her.

**GERTRUDE**

How fortunate we are, for if a crime had been committed in this establishment, which for twelve years has been so free from disturbance, I should have been horrified.

**THE GENERAL**

Here you see the effect of all this tittle-tattle. But are you quite certain, Vernon?

### VERNON

Am I certain?  That's a fine question to put to a retired surgeon-in-chief who has attended twelve French armies, from 1793 to 1815, and has practiced in Germany, in Spain, in Italy, in Russia, in Poland, and in Egypt!

### THE GENERAL (*poking him in the ribs*)

Away, you charlatan!  I reckon you have killed more peo ple than I have in those countries.

### GODARD

What is this talk that you are alluding to?

### GERTRUDE

This poor Champagne, our foreman, was supposed to have poisoned his wife.

### VERNON

Unhappily, the night before she died, they had had an altercation which ended in blows.  Ah! they don't take example from their masters.

### GODARD

Such happiness as reigns here ought to be contagious, but the virtues which are exemplified in the countess are very rare.

### GERTRUDE

Is there any merit in loving an excellent husband and a daughter such as these?

### THE GENERAL

Come, Gertrude, say no more! such words ought not to be spoken in public.

### VERNON (*aside*)

Such things are always said in this way, when it is necessary to make people believe them.

THE GENERAL (*to Vernon*)

What are you muttering about?


VERNON

I was saying that I was sixty-seven years old, and that I was younger than you are, and that I should wish to be loved like that. (*Aside*) If only I could be sure that it was love.


THE GENERAL (*to the doctor*)

I see you are dubious! (*To his wife*) My dear child, there is no need for me to bless the power of God on your behalf, but I think He must have lent it me, in order that I might love you sufficiently.


VERNON

You forget that I am a doctor, my dear friend. What you are saying to Madame is only good for the burden of a ballad.


GERTRUDE

The burdens of some ballads, doctor, are exceedingly true.


THE GENERAL

Doctor, if you continue teasing my wife, we shall quarrel; to doubt on such a subject as that is an insult.


VERNON

I have no doubt about it. (*To the General*) I would merely say, that you have loved so many women with the power of God, that I am in an ecstasy as a doctor to see you still so good a Christian at seventy! (*Gertrude glides softly towards the sofa, where the doctor is seated.*)


THE GENERAL

Pshaw! The last passions, my friend, are always the strongest.

### VERNON

You are right. In youth, we love with all our strength which grows weaker with age, while in age we love with all our weakness which is ever on the increase.

### THE GENERAL

Oh, vile philosophy!

### GERTRUDE (*to Vernon*)

Doctor, how is it that you, who are so good, try to infuse doubts into the heart of Grandchamp? You know that he is so jealous that he would kill a man on suspicion. I have such respect for his feelings that I have concluded upon seeing no one, but you, the mayor and the curé. Do you want me also to forego your society which is so pleasant, so agreeable to us? Ah! Here is Napoleon.

### VERNON (*aside*)

I take this for a declaration of war. She has sent away every one else, she intends to dismiss me.

### GODARD (*to Vernon*)

Doctor, you are an intimate friend of the house, tell me, pray, what do you think of Mlle. Pauline? (*The doctor rises from his seat, looks at the speaker, blows his nose, and goes to the middle of the stage. The dinner bell sounds.*)

---

*SCENE SIXTH.*

THE SAME PERSONS, NAPOLEON AND FELIX.

### NAPOLEON

Papa, papa, didn't you say I could ride Coco?

THE GENERAL

Certainly.

NAPOLEON (*to Felix*)

Do you hear that?

GERTRUDE (*wiping her son's forehead*)

He is quite warm!

THE GENERAL

But only on condition that some one goes with you.

FELIX

You see I was right, Master Napoleon. General, the little rascal wished to go on his pony alone into the country.

NAPOLEON

He was frightened for me! Do you think I am afraid of anything? (*Exit Felix. Dinner bell rings.*)

THE GENERAL

Come and let me kiss you for that word. He is a little soldier and belongs to the Young Guard

VERNON (*with a glance at Gertrude*)

He takes after his father!

GERTRUDE (*quickly*)

As regards courage, he is his father's counterpart; but as to physique, he resembles me.

FELIX

Dinner is served.

GERTRUDE

Very well! But do you know where Ferdinand is? He is generally so punctual. Here, Napoleon, go to the entrance of the factory and see if he is coming. Tell him to hurry; the bell has rung.

THE GENERAL

We need not wait for Ferdinand. Godard, give your arm to Pauline. (*Vernon offers his arm to .Gertrude.*) Excuse me, Vernon, you ought to be aware that I never permit anybody but myself to take my wife's arm.

VERNON (*aside*)

Decidedly, he is incurable.

NAPOLEON (*running back*)

I saw Ferdinand down in the main avenue.

VERNON

Give me your hand, you little tyrant!

NAPOLEON

Tyrant yourself! I'll bet I could tire you out. (*He turns Vernon round and round. All leave, chatting gaily.*)

_____

### SCENE SEVENTH.

FERDINAND (*cautiously stealing from Pauline's room*)

The youngster saved me, but I do not know how he happened to see me in the avenue! One more piece of carelessness like this may ruin us! I must extricate myself from this situation at any price. Here is Pauline refusing Godard's proposal. The General, and especially Gertrude, will try to find out the motives of her refusal! But I must hasten to reach the veranda, so that I may have the appearance of having come from the main avenue, as Leon said. I hope no one will catch sight of me from the dining-room. (*He meets Ramel.*) What, Eugène Ramel!

## SCENE EIGHTH.

### FERDINAND AND RAMEL.

#### RAMEL

You here, Marcandal!

#### FERDINAND

Hush! Don't pronounce that name in this place! If the General heard that my name was Mercandal, he would kill me at once as if I were a mad dog.

#### RAMEL

And why?

#### FERDINAND

Because I am the son of General Marcandal.

#### RAMEL

A general to whom the Bourbons are in part indebted for their second innings.

#### FERDINAND

In the eyes of General Grandchamp, to leave Napoleon for service under the Bourbons was treason against France. Alas! this was also my father's opinion, for he died of grief. You must therefore remember to call me by the name of Ferdinand Charny, my mother's maiden name.

#### RAMEL

And what are you doing here?

#### FERDINAND

I am the manager, the cashier, the factotum of Grandchamp's factory.

#### RAMEL

How is this? Do you do it from necessity?

### FERDINAND

From dire necessity! My father spent everything, even the fortune of my poor mother, who lived during her latter years in Brittany on the pension she received as widow of a lieutenant-general.

### RAMEL

How is it that your father, who had command of the Royal Guard, a most brilliant position, died without leaving you anything, not even a patron?

### FERDINAND

Had he never betrayed his friends, and changed sides, without any reason—

### RAMEL

Come, come, we won't talk any more about that.

### FERDINAND

My father was a gambler—that was the reason why he was so indulgent to me. But may I ask what has brought you here?

### RAMEL

A fortnight ago I was appointed king's attorney at Louviers.

### FERDINAND

I heard something about it. But the appointment was published under another name.

### RAMEL

De la Grandière, I suppose.

### FERDINAND

That is it.

### RAMEL

In order that I might marry Mlle. de Boudeville, I obtained

permission to assume my mother's name—as you have done.
The Boudeville family have given me their protection, and in
a year's time I shall doubtless be attorney-general at Rouen—
a stepping-stone towards a position at Paris.

### FERDINAND

And what brings you to our quiet factory?

### RAMEL

I came to investigate a criminal case, a poisoning affair,—a
fine introduction into my office.  (*Felix enters.*)

### FELIX

Monsieur, Madame is worrying about you—

### FERDINAND

Please ask her to excuse me for a few moments.  (*Exit
Felix.*)  My dear Eugène, in case the General—who like all
retired troopers is very inquisitive—should **inquire** how we
happen to meet here, don't forget to say that we came up
the main avenue.  It is important for me that you should
say so.  But go on with your story.  It is on account of the
wife of Champagne, our foreman, that you have come here;
but he is innocent as a new-born babe!

### RAMEL

You believe so, do you?  Well, the officers of justice are
paid for being incredulous.  I see that you still remain, as I
left you, the noblest, the most enthusiastic fellow in the world;
in short, a poet!  A poet who puts the poetry into his life
instead of writing it, and believes in the good and the beautiful!  And that reminds me—that angel of your dreams, that
Gertrude of yours, whatever has become of her?

### FERDINAND

Hush!  Not only has the minister of justice sent you here,

but some celestial influence has sent to me at Louviers the friend whose help I need in my terrible perplexity. Eugène, come here and listen to me awhile. I am going to appeal to you as my college friend, as the confidant of my youth; you won't put on the airs of the prosecuting attorney to me, will you? You will see from the nature of my admissions that I impose upon you the secrecy of the confessional.

### RAMEL

Is it anything criminal?

### FERDINAND

Oh, nonsense! My faults are such as the judges themselves would be willing to commit.

### RAMEL

Perhaps I had better not listen to you; or, if I do listen to you—

### FERDINAND

Well!

### RAMEL

I could demand a change of position.

### FERDINAND

You are always my best and kindest friend. Listen then! For over three years I have been in love with Mlle. Pauline de Grandchamp, and she—

### RAMEL

You needn't go on; I understand. You have been reviving *Romeo and Juliet*—in the heart of Normandy.

### FERDINAND

With this difference, that the hereditary hatred which stood between the two lovers of the play was a mere trifle in

comparison with the loathing with which the Comte de Grandchamp contemplates the son of the traitor Marcandal!

### RAMEL

Let me see! Mlle. Pauline de Grandchamp will be free
in three years; she is rich in her own right—I know this
from the Boudevilles. You can easily take her to Switzerland
and keep her there until the General's wrath has had time to
cool; and then you can make him the respectful apologies
required under the circumstances.

### FERDINAND

Do you think I would have asked your advice if the only
difficulty lay in the attainment of this trite and easy solution
of the problem?

### RAMEL

Ah! I see, my dear friend. You have already married
your Gertrude—your angel—who has become to you like all
other angels, after their metamorphoses into a lawful wives.

### FERDINAND

'Tis a hundred times worse than that! Gertrude, my dear
sir, is now Madame de Grandchamp.

### RAMEL

Oh, dear! how is it you've thrust yourself into such a
hornets' nest?

### FERDINAND

In the same way that people always thrust themselves into
hornets' nests; that is, with the hope of finding honey there.

### RAMEL

Oh, oh! This is a very serious matter! Now, really, you
must conceal nothing from me.

### FERDINAND

Mlle. Gertrude de Meilhac, educated at St. Denis, without doubt loved me first of all through ambition; she was glad to know that I was rich, and did all she could to gain my attachment with a view to marriage.

### RAMEL

Such is the game of all these intriguing orphan girls.

### FERDINAND

But how came it about that Gertrude has ended by loving me so sincerely? For her passion may be judged by its effects. I call it a passion, but with her it is first love, sole and undivided love, which dominates her whole life, and seems to consume her. When she found that I was a ruined man, towards the close of the year 1816, and knowing that I was like you, a poet, fond of luxury and art, of a soft and happy life, in short, a mere spoilt child, she formed a plan at once base and sublime, such a plan as disappointed passion suggests to women who, for the sake of their love, do all that despots do for the sake of their power; for them, the supreme law is that of their love—

### RAMEL

The facts, my dear fellow, give me the facts! You are making your defence, recollect, and I am prosecuting attorney.

### FERDINAND

While I was settling my mother in Brittany, Gertrude met General de Grandchamp, who was seeking a governess for his daughter. She saw nothing in this battered warrior, then fifty-eight years old, but a money-box. She expected that she would soon be left a widow, wealthy and in circumstances to claim her lover and her slave. She said to herself that her marriage would be merely a bad dream, followed quickly by a happy awakening. You see the dream has lasted twelve years! But you know how women reason.

#### RAMEL

They have a special jurisprudence of their own.

#### FERDINAND

Gertrude is a woman of the fiercest jealousy. She wishes for fidelity in her lover to recompense her for her infidelity to her husband, and as she has suffered martyrdom, she says, she wishes—

#### RAMEL

To have you in the same house with her, that she may keep watch over you herself.

#### FERDINAND

She has been successful in getting me here. For the last three years I have been living in a small house near the factory. I should have left the first week after my arrival, but that two days' acquaintance with Pauline convinced me that I could not live without her.

#### RAMEL

Your love for Pauline, it seems to me as a magistrate, makes your position here somewhat less distasteful.

#### FERDINAND

My position? I assure you, it is intolerable, among the three characters with whom I am cast. Pauline is daring, like all young persons who are innocent, to whom love is a wholly ideal thing, and who see no evil in anything, so long as it concerns a man whom they intend to marry. The penetration of Gertrude is very acute, but we manage to elude it through Pauline's terror lest my name should be divulged; the sense of this danger gives her strength to dissemble! But now Pauline has just refused Godard, and I do not know what may be the consequences.

#### RAMEL

I know Godard; under a somewhat dull exterior he conceals great sagacity, and he is the most inquisitive man in the department. Is he here now?

### FERDINAND

He dines here to-day.

### RAMEL

Do not trust him.

### FERDINAND

Good! If two women, between whom there is no love lost, make the discovery that they are rivals, one of them, I can't say which, would be capable of killing the other; for one is strong in innocence and lawful love; the other, furious to see the fruit of so much dissimulation, so many sacrifices, even crimes, lost to her forever. (*Enter Napoleon.*)

### RAMEL

You alarm me—me, the prosecuting attorney! Upon my word and honor, women often cost more than they are worth.

### NAPOLEON

Dear friend! Papa and mamma are impatient about you; they send word that you must leave your business, and Vernon says that your stomach requires it.

### FERDINAND

You little rogue! You are come eavesdropping!

### NAPOLEON

Mamma whispered in my ear: "Go and see what your friend is doing."

### FERDINAND

Run away, you little scamp! Be off! I am coming. (*To Ramel*) You see she makes this innocent child a spy over me. (*Exit Napoleon.*)

RAMEL

Is this the General's child?

FERDINAND

Yes.

RAMEL

He is twelve years old?

FERDINAND

About.

RAMEL

Have you anything more to tell me?

FERDINAND

Really, I think I have told you enough.

RAMEL

Very well! Go and get your dinner. Say nothing of my arrival, nor of my purpose here. Let them finish their dinner in peace. Now go at once. (*Exit Ferdinand.*)

---

## SCENE NINTH.

RAMEL (*alone*)

Poor fellow! If all young people had studied the annals of the court, as I have done in seven years of a magistrate's work, they would come to the conclusion that marriage must be accepted as the sole romance which is possible in life. But if passion could control itself, it would be virtue.

*Curtain to First Act.*

# ACT II.

---

## *SCENE FIRST.*

### *(Stage setting remains as in Act I.)*

### RAMEL AND MARGUERITE; LATER, FELIX.

*(Ramel is buried in his reflections, reclining on the sofa in such a way as to be almost out of sight. Marguerite brings in lights and cards. Night is approaching.)*

#### MARGUERITE

Four card tables—that will be enough, even though the curé, the mayor and his assistant come. (*Felix lights the candles.*) I'll wager anything that my poor Pauline will not be married this time. Dear child! If her late mother were to see that she was not the queen of the house, she would weep in her coffin! I only remain here in order to comfort and to wait upon her.

#### FELIX (*aside*)

What is this old woman grumbling about? (*Aloud*) Whom are you complaining of now, Marguerite? I'll bet it is the mistress.

#### MARGUERITE

No, it is not; I am blaming the master.

#### FELIX

The General? You had better mind your own business. He is a saint, is that man.

#### MARGUERITE

Yes, a stone saint, for he is blind.

FELIX

You had better say that he has been blinded.


MARGUERITE

You hit the nail on the head there.


FELIX

The General has but one fault—he is jealous.


MARGUERITE

Yes, and obstinate, too.


FELIX

Yes, obstinate; it is the same thing. When once he suspects anything he comes down like a hammer. That was the way he laid two men lifeless at a blow. Between ourselves, there is only one way to treat a trooper of that sort: you must stuff him with flattery. And the mistress certainly does stuff him. Besides, she is clever enough to put blinkers on him, such as they put on shying horses; he can see neither to the right nor to the left, and she says to him, "My dear, look straight ahead!" So she does!


MARGUERITE

Ah! You think with me that a woman of thirty-two does not love a man of seventy without some object. She is scheming something.


RAMEL (*aside*)

Oh, these servants! whom we pay to spy over us!


FELIX

What can be her scheme? She never leaves the house, she never sees any one.


MARGUERITE

She would skin a flint! She has taken away the keys from

me—from me who always had the confidence of the former
mistress; do you know why she did so?

### FELIX

I suppose she is saving up her pile.

### MARGUERITE

Yes, out of the fortune of Mlle. Pauline, and the profits
of the factory. That is the reason why she puts off the marriage of the dear child as long as she can, for she has to give
up her fortune when she marries her.

### FELIX

Yes, that's the law.

### MARGUERITE

I would forgive her everything, if only she made Made-
mioselle happy; but I sometimes catch my pet in tears, and
I ask her what is the matter, and she says nothing but "Good
Marguerite!" (*Exit Felix.*) Let me see, have I done everything? Yes, here are the card tables—the candles—the cards
—Ah! the sofa. (*She catches sight of Ramel*) Good Lord! a
stranger!

### RAMEL

Don't be startled, Marguerite.

### MARGUERITE

You must have heard all we said.

### RAMEL

Don't be alarmed. My business is to keep secrets. I am the
state's attorney.

### MARGUERITE

Oh!

## *SCENE SECOND.*

THE SAME PERSONS, PAULINE, GODARD, VERNON, NAPOLEON,
FERDINAND, THE GENERAL, MADAME
DE GRANDCHAMP.

(*Gertrude rushes to Marguerite and snatches the cushions
from her hands.*)

#### GERTRUDE

Marguerite, you know very well what pain you give me, by
not allowing me to do everything for your master; besides, I
am the only one who knows how to arrange the cushions to his
liking.

#### MARGUERITE (*to Pauline*)

What a to-do about nothing!

#### GODARD

Why, look! Here is the state's attorney!

#### THE GENERAL

The state's attorney at my house?

#### GERTRUDE

I am surprised!

#### THE GENERAL (*to Ramel*)

Sir, what brings you here?

#### RAMEL

I asked my friend, M. Ferdinand Mar—(*Ferdinand checks
him by a gesture. Gertrude and Pauline look at him in
alarm*).

#### GERTRUDE (*aside*)

It is his friend, Eugène Ramel.

### Ramel

My friend, Ferdinand de Charny, to whom I have told the object of my visit, to say nothing about it until you had finished your dinner.

### The General

Ferdinand then is your friend?

### Ramel

I have known him from childhood; and here we met in your avenue. On meeting, after nine years of separation, we had so many things to talk about, that I caused him to be late.

### The General

But, sir, to what circumstance am I to attribute your presence here?

### Ramel

I come in the matter of Jean Nicot, known as Champagne, your foreman, who is charged with a crime.

### Gertrude

But, sir, our friend, Doctor Vernon, has declared that Champagne's wife died a natural death.

### Vernon

Yes, sir, cholera.

### Ramel

Justice, sir, believes in nothing but investigations and convictions of its own. You did wrong to proceed before my arrival.

### Felix

Madame, shall I bring in the coffee?

### Gertrude

Wait awhile! (*Aside*) How changed this man is, this attorney. I shouldn't have recognized him. He terrifies me.

THE GENERAL

But how could you be brought here by the crime of Champagne, an old soldier for whom I would stand security?


RAMEL

You will learn that, on the arrival of the investigating magistrate.

THE GENERAL

Will you be pleased to take a seat?


FERDINAND (*to Ramel, pointing out Pauline*)

That is she!


RAMEL

A man might lay down his life for such a lovely girl.


GERTRUDE (*to Ramel*)

We do not know each other! You have never seen me, have you? You must have pity on us!


RAMEL

You may depend upon me for that.


THE GENERAL (*who sees Ramel and Gertrude talking together*)

Is my wife to be called to this investigation?


RAMEL

Certainly, General. I came here myself because the countess had not been notified that we required her presence.


THE GENERAL

My wife mixed up in such an affair? It is an outrage!

VERNON

Keep cool, my friend.

FELIX (*announcing*)

Monsieur, the investigating magistrate!

THE GENERAL

Let him come in.

---

## SCENE THIRD.

THE SAME PERSONS, THE INVESTIGATING MAGISTRATE, CHAMPAGNE, BAUDRILLON AND A GENDARME WHO IS GUARDING CHAMPAGNE.

THE MAGISTRATE (*bowing to the company*)

Monsieur the state's attorney, this is M. Baudrillon, the druggist.

RAMEL

Has M. Baudrillon seen the accused?

THE MAGISTRATE

No, monsieur, the accused came in charge of a gendarme.

RAMEL

We shall soon learn the truth in this case! Let M. Baudrillon and the accused approach.

THE MAGISTRATE

Come forward, M. Baudrillon; (*to Champagne*) and you also.

RAMEL

M. Baudrillon, do you identify this man as the person who bought arsenic from you two days ago?

BAUDRILLON

Yes, that is the very man.

CHAMPAGNE

Didn't I tell you, M. Baudrillon, that it was for the mice that were eating up everything, even in the house, and that I wanted it for Madame?

THE MAGISTRATE

Do you hear him, madame? This is his plea; he pretends that you yourself sent him to get this stuff, and that he handed the package to you just as he took it from M. Baudrillon.

GERTRUDE

It is true, sir.

RAMEL

Did you make any use of the arsenic, madame?

GERTRUDE

No, sir.

THE MAGISTRATE

You can then show us the package sent by M. Baudrillon; it should have his label, and if he acknowledges that it is entire and unbroken, the serious charges made against your foreman will in part be disproved. We shall then have nothing more to do than to receive the report of the physician who held the autopsy.

GERTRUDE

The package, sir, has never been taken from the desk in my bedroom. (*Exit.*)

CHAMPAGNE

Ah! General, I am saved!

THE GENERAL

Poor old Champagne!

RAMEL

General, we shall be very happy if we have to announce the

innocence of your foreman; unlike you soldiers, we are always delighted to be beaten.

### GERTRUDE (*returning*)

Here it is, gentlemen. (*The magistrate, Baudrillon and Ramel examine the package.*)

### BAUDRILLON (*putting on his glasses*)

It is intact, gentlemen, perfectly intact. Here is my seal on it unbroken.

### THE MAGISTRATE

Lock that up carefully, madame, for the assizes for some time have had to deal with nothing but poisoning cases.

### GERTRUDE

You see, sir, I have kept it in my desk, to which none but the General and myself have access. (*She returns to her bedroom.*)

### RAMEL

General, we will not wait for the report of the autopsy. The principal charge, which you will agree with me was very serious, for all the town was talking of it, has been disproved; and as we have full confidence in the skill and integrity of Doctor Vernon, (*Gertrude returns*) Champagne, you are at liberty. (*General expression of satisfaction.*) But you see, my friend, to what painful suspicions a man exposes himself when his home has a bad name.

### CHAMPAGNE

Ask the General, your Honor, if I am not mild as a lamb; but my wife, God forgive her, was the worst that was ever made. An angel could not have stood her. If I have sometimes tried to bring her to reason, the anxious moments you have made me pass here, have been punishment enough! To be taken up for a prisoner, and to know yourself innocent, while you are in the hands of justice! (*Weeps.*)

### The General

Well! well! You are acquitted now!

### Napoleon

Papa, what is justice?

### The General

Gentlemen, justice ought not to commit errors of this kind

### Gertrude

There seems to be always something fatal in this justice! And this poor man will always bear a bad name from your arrival here.

### Ramel

Madame, for the innocent there is nothing fatal in criminal justice. You see that Champagne has been promptly dis-charged. (*Fixing his eyes on Gertrude.*) Those who live without reproach, who indulge no passions, save the noble and the lawful, have nothing to fear from justice.

### Gertrude

Sir, you do not know the people of this country. Ten years from this time they will say that Champagne poisoned his wife, that the officers of justice came to investigate and, but for our protection—

### The General

Say no more, Gertrude. These gentlemen have done only their duty. (*Felix prepares the coffee.*) Gentlemen, can I offer you a cup of coffee?

### The Magistrate

Thank you, General; the urgency of this affair called me

away from home rather suddenly, and my wife is waiting din·
ner for me at Louviers. (*He goes on the veranda to talk with
the doctor.*)

### THE GENERAL (*to Ramel*)

You are a friend of Ferdinand's, I believe?

### RAMEL

Yes, General, and you have in him the noblest heart, the
most spotless integrity, the most charming character that I
have ever met.

### PAULINE

This state's attorney seems to be a very kind man!

### GODARD (*aside*)

And why does she say that? Is it because he praised M.
Ferdinand? Ah! there's something there!

### GERTRUDE (*to Ramel*)

Whenever you have any moments to spare, you must come
to see M. de Charny. (*To the General*) Would not that be
nice, dear?

### THE MAGISTRATE (*coming in from the veranda*)

M. de la Grandière, our physician, agrees with Doctor Vernon that this death resulted from Asiatic cholera. We beg,
therefore, that you, countess, and you, count, will excuse us
for having disturbed, even for a moment, the tranquillity
of your charming household.

### RAMEL (*to Gertrude in the front of the stage*)

Take care! God never protects undertakings so rash as
yours. I have discovered all. Give up Ferdinand, leave his
life free, and be satisfied with the happiness of a wife. The
path which you are following leads to crime.

GERTRUDE

I'll die before I give him up!

RAMEL (*aside*)

I must get Ferdinand away from this place. (*Beckons to Ferdinand, takes his arm, and goes out with him after exchange of formal bows.*)

THE GENERAL

At last we are rid of them! (*To Gertrude*) Let the coffee be handed round.

GERTRUDE

Pauline, kindly ring for the coffee. (*Pauline rings.*)

---

## SCENE FOURTH.

THE SAME PERSONS, EXCEPTING FERDINAND, RAMEL, THE MAGISTRATE AND BAUDRILLON.

GODARD (*aside*)

I shall find out presently whether Pauline loves Ferdinand. This urchin, who wants to know about justice, seems to me pretty cute; I'll make use of him. (*Felix appears.*)

GERTRUDE

The coffee. (*Felix brings in the tray.*)

GODARD (*who has taken Napoleon aside*)

Would you like to play a nice trick on somebody?

NAPOLEON

That I would. Do you know one?

#### GODARD

Come with me, and I'll tell you how you must do it. (*Godard goes on veranda with Napoleon.*)

#### THE GENERAL

Pauline, my coffee. (*Pauline brings it to him.*) It isn't sweet enough. (*Pauline gives him some sugar.*) Thank you, dear.

#### GERTRUDE

M. de Rimonville?

#### THE GENERAL

Godard?

#### GERTRUDE

M. de Rimonville?

#### THE GENERAL

Godard, my wife wants to know if you would like some coffee?

#### GODARD

Yes, thank you. (*He places himself in such way as to watch Pauline.*)

#### THE GENERAL

It is pleasant to sit down and take a little coffee in quiet!

#### NAPOLEON (*running in*)

Mamma, mamma! My good friend Ferdinand has just fallen down; he has broken his leg and they are carrying him into the house.

#### VERNON

That's dreadful!

#### THE GENERAL

How very unfortunate!

### PAULINE

Oh! (*Falls back on her chair.*)

### GERTRUDE

What is that you said?

### NAPOLEON

It is all a joke! I only wished to see if you all loved my good friend.

### GERTRUDE

It is very naughty of you to act in that way; how did you come to think of such a trick?

### NAPOLEON (*whispering*)

It was Godard.

### GODARD (*aside*)

She loves him! She was nicely caught by my trap, which I have never known to fail.

### GERTRUDE (*to Godard, as she offers him some coffee*)

Are you aware, sir, that you would make a very indifferent preceptor? It is very bad of you to teach a child such mischievous tricks.

### GODARD

You will come to the conclusion that I did pretty well, when you learn that I have been enabled by this little stratagem to discover my rival. (*He points to Ferdinand who is entering the room.*)

### GERTRUDE (*letting fall the sugar basin*)

He!

### GODARD (*aside*)

She is in the same box!

GERTRUDE (*aloud*)

You startled me.

THE GENERAL (*who has risen from his seat*)
What is the matter with you, my dear child?

GERTRUDE

Nothing; it is Godard's nonsense; he told me that the public prosecutor had come back. Felix, take away this sugar basin, and bring me another one.

VERNON

This is a day of surprises.

GERTRUDE

M. Ferdinand, they are going to bring some sugar for you. (*Aside*) He is not looking at her. (*Aloud*) How is it, Pauline, you did not put any sugar in your father's coffee?

NAPOLEON

Why, of course, it was because she was too scared; didn't you hear her say "oh!"?

PAULINE

Won't you hold your tongue, you little story-teller! You are always teasing me. (*She sits on her father's knee, and puts sugar in his cup.*)

GERTRUDE

Can it be true? And to think that I have taken such pains in dressing her! (*To Godard*) If you are right, your marriage will take place in a fortnight. (*Aloud*) M. Ferdinand, here is your coffee.

GODARD (*aside*)

It seems that I caught two in my mouse-trap! And all

the time the General is so calm, so tranquil, and this household is so peaceful! Things are getting mixed up. I shan't
go yet; I wish to have a game of whist! Oh! I give up all
thoughts of marriage for the present. (*Glancing at Ferdinand*) There's a lucky fellow! He is loved by two women—
two charming, delightful creatures! He is indeed a factotum!
But how is it that he is more successful than I am, who have
an income of forty thousand?

### GERTRUDE

Pauline, my dear, offer the cards to the gentlemen for a
game of whist. It is almost nine o'clock. If they are going
to have a game, there is no time to be lost. (*Pauline puts out
the cards.*) Come, Napoleon, bid good-night to the gentlemen, let them see you are a good boy, and don't try to stay
up as you usually do.

### NAPOLEON

Good-night, papa. What is justice like?

### THE GENERAL

Justice is blind! Good-night, my pet.

### NAPOLEON

Good-night, M. Vernon! What is justice made of?

### VERNON

It is made up of all our crimes. When you are naughty,
they whip you; that is justice.

### NAPOLEON

They never whip me.

### VERNON

Then they never do justice to you!

### NAPOLEON

Good-night, my good friend! Good-night, Pauline! Good-night, M. Godard—

### GODARD

De Rimonville.

### NAPOLEON

Have I been good? (*Gertrude kisses him.*)

### THE GENERAL

I have the king.

### VERNON

And I, the queen.

### FERDINAND (*to Godard*)

Monsieur, we are partners.

### GERTRUDE (*seeing Marguerite*)

Be sure to say your prayers, and don't provoke Marguerite—Now, go to bed, dear heart.

### NAPOLEON

Yes, dear heart! What is love made of? (*Exit Napoleon.*)

---

## SCENE FIFTH.

#### THE SAME PERSONS, EXCEPT NAPOLEON.

### THE GENERAL

When that child begins to ask questions, he is an amusing youngster.

### GERTRUDE

It is often very embarrassing to answer him. (*To Pauline*) Come, Pauline, let us go and finish our work.

VERNON

It is your lead, General.

THE GENERAL

Mine? You ought to get married, and we could visit at your house, as you visit here, and you would have all the happiness of a family. Don't forget, Godard, that there is no one in the department happier than I am.

VERNON

When a man reaches sixty-seven without reaching happiness, it is impossible to catch up. I shall die a bachelor. (*The two women set to work at the same piece of embroidery.*)

GERTRUDE (*seated with Pauline at the front of the stage*)

How is this my child! Godard tells me that you received his advances very coldly; yet he is a very good match for you.

PAULINE

My father, madame, has given me leave to choose a husband for myself.

GERTRUDE

Do you know what Godard will say? He will say that you refused him because you had already made your choice.

PAULINE

If it were true, you and my father would know it. What reason have I for not giving you my confidence?

GERTRUDE

I cannot say, and I do not blame you. You see in matters of love women keep their secret with heroic constancy, sometimes in the midst of the most cruel torments.

PAULINE (*aside, picking up the scissors, which she had let drop*)

Ferdinand was wise in telling me to distrust her—she is so insinuating!

GERTRUDE

Perhaps you have in your heart a love like that. If such a misfortune has befallen you, you may rely on my help—I love you, remember! I can win your father's consent; he has confidence in me, and I can sway both his mind and affections. Therefore, dear child, you may open your heart to me.

PAULINE

You can read my heart, madame, for I am concealing nothing from you.

THE GENERAL

Vernon, what in the name of everything are you doing? (*Faint murmurs are heard among the card players; Pauline casts a look at them.*)

GERTRUDE (*aside*)

The question point-blank does not do with her. (*Aloud*) How happy you make me! For this provincial joker, Godard, avers that you almost fainted when he prompted Napoleon to declare that Ferdinand had broken his leg. Ferdinand is a pleasant young fellow, our intimate friend for some four years; what is more natural than your attachment for the youth, whose birth and talents are both in his favor?

PAULINE

He is my father's clerk.

GERTRUDE

Thank God, you are not in love with him; I was a little anxious for the moment, for, my dear child, he is a married man.

#### PAULINE

What! he is married? Why then does he make a secret of it? (*Aside*) Married? That would be outrageous. I will ask him this evening. I will give him the signal on which we agreed to meet.

#### GERTRUDE (*aside*)

Not a line of her face changed! Godard is wrong, or this child is more self-possessed than I am. (*Aloud*) What is the matter with you, my pet?

#### PAULINE

Oh! nothing.

#### GERTRUDE (*touching Pauline's neck*)

Why, you are quite hot! Do you feel so? (*Aside*) She loves him, that is plain. But the question is, does he love her? I suffer the torments of the damned!

#### PAULINE

I have been working too closely at this frame! And what, pray, is the matter with you?

#### GERTRUDE

Nothing. But you asked me why Ferdinand kept his marriage secret.

#### PAULINE

Ah! yes!

#### GERTRUDE (*rising, aside*)

If she is in love, she has a will of iron. But where can they have met? I never leave her in the daytime, and Champagne sees him all the time at the factory. No! it is absurd—If she does love him, it is without his knowledge, and she is like all other young girls, who begin to love a man in secret. But if they have come to an understanding, I have given her such a start that she will be sure to communicate with him about it, if only through her eyes.  I will keep them both well in sight.

### GODARD

We have had wonderful luck, M. Ferdinand! (*Ferdinand leaves off playing and goes towards Gertrude.*)

### PAULINE (*aside*)

I did not know that it was possible to suffer so much and yet live on.

### FERDINAND (*to Gertrude*)

Madame, won't you take my place in the game?

### GERTRUDE

Pauline, will you go instead. (*Aside*)  I can't tell him that he loves Pauline, that would suggest what may be a new idea to him.  What shall I do? (*To Ferdinand*)  She has confessed all.

### FERDINAND

Confessed what?

### GERTRUDE

Why, all!

### FERDINAND

I don't understand—Do you refer to Mlle. de Grandchamp?

### GERTRUDE

Yes.

### FERDINAND

And what has she been doing?

### GERTRUDE

You have not been false to me?  You do not want to kill me?

FERDINAND

Kill you? She?—I?—

GERTRUDE

Am I the victim of one of Godard's jokes?

FERDINAND

Gertrude, you are beside yourself!

GODARD (*to Pauline*)

Ah! Mademoiselle, that is bad play!

PAULINE

You lost a great deal by not taking my stepmother for a partner

GERTRUDE (*to Ferdinand*)

Ferdinand, I do not know whether I am rightly or wrongly informed; but this I do know; I prefer death to the loss of our hopes.

FERDINAND

Take care! The doctor has been watching us very keenly for the last few days.

GERTRUDE (*aside*)

She has not once looked back at him! (*Aloud*) She will marry Godard, for her father will compel her to do so.

FERDINAND

Godard would make an excellent match for any one.

THE GENERAL

I can't stay here any longer! My daughter plays vilely, and you, Vernon, have trumped my king!

VERNON

My dear General, it was a finesse.

THE GENERAL

You stupid! Come, it is ten o'clock, and time to go to sleep instead of playing cards. Ferdinand, be good enough to take Godard to his room. As for you, Vernon, you deserve to sleep on the floor as a punishment, for trumping my king.

GODARD

It is, after all, merely a matter of five francs, General.

THE GENERAL

It is also a matter of honor. (*To Vernon*) Come, now, although you have played so badly, let me hand you your hat and cane. (*Pauline takes a flower from the vase and plays with it.*)

GERTRUDE (*aside*)

A signal! I will watch her this night, even though my husband should afterwards kill me for it!

FERDINAND (*taking a candlestick from Felix*)

M. de Rimonville, I am at your service.

GODARD

I wish you good-night, madame. My respects to you, mademoiselle. General, good-night.

THE GENERAL

Good-night, Godard.

GODARD

De Rimonville—Doctor, I—

VERNON (*looking at him and blowing his nose*)

Good-bye, my friend.

THE GENERAL (*attending the doctor on his way out*)

Good-bye till to-morrow, Vernon, but come early.

## SCENE SIXTH.

GERTRUDE, PAULINE AND THE GENERAL.

GERTRUDE

My dear, Pauline refuses Godard.

THE GENERAL

And what are your reasons, my daughter?

PAULINE

I do not like him sufficiently to take him for a husband.

THE GENERAL

Well, never mind! We will look out some one else for you; but it is time for this to end, for you are now twenty-two, and people will begin to talk about you, my wife and me unless you make an early choice.

PAULINE

May I not be permitted, if I choose, to remain single?

GERTRUDE

She has made her choice, but probably wishes to tell you by yourself. I will leave you, and she will confess it. (*To Pauline*) Good-night, my child; talk freely with your father. (*Aside*) I will listen. (*She enters her chamber and proceeds to close the door.*)

## SCENE SEVENTH.

THE GENERAL AND PAULINE.

THE GENERAL (*aside*)

Act as my daughter's confessor! I am utterly unfitted for

such a task! She might rather act as confessor to me. (*Aloud*) Pauline, come here. (*He takes her on his knee*) Now, do you really think, my pet, that an old trooper like me doesn't understand your resolution to remain single? Why, of course, that means, in every language in which it has ever been uttered, that a young person is in a special hurry to be married—to some one that she is in love with.

### PAULINE

Papa, I would like to tell you something, but I cannot have confidence in you.

### THE GENERAL

And why not, mademoiselle?

### PAULINE

Because you tell everything to your wife.

### THE GENERAL

And you mean to tell me that you have a secret of such a kind that it cannot be revealed to an angel, to the woman who has educated you—to your second mother!

### PAULINE

Oh! If you are going to be vexed, I shall get off to bed. I used to think that a father's heart would be a place of unfailing refuge for a daughter.

### THE GENERAL

You silly child! Come, I am going to be in a good humor.

### PAULINE

, How kind you are! But listen! Suppose I were in love with the son of one of those whom you detest?

### THE GENERAL (*rising abruptly to his feet and repulsing her*)

I should detest you!

PAULINE

And this is what you call being good humored? (*Gertrude appears.*)

THE GENERAL

My child, there are feelings in my heart which you should never rouse in me; you ought to know this. They are my very life. Do you wish to be the death of your father?

PAULINE

Oh!

THE GENERAL

Dear child! I have had my day. My lot, with you and Gertrude at my side, is an enviable one. But, however sweet and charming is my life, I would quit it without regret, if by that means I could render you happy; for happiness is a debt we owe to those who owe to us their existence.

PAULINE (*noticing the door ajar, aside*)

Ah! she is listening. (*Aloud*) Father, I didn't mean what I said, but suppose I felt a love of that kind and it was so violent that I was likely to die of it?

THE GENERAL

It would be best for you to tell me nothing about it, and wait for your happiness until my death. And yet, since there is nothing more sacred, nothing more dear next to God and country, than children to their parents, children in their turn ought to hold sacred their parents' wishes and never to disobey them, even after their death. If you do not remain faithful to this hatred of mine, I think I should come forth from my grave to curse you!

PAULINE (*kissing her father*)

Oh! you bad, bad man! At any rate, I shall now find out whether you can keep a secret or not. Swear to me on your honor that you'll not repeat a syllable of what I told you.

THE GENERAL

I promise you that. But what reason have you for distrusting Gertrude?

PAULINE

If I told you, you would not believe it.

THE GENERAL

Are you trying to torture your father?

PAULINE

No. But which do you place first,—this hatred for traitors, or your own honor?

THE GENERAL

They are both first with me, for they are based upon a common principle.

PAULINE

Very well; if you throw away your honor by violating your oath, you may as well throw away your hatred. That is all I wanted to find out.

THE GENERAL

If women are angelic, they have in them also something of the diabolical. Tell me, who has filled the head of such an innocent girl as you are with ideas like these? This is the way they·lead us by the—

PAULINE (*interrupting him*)

Good-night, father.

THE GENERAL

You naughty child!

PAULINE

Keep my secret, or I will bring you a son-in-law that will drive you wild. (*Enters her own apartment.*)

## SCENE EIGHTH.

THE GENERAL (*alone*)
There must certainly be some key to this enigma! It must be discovered! Yes, and Gertrude shall discover it!

(*Scene curtain.*)

---

## SCENE NINTH.

(*Pauline's chamber; a small plain room with a bed in the centre and a round table at the left; the entrance is at the right, but there is a secret entrance on the left.*)

### PAULINE

At last I am alone! At last I can be natural! Married? My Ferdinand married? If this is so, he is the falsest, foulest, vilest of men! And I could kill him! Kill him? But I myself could not survive one hour the knowledge that he was actually married. My stepmother I detest! and if she becomes my enemy, there will be war between us, and war in earnest. It would be terrible, for I should tell my father all I know. (*She looks at her watch.*) Half-past eleven, and he cannot come before midnight, when the whole household is asleep. Poor Ferdinand! He has to risk his life for a few minutes' chat with her he loves! That is what I call true love! Such perils men will not undergo for every woman! But what would not I undergo for him! If my father surprised us, I would be the one to take the first blow. Oh! To suspect the man you love is to suffer greater torment than to lose him! If he dies, you can follow him in death; but doubt—is the cruelest of separations!—Ah! I hear him.

## SCENE TENTH.

FERDINAND AND PAULINE (*who locks the door*)
Are you married?

### FERDINAND

What a joke! Wouldn't I have told you?

### PAULINE

Ah! (*She sinks back on a chair, then falls upon her knees.*) Holy Virgin, what vows shall I make to thee? (*She kisses Ferdinand's hand.*) And you, a thousand blessings on your head!

### FERDINAND

Who could have told you such a foolish thing?

### PAULINE

My stepmother.

### FERDINAND

Why, she knows all about me, and if she did not, she would set spies to discover all; for suspicion with such women as that is certitude! Listen, Pauline, moments now are precious. It was Madame de Grandchamp who brought me into this house.

### PAULINE

And why?

### FERDINAND

Because she is in love with me.

### PAULINE

How horrible! And what of my father?

### FERDINAND

She was in love with me before her marriage.

PAULINE

She is in love with you; but you, are you in love with her?

FERDINAND

Do you think if I were, I should have remained in this house?

PAULINE

And she is still in love with you?

FERDINAND

Yes, unhappily she is! I ought to tell you that she was at one time beloved by me; but to-day I hate her from the bottom of my heart, and I sometimes ask myself why. Is it because I am in love with you, and every genuine and pure love is by nature exclusive? Is it because the contrast between an angel of purity, such as you, and a devil like her excites in me just as much hatred towards her as it rouses love towards you, my joy, my bliss, my beauteous treasure? I cannot say. But I hate her, and I love you so much that I should not regret dying if your father killed me; for one talk with you, one hour spent in this chamber by your side, seems, even when it is passed away, a whole lifetime to me.

PAULINE

Oh, say those dear words again! For they bring back my confidence once more. After hearing you speak thus, I forgive you the wrong you have done me in telling that I am not your first and only love, as you are mine. It is but a lost illusion, that is all! Do not be vexed with me. Young girls are foolish, they have no ambition but in their love, and they would fain rule over the past as they rule over the future of their beloved! But you hate her! And in that word, you give to me more proof of love than you have given me for the two years that we have loved. If only you knew with what cruelty this stepmother has put me on the rack, by her questions! But I will be avenged!

### FERDINAND

You must be very careful! She is a very dangerous woman! She rules your father. She is a woman who will fight to the death!

### PAULINE

To the death! That is as I wish it!

### FERDINAND

Be prudent, dear Pauline! We are going to act in harmony, are we not? Well, my love, the prosecuting attorney is of opinion that if we would triumph over the difficulties that prevent our union, we must have fortitude enough to part for some time.

### PAULINE

Oh! Give me two days and I will win over my father!

### FERDINAND

But you do not know Madame de Grandchamp. She has gone too far to leave off without ruining you, and to do that she will go to any lengths. But I will not go away without giving you what may prove most effective weapons against her.

### PAULINE

Oh, give them, give them to me!

### FERDINAND

Not yet. And you must promise me not to make use of them, unless your life is in danger; for what I am doing is certainly a breach of confidence. But it is for your sake I do it.

### PAULINE

Tell me what it is?

### FERDINAND

To-morrow I shall put into **your** hands the letters which

she wrote to me, some of them before, some of them after her marriage. Pauline, do not read them! Swear this to me, in the name of our love, in the name of our happiness! It will be sufficient, should it ever become absolutely necessary, that she knows that they are in your possession; at that moment you will see her trembling and groveling at your feet, for all her machinations then are foiled. But do not use them excepting as a last resort, and keep them well concealed.

PAULINE

What a terrible duel it will be!

FERDINAND

Terrible! But, Pauline, be courageous, as you have so far been, in keeping the secret of our love; do not acknowledge it, until you find it no longer possible to deny it.

PAULINE

Oh, why did your father betray the Emperor? If fathers knew how their children would be punished for the sins of their parents, there would be none but good men!

FERDINAND

Perhaps this sad interview will prove the last moment of happiness we shall have!

PAULINE (aside)

I will rejoin him, if he leaves me—(Aloud) See, I no longer weep, I am full of courage! But tell me, will your friend know the place where you are hiding?

FERDINAND

Eugène will be our confidential friend.

PAULINE

And the letters?

FERDINAND

To-morrow! To-morrow! But where will you conceal them?

PAULINE

I shall keep them about me.

FERDINAND

Good! Farewell!

PAULINE

Oh no, not yet!

FERDINAND

A moment more may ruin us.

PAULINE

Or unite us for life. Come, let me show you out, I shall not rest until I see you in the garden. Come!

FERDINAND

Let me take one more glance at this maiden chamber, in which you will think of me—where all things speak of you.

(*Scene curtain.*)

---

## SCENE ELEVENTH.

(*The drawing-room before described.*)

PAULINE *on the veranda;* GERTRUDE *at the door of the room.*

GERTRUDE

She is seeing him out! He has been deceiving me! So has she! (*Taking Pauline by the hand, she leads her to the front of the stage.*) Will you dare tell me, now, mademoiselle, that you do not love him?

PAULINE

Madame, I am deceiving no one.

GERTRUDE

You are deceiving your father.

PAULINE

And you, madame?

GERTRUDE

So both of you are against me—Oh, I shall—

PAULINE

You shall do nothing, either against me or against him.

GERTRUDE

Do not compel me to show my power! You must be obedient to your father, and—he is obedient to me.

PAULINE

We shall see!

GERTRUDE (*aside*)

Her coolness makes my blood boil. My brain reels! (*Aloud*) Do you know that I would rather die than live without him?

PAULINE

And so would I, madame. But I am free. I have not sworn as you have to be faithful to a husband—And your husband is my father!

GERTRUDE (*kneeling before Pauline*)

What have I done to you? I have loved you, I have educated you, I have been a good mother to you.

PAULINE

Be a faithful wife, and I will say no more.

GERTRUDE

Nay! Speak! Say all you like—Ah! the struggle has
begun.

————————

### SCENE TWELFTH.

THE SAME PERSONS AND THE GENERAL.

THE GENERAL

How is this? What is going on here?

GERTRUDE (*to Pauline*)

You must feign sickness. Come lie down. (*She makes
her lie down.*) I happened, my dear, to hear moans. Our
dear child was calling for help; she was almost suffocated by
the flowers in her bedroom.

PAULINE

Yes, papa, Marguerite had forgotten to take away the vase
of flowers, and I almost died.

GERTRUDE

Come, my daughter, come into the open air. (*They go towards the door.*)

THE GENERAL

Stay a moment. What have you done with the flowers?

PAULINE

I do not know where Madame has put them.

GERTRUDE

I threw them into the garden. (*The General abruptly
rushes out, after setting his candle on the card table.*)

## *SCENE THIRTEENTH.*

Pauline and Gertrude; later, the General.

#### Gertrude

Go back to your room, lock yourself in! I'll take all the'
blame. (*Pauline goes to her room.*)   I will wait for him here.
(*She goes back into her room.*)

#### The General (*coming in from the garden*)

I can find the vase of flowers nowhere.  There is some mystery in all these things.  Gertrude?—There is no one here!
Ah!  Madame de Grandchamp, you will have to tell me!—It
is a nice thing that I should be deceived by both wife and
daughter!  (*He takes up his candlestick and goes into Gertrude's room.*)

*Curtain to the Second Act.*

# ACT III.

---

## *SCENE FIRST.*

*(Same stage-setting. Morning.)*

GERTRUDE; THEN CHAMPAGNE.

GERTRUDE (*brings a flower vase from the garden and puts it down on the table*)

What trouble I had to allay his suspicions! One or two more scenes like that and I shall lose control of him. But I have gained a moment of liberty now—provided Pauline does not come to trouble me! She must be asleep—she went to bed so late!—would it be possible to lock her in her room? (*She goes to the door of Pauline's chamber, but cannot find the key.*) I am afraid not.

CHAMPAGNE (*coming in*)

M. Ferdinand is coming, madame.

GERTRUDE

Thank you, Champagne. He went to bed very late, did he not?

CHAMPAGNE

M. Ferdinand makes his rounds, as you know, every night, and he came in at half-past one o'clock. I sleep over him, and I heard him.

GERTRUDE

Does he ever go to bed later than that?

CHAMPAGNE

Sometimes he does, but that is according to the time he makes his rounds.

GERTRUDE

Very good. Thank you, Champagne. (*Exit Champagne.*) As the reward for a sacrifice which has lasted for twelve years, and whose agonies can only be understood by women,— for what man can guess at such tortures!—what have I asked? Very little! Merely to know that he is here, near to me, without any satisfaction saving, from time to time, a furtive glance at him. I wished only to feel sure that he would wait for me. To feel sure of this is enough for us, us for whom a pure, a heavenly love is something never to be realized. Men never believe that they are loved by us, until they have brought us down into the mire! And this is how he has rewarded me! He makes nocturnal assignations with this stupid girl! Ah! He may as well pronounce my sentence of death; and if he has the courage to do so, I shall have the courage at once to bring about their eternal separation; I can do it! But here he comes! I feel faint! My God! Why hast Thou made me love with such desperate devotion him who no longer loves me!

*SCENE SECOND.*

FERDINAND AND GERTRUDE.

GERTRUDE

Yesterday you deceived me. You came here last night, through this room, entering by means of a false key, to see Pauline, at the risk of being killed by M. de Grandchamp! Oh! you needn't lie about it. I saw you, and I came upon Pauline just as you had concluded your nocturnal promenade

You have made a choice upon which I cannot offer you my congratulations. If only you had heard us discussing the matter, on this very spot! If you had seen the boldness of this girl, the effrontery with which she denied everything to me, you would have trembled for your future, that future which belongs to me, and for which I have sold myself, body and soul.

### FERDINAND (*aside*)

What an avalanche of reproach! (*Aloud*) Let us try, Gertrude, both of us, to behave wisely in this matter. Above all things, let us try to avoid base accusations. I shall never forget what you have been to me; I still entertain towards you a friendship which, is sincere, unalterable and absolute; but I no longer love you.

### GERTRUDE

That is, since eighteen months ago.

### FERDINAND

No. Since three years ago.

### GERTRUDE

You must admit then that I have the right to detest and make war upon your love for Pauline; for this love has rendered you a traitor and criminal towards me.

### FERDINAND

Madame!

### GERTRUDE

Yes, you have deceived me. In standing as you did between us two, you made me assume a character which is not mine. I am violent as you know. Violence is frankness, and I am living a life of outrageous duplicity. Tell me, do you know what it is to have to invent new lies, on the spur of the moment, every day,—to live with a dagger at your heart? Oh! This lying! But for us, it is the Nemesis of happiness. It is disgraceful, when it succeeds; it is death, when it fails. And you, other men envy you because you make women love you. You will be applauded, while I shall be despised. And you do not wish me to defend myself! You have nothing but bitter words for a woman who has hidden from you everything—her remorse—her tears! I have suffered alone and without you the wrath of heaven; alone and without you I have descended into my soul's abyss, an abyss which has been opened by the earthquake of sorrow; and, while repentance was gnawing at my heart, I had for you nothing but looks of tenderness, and smiles of gaiety! Come, Ferdinand, do not despise a slave who lies in such utter subjection to your will!

### FERDINAND (*aside*)

I must put an end to this. (*Aloud*) Listen to me, Gertrude. When first we met it was youth alone united us in love. I then yielded, you may say, to an impulse of that egotism which lies at the bottom of every man's heart, though he knows it not, concealed under the flowers of youthful passion. There is so much turbulence in our sentiments at twenty-two! The infatuation which may seize us then, permits us not to reflect either upon life as it really is, or upon the seriousness of its issues—

### GERTRUDE (*aside*)

How calmly he reasons upon it all! Ah! It is infamous!

### FERDINAND

And at that time I loved you freely, with entire devotion; but afterwards—afterwards, life changed its aspect for both of us. If you ask why I remained under a roof which I should never have approached, it is because I chose in Pauline the only woman with whom it was possible for me to end my days. Come, Gertrude, do not break yourself to pieces against the barrier raised by heaven. Do not torture two beings who ask you to yield them happiness, and who will ever love you dearly.

### GERTRUDE

Ah, I see! You are the martyr—and I—I am the executioner! Would not I have been your wife to-day, if I had not set your happiness above the satisfaction of my love?

### FERDINAND

Very well! Do the same thing to-day, by giving me my liberty.

### GERTRUDE

You mean the liberty of loving some one else. That is not the way you spoke twelve years ago. Now it will cost my life.

### FERDINAND

It is only in romance that people die of love. In real life they seek consolation.

### GERTRUDE

Do not you men die for your outraged honor, for a word, for a gesture? Well, there are women who die for their love, that is, when their love is a treasure which has become their all, which is their very life! And I am one of these women. Since you have been under this roof, Ferdinand, I have feared a catastrophe every moment. Yes. And I always carry about me something which will enable me to quit this life, the very moment that misfortune falls on us. See! (*She shows him a phial.*) Now you know the life that I have lived!

### FERDINAND

Ah! you weep!

### GERTRUDE

I swore that I would keep back these tears, but they are

strangling me! For you—While you speak to me with that cold politeness which is your last insult,—your last insult to a love which you repudiate!—you show not the least sympathy towards me! You would like to see me dead, for then you would be unhampered by me. But, Ferdinand, you do not know me! I am willing to confess everything to the General, whom I would not deceive. This lying fills me with disgust! I shall take my child, I shall come to your house, we will flee together. But no more of Pauline!               ·

FERDINAND

If you did this, I would kill myself.

GERTRUDE

And I, too, would kill myself! Then we should be united in death, and you would never be hers!

FERDINAND (*aside*)

What an infernal creature!

GERTRUDE

And there is this consideration. What would you do if the barrier which separates you from Pauline were never broken down?

FERDINAND

Pauline will be able to maintain her own independence.

GERTRUDE

But if her father should marry her to some one else?

FERDINAND

It would be my death.

GERTRUDE

People die of love in romance. In real life they console

themselves with some one else, and a man only does his duty by being true to her with whom he has plighted troth.

THE GENERAL (*outside*)

Gertrude!   Gertrude!

GERTRUDE

I hear the General calling. (*The General appears.*)  You will then finish your business as quickly as you can, M. Ferdinand, and return promptly; I shall wait for you here. (*Exit Ferdinand.*)

---

## SCENE THIRD.

### THE GENERAL, GERTRUDE, THEN PAULINE.

THE GENERAL

This is rather early in the morning for you to be holding a conference with Ferdinand! What were you discussing? The factory?

GERTRUDE

What were we discussing? I will tell you; for you are exactly like your son; when once you begin to ask questions, you must have a direct answer. I had an impression that Ferdinand had something to do with Pauline's refusal to marry Godard.

THE GENERAL

When I come to think of it, you were perhaps right.

GERTRUDE

I got M. Ferdinand to come here for the purpose of clearing up my suspicions, and you interrupted us at the very moment when I seemed likely to gain some information. (*Pauline pushes the door ajar unseen.*)

THE GENERAL

But if my daughter is in love with M. Ferdinand—

PAULINE (*aside*)

I must listen.

THE GENERAL

I do not see why, when I questioned her yesterday in a paternal manner and with absolute kindness, she should have concealed it from me, for I left her perfectly free, and her feeling for him would be absolutely natural.

GERTRUDE

She probably misunderstood you or you questioned her before she had made up her mind. The heart of a young girl, as you ought to know, is full of contradictions.

THE GENERAL

And why should there not be something between them? This young man toils with the courage of a lion, he is the soul of honor, he is probably of good family.

PAULINE (*aside*)

I understand the situation now. (*She withdraws.*)

THE GENERAL

He will give us information on this point. He is above all things trustworthy; but you ought to know his family, for it was you who discovered this treasure for us.

GERTRUDE

I proposed him to you on the recommendation of old Madame Morin.

THE GENERAL

But she is dead!

GERTRUDE (*aside*)

It is very lucky that I quoted her then! (*Aloud*) She told me that his mother was Madame de Charny to whom he is devoted; she lives in Brittany and belongs to the Charnys, an old family of that country.

THE GENERAL

The Charnys. Then if he is in love with Pauline, and Pauline with him, I, for my part, would prefer him to Godard in spite of Godard's fortune. Ferdinand understands the business of the factory, he could buy the whole establishment with the dowry of Pauline. That would be understood. All he has to do is to tell us where he comes from, who he is, and who his father was. But we will see his mother.

GERTRUDE

Madame Charny?

THE GENERAL

Yes, Madame Charny. Doesn't she live near Saint-Melo? That is by no means at the other end of the world.

GERTRUDE

Just use a little tact, some of the manœuvres of an old soldier, and be very gentle, and you will soon learn whether this child—

THE GENERAL

Why should I worry about it? Here comes Pauline herself.

_____

SCENE FOURTH.

THE SAME PERSONS, MARGUERITE, THEN PAULINE.

THE GENERAL

'Ah! It is you, Marguerite. You came near causing the

death of my daughter last night by your carelessness. You
forgot—

THE GENERAL

MARGUERITE

I, General, cause the death of my child!

THE GENERAL

You forgot to take away the vase containing flowers of a
'strong scent, and she was almost suffocated.

MARGUERITE

Impossible! I took away the vase before the arrival of
M. Godard, and Madame must have seen that it was not
there while we were dressing Mademoiselle—

GERTRUDE

You are mistaken. It was there.

MARGUERITE (*aside*)

She's a hard one. (*Aloud*) Does not Madame remember
that she wished to put some natural flowers in Mademoiselle's
hair, and that she remarked about the vase being gone?

GERTRUDE

You are inventing a story. But where did you carry it?

MARGUERITE

To the foot of the veranda.

GERTRUDE (*to the General*)

Did you find it there last night?

THE GENERAL

No.

GERTRUDE

I took it from the chamber myself last night, and put it

where it now stands. (*Points to the vase of flowers on the veranda.*)

#### MARGUERITE

Sir, I swear to you by my eternal salvation—

#### GERTRUDE

Do not swear. (*Calling.*) Pauline!

#### THE GENERAL

Pauline! (*She appears.*)

#### GERTRUDE

Was the vase of flowers in your room last night?

#### PAULINE.

Yes. Marguerite, my dear old friend, you must have forgotten it.

#### MARGUERITE

Why don't you say, Mademoiselle, that some one put it there on purpose to make you ill!

#### GERTRUDE

Whom do you mean by some one?

#### THE GENERAL

You old fool, if your memory failed you, it is unnecessary for you, at any rate, to accuse anybody else.

#### PAULINE (*aside to Marguerite*)

Keep silence! (*Aloud*) Marguerite, it was there! You forgot it.

#### MARGUERITE

It is true, sir, I was thinking of the day before yesterday.

THE GENERAL (*aside*)

She has been in my service for twenty years. Strange that she should be so persistent! (*Takes Marguerite aside.*) Come! What did you say about the flowers for my daughter's hair?

MARGUERITE (*while Pauline makes signs to her*)

I said that, sir,—I am so old that my memory is treacherous.

THE GENERAL

But even then, why did you suppose that any one in the house had an evil thought towards—

PAULINE

Say no more, father! She has so much affection for me, dear Marguerite, that she is sometimes distracted by it.

MARGUERITE (*aside*)

I am quite sure I took away the flowers.

THE GENERAL (*aside*)

Why should my wife and my daughter deceive me? An old trooper like me doesn't permit himself to be caught between two fires, and there is something decidedly crooked—

GERTRUDE

Marguerite, we will take tea in this room when M. Godard comes down. Tell Felix to bring in all the newspapers.

MARGUERITE

Very good, madame.

## SCENE FIFTH.

### GERTRUDE, THE GENERAL AND PAULINE.

#### THE GENERAL (*kissing his daughter*)

You've not even said good-morning to me, you unnatur͏ʼ
child.

#### PAULINE (*kissing him*)

But, you began by scolding about nothing. I declare,
father, I am going to undertake your education. It is quite
time for you, at your age, to control yourself a little,—a
young man would not be so quick as you are! You have terrified Marguerite, and when women are in fear, they tell little
falsehoods, and you can get nothing out of them.

#### THE GENERAL (*aside*)

I'm in for it now! (*Aloud*) Your conduct, young lady,
does not do much towards promoting my self-control. I wish
you to marry, and I propose a man who is young—

#### PAULINE

Handsome and well educated!

#### THE GENERAL

Please keep silence, when your father addresses you, mademoiselle. A man who possesses a magnificent fortune, at
least six times as much as yours, and you refuse him. You are
well able to do so, because I leave you free in the matter; but
if you do not care for Godard, tell me who it is you choose,
if I do not already know.

#### PAULINE

Ah, father, you are much more clear-sighted than I am.
Tell me who he is?

#### THE GENERAL

He is a man from thirty to thirty-five years old, who

pleases me much more than Godard does, although he is
without fortune. He is already a member of our family.

PAULINE

I don't see any of our relations here.

THE GENERAL

I wonder what you can have against this poor Ferdinand,
that you should be unwilling—

PAULINE.

Ah! Who has been telling you this story? I'll warrant
that it is Madame de Grandchamp.

THE GENERAL

A story? I suppose, you will deny the truth of it! Have
you never thought of this fine young fellow?

PAULINE

Never!

GERTRUDE (*to the General*)

She is lying! Just look at her.

PAULINE

Madame de Grandchamp has doubtless her reasons for
supposing that I have an attachment for my father's clerk.
Oh! I see how it is, she wishes you to say: "If your heart,
my daughter, has no preference for any one, marry Godard."
(*In a low voice to Gertrude*) This, madame, is an atrocious
move! To make me abjure my love in my father's presence!
But I will have my revenge.

GERTRUDE (*aside to Pauline*)

As you choose about that; but marry Godard you shall!

The General (*aside*)

Can it be possible that these two are at variance? I must question Ferdinand. (*Aloud*) What were you saying to each other?

Gertrude

Your daughter, my dear, did not like my idea that she was taken with a subordinate; she is deeply humiliated at the thought.

The General

Am I to understand, then, my daughter, that you are not in love with him?

Pauline

Father, I—I do not ask you to marry me to any one! I am perfectly happy! The only thing which God has given us women, as our very own, is our heart. I do not understand why Madame de Grandchamp, who is not my mother, should interfere with my feelings.

Gertrude

My child, I desire nothing but your happiness. I am merely your stepmother, I know, but if you had been in love with Ferdinand, I should have—

The General (*kissing Gertrude's hand*)

How good you are!

Pauline (*aside*)

I feel as if I were strangled! Ah! If I could only undo her!

Gertrude

Yes, I should have thrown myself at your father's feet, to win his consent, if he had refused it.

The General

Here comes Ferdinand. (*Aside*) I shall question him at

my discretion; and then perhaps the mystery will be cleare
up.

## SCENE SIXTH.

### THE SAME PERSONS AND FERDINAND.

THE GENERAL (*to Ferdinand*)

Come here, my friend. You have been with us over three
years now, and I am indebted to you for the power of sleeping soundly amid all the cares of an extensive business. You
are almost as much as I am the master of my factory. You
have been satisfied with a salary, pretty large it is true, but
scarcely proportionate perhaps to the services rendered by
you. I think at last I understand the motive of your disinterestedness.

FERDINAND

It is my duty, General.

THE GENERAL

Granted; but does not the heart count for a good deal in
this? Come now, Ferdinand, you know my way of considering the different ranks of society, and the distinctions per-
taining to them. We are all the sons of our own works. I
have been a soldier. You may therefore have full confidence
in me. They have told me all; how you love a certain young
person, here present. If you desire it, she shall be yours. My
wife has pleaded your cause, and I must acknowledge that
she has gained it before the tribunal of my heart.

FERDINAND

General, can this be true? Madame de Grandchamp has
pleaded my cause? Ah, madame! (*He falls on his knees
before her.*) I acknowledge in this your greatness of heart!
You are sublime, you are an angel! (*Rising and rushing
forward to Pauline.*) Pauline, my Pauline!

GERTRUDE (*to the General*)

I guessed aright; he is in love with Pauline.

PAULINE

Sir, have I ever given you the right, by a single look, or by a single word, to utter my name in this way? No one could be more astonished than I am to find that I have inspired you with sentiments which might flatter others, but which I can never reciprocate; I have a higher ambition.

THE GENERAL

Pauline, my child, you are more than severe. Come, tell me, is there not some misunderstanding here? Ferdinand, come here, come close to me.

FERDINAND

How is it, mademoiselle, when your stepmother, and your father agree?

PAULINE (*in a low voice to Ferdinand*)

We are lost!

THE GENERAL

Now I am going to act the tyrant. Tell me, Ferdinand, of course your family is an honorable one?

PAULINE (*to Ferdinand*)

You hear that!

THE GENERAL

Your father must certainly have been a man of as honorable a profession as mine was; my father was sergeant of the watch.

GERTRUDE (*aside*)

They are now separated forever.

FERDINAND

Ah! (*To Gertrude*) I understand your move. (*To the General*) General, I do not deny that once in a dream, long ago, in a sweet dream, in which it was delicious for a man poor and without family to indulge in—dreams we are told are all the fortune that ever comes to the unfortunate—I do not deny that I once regarded it as a piece of overwhelming happiness to become a member of your family; but the reception which mademoiselle accords to those natural hopes of mine, and which you have been cruel enough to make me reveal, is such that at the present moment they have left my heart, never again to return! I have been rudely awakened from that dream, General. The poor man has his pride, which it is as ungenerous in the rich man to wound, as it would be for any one to insult—mark what I say—your attachment to Napoleon. (*In a low voice to Gertrude*) You are playing a terrible part!

GERTRUDE (*aside to Ferdinand*)

She shall marry Godard.

THE GENERAL

Poor young man! (*To Pauline*) He is everything that is good! He inspires me with affection. (*He takes Ferdinand aside.*) If I were in your place, and at your age, I would have—No, no, what the devil am I saying?—After all she is my daughter!

FERDINAND

General, I make an appeal to your honor; swear that you will keep, as the most profound secret, what I am going to confide to you; and this secrecy must extend so far even as to Madame de Grandchamp.

THE GENERAL (*aside*)

What is this? He also, like my daughter, seems to distrust my wife. But, by heaven, I will learn what it means!

(*Aloud*) I consent; you have the word of a man who has never once broken a promise given.

### FERDINAND

After having forced me to reveal that which I had buried in the recesses of my heart, and after I have been thunder-struck, for that is the only word in which to express it, by the disdain of Mademoiselle Pauline, it is impossible for me' to remain here any longer. I shall therefore put my accounts in order; this evening I shall quit this place, and to-morrow will leave France for America, if I can find a ship sailing from Havre.

### THE GENERAL (*aside*)

It is as well that he should leave, for he will be sure to return. (*To Ferdinand*) May I tell this to my daughter?

### FERDINAND

Yes, but to no one else.

### THE GENERAL (*aside to Pauline*)

Pauline! my daughter, you have so cruelly humiliated this poor youth, that the factory is on the point of losing its manager; Ferdinand is to leave this evening for America.

### PAULINE (*to the General*)

He is right, father. He is doing of his own accord, what you doubtless would have advised him to do.

### GERTRUDE (*to Ferdinand*)

She shall marry Godard.

### FERDINAND (*to Gertrude*)

If I do not punish you for your atrocious conduct, God Himself will!

THE GENERAL (*to Pauline*)

America is a long way off and the climate is deadly.


PAULINE (*to the General*)

Many a fortune is made there.


THE GENERAL (*aside*)

She does not love him. (*To Ferdinand*) Ferdinand, you must not leave before I have put in your hands sufficient to start you on the road to fortune.


FERDINAND

I thank you, General; but what is due me will be sufficient. Moreover, I shall not be missed in your factory, for I have trained Champagne so thoroughly as a foreman, that he is skillful enough to become my successor; and if you will go with me to the factory, you will see—


THE GENERAL

I will gladly accompany you. (*Aside*) Everything is in such a muddle here, that I must go and look for Vernon. The advice and clear-sightedness of my old friend, the doctor, will be of service in ferreting out what it is that disturbs this household, for there is something or other. Ferdinand, I will follow you. Ladies, we will soon be back again. (*Aside*) There is something or other! (*The General follows Ferdinand out.*)

---

## SCENE SEVENTH.

### GERTRUDE AND PAULINE.

PAULINE (*locking the door*)

Madame, do you consider that a pure love, a love which comprises and enhances all human happiness, which makes us understand that happiness which is divine,—do you consider such a love to be dearer and more precious to us than life?

### GERTRUDE

You have been reading the *Nouvelle Héloise,* my dear. What you say is rather stilted in diction, but it is nevertheless true.

### PAULINE

Well, madame, you have just caused me to commit suicide.

### GERTRUDE

The very act you would have been happy to see me commit; and if you had succeeded in forcing me to it, you would have felt in your heart the joy which fills mine at present.

### PAULINE

According to my father, war between civilized nations has its laws; but the war which you wage against me, madame, is that of savages.

### GERTRUDE

You may do as I do, if you can—but you can do nothing! You shall marry Godard. He is a very good match for you; you will be very happy, I assure you, for he has fine qualities.

### PAULINE

And you think that I will quietly let you marry Ferdinand?

### GERTRUDE

After the few words which we have exchanged this evening, why should we now indulge in the language of hypocrisy? I was in love with Ferdinand, my dear Pauline, when you were but eight years old.

### PAULINE

But now you are more than thirty—and I am still young.

Moreover, he hates you, he abhors you! He has told me so, and he wishes to have nothing to do with a woman capable of the black treachery with which you have acted towards my father.

GERTRUDE

In the eyes of Ferdinand, my love will serve as my vindication.

PAULINE

He shares the feelings which I have for you; he despises you, madame.

GERTRUDE

Do you really believe it? Well, if it so, my dear, I have one more reason for the position I take, for if he refuses to become my husband, to gratify his love, Pauline, you will force me to marry him for the sake of satisfying my revenge. When he came to this house, was he not aware that I was here?

PAULINE

You probably caught him by some such snare as you have just set for us. and into which both of us have fallen.

GERTRUDE

Now, my child, a single word more will put an end to everything between us. Have you not said a hundred times, a thousand times, in moments when you were all feeling, all soul, that you would make the greatest sacrifices for Ferdinand?

PAULINE.

Yes, madame.

GERTRUDE.

You said you would leave your father, would flee from France; you would give your life, your honor, your salvation for Ferdinand?

PAULINE

Yes, and if there is anything else that I can offer besides myself—this world and heaven!

GERTRUDE

Let me tell you, then, that all that you have wished to do, I have done! It is enough therefore to assure you that nothing, not even death itself, can arrest my course.

PAULINE

In saying this, you give me the right to defend myself before my father  (*Aside*)  O Ferdinand!  Our love, (*Gertrude takes a seat on the sofa during the soliloquy of Pauline*) as she has said, is greater than life.  (*To Gertrude*)  Madame, you must repair all the evil that you have done to me; the sole difficulties which lie in the way of my marriage with Ferdinand, you must overcome.  Yes, you, who have complete control over my father, you must make him forego his hatred of the son of General Marcandal.

GERTRUDE

And do you really mean that?

PAULINE

Yes, madame.

GERTRUDE

And what means do you possess formidable enough to compel me to do so?

PAULINE

Are we not carrying on a warfare of savages?

GERTRUDE

Say rather, of women, which is even more terrible!  Savages torment the body alone; while we direct our arrows against the heart, the self-love, the pride, the soul of those whom we attack in the very midst of their happiness.

### PAULINE

That is truly said. It is the whole woman-nature that I attack. Therefore, my dear and truly honored stepmother, you must eliminate by to-morrow, and not later, all the obstacles that stand between me and Ferdinand; or you may be sure my father shall learn from me the whole course of your conduct, both before and after your marriage.

### GERTRUDE

Ah! That is the way you are going to do it! Poor child! He will never believe you.

### PAULINE

Oh, I know the domination you exercise over my father; but I have proofs.

### GERTRUDE

Proofs! Proofs!

### PAULINE

I went to Ferdinand's house—I am very inquisitive—and I found there your letters, madame; I took from among them those which would convince even the blindness of my father, for they will prove to him—

### GERTRUDE

What will they prove?

### PAULINE

Everything!

### GERTRUDE

But, this will be, unhappy child, both theft and murder! For think of his age.

### PAULINE

And have not you accomplished the murder of my happiness? Have you not forced me to deny, both to my father and to Ferdinand, my love, my glory, my life?

### GERTRUDE (*aside*)

This is a mere trick; she knows nothing. (*Aloud*) This is a clever stratagem, but I never wrote a single line. What you say is not true. It is impossible. Where are the letters?

### PAULINE

They are in my possession.

### GERTRUDE

In your room?

### PAULINE

They are where you can never reach them.

### GERTRUDE (*aside*)

Madness with its wildest dreams spins through my brain! My fingers itch for murder. It is in such moments as this that men kill each other! How gladly would I kill her! My God! do not forsake me! Leave me my reason!—(*Aloud*) Wait a moment.

### PAULINE (*aside*)

My thanks to you, Ferdinand! I see how much you love me; I have been able to pay back to her all the wrongs she did us a short time ago—and—she shall save us from all we feared!

### GERTRUDE (*aside*)

She must have them about her,—but how can I be sure of that? Ah! (*Aloud*) Pauline! If you have had these letters for long, you must have known that I was in love with Ferdinand. You can only lately have received them.

## PAULINE

They came into my hands this morning.

## GERTRUDE

You have not read them all?

## PAULINE

Enough to find out that they would ruin you.

## GERTRUDE

Pauline, life is just beginning for you. (*A knock is heard.*) Ferdinand is the first man, young, well educated and distinguished, for he is distinguished, by whom you have been attracted; but there are many others in the world such as he is. Ferdinand has been in a certain sense under the same roof with you, and you have seen him every day; the first impulses of your heart have therefore directed you to him. I understand this, and it is quite natural. Had I been in your place I should doubtless have experienced the same feelings. But, my dear, you know not the ways either of the world or of society. And if, like so many other women, you have been deceiving yourself—for we women, ah, how often are we thus deceived!— you still can make another choice. But for me the deed has been done, I have no other choice to make. Ferdinand is all I have, for I have passed my thirtieth year, and I have sacrificed to him what I should have kept unsullied— the honor of an aged man. The field is clear for you, you may yet love some other man more ardently than you can love to-day—this is my experience. Pauline, child, give him up, and you will learn what a devoted slave you will have in me! You will have more than a mother, more than a friend, you will have the unstinted help of a soul that is lost! Oh! listen to me! (*She kneels, and raises her hands to Pauline's corsage.*) Behold me at your feet, acknowledging you my rival! Is this sufficient humiliation for me? Oh, if you only knew what this costs a woman to undergo! Relent! Relent, and save me.

(*A loud knocking is heard, she takes advantage of Pauline's confusion to feel for the letters.*)   Give back my life to me! (*Aside*)   She has them!

### PAULINE

Oh, leave me, madame!   Will you  force me  to call for some one?   (*She pushes Gertrude away, and proceeds to open the door.*)

### GERTRUDE (*aside*)

I was not deceived, she has them about her; but I must not leave them with her one single hour.

---

## SCENE EIGHTH.

### THE SAME PERSONS, THE GENERAL AND VERNON.

### THE GENERAL

You two, locked in together!   Why  did  you  call out, Pauline?

### VERNON

How pale you are, my child!   Let me feel your pulse.

### THE GENERAL (*to Gertrude*)

And you also seem to be very much excited.

### GERTRUDE

There was a joke between us and we were indulging in a laugh; weren't we, Pauline?   You were laughing, my pet?

### PAULINE

Yes, papa.   Dear mamma and I were in a gale of laughter.

### VERNON (*in a low voice to Pauline*)

That's a pretty big lie!

THE GENERAL

Didn't you hear us knocking?

PAULINE

We heard quite plainly, papa; but we didn't know it was you.

THE GENERAL (*in a low voice to Vernon*)

They seem to be leagued against me. (*Aloud*) But what was it all about?

GERTRUDE

Dear husband, you always want to know everything! We were speaking for the moment about the tenants, about some acquaintances of ours.—But let me go and ring for tea.

THE GENERAL

But tell me all about it?

GERTRUDE

Why this is sheer tyranny! To tell the truth, we locked ourselves in so that no one should disturb us. Is that plain enough?

VERNON

I should think it quite plain.

GERTRUDE (*whispering to the General*)

I wished to worm her secrets out of your daughter, for it is evident that she has some secrets! And you come interrupting us, while I am working in your service—for Pauline is not my daughter; you arrive, as if you were charging a hostile squadron, and interrupt us, at the very moment I was going to learn something.

THE GENERAL

Madame the Countess of Grandchamp, ever since the arrival of Godard—

GERTRUDE

Ah! yes, Godard. Well! he is here still.


THE GENERAL

Do not ridicule my words! Ever since yesterday nothing has gone as usual! By God! I'd like to know—


GERTRUDE

Sir, this oath is the first I have ever heard from you. Felix, bring in the tea. (*To the General*) You are tired, it seems, of twelve years of happiness?


THE GENERAL

I am not, and never will be a tyrant. A little time ago I came unexpectedly upon you and Ferdinand engaged in conversation, and I felt I was in the way. Again, I come here and you are locked in with my daughter, and my appearance seemed to put you out. And to cap all, last night—


VERNON

Come, General, you can quarrel with Madame as much as you like, but not before other people. (*Godard is heard approaching.*) I hear Godard. (*Whispers to the General*) Is this keeping your promise to me? In treating with women—I am bound as a doctor to admit it—you must leave them to betray themselves; while at the same time you watch them carefully; otherwise your violence draws forth their tears, and when once the hydraulic machinery begins to play, they drown a man as if they had the strength of a triple Hercules!

----

*SCENE NINTH.*

THE SAME PERSONS AND GODARD.

GODARD

Ladies, I came once before to present my compliments and

respects to you, but I found the door closed.  General, I wish you good-day.  (*The General takes up a newspaper and waves his hand in greeting.*)   Ah! Here is my adversary of yesterday's game.  Have you come to take your revenge, doctor?

### VERNON

No, I came to take some tea.

### GODARD

Ah!  I see you keep up here the custom of the English, Russians and Chinese.

### PAULINE

Would you prefer some coffee?

### GERTRUDE

Marguerite, bring in some coffee.

### GODARD

No, no; allow me to have some tea; I will, for once, deviate from my every-day custom.  Moreover, you have your luncheon at noon, I see, and a cup of coffee with cream would take away my appetite for that meal.  And then the English, the Russians and the Chinese are not entirely incorrect in taste.

### VERNON

Tea, sir, is an excellent thing.

### GODARD

Yes, when it is good.

### PAULINE

This is caravan tea.

### GERTRUDE

Doctor, have you seen the papers?  (*To Pauline*)  Go and talk to M. de Rimonville, my daughter; I, myself, will make tea.

GODARD

Perhaps Mlle. de Grandchamp likes my conversation no better than my person?

PAULINE

You are mistaken, sir.

THE GENERAL

Godard—

PAULINE

Should you do me the favor of no longer seeking me in marriage, you would still possess in my eyes qualities of sufficient brilliancy to captivate the young ladies Boudeville, Clinville, Derville, etc.

GODARD

That is enough, mademoiselle. Ah! How you do ridicule an unfortunate lover, in spite of his income of forty thousand francs! The longer I stay here, the more I regret it. What a lucky fellow M. Ferdinand de Charny is!

PAULINE

Lucky? Why is he lucky? Poor fellow! Does his good fortune consist in the fact that he is my father's clerk?

GERTRUDE

M. de Rimonville—

THE GENERAL

Godard—

GERTRUDE

M. de Rimonville—

THE GENERAL

Godard, my wife is speaking to you.

GERTRUDE

Do you like much or little sugar?

GODARD

A moderate quantity.

GERTRUDE

Not much cream, I suppose?

GODARD

On the contrary, plenty of cream, countess. (*To Pauline*) Ah! M. Ferdinand is not then, after all, the man who—whom you have distinguished by your favor? I can at least assure you that he is very much to the taste of your stepmother.

PAULINE (*aside*)

How annoying these inquisitive provincials are!

GODARD (*aside*)

It is fair that I should amuse myself a little at her expense before I take leave. I must get something out of this visit.

GERTRUDE

M. de Rimonville, if you desire anything solid, there are sandwiches here.

GODARD

Thank you, madame.

GERTRUDE (*whispering to Godard*)

Your cause is not wholly lost.

GODARD

O madame! I have thought a great deal over my rejection by Mlle. de Grandchamp.

GERTRUDE

Ah! (*To the doctor*) Doctor, you will take yours as usual, I suppose?

VERNON

If you please, madame.

GODARD (*to Pauline*)

Did you say, "poor fellow," mademoiselle? for M. Ferdinand is not so poor as you think him. He is richer than I am!

PAULINE

How do you know that?

GODARD

I am certain of it, and I will tell you why. This M. Ferdinand, whom you think you know, is an exceedingly crafty fellow—

PAULINE (*aside*)

Can he possibly know his real name?

GERTRUDE (*aside*)

A few drops of opium in her tea will put her to sleep, and I shall be saved.

GODARD (*to Pauline*)

You cannot deny the authority of him who has put me on the track.

PAULINE

Oh, sir! Kindly tell—

GODARD

It was the prosecuting attorney. I remembered that at the house of the Boudevilles it was said that your clerk—

PAULINE (*aside*)

He is putting me on the rack.

GERTRUDE (*offering a cup to Pauline*)

Here, Pauline.

VERNON (*aside*)

Am I dreaming? I thought I saw her put something into Pauline's cup.

PAULINE (*to Godard*)

And what did they say?

GODARD

Ah! Ah! How attentive you are! I should have been exceedingly flattered to think that you put on that air when any one was talking about me, as I am now talking about M. Ferdinand de Charny.

PAULINE

What a strange taste this tea has! You find yours good?

GODARD

You talk about the tea in order to distract my attention from the interest you take in what I am telling you. I see through it all! Well, come now, I am going to astonish you. You must know that M. Ferdinand is—

PAULINE

Is—?

GODARD

A millionaire.

PAULINE

You are joking, M. Godard.

GODARD

On my word of honor, mademoiselle, he possesses a treasure. (*Aside*) She is madly in love with him.

PAULINE (*aside*)

How this fool startled me. (*She rises from her seat and Vernon takes the teacup from her hand.*)

VERNON

Let me take it, my child.

THE GENERAL (*to his wife*)

What ails you, dearest? you seem—

VERNON (*who has retained Pauline's cup and returned his own in its place to Gertrude. Aside*)

It is laudanum; fortunately the dose is light; but it is very certain that something is about to happen. (*To Godard*) M. Godard, you are a crafty fox. (*Godard takes out his handkerchief as if to blow his nose.*) Ah!

GODARD

Doctor, I bear no ill-will.

VERNON

Listen! Do you think that you could carry off the General to the factory and keep him there for an hour?

GODARD

I would like to have that youngster to help me.

VERNON

He is at school until dinner-time.

GODARD

Why do you wish me to do this?

VERNON

Now I beg of you, for you are a good fellow, to do as I bid you; it is necessary. Do you love Pauline?

GODARD

I did love her yesterday, but this morning— (*Aside*) I

must find out what he is concealing from me.  (*To Vernon*)
It shall be done!  I will go on to the veranda and come back
again with a message that Ferdinand sends for the General.
You may rely upon me.  Ah!  Here is Ferdinand himself, that
is all right!  (*Goes on the veranda.*)


### PAULINE

'Tis peculiar, how drowsy I feel.  (*She lies down on th
divan; Ferdinand appears and talks with Godard.*)

---

## SCENE TENTH.

### THE SAME PERSONS AND FERDINAND.

### FERDINAND

General, it will be necessary for you to come to the office
and the factory in order to verify my accounts.


### THE GENERAL

That is only just to you.


### PAULINE  (*drowsily*)

Ferdinand!

### GODARD

Ah, General, I'll take advantage of this occasion to visit
your establishment with you, for I have never seen it.


### THE GENERAL

Very good, come along Godard.


### GODARD

De Rimonville.

### GERTRUDE  (*aside*)

If they go away, fortune will favor me indeed.

VERNON (*who has overheard her; aside*)
Fortune, in this case, is represented by me—

---

## SCENE ELEVENTH.

GERTRUDE, VERNON, PAULINE, AND LATER MARGUERITE.

GERTRUDE

Doctor, would you like another cup of tea?

VERNON

Thank you, but I am so deep in the election returns that I have not yet finished my first cup.

GERTRUDE (*pointing to Pauline*)
Poor child, you see she is sleeping?

VERNON

How is this? She is sleeping?

GERTRUDE

It is no wonder. Imagine, doctor, she did not go to sleep until three o'clock this morning. We were greatly disturbed last night.

VERNON

Let me assist you to carry her to her room.

GERTRUDE

It is not necessary. Marguerite, help me put this poor child to bed. She will be more comfortable there.

(*Marguerite comes forward and assists Gertrude to carry Pauline away.*)

## SCENE TWELFTH.

VERNON, AND FELIX (*who enters at this juncture*)

#### VERNON

Felix!

#### FELIX

Is there anything I can do for you, sir?

#### VERNON

Is there a closet anywhere here in which I can lock up something?

FELIX (*pointing to the closet*)

Here is a place, sir.

#### VERNON

Good! Felix, don't say a word of this to a single soul. (*Aside*) He will be sure to remember it. (*Aloud*) I am playing a trick on the General, and the trick will fail if you say anything.

#### FELIX

I will be as dumb as a fish. (*The doctor takes from him the key of the closet.*)

#### VERNON

And now leave me alone with your mistress, who is coming back here, and be on the watch that no one interrupts us for a moment.

FELIX (*going out*)

Marguerite was right; there is something in the wind, that's certain.

MARGUERITE (*returning*)

There is nothing the matter. Mademoiselle is sleeping quietly. (*Exit.*)

## SCENE THIRTEENTH.

### VERNON (*alone*)

What can have set by the ears two women who have hitherto lived in peace? All doctors, little though they be philosophers, can tell. The poor General, who all his life has had no other idea excepting that of escaping the common lot! Yet I see no one here likely to cause him jealousy, but myself and Ferdinand. It is not probable that I am the man; but Ferdinand—Yet I have so far noticed nothing—I hear her coming! Now for the tug-of-war!

---

## SCENE FOURTEENTH.

### VERNON AND GERTRUDE.

### GERTRUDE (*aside*)

I have them!—I am going to burn them in my chamber. (*She meets Vernon.*) Ah!

### VERNON

Madame, I have sent everybody away.

### GERTRUDE

May I ask you why?

### VERNON

In order that we may have our explanation without witnesses.

### GERTRUDE

Explanation! By what right do you—you, the parasite of the house, pretend to have an explanation with the Comtesse de Grandchamp?

### VERNON

I, a parasite? Madame! I have an income of ten thousand francs, besides my pension; I have the rank of general, and my fortune will be bequeathed to the children of my old friend! A parasite indeed! You forget that I am not only here as a friend but as a doctor, and—you poured certain drops of laudanum into Pauline's tea.

### GERTRUDE

**I?**

### VERNON

I saw you do it, and I have the cup.

### GERTRUDE

You have the cup? Why, I washed it myself!

### VERNON

Yes, you washed mine, which I gave you in exchange for that of Pauline! I was not reading the newspaper, I was watching you.

### GERTRUDE

Oh! sir, how unworthy of you!

### VERNON

You must confess that what I did then is of great service to you, for if you had by the effect of that draught brought Pauline to the brink of the grave, you would have been very glad of my services.

### GERTRUDE

The brink of the grave—why, doctor, I put in only a very few drops.

### VERNON

You admit, then, that you put opium in her tea.

### GERTRUDE

Doctor—this is outrageous!

### VERNON

That I have obtained a confession from you? Every woman under the same circumstances would have said the same thing. I know it by experience. But that is not all. You have several other things to confide in me.

### GERTRUDE (*aside*)

He is a spy! The only thing I can do is to make him my accomplice. (*Aloud*) Doctor, you are too useful to me to admit of our quarreling. In a moment, if you will wait here, I will return and speak frankly to you. (*She goes into her chamber and locks the door.*)

### VERNON

She has turned the key! I am caught, tricked! I cannot after all resort to violence. What is she doing? She is going to hide her flask of opium. A man is always wrong when he undertakes to discharge for a friend the offices which my old friend, this poor General, expects of me. She is going to entangle me—Ah! Here she comes.

### GERTRUDE (*aside*)

I have burnt them! There is not a trace left—I am saved! (*Aloud*) Doctor!

### VERNON

Madame?

### GERTRUDE

My stepdaughter Pauline, whom you believed to be an innocent girl, an angel, had carried off furtively and criminally something whose discovery would have compromised the honor and the life of four persons.

#### VERNON

Four! (*Aside*) That is herself, the General—Ah! her son, perhaps—and the unknown.

#### GERTRUDE

This secret, concerning which she is forced to keep silence, even though it imperilled her life to do so—

#### VERNON

I don't quite catch your meaning.

#### GERTRUDE

In short, the proofs of this secret are now destroyed! And you, doctor, who love us all, you would be as base, as infamous as she is—even more so, because you are a man, and have not the insensate passions of a woman!—You would be a monster if you were to take another step along the path on which you have now started—

#### VERNON

You mean that for intimidation? Madame, since civilized society first sprang into being, the seed which you are sowing has produced a crop whose name is crime.

#### GERTRUDE

But there are four lives at stake; remember that. (*Aside*) He is giving way. (*Aloud*) In spite of this danger I demand that you will assist me in maintaining peace here, and that you will immediately go and get something by which Pauline may be roused from her slumber. And you will explain, if necessary, her drowsiness to the General. Further, you will give me back the cup, for I am sure you intend to do so, and each step that we take together in this affair shall be fully explained to you.

#### VERNON

Madame!

GERTRUDE

We must separate now, for the General will soon be back.

VERNON (*aside*)

I shall still look after you! I have now a weapon that I can use and— (*Exit*).

---

*SCENE FIFTEENTH.*

GERTRUDE (*alone, leaning against the closet in which the cup is locked up*)

Where can he have hidden that cup?

*Curtain to the Third Act.*

## ACT IV.

---

### SCENE FIRST.

(*Pauline's chamber.*)

GERTRUDE AND PAULINE (*the latter sleeping on a large arm-chair on the left*).

GERTRUDE (*cautiously entering*)

She is sleeping, and the doctor said that she would wake up at once. Her slumber alarms me. This then is the girl that he is in love with. I do not find her pretty at all. Oh, yes, after all, she is beautiful! But how is it that men do not see that beauty is nothing but a promise, and that love is the—(*some one knocks*). How is this; there are people coming.

VERNON (*outside*)

May I come in, Pauline?

GERTRUDE

It is the doctor.

---

### SCENE SECOND.

THE SAME PERSONS AND VERNON.

GERTRUDE

You told me that she would soon awake.

VERNON

Don't be alarmed. (*Calling aloud*) Pauline! Pauline!

PAULINE (*awakening*)

O M. Vernon! Where am I? Ah! In my own room. What has happened to me?

VERNON

My child, you fell asleep while you were taking your tea. Madame de Grandchamp feared as I did that this was the beginning of a sickness; but it is no such thing. It is altogether, as it seems to me, the consequence of a night without sleep.

GERTRUDE

And now, Pauline, how do you feel?

PAULINE

I have been sleeping—and madame was here while I slept! (*She starts up; puts her hand upon her bosom.*) Ah! it is outrageous! (*To Vernon*) Doctor, can you have been an accomplice?

GERTRUDE

An accomplice in what? What were you going to say?

VERNON

I! my child! Could you suppose that I was the accomplice of an evil action wrought against you, whom I love as if you were my daughter? Don't speak of such a thing as that! But come, tell me?

PAULINE

There is nothing, doctor, nothing to say!

GERTRUDE

Let me speak a few words to her.

VERNON (*aside*)

What possible motive can there be for a young child to

keep silence, when she is the victim of such an act of treachery as this?

GERTRUDE (*in a low voice to Pauline*)

So you see, Pauline, you didn't long keep in your possession the proofs which you intended taking to your father in your ridiculous accusation of me!

PAULINE

I understand all; you gave me a narcotic in order to deprive me of them.

GERTRUDE

We are equally inquisitive. I have done to you what you did to me in Ferdinand's apartments.

PAULINE

You are triumphant now, madame, but it will soon be my turn.

GERTRUDE

The war, then, is to continue?

PAULINE

War, madame? Call it a duel! One or the other of us must go.

GERTRUDE

You are tragic.

VERNON (*aside*)

There appears to be no outbreak between them, nor the least misunderstanding!—But stay, an idea strikes me; suppose I go and look for Ferdinand? (*He prepares to go out.*)

GERTRUDE

Doctor!

**VERNON**

Madame?

**GERTRUDE**

We must have a talk together. (*Whispering*) I shall not leave you until you have given me back—

**VERNON**

I stated to you the sole condition—

**PAULINE**

Doctor!

**VERNON** (*going to her*)

My child?

**PAULINE**

Are you aware that my sleep just now was not a natural one?

**VERNON**

Yes, you were put to sleep by your stepmother. I have proof of it. But do you know the reason why?

**PAULINE**

Oh! doctor, it is—

**GERTRUDE**

Doctor!

**PAULINE**

Later on, I will tell you all.

**VERNON**

Already from each one of them I have learned something of what lies beneath. Ah! poor General!

**GERTRUDE**

I am waiting, doctor. (*He bows and escorts Gertrude out.*)

## SCENE THIRD.

PAULINE (*alone; she rings*)

Yes, the only alternative left me is to flee with him; if we continue this conflict, my stepmother and I, it can but result in my father's dishonor. Would it not be better to disobey him? Then I will write to him—I will be generous, because my triumph over her will be complete—I will let my father still believe in her, and will explain my flight by attributing it to the hatred which he bears to the name of Marcandal and to my love for Ferdinand.

## SCENE FOURTH.

PAULINE AND MARGUERITE.

MARGUERITE

Does mademoiselle feel well again?

PAULINE

Yes, I am well enough in body; but in mind—Oh, I am in despair! My poor Marguerite, unfortunate is the girl who has lost her mother—

MARGUERITE

And whose father has for his second wife such a woman as Madame de Grandchamp. But tell me, mademoiselle, am I not to you a humble and devoted mother? My affection for you as a nurse has grown in proportion to the hate with which this stepmother regards you.

PAULINE

Yes, Marguerite, you may believe it, but you delude yourself. Your love can never be as great as her hatred.

MARGUERITE

Oh! mademoiselle! If you would only put me to the proof!

PAULINE

Really?—Would you leave France for me?

MARGUERITE

To be with you, I would travel to the Indies.

PAULINE

And would you start at once?

MARGUERITE

At once!—My baggage is not heavy.

PAULINE

Well, Marguerite, we will start to-night, and secretly.

MARGUERITE

But why is this?

PAULINE

You ask me why? Do you not know that Madame de Grandchamp put me to sleep with opium?

MARGUERITE

I know it, mademoiselle, and Doctor Vernon knows it also, for Felix told me that he put under lock and key your tea-cup.—But why did she do it?

PAULINE

Say not a word about it, if you love me! And if you are as devoted to me as you profess to be, go to your room and gather together all that you possess, so quietly that none shall suspect that you are preparing for a journey. We will start after midnight. You must now take from me here, and carry to your room, my jewels and all that I shall need for a long journey. Use the utmost caution; for if my stepmother had the least idea of what we are doing, I should be ruined.

### MARGUERITE

Ruined!—But, mademoiselle, what is come over you? Think seriously before you leave your home.

### PAULINE

Do you wish to see me die?

### MARGUERITE

Die?—Oh, mademoiselle, I will at once obey your wishes.

### PAULINE

Marguerite, tell M. Ferdinand to bring me my year's allowance; bid him come this moment.

### MARGUERITE

He was under your windows when I came in.

### PAULINE (*aside*)

Under my windows!—doubtless he thought that he would never see me again.—Poor Ferdinand! (*Exit Marguerite.*)

---

## SCENE FIFTH.

### PAULINE (*alone*)

When I think of leaving my father's house, it at once comes home to me that my father will seek me many a day, far and wide.—With what treasures love ought to repay me, for such sacrifices, for I abandon to follow Ferdinand my country, my father, and my home! But at any rate, this

shameless woman will lose him without hope of restoration!
Moreover, I shall return! The doctor and M. Ramel will win
for me forgiveness from my father. I think I hear the step of
Ferdinand!—Yes, it is actually he!

---

## SCENE SIXTH.

### PAULINE AND FERDINAND.

#### PAULINE

Oh, my love, my Ferdinand!

#### FERDINAND

And I thought that I should never see you again! Marguerite, I see, knows all.

#### PAULINE

She knows nothing yet; but this night she shall learn of
our flight, for we shall be free; and you shall take your wife
with you.

#### FERDINAND

Oh, Pauline, do not deceive me!

#### PAULINE

I was making arrangements to rejoin you in your place of
exile; but this odious woman has hurried on my resolution.—
There is no merit in what I am doing, it is a question of life
and death to me.

#### FERDINAND

Of life and death!—Tell me what has she been doing?

#### PAULINE

She almost poisoned me; she drugged me, in order to take

the letters I carried about me! By what she has dared to do, in order to keep you for herself, I judge what she yet may do. If therefore we wish to be united, our only hope lies in flight. Therefore let us not say farewell! This night we must find some refuge or other—But where? That lies with you.

### FERDINAND

Ah! These words,—how wild with joy they make me!

### PAULINE

Ferdinand! Take every precaution; hurry to Louviers, go to the house of your friend, the prosecuting attorney; secure our passports, and a carriage with fast horses. I fear that my father, urged on by this stepmother, may try to overtake us! May he fail to do so; he would kill us, for I am telling him in this letter the fatal secret of your birth which compels me thus to leave him.

### FERDINAND

Dismiss your fears. Eugène completed his preparations for my departure yesterday. Here is the sum of money which your father owed me. (*He shows her a pocket-book.*) Give me your receipt. (*He puts down some money on the table.*) I have only to give in my balance sheet in order to be free. We shall reach Rouen in three hours, and at Havre we shall take an American ship. Eugène has sent a trusty man to secure me a passage on board. The officers of the vessel will think it only natural that a man should take his wife abroad with him, so we shall meet with no obstacle—

---

### SCENE SEVENTH.

#### THE SAME PERSONS AND GERTRUDE.

#### GERTRUDE

Excepting me.

PAULINE

We are lost!

GERTRUDE

So you are going to start without telling me, Ferdinand?
Oh, indeed!—But I have heard it all.

FERDINAND (*to Pauline*)

Mademoiselle, have the goodness to give me your receipt, it
is indispensable in completing the account which I must give
to your father before leaving. (*To Gertrude*) Madame, you
may be able, perhaps, to prevent mademoiselle from going
away; but I can no longer remain here, and I must absolutely
start to-night.

GERTRUDE

You must stay here, and you shall stay here, sir!

FERDINAND

Against my will?

GERTRUDE

What mademoiselle wishes to do, I myself will do, and without fear. I will make M. de Grandchamp come into this very
room, and you will at once see that he will compel you to leave,
but—with me and my child. (*Felix appears.*) Beg M. de
Grandchamp to come here.

FERDINAND (*to Pauline*)

I see her object. Detain her here, while I overtake Felix,
and prevent him from speaking to the General! Eugène will
tell you how you must act after my departure. When once
we have left this place, Gertrude will be powerless to oppose
us. (*To Gertrude*) Farewell, madame. You lately made an
attack on Pauline's life, and by this act have broken the last
ties that bound me to your friendship.

### GERTRUDE

You have nothing but accusations for me! But you do not know what mademoiselle intended telling her father concerning you and me.

### FERDINAND

I love her, and will love her all my life; I shall be able to defend her against you, and I prize her high enough to suffer banishment in order to obtain her. Farewell.

### PAULINE

Dear, dear Ferdinand!

------

## SCENE EIGHTH.

### GERTRUDE AND PAULINE.

### GERTRUDE

Now that we are alone, do you know why I have summoned your father? It is in order to tell him the name and family of Ferdinand.

### PAULINE

Madame, what are you going to do? My father, as soon as he learns that the son of General Marcandal has won the love of his daughter, will get to Havre as quickly as Ferdinand does. He will come up with him, and then—

### GERTRUDE

I would sooner see Ferdinand dead than united to any one but myself, especially when I feel in my heart as much hatred for that other one as I have love for him. Such is my final word in our mortal duel.

### PAULINE

Madame, I am now at your feet, as you but now were at

mine. Let us slay each other if you like, but let us not murder
him! Let his life be spared, though it be at the cost of mine!


GERTRUDE

Will you give him up?


PAULINE

I will, madame.


GERTRUDE (*she lets her handkerchief fall in the excitement of
her passionate speech*)

You are deceiving me! You tell me this, because he loves
you, because he has already insulted me by avowing it, and
because you believe that he will not love me any longer. Now
this will not do, Pauline, you must give me some pledges of
your sincerity.


PAULINE (*aside*)

Her handkerchief! Ah! I see with it the key of her desk.—
It is there that the poison is locked up! (*Aloud*) Did you
say pledges of my sincerity? I will give them to you.—What
do you demand?


GERTRUDE

Really, I do not care for more than one proof that you mean
what you say, and that is, that you should marry the other
suitor.

PAULINE

I will marry him.


GERTRUDE

And you must, at this very moment, plight your troth with
him.


PAULINE

Go to him yourself, madame, and tell him; and then come
here with my father, and—

GERTRUDE

And what?—

PAULINE

And I will give him my word; even though this be to give away my life.

GERTRUDE (*aside*)

In what a tone she uttered that. With what resolution! And without tears—I feel sure she is keeping something back! (*Aloud*) And so you are quite resigned to this?

PAULINE

I am.

GERTRUDE (*aside*)

I hope she is. (*To Pauline*) If you are sincere—

PAULINE

You are mendacity itself, and you always see a lie in other's words—Oh! Leave me, madame, you make me shudder.

GERTRUDE (*aside*)

Well, she is candid at any rate. (*Aloud*) I am going to tell Ferdinand of your resolution—(*Pauline nods in acquiescence.*) But he will not believe me. Suppose you write a word to him?

PAULINE

Yes, I will write to him, and tell him not to go away. (*Sits down and writes.*) Here is the letter, madame.

GERTRUDE (*reads*)

"I am going to marry M. de Rimonville—so that you may remain here. Pauline." (*Aside*) I do not quite understand this—I fear that there is some trick in it. I am going to let him leave; he will learn of the marriage when he is far away from this. (*Exit.*)

## *SCENE NINTH.*

PAULINE (*alone*)

Ferdinand is utterly lost to me now—I have always expected it; the world is either a paradise or a prison cell; and I, a young girl, have dreamed only of the paradise. But anyway I have the key of the desk, and I can return it after having taken out something which may serve to put an end to this terrible situation. Yes, that is what I will do!

## *SCENE TENTH.*

PAULINE AND MARGUERITE.

MARGUERITE

Mademoiselle, my trunks are all packed. I am now going to begin packing here.

PAULINE

Yes. (*Aside*) It is best to let her do so. (*Aloud*) Come here, Marguerite, take this gold and conceal it among your things.

MARGUERITE

You are sure that your reasons for starting away are very urgent?

PAULINE

My poor Marguerite, who knows whether I shall be able to get away! But come, go on with your work. (*Exit.*)

## *SCENE ELEVENTH.*

MARGUERITE (*alone*)

And to think that I believed this fury was unwilling that

mademoiselle should marry! Is it possible that mademoiselle should have concealed from me that her real love was being opposed? Yet her father is so good to her! He leaves her free to choose—Suppose I were to speak to the General—Oh! no, I would not run the risk of injuring my child.

## SCENE TWELFTH.

### MARGUERITE AND PAULINE.

#### PAULINE

No one has seen me. Listen, Marguerite, first of all, take away the money that I gave you, and then let me think about the resolution which I have taken.

#### MARGUERITE

If I were in your place, mademoiselle, I would tell everything to the General.

#### PAULINE

To my father? Unhappy woman, do not betray me! And let both of us respect the illusions, in the midst of which he lives.

#### MARGUERITE

Ah! Illusions! That is the very word.

#### PAULINE

You may leave me now. (*Exit Marguerite.*)

## *SCENE THIRTEENTH.*

### PAULINE, THEN VERNON.

PAULINE (*holding in her hand the parcel of poison, which
was shown in the first act*)

Here stands death before me! The doctor told us yesterday, in reference to Champagne's wife, that this terrible substance required some hours, almost a whole night, to produce
its deadly effects, and that it was possible, during the first
hours, to nullify these effects; if the doctor remains at the
house, he will provide this antidote. (*Some one knocks.*)
Who is that?

### VERNON (*from without*)

It is I.

### PAULINE

Come in, doctor! (*Aside*) Curiosity brings him to see me,
curiosity will take him away.

### VERNON

I see, my child, that between you and your stepmother,
there are secrets of life and death?

### PAULINE

Yes, and, above all, death.

### VERNON

I was afraid so! And that, of course, I must attend to.
But tell me—You must have had some terrible quarrel with
your stepmother.

### PAULINE

Let me hear no more of that creature. She deceives my
father.

### VERNON

I know it.

### PAULINE

She never loved him.

### VERNON

I was quite sure of that!

### PAULINE

She has sworn to ruin me.

### VERNON

How? Is it in an affair of your heart that she wishes to do you harm?

### PAULINE

Rather say, it is my life she threatens.

### VERNON

What a horrible suspicion! Pauline, my child, I love you well, you know I do. Tell me, can nothing save you?

### PAULINE

In order to change my fate, it would be necessary that my father change his ideas. Listen; I am in love with M. Ferdinand.

### VERNON

I already know that. But who would hinder you from marrying him?

### PAULINE

Can you keep a secret? Well, he is the son of General Marcandal!—

### VERNON

My God! You may rely on my keeping that secret! Why, your father would fight with him to the death, if for nothing else, because he has had him under his roof for three years.

PAULINE

You will then see very plainly that there is no hope for me. (*She sinks back overwhelmed with emotion in an arm-chair.*)

VERNON

Poor child! I fear she is going to faint! (*He rings and calls*) Marguerite! Marguerite!

## SCENE FOURTEENTH.

THE SAME PERSONS, GERTRUDE, MARGUERITE AND THE GEN-ERAL.

MARGUERITE (*running in*)

What is it, sir?

VERNON

Get me a tea-urn of boiling water, into which you must drop some orange leaves.

GERTRUDE

What is the matter with you, Pauline?

THE GENERAL

Dear child, do tell us?

GERTRUDE

Oh, it is nothing! We can understand her feelings. It is because she sees her lot in life decided—

VERNON (*to the General*)

Her lot decided? And in what way?

THE GENERAL

She is going to marry Godard! (*Aside*)It seems to me as

if she were giving up some love affair of which she did not
wish to tell me. As far as I can understand from what my
wife has told me, the unknown one is ineligible, and Pauline
did not discover his unworthiness until yesterday.

### VERNON

And you believe this? Do not precipitate matters, General.
We will talk it over this evening. (*Aside*) Before then I am
going to have a few words with Madame de Grandchamp.

### PAULINE (*to Gertrude*)

The doctor knows all!

### GERTRUDE

Ah!

### PAULINE (*she puts back into the pocket of Gertrude the hand-kerchief and the key, while the latter is looking at Vernon, who converses with the General*)

Keep him away, for he is capable of telling all he knows to
the General. We must at least protect Ferdinand.

### GERTRUDE (*aside*)

She is right. (*Aloud*) Doctor, I have just been informed
that Francis, one of our best workmen, is sick; he hasn't
appeared this morning, and you might go and visit him.

### THE GENERAL

Francis? Oh! Vernon, you had better go and see him—

### VERNON

Doesn't he live at Pré-l'Evêque? (*Aside*)    More than
three leagues away.

### THE GENERAL

Are you alarmed about Pauline?

VERNON

It is simply an attack of nerves.


GERTRUDE

I can take your place here, doctor, if that is so, can't I?—


VERNON

Yes. (*To the General*) I'll undertake to say that Francis is about as sick as I am! The fact of it is, I see rather too much and my presence is not desired—


THE GENERAL (*in a rage*)

What are you talking about? To whom do you refer?


VERNON

Are you going to fly into a passion again? Do calm yourself, my old friend, or you will cause yourself eternal remorse.


THE GENERAL

Remorse?

VERNON

Just keep these people talking, till I return.


THE GENERAL

But—

GERTRUDE (*to Pauline*)

Tell me, how do you feel now, my sweet angel?


THE GENERAL

Just look at them.

VERNON

Ah! well, women stab each other with a smile and a kiss.

## *SCENE FIFTEENTH.*

THE SAME PERSONS (EXCEPT VERNON) AND MARGUERITE.

GERTRUDE (*to the General, who seems as if he were bewildered by the last words of Vernon*)

What is the matter with you?

THE GENERAL (*passing before Gertrude to the side of Pauline*)

Nothing, nothing! Tell me, my little Pauline, is your engagement with Godard to be quite voluntary?

PAULINE

Quite voluntary.

GERTRUDE (*aside*)

Ah!

THE GENERAL

He will be here soon.

PAULINE

I am expecting him.

THE GENERAL (*aside*)

There is a tremendous amount of bitterness in her tone. (*Marguerite appears with a tea-cup.*)

GERTRUDE

It is too soon, Marguerite, the infusion can't yet be strong enough! (*She tastes it.*) I must go and prepare it myself.

MARGUERITE

I have always been in the habit of waiting upon Mlle. Pauline.

GERTRUDE

What do you mean by speaking to me in this tone?

MARGUERITE

But—madame—

THE GENERAL

Maguerite, if you say another word, we shall fall out.

PAULINE

Marguerite, you may just as well let Madame de Grand-champ have her way. (*Gertrude goes out with Marguerite.*)

THE GENERAL

And so my little girl has not much confidence in the father who loves her so? Come now! Tell me why you so distinctly refused Godard yesterday, and yet, accept him to-day?

PAULINE

I suppose it is a young girl's whim.

THE GENERAL

Are you in love with anybody else?

PAULINE

It is because I am not in love with anybody else that I consent to marry your friend M. Godard! (*Gertrude comes in with Marguerite.*)

THE GENERAL

Ah!

GERTRUDE

Take this, my darling, but be careful, for it is a little hot.

PAULINE

Thank you, mother!

### THE GENERAL

Mother!—Truly, this is enough to drive one crazy with perplexity!

### PAULINE

Marguerite, bring me the sugar basin! (*While Marguerite goes out and Gertrude talks with the General, she drops the poison into the cup and lets fall the paper which contained it.*)

### GERTRUDE (*to the General*)

You seem to be indisposed?

### THE GENERAL

My dear, I cannot understand women; I am like Godard. (*Marguerite comes back.*)

### GERTRUDE

You are like all other men.

### PAULINE (*hurriedly drinking the poisoned cup*)

Ah!

### GERTRUDE

How are you now, my child?

### PAULINE

I am better.

### GERTRUDE

I am going to prepare another cup for you.

### PAULINE

Oh, no, madame, this will be quite enough! I would sooner wait for the doctor. (*She sets down the empty cup on the table.*)

## SCENE SIXTEENTH.

THE SAME PERSONS AND FELIX, THEN GODARD.

FELIX

M. Godard asks if you will see him? (*He looks inquiringly at Pauline.*)

PAULINE

Certainly.

GERTRUDE (*leaving the room*)

What do you intend saying to him?

PAULINE

Wait and see.

GODARD (*entering*)

I am sorry that mademoiselle is indisposed. I did not know it. I will not intrude. (*They offer him a chair.*) Mademoiselle, allow me to thank you above all for the kindness you have shown in receiving me in this sanctuary of innocence. Madame de Grandchamp and your father have just informed me of something which would have overwhelmed me with happiness yesterday, but rather astonishes me to-day.

THE GENERAL

That is to say, M. Godard—

PAULINE

Do not be hasty, father, M. Godard is right. You do not know all I said to him yesterday.

GODARD

You are far too clever, mademoiselle, not to consider as quite natural the curiosity of an honorable young man, who has an income of forty thousand francs, besides his savings, to learn the reason why he should be accepted after a lapse of twenty-four hours from his rejection— For, yesterday, it was at this very hour—(*He pulls out his watch*)  Half-past five—

### THE GENERAL

What do you mean by all this?  It looks as if you are not as much in love as you said you were.  You have come here to complain of a charming girl at the very moment when she has told you—

### GODARD

I would not complain, if the subject were not marriage. Marriage, General, is at once the cause and the effect of sentiment.

### THE GENERAL

Pardon me, Godard, I am a little hasty, as you know.

### PAULINE (*to Godard*)

Sir—(*Aside*)  Oh, how I suffer!  Sir, why should poor young girls—

### GODARD

Poor?—No, no, mademoiselle; you are not poor.  You have four hundred thousand francs.

### PAULINE

Why should weak young girls—

### GODARD

Weak?

### PAULINE

Well, then, innocent young persons—be so very fastidious about the character of the man who presents himself as their lord and master?  If you love me, will you punish yourself— will you punish me—because your love has been submitted to a test?

GODARD

Of course, from that point of view—

THE GENERAL

Oh! These women! These women!

GODARD

You may just as well say, "These daughters."

THE GENERAL

Yes, for I am quite sure that mine has more brains than I have.

---

*SCENE SEVENTEENTH.*

THE SAME PERSONS, GERTRUDE AND NAPOLEON.

GERTRUDE

How has it turned out, M. Godard?

GODARD

Ah, Madame! General! My happiness is complete, and my dream fulfilled. For now I am to be admitted into a family like yours. To think that I—Ah! Madame! General! (*Aside*) I'd like to find out the mystery, for she has precious little love for me.

NAPOLEON (*entering*)

Papa, I have won the school medal—Good-day, mamma— and where is Pauline? And so you are sick? Poor little sister!

I'll tell you something—I have found out where justice comes from.

### GERTRUDE

And who told you? Ah! see what a lovely boy he is!

### NAPOLEON

The master told me that justice came from God.

### GODARD

It is very plain that your master was not born in Normandy.

### PAULINE (*in a low voice to Marguerite*)

O Marguerite! Dear Marguerite! Do send them all away.

### MARGUERITE

Gentlemen, Mlle. Pauline desires to take a little nap.

### THE GENERAL

Just so, Pauline, we will leave you, and you need not get up till dinner time.

### PAULINE

I will certainly get up then if I can. Father, kiss me before you go.

### THE GENERAL (*kissing her*)

My darling child! (*To Napoleon*) Come, my boy. (*They all go out, except Pauline, Marguerite and Napoleon.*)

### NAPOLEON (*to Pauline*)

And how is it you do not kiss me? Tell me what ails you?

PAULINE

Oh! I am dying!

NAPOLEON

Do people die? Pauline, what is death made of?

PAULINE

Death—is made—like this—(*she falls back into Marguerite's arms*).

MARGUERITE

Oh! My God! Help! Help!

NAPOLEON

Oh! Pauline, you frighten me! (*Running away.*) Mamma! Mamma!

*Curtain to the Fourth Act.*

# ACT V.

### *SCENE FIRST.*

**(*The* chamber of Pauline as before.)**

PAULINE, FERDINAND AND VERNON.

*(Pauline lies stretched upon her bed. Ferdinand holds her hand in an attitude of profound grief and despair. It is just before dawn and a lamp is burning.)*

VERNON *(seated near the table)*

I have seen thousands of dead men on the field of battle and in the ambulances, yet the death of this young girl under her father's roof moves me more profoundly than all those heroic sufferings. Death is perhaps a thing foreseen on the field of battle—it is even expected there; while here, it is not only the passing away of a single person, but a whole family is plunged in tears and fond hopes vanish. Here is this child, of whom I was so fond, murdered, poisoned—and by whom? Marguerite has rightly guessed the secret of this struggle between two rivals. It was impossible to refrain from communicating at once with the authorities. In the meantime, God knows I have used every effort to snatch this young life from the grave. *(Ferdinand raises his head and listens to the doctor.)* I have even brought this poison, which may act as an antidote to the other; but the princes of medical science should have been present to witness the experiment! No one man ought to venture upon such a throw of the dice.

FERDINAND *(rises and approaches the doctor)*

Doctor, when the magistrates arrive, will you explain this

experiment of yours; they will be sure to sanction it; and you may be sure that God, yes God, will hear me. He will work some miracle, He will give her back to me!

### VERNON

I should have ventured upon it before the action of the poison had wrought its full effects. If I did so now, I should be looked upon as the poisoner. No (*he places a little flask upon the table*), it would be useless now, and to give it with the most disinterested motives would be looked upon as a crime.

FERDINAND (*after holding a mirror before Pauline's lips*)

Anything, everything is yet possible; she still breathes.

### VERNON

She will not live till daylight.

### PAULINE

Ferdinand!

### FERDINAND

She has just uttered my name.

### VERNON

The vitality of a girl of twenty-two is very tenacious! Moreover, she will preserve consciousness, even to her last gasp. She might possibly rise from her bed and talk with us, although the sufferings caused by this terrible poison are inconceivable.

## SCENE SECOND.

THE SAME PERSONS AND THE GENERAL.

THE GENERAL (*outside*)

**Vernon!**

VERNON (*to Ferdinand*)

It is the General. (*Ferdinand, overcome with grief, falls back on the arm-chair, where he is concealed by the curtains of the bed.*) What do you want?

THE GENERAL

**I want to see Pauline!**

VERNON

If you take my advice, you will wait awhile; she is **very much worse.**

THE GENERAL (*entering*)

For that reason I shall come in.

VERNON

Do not come in, General. Listen to me!

THE GENERAL

No, no! Ah, how motionless, how cold she is, Vernon!

VERNON

Listen! General! (*Aside*) We must get him away somehow. (*Aloud*) There is but a faint hope of saving her.

THE GENERAL

You told me—You must have been deceiving me!

VERNON

My friend, we have to look this catastrophe in the face, as

we had to look towards the batteries through a shower of bullets! On such occasions, when I hesitated, you always went forward. (*Aside*) That is a good idea! (*Aloud*) You had better bring to her the consolations of religion.

#### THE GENERAL
Vernon, I wish to see her, to give her my last kiss.

#### VERNON
Be careful!

#### THE GENERAL (*kissing her*)
Oh! How icy cold she is!

#### VERNON
That is a peculiarity of her sickness, General. Hurry to the priest's house, for in case my remedies fail, it is not right that your daughter, who has been reared as a Christian, should be forgotten by the Church.

#### THE GENERAL
Ah! yes. I will go. (*He moves towards the bed.*)

#### VERNON (*pointing towards the door*)
This way!

#### THE GENERAL
I quite lose my head; I am distracted—O Vernon, work a miracle for us! You have saved so many people—and here you cannot save the life of my child!

#### VERNON
Come, come be off. (*Aside*) I must go with him, for if he meets the magistrates there will be more trouble still. (*Exeunt.*)

## *SCENE THIRD.*

PAULINE AND FERDINAND.

PAULINE

Ferdinand!

FERDINAND

Ah! My God! Can this be her last sigh? Pauline, you are my very life; if Vernon does not save you, I will follow you, and we shall still be united.

PAULINE

I shall expire, then, without a single regret.

FERDINAND (*takes up the flask*)

That which would have saved you, if the doctor had arrived earlier, shall deliver me from life.

PAULINE

No, for you may still be happy.

FERDINAND

Never, without you.

PAULINE

Your words revive me.

---

## *SCENE FOURTH.*

THE SAME PERSONS AND VERNON.

FERDINAND

She speaks; her eyes once more are open.

## VERNON

Poor child! There she falls asleep again. What shall the waking be? (*Ferdinand sits down again and takes the hand of Pauline.*)

---

## SCENE FIFTH.

THE SAME PERSONS, RAMEL, THE INVESTIGATING MAGIS-
TRATE, A DOCTOR, A CORPORAL OF POLICE
AND MARGUERITE.

## MARGUERITE

M. Vernon, the magistrates are here. M. Ferdinand, you must leave the room! (*Exit Ferdinand.*)

## RAMEL

Take care, corporal, that all the entrances of this house are guarded, and observe our orders! Doctor, can we remain here a few moments without danger to the sick lady?

## VERNON

She is asleep, sir; and it is her last slumber.

## MARGUERITE

Here is the cup into which the infusion was poured and which still has traces of arsenic; I perceived it there as soon as I took hold of it.

THE DOCTOR (*examining the cup and tasting the contents*)

It is evident that the liquid contains some poisonous substance.

## THE MAGISTRATE

Please to make an analysis of it. (*He sees Marguerite pick-*

*ing up a small piece of paper from the ground.*)    What paper
is that?

### MARGUERITE

**Oh,** it is nothing.

### RAMEL

In such cases as these, nothing is insignificant in the eyes
of magistrates! Yes, gentlemen, we shall have to examine
this paper later.  What can have delayed M. de Grandchamp?

### VERNON

He is at the priest's house, but he will not stay there long.

### THE MAGISTRATE (*to the doctor*)

Have you made your examination yet, sir? (*The two physicians converse together at the head of the bed.*)

### RAMEL (*to the magistrate*)

If the General returns, we must deal with him according to
the circumstances.   (*Marguerite is weeping, kneeling at the
foot of the bed; the two physicians, the judge and Ramel are
grouped in the front of the stage.*)

### RAMEL (*to the doctor*)

It is therefore your opinion, sir, that the illness of Mlle. de
Grandchamp, whom we saw two days ago full of health, and
even of happiness, is the result of a crime?

### THE DOCTOR

**The** symptoms of poisoning are undeniable.

### RAMEL

And are the remains of the poison contained in this cup
so discernible, and present in such a quantity, as to furnish
legal proof?

THE DOCTOR

Yes, sir.

THE MAGISTRATE (*to Vernon*)

This woman alleges, sir, that yesterday, at four o'clock, you prescribed for Mlle. de Grandchamp an infusion of orange leaves, as a soothing draught for the nervous excitement which followed upon an interview between the stepmother and her stepdaughter; she says, moreover, that Madame de Grandchamp, who had despatched you on an empty errand to a place four leagues away, had insisted upon preparing and giving everything to her daughter herself; is this true?

VERNON

Yes, sir.

MARGUERITE

When I persisted in my purpose of attending myself upon my young mistress, my poor master was incensed to the point of reproaching me.

RAMEL (*to Vernon*)

Where did Madame de Grandchamp send you?

VERNON

Everything is ominous in this mysterious affair. Madame de Grandchamp was so anxious to get me out of the way that she sent me three leagues to visit a sick man, who, I found when I reached his home, was drinking in the inn. I blamed Champagne for deceiving Madame de Grandchamp, and Champagne positively told me that the workman had not appeared at the factory, but that he himself knew nothing about his alleged sickness.

FELIX

Gentlemen, the clergy are here.

RAMEL

We can continue our proceedings in the drawing-room.

### VERNON

This way, gentlemen, this way.

*(Scene curtain.)*

---

## SCENE SIXTH.

*(The drawing-room.)*

RAMEL, THE MAGISTRATE, THE SHERIFF'S OFFICER AND
VERNON.

### RAMEL

Here, then, is the result so far of our inquiry, in accordance with the evidence of Felix and Marguerite. Madame
de Grandchamp, in the first place, administered to her stepdaughter a dose of opium, and you, M. Vernon, who were
present and saw the criminal attempt, managed to secure and
lock up the cup.

### VERNON

It is true, gentlemen, but—

### RAMEL

How is it, M. Vernon, that when you witnessed this criminal attempt, you did not check Madame de Grandchamp in
the fatal course which she was then pursuing?

### VERNON

Believe me, gentlemen, I did everything which I thought
could be done with prudence, and all that my long experience
suggested was attempted by me.

### THE MAGISTRATE

Your conduct, sir, was peculiar, and you will be called upon to explain it. You did your duty yesterday in preserving the cup as evidence; but why did you not go further?

### RAMEL

Pardon me, M. Cordier, this gentleman is advanced in years; he is an honest and trustworthy man. (*He takes Vernon aside*) You have found out, I suppose, the cause of this crime?

### VERNON

It springs from a rivalry between two women, who have been urged on to the most violent extremes by their reckless passions. And I was obliged to keep silence on the subject.

### RAMEL

I know the whole business.

### VERNON

You! sir?

### RAMEL

Yes, and, like you, I have done everything to prevent this catastrophe; for Ferdinand was to leave this very night. I knew Mlle. Gertrude de Meilhac in former years, having met her at the house of my friend.

### VERNON

Oh! sir, show clemency! Have pity on an old soldier, crippled with wounds, and enslaved by delusions. He is in danger of losing both his daughter and his wife. Heaven grant he may not lose his honor also!

### RAMEL

We understand each other. So long as Gertrude does not make such admissions as force us to see the real situation, I shall endeavor to persuade the investigating magistrate—who is an extremely sagacious and honest man of ten years' experience—I shall try to make him believe that cupidity alone has influenced Madame de Grandchamp. You must assist me. (*The magistrate approaches; Ramel nods to Vernon and puts on an expression of severity*) Why did Madame de Grandchamp wish to drug her stepdaughter? You, who are the friend of the household, ought to know this.

### VERNON

Pauline was about to confide her secrets to me. Her step-mother thought that I was learning certain things which her interest required should be concealed; and that, sir, is doubtless the reason why she sent me to treat a workman who was in good health, and not to prevent help from being brought to Pauline, for Louviers is not so far off.

### THE MAGISTRATE

What forethought she has! She won't be able to escape, if we find the proofs of crime in her desk. She does not expect us here; she will be thunderstruck.

---

## SCENE SEVENTH.

### THE SAME PERSONS, GERTRUDE AND MARGUERITE.

### GERTRUDE

I hear the strains of church music! What, is there another trial going on here? What can be happening? (*She goes to the door of Pauline's chamber and starts back terrified, on the appearance of Marguerite.*) Ah!

### MARGUERITE

They are offering prayers over the body of your victim!

### GERTRUDE

Pauline! Pauline! Dead!

THE MAGISTRATE

And it is you, madame, who have poisoned her.

GERTRUDE

I! I! I! Ah! what is this? Am I asleep or awake? (*To Ramel*) Ah! How extremely fortunate for me is this meeting! For you know the whole affair, don't you? Do you believe me capable of a crime like this? What! Am I actually accused of it? Do you think that I would have made an attack' upon her life? I, the wife of a veteran who is the soul of honor? I, the mother of a child, before whom I would not wish to be disgraced? Justice will vindicate me—Marguerite, let no one leave the room. Gentlemen, tell me what has taken place since yesterday evening, when I left Pauline slightly indisposed?

THE MAGISTRATE

Madame, collect yourself! You stand before the tribunal of your country.

GERTRUDE

You chill me with such words—

THE MAGISTRATE

The administration of justice in France is the most perfect of criminal procedures. No traps are set, for justice proceeds, acts, and speaks with open face, for she is solely intent upon her mission, which is, the discovery of the truth. At the present moment, you are merely inculpated, and in me you must see your protector. But tell the truth, whatever it may be; the final result will be decided at a higher tribunal.

GERTRUDE

Ah! sir, take me into her chamber, and in presence of Pauline I will cry out, what I cry out before you—I am guiltless of her death!—

### THE MAGISTRATE

Madame !—

### GERTRUDE

Sir, let us have none of those long phrases, with which you blind the eyes of people. I suffer pains unheard of! I weep for Pauline as though she were my child, and—I forgive her everything! What do you want with me? Proceed, and I will answer you.

### RAMEL

What is it that you will forgive her?

### GERTRUDE

I mean—

### RAMEL (*in a low voice*)

Be cautious in your replies.

### GERTRUDE

You are right, for precipices yawn on every side!

### THE MAGISTRATE (*to the sheriff's officer*)

Names and titles may be taken later; now write down the notes of the investigation, and the inquiry. (*To Gertrude*) Did you yesterday forenoon put opium into the tea of Mlle. de Grandchamp?

### GERTRUDE

Ah! doctor—this is you.

### RAMEL

Do not accuse the doctor. He has already too seriously compromised himself for you! Answer the magistrate!

### GERTRUDE

It is true.

### THE MAGISTRATE

Madame recognizes the cup and admits that she put opium

in it. That will be enough for the present, at this stage of the inquiry.

### GERTRUDE

Do you accuse me then of something further? What is it?

### THE MAGISTRATE

Madame, if you cannot free yourself from blame with regard to a later event, you may be charged with the crime of poison-ing. We must now proceed to seek proofs either of your inno-cence or of your guilt.

### GERTRUDE

Where will you seek them?

### THE MAGISTRATE

From you! Yesterday you gave Mlle. de Grandchamp an infusion of orange leaves, in another cup which contained arsenic.

### GERTRUDE

Can it be possible!

### THE MAGISTRATE

The day before yesterday you declared that the key of your desk, in which the arsenic was locked, never left your posses-sion.

### GERTRUDE

It is in my dress pocket.—

### THE MAGISTRATE

Have you ever made any use of that arsenic?

### GERTRUDE

No; you will find the parcel still sealed.

### RAMEL

Ah! madame, I sincerely hope so.

THE MAGISTRATE

I very much doubt it; this is one of those audacious criminals—

GERTRUDE

The chamber is in disorder, permit me—

THE MAGISTRATE

No, no! All three of us will enter it.

RAMEL

Your innocence is now at stake.

GERTRUDE

Gentlemen, let us go in together.

------

## SCENE EIGHTH.

VERNON (*alone*)

My poor General! He kneels by the bed of his daughter; he weeps, he prays!—Alas! God alone can give her back to him.

------

## SCENE NINTH.

VERNON, GERTRUDE, RAMEL, THE MAGISTRATE AND THE SHERIFF'S OFFICER.

GERTRUDE

I scarce can believe my senses; I am dreaming—I am—

RAMEL

You are ruined, madame.

GERTRUDE

Yes, sir—But by whom?

THE MAGISTRATE (*to the sheriff's officer*)

Write down that Madame de Grandchamp having herself
unlocked for us the desk in her bedchamber and having herself given into our hands the parcel sealed by M. Baudrillon,
this parcel which two days ago was intact is found unsealed
and from it has been taken a dose, more than sufficient to
produce death.

GERTRUDE

Death!—And I?

THE MAGISTRATE

Madame, it was not without reason that I took from your
desk this torn piece of paper. We have also picked up in
Mlle. de Grandchamp's chamber a piece of paper, which
exactly fits to it; and this proves that when you reached your
desk, in that confusion which crime always brings upon criminals, you took up this paper to wrap up the dose, which you
intended to mix with the infusion.

GERTRUDE

You said that you were my protector! And there, see now—

THE MAGISTRATE

Give me your attention, madame. In face of such suspicions, I feel I shall have to change the writ of summons into a
writ of bail or imprisonment. (*He signs the document.*) And
now, madame, you must consider yourself under arrest.

GERTRUDE

Of course, I will do all that you wish!—But you told me
that your mission was to search for the truth—Oh! Let us
search for it here—Let us search for it here!

### THE MAGISTRATE

Certainly, madame.

### GERTRUDE (*to Ramel; she is weeping*)

O M. Ramel!

### RAMEL

Have you anything to say in your defence which would lead us to cancel this terrible sentence?

### GERTRUDE

Gentlemen, I am innocent of the crime of poisoning, and yet all is against me! I implore you, give me your help instead of torturing me!—And listen to me—Some one must have taken my key,—can you not understand? Some one must have come into my room—Ah! I see it all now— (*To Ramel*) Pauline loved as I loved; she has poisoned herself!

### RAMEL

For the sake of your honor, do not say that, without the most convincing proofs, otherwise—

### THE MAGISTRATE

Madame, is it true that, yesterday, you, knowing Doctor Vernon was to dine with you, sent him—

### GERTRUDE

Oh! you,—your questions are so many daggers at my heart! and yet you go on, you still go on.

### THE MAGISTRATE

Did you send him away to attend a workman at Pré-l'Evêque?

### GERTRUDE

I did, sir.

### THE MAGISTRATE

This workman, madame, was found in a tavern, and in excellent health.

### GERTRUDE

Champagne had told me that he was sick

### THE MAGISTRATE

We have questioned Champagne, and he denies this, averring that he said nothing about sickness. The fact of it was, you wished to preclude the possibility of medical aid.

### GERTRUDE (*aside*)

It was Pauline! It was she who made me send away Vernon! O Pauline! You have dragged me down with yourself into the tomb, to which I sink bearing the name of criminal! No! No! No! (*To Ramel*) Sir, I have but one avenue of escape. (*To Vernon*) Is Pauline still alive?

### VERNON (*pointing to the General*)

Here is my answer.

---

## SCENE TENTH.

### THE SAME PERSONS AND THE GENERAL

### THE GENERAL (*to Vernon*)

She is dying, my friend! If I lose her, I shall never survive it.

### VERNON

My friend!

### THE GENERAL

It seems to me that there are a great many people here——

What must be done? Oh, try to save her! I wonder where
Gertrude is. (*They give him a seat.*)

### GERTRUDE (*sinking at the feet of the General*)

My friend!—Poor father!—I would this instant I might
be killed without a trial. (*She rises.*) No, Pauline has
wrapped me in her shroud, I feel her icy hands about my neck.
And yet I was resigned. Yes, I would have buried with me the
secret of this terrible drama, which every woman should understand! But I am weary of this struggle with a corpse that
holds me tight, and communicates to me the coldness and the
stiffness of death! I have made up my mind that my innocence of this crime shall come forth victorious at the expense
of somebody's honor; for never, never could I become a vile
and cowardly poisoner. Yes, I shall tell the whole, dark tale.

### THE GENERAL (*rising from his seat and coming forward*)

Ah! so you are going to say in the face of justice all that
for two days you have concealed by such obstinate silence—
vile and ungrateful creature, fawning liar!—you have killed
my daughter. Are you going to kill me also?

### GERTRUDE

Ought I to keep silence?—Ought I to speak?

### RAMEL

General, be kind enough to retire. The law commands.

### THE GENERAL

The law? You represent the justice of men, I represent the
justice of God, and am higher than you all! I am at once
accuser, tribunal, sentence and executioner—Come, madame,
tell us what you have to say?

### GERTRUDE (*at the General's feet*)

Forgive me, sir—Yes—I am—

RAMEL (*aside*)

Oh, poor wretch!

GERTRUDE (*aside*)

I cannot say it! Oh! for his honor's sake, may he never know the truth. (*Aloud*) I am guilty before all the world, but to you I say, and will repeat it to my last breath, I am innocent! And some future day the truth shall speak from out two tombs, the cruel truth, which will show to you that you also are not free from reproach, but from the very blindness of your hate are culpable in all.

THE GENERAL

I? I? Am I losing my senses? Do you dare to accuse me? (*Perceiving Pauline.*) Ah! Ah! My God!

---

## SCENE ELEVENTH.

THE SAME PERSONS, AND PAULINE (*supported by Ferdinand*).

PAULINE

They have told me all! This woman is innocent of the crime whereof she is accused. Religion has at last taught me that pardon cannot be obtained on high except by those who leave it behind them here below. I took from Madame the key of her desk, I myself sought the poison. I myself tore off the paper to wrap it up, for I wished to die.

GERTRUDE

O Pauline! Take my life, take all I love—Oh, doctor, save her!

THE MAGISTRATE

Is this the truth, mademoiselle?

PAULINE

The truth, yes, for the dying alone speak it—

THE MAGISTRATE

We know then actually nothing about this business.

PAULINE (*to Gertrude*)

Do you know why I came to draw you from the abyss which had engulfed you? It is because Ferdinand spoke to me a word which brought me back from the tomb. He has so great a horror of being left with you in life that he follows me, and will follow me to the grave, where we shall rest together, wedded in death.

GERTRUDE

Ferdinand! Ah, my God! At what a price have I been saved!

THE GENERAL

But unhappy child, wherefore must you die? Am I not, have I ceased for one moment to be a good father? And yet they say that I am culpable.—

FERDINAND

Yes, General, I alone can give the answer to the riddle, and can explain to you your guilt.

THE GENERAL

You, Ferdinand, you to whom I offered my daughter, you who loved her—

FERDINAND

My name is Ferdinand Comte de Marcandal, son of General Marcandal. Do you understand?

THE GENERAL

Ah! son of a traitor! What could you bring to my home but death and treachery!—Defend yourself!—

FERDINAND

Would you fight, General, with the dead? (*He falls.*)


GERTRUDE (*rushes to Ferdinand with a cry*)

Oh! (*She recoils before the General, and approaches his daughter, then draws forth a phial, but immediately flings it away.*) I will condemn myself to live for this old man! (*The General kneels beside his dying daughter.*) Doctor, what will become of him? Is he likely to lose his reason?


THE GENERAL (*stammering like a man who has lost his speech*)

I— I— I—

VERNON

General, what is it?


THE GENERAL

I—I am trying— to pray—for my daughter!


*Final Curtain*

# MERCADET

## A COMEDY IN THREE ACTS

Presented for the First Time in Paris, at the Théâtre du Gymnase
Dramatique, August 24, 1851.

# PERSONS OF THE PLAY

MERCADET, a speculator.
MADAME MERCADET, his wife.
JULIE, their daughter.
MINARD, clerk of Mercadet.
VERDELIN, friend of Mercadet.
GOULARD,
PIERQUIN, } creditors of Mercadet.
VIOLETTE,
MERICOURT, acquaintance of Mercadet.
DE LA BRIVE, suitor to Julie.
JUSTIN, valet,
THÉRÈSE, lady's-maid, } servants of Mercadet.
VIRGINIE, cook,
VARIOUS CREDITORS OF MERCADET.

SCENE: *Paris, in the house of Mercadet.* TIME, *about* 1845.)

# MERCADET

---

## ACT I.

### *SCENE FIRST.*

*(A drawing-room.  A door in the centre.  Side doors.  At the front, to the left, a mantel-piece with a mirror.  To the right, a window, and next it a writing table.  Armchairs.)*

JUSTIN, VIRGINIE AND THÉRÈSE.

JUSTIN (*finishing dusting the room*)

Yes, my dears, he finds it very hard to swim; he is certain to drown, poor M. Mercadet.

VIRGINIE (*her basket on her arm*)
Honestly, do you think that?

JUSTIN

He is ruined!  And although there is much fat to be stewed from a master while he is financially embarrassed, you must not forget that he owes us a year's wages, and we had better get ourselves discharged.

THÉRÈSE

Some masters are so frightfully stubborn!  I spoke to the mistress disrespectfully two or three times, and she pretended not to hear me.

VIRGINIE

**Ah!**  I have been at service in many middle-class houses;

(173)

but I have never seen one like this!—I am going to leave my
stove, and become an actress in some theatre.

### JUSTIN

All of us here are nothing but actors in a theatre.

### VIRGINIE

Yes, indeed, sometimes one has to put on an air of astonishment, as if just fallen from the moon, when a creditor
appears: "Didn't you know it, sir?"—"No."—"M. Mercadet
has gone to Lyons."—"Ah!—He is away?"—"Yes, his prospects are most brilliant; he has discovered some coal-mines."—
"Ah! So much the better!—When does he return?"—"I do
not know." Sometimes I put on an expression as if I had
lost the dearest friend I had in the world.

### JUSTIN (aside)

That would be her money.

### VIRGINIE (pretending to cry)

"Monsieur and mademoiselle are in the greatest distress.
It seems that we are going to lose poor Madame Mercadet.—
They have taken her away to the waters!—Ah!"

### THÉRÈSE

And then, there are some creditors who are actual brutes!
They speak to you as if you were the masters!

### VIRGINIE

There's an end of it.—I ask them for their bill and tell
them I am going to settle.—But now, the tradesmen refuse to
give anything without the money! And you may be sure that
I am not going to lend any of mine.

### JUSTIN

Let us demand our wages.

### VIRGINIE AND THÉRÈSE

Let us demand our wages.


### VIRGINIE

Who are middle-class people?—Middle-class people are those who spend a great deal on their kitchen—


### JUSTIN

Who are devoted to their servants—


### VIRGINIE

And who leave them a pension. That is how middle-class people ought to behave to their servants.


### THÉRÈSE

The lady of Picardy speaks well.—But all the same, I pity mademoiselle and young Minard, her suitor.


### JUSTIN

M. Mercadet is not going to give his daughter to a miserable bookkeeper who earns no more than eighteen hundred francs a year;—he has better views for her than that.


### THÉRÈSE AND VIRGINIE.

Who is the man he thinks of?


### JUSTIN

Yesterday two fine young gentlemen came here in a carriage, and their groom told old Gruneau that one of them was going to marry Mlle. Mercadet.


### VIRGINIE

You don't mean to say so! Are those gentlemen in yellow gloves, with fine flowered waistcoats, going to marry mademoiselle?

### JUSTIN

Not both of them, lady of Picardy.

### VIRGINIE

The panels of their carriage shone like satin.—Their horse had rosettes here. (*She points to her ears.*) It was held by a boy of eight, fair, with frizzed hair and top boots. He looked as sly as a mouse—a very Cupid, though he swore like a trooper. His master is as fine as a picture, with a big diamond in his scarf. It ain't possible that a handsome young man, who owns such a turnout as that is going to be the husband of Mlle. Mercadet? I can't believe it!

### JUSTIN

You don't know M. Mercadet! I, who have been in his house for the last six years, and have seen him since his troubles fighting with his creditors, can believe him capable of anything, even of growing rich; sometimes I say to myself he is utterly ruined! Yellow auction placards flame at his door. He receives reams of stamped creditor's notices, which I sell by the pound for waste paper without being noticed.— But presto! Up he bobs again.—He is triumphant. And what devices he has!—There is a new one every day! First of all, it is a scheme for wooden pavements—then it is duke- doms, ponds, mills. I don't know where the leakage is in his cash box; he finds it so hard to fill; for it empties itself as easily as a drained wine-glass! And always crowds of credi- tors!—How well he turns them away!—Sometimes I have seen them come with the intention of carrying off everything and throwing him into prison. But when he talks to them they end by being the best of friends, and part with cordial hand- shakes! There are some men who can tame jackals and lions. That's not a circumstance; M. Mercadet can tame creditors!

### THÉRÈSE

One of them is not quite so easily managed; and that is M. Pierquin.

##### JUSTIN

He is a tiger who feeds on bankrupts. And to think of poor old Violette!

##### VIRGINIE

He is both creditor and beggar—I always feel inclined to give him a plate of soup.

##### JUSTIN

And Goulard!

##### THÉRÈSE

A bill discounter who would like very much to—to discount me.

##### VIRGINIE (*amid a general laugh*)

I hear madame coming.

##### JUSTIN

Let us keep a civil tongue in our heads, and we shall learn something about the marriage.

---

### SCENE SECOND.

#### THE SAME PERSONS AND MME. MERCADET.

##### MME. MERCADET

Justin, have you executed the commissions I gave you?

##### JUSTIN

Yes, madame, but they refused to deliver the dresses, the hats, and indeed all the things you ordered until—

##### VIRGINIE

And I also have to inform madame that the tradesmen are no longer willing—

### MME. MERCADET

I understand.

### JUSTIN

The creditors are the cause of the whole trouble. I wish I knew how to get even with them.

### MME. MERCADET

The best way to do so would be to pay them.

### JUSTIN

They would be mightily surprised.

### MME. MERCADET

It is useless to conceal from you the excessive anxiety which I suffer over the condition of my husband's affairs. We shall doubtless be in need of your discretion—for we can depend upon you, can we not?

### ALL

You need not mention it, madame.

### VIRGINIE

We were just saying, what excellent employers we had.

### THÉRÈSE

And that we would go through fire and water for you!

### JUSTIN

We were saying—(*Mercadet appears unnoticed.*)

### MME. MERCADET

Thank you all, you are good creatures—(*Mercadet shrugs his shoulders.*) Your master needs only time, he has so many schemes in his head!—a rich suitor has offered himself for Mlle. Julie, and if—

## *SCENE THIRD.*

### THE SAME PERSONS AND MERCADET.

MERCADET (*interrupting his wife*)

My dearest! (*The servants draw back a little. In a low voice to madame*) And so this is how you speak to the serv· ants! To-morrow they laugh at us. (*To Justin*) Justin, go at once to M. Verdelin's house, and ask him to come here, as I want to speak to him about a piece of business that will not admit of delay. Assume an air of mystery, for I must have him come. You, Thérèse, go to the tradesmen of Madame de Mercadet, and tell them, sharply, that they must send the things that have been ordered.—They will be paid for— yes—and cash, too—go at once. (*Justin and Thérèse start.*) Ah!—(*They stop.*) If—these people come to the house again, ask them to enter. (*Mme. Mercadet takes a seat.*)

JUSTIN

These—these people?—

THÉRÈSE AND VIRGINIE.

These people? Eh!

MERCADET

Yes, these people—these creditors of mine!—

MME. MERCADET

How is this, my dear?

MERCADET (*taking a seat opposite his wife*)

I am weary of solitude—I want their society. (*To Justin and Thérèse*) That will do. (*They leave the room.*)

## SCENE FOURTH.

MERCADET, MME. MERCADET AND VIRGINIE.

MERCADET (*to Virginie*)

Has madame given you any orders?

VIRGINIE

No, sir, and besides the tradespeople—

MERCADET

I hope you will do yourself credit to-day. We are going to
have four people to dinner—Verdelin and his wife, M. de
Mericourt and M. de la Brive—so there will be seven of us.
Such dinners are the glory of great cooks! You must have
a fine fish after the soup, then two entrées, very delicately
looked—

VIRGINIE

But, sir, the trades—

MERCADET

For the second course—ah, the second course ought to be at
once rich and brilliant, yet solid. The second course—

VIRGINIE

But the tradespeople—

MERCADET

Nonsense! You annoy me—To talk about tradespeople on
the day when my daughter and her intended are to meet!—

VIRGINIE

They won't supply anything.

MERCADET

What have we got to do with tradespeople that won't take

our trade? We must get others. You must go to their com-
petitors, you must give them my custom, and they will tip you
for it.

VIRGINIE

And how shall I pay those that I am giving up?

MERCADET

Don't worry yourself about that,—it is my business.

VIRGINIE

But if they ask me to pay them—

MERCADET (*aside, rising to his feet*)

This girl has money of her own. (*Aloud*) Virginie, in
these days, credit is the sole wealth of government. My tradespeople misunderstand the laws of their country, they will
show themselves unconstitutional and utter radicals, unless
they leave me alone.—Don't you trouble your head about
people who raise an insurrection against the vital principles
of all rightly constituted states! What you have got to attend
to, is dinner,—that is your duty, and I hope that on this
occasion you will show yourself to be what you are, a first-
class cook!—And if Mme. Mercadet, when she settles with
you on the day after my daughter's wedding, finds that she
owes you anything, I will hold myself liable for it all.

VIRGINIE (*hesitating*)

Sir—

MERCADET

Now go about your business. I give you here an opportunity
of gaining an interest of ten per cent every six months!—and
that is better than the savings banks will do for you.

VIRGINIE

That it is; they only give four per cent a year!

MERCADET (*whispering to his wife*)

What did I tell you!—(*To Virginie*) How can you run the risk of putting your money into the hands of strangers—You are quite clever enough to invest it yourself, and here your little nest-egg will remain in your own possession.

### VIRGINIE

Ten per cent every six months!—I suppose that madame will give me the particulars with regard to the second course. I must start to work on it. (*Exit.*)

## SCENE FIFTH.

### MERCADET AND MME. MERCADET.

MERCADET (*watching Virginie as she goes out*)

That girl has a thousand crowns of our good money in the savings bank, so that we needn't worry about the kitchen for awhile.

### MME. MERCADET

Ah! sir, how can you stoop to such a thing as this?

### MERCADET

Madame, these are mere petty details; don't bother about the means to the end. You, a little time ago, were trying to control your servants by kindness, but it is necessary to command and compel them, and to do it briefly, like Napoleon.

### MME. MERCADET

How can you order them when you don't pay them?

### MERCADET

You must pay them by a bluff.

### Mme. Mercadet

Sometimes you can obtain by affection what is not attainable by—

### Mercadet

By affection! Ah! Little do you know the age in which we live—To-day, madame, wealth is everything, family is nothing; there are no families, but only individuals! The future of each one is to be determined by the public funds. A young girl when she needs a dowry no longer appeals to her family, but to a syndicate. The income of the King of England comes from an insurance company. The wife depends for funds, not upon her husband, but upon the savings bank!—Debts are paid, not to creditors, but to the country, through an agency, which manages a sort of slave-trade in white people! All our duties are arranged by coupons—The servants which we exchange for them are no longer attached to their masters, but if you hold their money they will be devoted to you.

### Mme. Mercadet

Oh, sir, you who are so honorable, so upright, sometimes say things to me which—

### Mercadet

And what is said may also be done, that is what you mean, isn't it? Undoubtedly I would do anything to save myself, for (*he pulls out a five-franc piece*) this represents modern honor. Do you know why the dramas that have criminals for their heroes are so popular? It is because all the audience flatter themselves and say, "at any rate, I am much better than that fellow!"

### Mme. Mercadet

My dear!

### Mercadet

For my part I have an excuse, for I am bearing the burden of my partner's crime—of that fellow Godeau, who absconded,

carrying with him the cash box of our house!—And besides
that, what disgrace is it to be in debt? What man is there
who does not owe his father his existence? He can never
repay that debt. The earth is constantly bankrupt to the sun.
Life, madame, is a perpetual loan! Am I not superior to my
creditors? I have their money, when they can only expect
mine. I do not ask anything of them, and yet they are constantly importuning me.—A man who does not owe anything
is not thought about by any one, while my creditors take a
keen interest in me.

### MME. MERCADET

They take rather too much! To owe and to pay is well
enough—but to borrow without any prospect of returning—

### MERCADET

You feel a great deal of compassion for my creditors, but
our indebtedness to them springs from—

### MME. MERCADET

Their confidence in us, sir.

### MERCADET

No, but from their greed of gain! The speculator and the
broker are one and the same—each of them aims at sudden
wealth. I have done a favor to all my creditors, and they all
expect to get something out of me! I should be most unhappy
but for the secret consciousness I have that they are selfish and
avaricious—so that you will see in a few moments how I will
make each of them play out his little comedy. (*He sits down.*)

### MME. MERCADET

You have actually ordered them to be admitted?

### MERCADET

That I may meet them as I ought to!—(*taking her hand.*)

I am at the end of my resources; the time has come for a master-stroke, and Julie must come to our assistance.

### MME. MERCADET

What, my daughter!

### MERCADET

My creditors are pressing me, and harassing me. I must manage to make a brilliant match for Julie. This will dazzle them; they will give me more time. But in order that this brilliant marriage may take place, these gentlemen must give me more money.

### MME. MERCADET

They give you more money!

### MERCADET

Isn't there need of it for the dresses which they are sending to you, and for the trousseau which I am giving? And a suitable trousseau to go with the dowry of two hundred thousand francs, will cost fifteen thousand.

### MME. MERCADET

But you are utterly unable to give such a dowry.

### MERCADET (*rising*)

All the more reason why I should give the trousseau. Now this is what we stand in need of: twelve or fifteen thousand francs for the trousseau, and a thousand crowns to pay the tradesmen and to prevent any appearance of straitened circumstances in our house, when M. de la Brive arrives.

### MME. MERCADET

How can you count on your creditors for that?

### MERCADET

Don't they now belong to the family? Can you find any

relation who is as anxious as they are to see me wealthy and rich? Relations are always a little envious of the happiness or the wealth which comes to us; the creditor's joy alone is sincere. If I were to die, I should have at my funeral more creditors than relations, and while the latter carried their mourning in their hearts or on their heads, the former would carry it in their ledgers and purses. It is here that my departure would leave a genuine void! The heart forgets, and crape disappears at the end of a year, but the account which is unpaid is ineffaceable, and the void remains eternally unfilled.

### Mme. Mercadet

My dear, I know the people to whom you are indebted, and I am quite certain that you will obtain nothing from them.

### Mercadet

I shall obtain both time and money from them, rest assured of that. (*Mme. Mercadet is perturbed.*) Don't you see, my dear, that creditors when once they have opened their purses are like gamblers who continue to stake their money in order to recover their first losses? (*Growing excited.*) Yes! they are inexhaustible gold mines! If a man has no father to leave him a fortune, he finds his creditors are so many indefatigable uncles.

### Justin (*entering*)

M. Goulard wishes to know if it is true that you desire to see him?

### Mercadet (*to his wife*)

My message astounded him. (*To Justin*) Beg him to come in. (*Justin goes out.*) Goulard! The most intractable of them all!—who has three bailiffs in his employ. But fortunately he is a greedy though timid speculator who engages in the most risky affairs and trembles all the time they are being conducted.

JUSTIN (*announcing*)

M. Goulard! (*Exit Justin.*)

---

## SCENE SIXTH.

### THE SAME PERSONS AND GOULARD.

GOULARD (*in anger*)

Ah! you can be found, sir, when you want to be!

MME. MERCADET (*aside to her husband*)

My dear, how angry he seems!

MERCADET (*making a sign that she should be calm*)

This is one of my creditors, my dear.

GOULARD

Yes, and I shan't leave this house until you pay me.

MERCADET (*aside*)

You shan't leave this house until you give me some money—
(*Aloud*) Ah! you have persecuted me most unkindly—me, a
man with whom you have had such extensive dealings!—

GOULARD

Dealings which have not always been to my advantage.

MERCADET

All the more credit to you, for if advantages were the sole
results of business, everybody would become a money-lender.

GOULARD

I hope you haven't asked me to come here, in order to show

me how clever you are! I know that you are cleverer than I
am, for you have got over me in money matters.

### MERCADET

Well, money matters have some importance. (*To his wife*)
Yes, yes, you see in this man one who has hunted me as if I
were a hare. Come, come, Goulard, admit it, you have behaved badly. Anybody but myself would have taken vengeance on you—for of course I could cause you to lose a considerable sum of money.

### GOULARD

So you could, if you didn't pay me; but you shall pay me—
your obligations are now in the hands of the law.

### MME. MERCADET

Of the law?

### MERCADET

Of the law! You are losing your senses, you don't know
what you are doing, you are ruining us both—yourself and
me—at the same time.

### GOULARD (*anxiously*)

How?—You—that of course is possible—but—but—me?

### MERCADET

Both of us, I tell you!—Quick, sit down there—write,
write—!

### GOULARD (*mechanically taking the pen*)

Write—write what?

### MERCADET

Write to Delannoy that he must make them stay the pro·
ceedings, and give me the thousand crowns which I absolutely
need.

GOULARD (*throwing down the pen*)

That is very likely, indeed!

MERCADET

You hesitate, and, when I am on the eve of marrying my daughter to a man immensely wealthy—that is the time you choose to cause my arrest. And by that means you are killing both your capital and interest!

GOULARD

Ah! you are going to marry your daughter—

MERCADET

To the Comte de la Brive; he possesses as many thousand francs as he is years old!

GOULARD

Then if he is up in years, there is reason for giving you some delay. But the thousand crowns—the thousand crowns—never.—I am quite decided on that point. I will give you nothing, neither delay nor—I must go now—

MERCADET (*with energy*)

Very well! You can go if you like, you ungrateful fellow!—But don't forget that I have done my best to save you.

GOULARD (*turning back*)

Me?—To save me—from what?

MERCADET (*aside*)

I have him now. (*Aloud*) From what?—From the most complete ruin.

GOULARD

Ruin? It is impossible.

MERCADET (*taking a seat*)

What is the matter with you? You, a man of intelligence, of ability—a strong man, and yet you cause me all this trouble! You came here and I felt absolutely enraged against you—not because I was your friend, I confess it, but through selfishness. I look upon our interests as identical. I said to myself: I owe him so much that he is sure to give me his assistance when I have such a grand chance—like the one at this moment! And you are going to let out the whole business and to lose everything for the sake of a paltry sum! Everything! You are perhaps right in refusing me the thousand crowns—It is better, perhaps, to bury them in your coffers with the rest. All right! Send me to prison! Then, when all is gone, you'll have to look somewhere else for a friend!

GOULARD (*in a tone of self-reproach*)

Mercadet!—my dear Mercadet!—But is it actually true?

MERCADET (*rising from his seat*)

Is it true? (*To his wife*) You would not believe he was so stupid. (*To Goulard*) She has ended by becoming a daring speculator. (*To his wife*) I may tell you, my dear, that Goulard is going to invest a large sum in our great enterprise.

MME. MERCADET (*ashamed*)

Sir!

MERCADET

What a misfortune it will be if it does not turn out well.

GOULARD

Mercadet!—Are you talking about the Basse-Indre mines?

MERCADET

Of course I am. (*Aside*) Ah! You have some of the Basse-Indre stock, I see.

GOULARD

But the investment seems to me first-class.

MERCADET

First-class—Yes, for those who sold out yesterday.

GOULARD

Have any stockholders sold out?

MERCADET

Yes, privately.

GOULARD

Good-bye. Thanks, Mercadet; madame, accept my respects.

MERCADET (*stopping him*)

Goulard!

GOULARD

Eh?

MERCADET

What about this note to Delannoy?

GOULARD

I will speak to him about the postponement—

MERCADET

No; write to him; and in the meantime I will find some one who will buy your stock.

GOULARD (*sitting down*)

All my Basse-Indre? (*He takes up the pen.*)

MERCADET (*aside*)

Here you see the honest man, ever ready to rob his neighbor. (*Aloud*) Very well, write—ordering a postponement of three months.

GOULARD (*writing*)

Three months! There you have it.


MERCADET

The man I allude to, who buys in secret for fear of causing
a rise, wants to get three hundred shares; do you happen to
have three hundred?

GOULARD

I have three hundred and fifty.


MERCADET

Fifty more! Never mind! he'll take them all. (*Examining
what Goulard has written*) Have you mentioned the thousand
crowns?

GOULARD

And what is your friend's name?


MERCADET

His name? You haven't mentioned?—


GOULARD

His name!

MERCADET

The thousand crowns.


GOULARD

What a devil of a man he is! (*He writes.*) There, you have
it!

MERCADET

His name is Pierquin.


GOULARD (*rising*)

Pierquin.

MERCADET

He at least is the nominal buyer.—Go to your house and I

will send him to you; it is never a good thing to run after a purchaser.

### GOULARD

Never!—You have saved my life. Good-bye, my friend. Madame, accept my prayers for the happiness of your daughter. (*Exit.*)

### MERCADET

One of them captured! Now watch me get the others!

---

## SCENE SEVENTH.

### MME. MERCADET, MERCADET, THEN JULIE.

### MME. MERCADET

Is there any truth in what you just now said? I could not quite follow you.

### MERCADET

It is to the interest of my friend Verdelin to cause a panic in Basse-Indre stock; this stock has been for a long time very risky and has suddenly become of first-class value, through the discovery of certain beds of mineral, which are known only to those on the inside.—Ah! If I could but invest a thousand crowns in it my fortune would be made. But, of course, our main object at present is the marriage of Julie.

### MME. MERCADET

You are well acquainted with M. de la Brive, are you not?

### MERCADET

I have dined with him. He has a charming apartment, fine plate, a silver dessert service, bearing his arms, so that it could not have been borrowed. Our daughter is going to make a fine match, and he—when either one of a married couple is happy, it is all right. (*Julie enters.*)

### MME. MERCADET

Here comes our daughter. Julie, your father and I have something to say to you on a subject which is always agreeable to a young girl.

### JULIE

M. Minard has then spoken to you, father?

### MERCADET

M. Minard! Did you expect, madame, to find a M. Minard reigning in the heart of your daughter? Is not this M. Minard that under clerk of mine?

### JULIE

Yes, papa.

### MERCADET

Do you love him?

### JULIE

Yes, papa.

### MERCADET

But besides loving, it is necessary for a person to be loved.

### MME. MERCADET

Does he love you?

### JULIE

Yes, mamma!

### MERCADET

. Yes, papa; yes, mamma; why don't you say mammy and daddy?—As soon as daughters have passed their majority they begin to talk as if they were just weaned. Be polite enough to address your mother as madame.

### JULIE

Yes, monsieur.

### MERCADET

Oh! you may address me as papa. I shan't be annoyed at that. What proof have you that he loves you?

### JULIE

The best proof of all; he wishes to marry me.

### MERCADET

It is quite true, as has been said, that young girls, like little children, have answers ready enough to knock one silly. Let me tell you, mademoiselle, that a clerk with a salary of eighteen hundred francs does not know how to love. He hasn't got the time, he has to work too hard—

### MME. MERCADET

But, unhappy child—

### MERCADET

Ah! A lucky thought strikes me! Let me talk to her. Julie, listen to me. I will marry you to Minard. (*Julie smiles with delight.*) Now, look here, you haven't got a single sou, and you know it; what is going to become of you a week after your marriage? Have you thought about that?

### JULIE

Yes, papa—

### MME. MERCADET (*with sympathy, to her husband*)

The poor child is mad.

### MERCADET

Yes, she is in love. (*To Julie*) Tell me all about it, Julie. I am not now your father, but your confidant; I am listening.

### JULIE

After our marriage we will still love each other.

MERCADET

But will Cupid shoot you bank coupons at the end of his arrows?

JULIE

Father, we shall lodge in a small apartment, at the extremity of the Faubourg, on the fourth story, if necessary!—And if it can't be helped, I will be his house-maid. Oh! I will take an immense delight in the care of the household, for I shall know that it will all be done for him. I will work for him, while he is working for me. I will spare him. every anxiety, and he will never know how straitened we are. Our home will be spotlessly clean, even elegant—You shall see! Elegance depends upon such little things; it springs from the soul, and happiness is at once the cause and the effect of it. I can earn enough from my painting to cost him nothing and even to contribute to the expenses of our living. Moreover, love will help us to pass through days of hardship. Adolphe has ambition, like all those who are of lofty soul, and these are the successful men—

MERCADET

Success is within reach of the bachelor, but, when a man is married, he exhausts himself in meeting his expenses, and runs after a thousand franc bill as a dog runs after a carriage.

JULIE

But, papa, Adolphe, has strength of will, united with such capacity that I feel sure I shall see him some day a Minister, perhaps—

MERCADET

In these days, who is there that does not indulge more or less the hope of being a Minister? When a man leaves college he thinks himself a great poet, or a great orator! Do you know what your Adolphe will really become?—Why, the father of several children, who will utterly disarrange your plans of work and economy, who will end by landing his excellency in the debtor's prison, and who will plunge you into the most frightful poverty. What you have related to me is the romance and not the reality of life.

### MME. MERCADET

Daughter, there can be nothing serious in this love of yours.

### JULIE

It is a love to which both of us are willing to sacrifice every-thing.

### MERCADET

I suppose that your friend Adolphe thinks that we are rich?

### JULIE

He has never spoken to me about money.

### MERCADET

Just so. I can quite understand it. (*To Julie*) Julie, write to him at once, telling him to come to me.

### JULIE (*kissing him*)

Dear papa!

### MERCADET

And you must marry M. de la Brive. Instead of living on a fourth floor in a suburb, you will have a fine house in the Chaussée-d'Antin, and, if you are not the wife of a Minister, you perhaps will be the wife of a peer of France. I am sorry, my daughter, that I have no more to offer you. Remember, you can have no choice in the matter, for M. Minard is going to give you up.

### JULIE

Oh! he will never do that, papa. He will win your heart—

### MME. MERCADET

My dear, suppose he loves her?

**MERCADET**

He is deceiving her—

**JULIE**

I shouldn't mind being always deceived in that way. (*A bell is heard without.*)

**MME. MERCADET**

Some one is ringing, and we have no one to open the door.

**MERCADET**

That is all right. Let them ring.

**MME. MERCADET**

I am all the time thinking that Godeau may return.

**MERCADET**

After eight years without any news, you are still expecting Godeau! You seem to me like those old soldiers who are waiting for the return of Napoleon.

**MME. MERCADET**

They are ringing again.

**MERCADET**

Julie, go and see who it is, and tell them that your mother and I have gone out. If any one is shameless enough to disbelieve a young girl—it must be a creditor—let him come in. (*Exit Julie.*)

**MME. MERCADET**

This love she speaks of, and which, at least on her side, is sincere, disturbs me greatly.

**MERCADET**

You women are all too romantic.

JULIE (*returning*)

It is M. Pierquin, papa.

MERCADET

A creditor and usurer—a vile and violent soul, who humors me because he thinks me a man of resources; a wild beast only half-tamed yet cowed by my audacity. If I showed fear he would devour me. (*Going to the door.*) Come in, Pierquin, come in.

---

## SCENE EIGHTH.

THE SAME PERSONS AND PIERQUIN.

PIERQUIN

My congratulations to you all. I hear that you are making a grand marriage for your daughter. Mademoiselle is to marry a millionaire; the report has already gone abroad.

MERCADET

A millionaire?—No, he has only nine hundred thousand francs, at the most.

PIERQUIN

This magnificent prospect will induce a lot of people to give you time. They are becoming devilishly tired of your talk about Godeau's return. And I myself—

MERCADET

Were you thinking about having me arrested?

JULIE

Arrested!

MME. MERCADET (*to Pierquin*)

Ah! sir.

PIERQUIN

Now listen to me, you have had two years, and I never before let a bond go over so long; but this marriage is a glorious invention and—

MME. MERCADET

An invention!

MERCADET

Sir, my future son-in-law, M. de la Brive, is a young man—

PIERQUIN

So that there is a real young man in the case? How much are you going to pay the young man?

MME. MERCADET

Oh!

MERCADET (*checking his wife by a sign*)

No more of this insolence! otherwise, my dear sir, I shall be forced to demand a settlement of our accounts—and, my dear M. Pierquin, you will lose a good deal of the price at which you sold your money to me. And at the rate of interest you charge, I shall cost you more than the value of a farm in Bauce.

PIERQUIN

Sir—

MERCADET (*haughtily*)

Sir, I shall soon be so rich that I will not endure to be twitted by any one—not even by a creditor.

PIERQUIN

But—

MERCADET

Not a word—or I will pay you! Come into my private room and we will settle the business about which I asked you to come.

PIERQUIN

I am at your service, sir. (*Aside*) What a devil of a man !
(*They bow to the ladies and enter Mercadet's room.*)


MERCADET (*following Pierquin; aside to his wife*)
The wild beast is tamed. I'll get this one, too.

---

## SCENE NINTH.

MME. MERCADET, JULIE, AND LATER, SERVANTS.


JULIE

O mamma ! I cannot marry this M. de la Brive!


MME. MERCADET

But he is rich, you know.


JULIE

But I prefer happiness and poverty, to unhappiness and
wealth.

MME. MERCADET

My child, happiness is impossible in poverty, while there
is no misfortune that wealth cannot alleviate.


JULIE

How can you say such sad words to me?


MME. MERCADET

Children should learn a lesson from the experience of
parents. We are at present having a very bitter taste of life's
vicissitudes. Take my advice, daughter, and marry wealth.


JUSTIN (*entering, followed by Thérèse and Virginie*)
Madame, we have carried out the master's orders.

VIRGINIE

My dinner will be ready.

THÉRÈSE

And the tradesmen have consented.

JUSTIN

As far as concerns M. Verdelin—

---

## SCENE TENTH.

THE SAME PERSONS AND MERCADET (*carrying a bundle of papers*)

MERCADET

What did my friend Verdelin say?

JUSTIN

He will be here in a moment. He was just on his way here to bring some money to M. Bredif, the owner of this house.

MERCADET

Bredif is a millionaire. Take care that Verdelin speaks to me before going up to him. How did you get on, Thérèse, with the milliners and dressmakers?

THÉRÈSE

Sir, as soon as I gave them a promise of payment, every one greeted me with smiles.

MERCADET

Very good. And shall we have a fine dinner, Virginie?

VIRGINIE

You will compliment it, sir, when you eat it.

MERCADET

And the tradespeople?

VIRGINIE

They will wait your time.

MERCADET

I shall settle with you all to-morrow.  You can go now.
(*They go out.*)   A man who has his servants with him is like
a minister who has the press on his side!—

MME. MERCADET

And what of Pierquin?

MERCADET (*showing the papers*)

All that I could extort from him is as follows.—He will
give me time, and this negotiable paper in exchange for stock.
—Also notes for forty-seven thousand francs, to be collected
from a man named Michonnin, a gentleman broker, not considered very solvent, who may be a crook but has a very rich
aunt at Bordeaux; M. de la Brive is from that district and I
can learn from him if there is anything to be got out of it.

MME. MERCADET

But the tradesmen will soon arrive.

MERCADET

I shall be here to receive them.  Now leave me, leave me,
my dears.  (*Exeunt the two ladies.*)

---

## SCENE ELEVENTH.

MERCADET, THEN VIOLETTE.

MERCADET (*walking up and down*)

Yes, they will soon be here!  And everything depends upon

the somewhat slippery friendship of Verdelin—a man whose fortune I made! Ah! when a man has passed forty he learns that the world is peopled by the ungrateful—I do not know where all the benefactors have gone to. Verdelin and I have a high opinion of each other. He owes me gratitude, I owe him money, and neither of us pays the other. And now, in order to arrange the marriage of Julie, my business is to find a thousand crowns in a pocket which pretends to be empty—to find entrance into a heart in order to find entrance into a cashbox! What an undertaking! Only women can do such things, and with men who are in love with them.

#### JUSTIN (*without*)

Yes, he is in.

#### MERCADET

It is he. (*Violette appears.*) Ah! my friend! It is dear old Violette!

#### VIOLETTE

This is the eleventh call within a week, my dear M. Mercadet, and my actual necessity has driven me to wait for you three hours in the street; I thought the truth was told me when I was assured that you were in the country. But I came to-day—

#### MERCADET

Ah! Violette, old fellow, we are both hard up!

#### VIOLETTE

Humph! I don't think so. For my part, I've pledged everything I could put in the pawn-shop.

#### MERCADET

So have we.

#### VIOLETTE

I have never reproached you with my ruin, for I believe it is your intention to enrich me, as well as yourself; but still,

fine words butter no parsnips, and I am come to implore you
to give me a small sum on account, and by so doing you will
save the lives of a whole family.


### MERCADET

My dear old Violette, you grieve me deeply! Be reasonable
and I will share with you. (*In a low voice*) We have scarcely
a hundred francs in the house, and even that is my daughter's
money.

### VIOLETTE

Is it possible! You, Mercadet, whom I have known so rich?


### MERCADET

I conceal nothing from you.


### VIOLETTE

Unfortunate people owe it to each other to speak the truth.


### MERCADET

Ah! If that were the only thing they owed how prompt
would be the payment! But keep this as a secret, for I am on
the point of making a good match for my daughter.


### VIOLETTE

I have two daughters, sir, and they work without hope of
being married! In your present circumstances I cannot press
you, but my wife and my daughters await my return in the
deepest anxiety.

### MERCADET

Stay a moment. I will give you sixty francs.


### VIOLETTE

Ah! my wife and my girls will bless you. (*Aside, while
Mercadet leaves the room for a moment.*) The others who
abuse him get nothing out of him, but by appealing to his

pity, little by little I get back my money! (*Chuckles and slaps his pocket.*)

MERCADET (*on the point of re-entering sees this action*)

The beggarly old miser! Sixty francs on account paid ten times makes six hundred francs. Come now, I have sown enough, it is time to reap the harvest. (*Aloud*) Take this.

VIOLETTE

Sixty francs in gold! It is a long time since I have seen such a sum. Good-bye, we shan't forget to pray for the speedy marriage of Mlle. Mercadet.

MERCADET

Good-bye, dear old Violette. (*Holding him by the hand.*) Poor man, when I look at you, I think myself rich—your misfortunes touch me deeply. And yesterday I thought I would soon be on the point of paying back to you not only the interest but the principal of what I owe you.

VIOLETTE (*turning back*)

Paying me back! In full!—

MERCADET

It was a close shave.

VIOLETTE

What was?

MERCADET

Imagine, my dear fellow, that there exists a most brilliant opportunity, a most magnificent speculation, the most sublime discovery—an affair which appeals to the interest of every one, which will draw upon all the exchanges, and for the realization of which a stupid banker has refused me the miserable sum of a thousand crowns—when there is more than a million in sight.

VIOLETTE

A million!

MERCADET

Yes, a million, from the start. Afterwards no one can calculate where the rage for protective pavement will stop.

VIOLETTE

Payment?

MERCADET

Protective pavement.  A pavement on which no barricade
can be raised.

VIOLETTE

Really!

MERCADET

You see, that from henceforth all governments interested
in the preservation of order will become our chief sharehold-
ers—Ministers, princes and kings will be our chief partners.—
Next come the gods of finance, the great bankers, those of
independent income in commerce and speculation; even the
socialists, seeing that their industry is ruined, will be forced
to buy stocks for a living from me!

VIOLETTE

Yes, it is fine!  It is grand!

MERCADET

It is sublime and philanthropic!—And to think that I have
been refused four thousand francs, wherewith to send out
advertisements and launch my prospectus!

VIOLETTE

Four thousand francs!  I thought it was only—

MERCADET

Four thousand francs, no more!  And I was to give away

for the loan a half interest in the enterprise—that is to say a
fortune! Ten fortunes!

VIOLETTE

Listen—I will see—I will speak to some one—

MERCADET

Speak to no one! Keep it to yourself! The idea would at
once be snatched up—or perhaps they wouldn't understand it·
so well as you have immediately done. These money dealers
are so stupid. Besides, I am expecting Verdelin here—

VIOLETTE

Verdelin—but—we might perhaps—

MERCADET

'Twill be lucky for Verdelin, if he has the brains to risk
six thousand francs in it.

VIOLETTE

But you said four thousand just now.

MERCADET

It was four thousand that they refused me, but I need six
thousand! Six thousand francs, and Verdelin, whom I have
already made a millionaire once, is likely to become so three,
four, five times over! But he will deserve it, for he is a clever
fellow, is Verdelin.

VIOLETTE

Mercadet, I will find you the money.

MERCADET

No, no, don't think of it. Besides, he will be here in a
moment, and if I am to send him away without concluding
the business with him, it will be necessary to have it settled

with some one else before Verdelin comes—and, as that is
impossible—good-bye—and good luck—I shall certainly be
able to pay you your thirty thousand francs.

### VIOLETTE

But say—why couldn't I—?

### MME. MERCADET (*entering*)

M. Verdelin has come, my dear.

### MERCADET (*aside*)

Good, good! (*Aloud*) Just detain him a minute. (*Mme.
Mercadet goes out.*) Well, good-bye, dear old Violette—

### VIOLETTE (*pulling out a greasy pocketbook*)

Wait a moment—here, I have the money with me—and will
give it you beforehand.

### MERCADET

You! Six thousand francs!—

### VIOLETTE

A friend asked me to invest it for him, and—

### MERCADET

And you couldn't find a better opening. We'll sign the
contract presently! (*He takes the bills.*) This closes the
deal—and so much the worse for Verdelin—he has missed a
gold mine!

### VIOLETTE

Well, I'll see you later.

### MERCADET

Yes—see you later! You can get out through my study.
(*He shows him the way out. Mme. Mercadet enters.*)

##### MME. MERCADET

Mercadet!

##### MERCADET (*reappearing*)

Ah! my dear! I am an unfortunate man! I ought to blow my brains out!

##### MME. MERCADET

Good heavens! What is the matter?

##### MERCADET

The matter is that a moment ago I asked this sham bankrupt Violette for six thousand francs.

##### MME. MERCADET

And he refused to give them to you?

##### MERCADET

On the contrary, he handed them over.

##### MME. MERCADET

What, then, do you mean?

##### MERCADET

I am an unlucky man, as I told you, because he gave them so quickly that I could have gotten ten thousand if I had only known it.

##### MME. MERCADET

What a man you are! I suppose you know that Verdelin is waiting for you.

##### MERCADET

Beg him to come in. At last I have Julie's trousseau; and we now need only enough money for your dresses and for household expenses until the marriage. Send in Verdelin.

### MME. MERCADET

Yes, he is your friend, and of course you will gain your end with him.  (*She goes out.*)

### MERCADET (*alone*)

Yes, he is my friend!  And he has all the pride that comes with fortune; but he has never had a Godeau (*looking round to see if he is alone*).  After all, Godeau!  I really believe that Godeau has brought me in more money than he has taken from me.

---

## SCENE TWELFTH.

### MERCADET AND VERDELIN.

### VERDELIN

Good-day, Mercadet.  What is doing now?  Tell me quickly for I was stopped here on my way up-stairs to Bredif's apartment.

### MERCADET

Oh, he can wait!  How is it that you are going to see a man like Bredif?

### VERDELIN (*laughing*)

My dear friend, if people only visited those they esteem they would make no visits at all.

### MERCADET (*laughing and taking his hand*)

A man wouldn't go even into his own house.

### VERDELIN

But tell me what you want with me?

MERCADET

Your question is so sudden that it hasn't left me time to gild the pill!

VERDELIN

Oh! my old comrade. I have nothing, and I am frank to say that even if I had I could give you nothing. I have already lent you all that my means permit me to dispose of; I have never asked you for payment, for I am your friend as well as your creditor, and indeed, if my heart did not overflow in gratitude towards you, if I had not been a man different from ordinary men, the creditor would long ago have killed the man. I tell you everything has a limit in this world.

MERCADET

Friendship has a limit, that's certain; but not misfortune.

VERDELIN

If I were rich enough to save you altogether, to cancel your debt entirely, I would do so with all my heart, for I admire your courage. But you are bound to go under. Your last schemes, although cleverly projected, have collapsed. You have ruined your reputation, you are looked upon as a dangerous man. You have not known how to take advantage of the momentary success of your operations. When you are utterly beggared, you will always find bread at my house; but it is the duty of a friend to speak these plain truths.

MERCADET

What would be the advantage of friendship unless it gave us the pleasure of finding ourselves in the right, and seeing a friend in the wrong—of being comfortable ourselves and seeing our friend in difficulties and of paying compliment to ourselves by saying disagreeable things to him? Is it true then that I am little thought of on 'Change?

VERDELIN

I do not say so much as that. No; you still pass for an honest man, but necessity is forcing you to adopt expedients—

MERCADET

Which are not justified by the success which luckier men enjoy! Ah, success! How many outrageous things go to make up success. You'll learn that soon enough. Now, for instance, this morning I began to bear the market on the mines of Basse-Indre, in order that you may gain control of that enterprise before the favorable report of the engineers is published.

VERDELIN

Hush, Mercadet, can this be true? Ah! I see your genius there! (*Puts his arm round him.*)

MERCADET

I say this in order that you may understand that I have no need of advice, nor of moralizing,—merely of money. Alas! I do not ask any thing of you for myself, my dear friend, but I am about to make a marriage for my daughter, and here we are actually, although secretly, fallen into absolute destitution. You are in a house where poverty reigns under the appearance of luxury. The power of promises, and of credit, all is exhausted! And if I cannot pay in cash for certain necessary expenses, this marriage must be broken off. All I want here is a fortnight of opulence, just as all that you want is twenty-four hours of lying on the Exchange. Verdelin, this request will never be repeated, for I have only one daughter. Must I confess it to you? My wife and daughter are absolutely destitute of clothes! (*Aside*) He is hesitating.

VERDELIN (*aside*)

He has played me so many tricks that I really do not know whether his daughter is going to be married or not. How can she marry?

## MERCADET

This very day I have to give a dinner to my future son-in-law, whom a mutual friend is introducing to us, and I haven't even my plate remaining in the house. It is—you know where it is—I not only need a thousand crowns, but I also hope that you will lend me your dinner service and come and dine here with your wife.

## VERDELIN

A thousand crowns!—Mercadet! No one has a thousand crowns to lend. One scarcely has them for himself; if he were to lend them whenever he was asked, he would never have them. (*He retires to the fire-place.*)

## MERCADET (*following him, aside*)

He will yet come to the scratch. (*Aloud*) Now look here, Verdelin, I love my wife and my daughter; these sentiments, my friend, are my sole consolation in the midst of my recent disasters; these women have been so gentle, so patient! I should like to see them placed beyond the reach of distress. Oh! It is on this point that my sufferings are most real! (*They walk to the front of the stage arm in arm.*) I have recently drunk the cup of bitterness, I have slipped upon my wooden pavement,—I organized a monopoly and others drained me of everything! But, believe me, this is nothing in comparison with the pain of seeing you refuse me help in this extremity! Nevertheless, I am not going to dwell upon the consequences—for I do not wish to owe anything to your pity.

## VERDELIN (*taking a seat*)

A thousand crowns!—But what purpose would you apply them to?

## MERCADET (*aside*)

I shall get them. (*Aloud*) My dear fellow, a son-in-law is a bird who is easily frightened away. The absence of one

piece of lace on a dress reveals everything to him.   The ladies'
costumes are ordered, the merchants are on the point of
delivering them—yes, I was rash enough to say that I would
pay for everything, for I counted on you!   Verdelin, a thousand crowns won't kill you, for you have sixty thousand francs
a year.   And the life of a young girl of whom you are fond is
now at stake—for you are fond of Julie!   She has a sincere
attachment for your little girl, they play together like the
happiest of creatures.   Would you let the companion of your
daughter pine away with despair?   Misfortune is contagious!
It brings evil on all around!

VERDELIN

My dear fellow, I have not got a thousand crowns.   I can
lend you my plate; but I have not—

MERCADET

You can give me your note on the bank.   It is soon signed—

VERDELIN (rising)

I—no—

MERCADET

Ah! my poor daughter!   It is all over.   (*Falls back overcome in an armchair near the table.*)   God forgive me, if I put
an end to the painful dream of life, and let me awaken in Thy
bosom!

VERDELIN (after a short silence)

But—  Have you really found a son-in-law?

MERCADET (rising abruptly to his feet)

You ask if I have found a son-in-law!—You actually throw
a doubt upon this!   You may refuse me, if you like, the means
of effecting the happiness of my daughter, but do not insult
me!—I am fallen low indeed!   O Verdelin!   I would not
for a thousand crowns have had such an idea of you, and you
can never win absolution from me excepting by giving them.

VERDELIN (*wishing to leave*)

I must go and see if I can—

MERCADET

No! This is only another way of refusing me!—Can I believe it? Will not you whom I have seen spend the same sum upon some such trifle as a passing love affair—will you not apply a thousand crowns to the performance of a good action?

VERDELIN (*laughing*)

At the present time there are very few good actions, or transactions.

MERCADET

Ha! ha! ha! How witty!—You are laughing, I see there is a reaction!

VERDELIN

Ha! ha! ha! (*He drops his hat.*)

MERCADET (*picking up the hat and dusting it with his sleeve*)

Come now, old fellow. Haven't we seen life! We two began it together. What a lot of things we have said and done!—Don't you recollect the good old time when we swore to be friends always through thick and thin?

VERDELIN

Indeed, I do. And don't you recollect our party at Rambouillet, where I fought with an officer of the Guard on your account?

MERCADET

I thought it was for the lovely Clarissa! Ah! But we were gay!—We were young!—And to-day we have our daughters, daughters old enough to marry! If Clarissa were alive now, she would blame your hesitation!

VERDELIN

If she had lived, I should never have married.


MERCADET

Because you know what love is, that you do!—So I may count upon you for dinner, and you give me your word of honor that you will send me—


VERDELIN

The plate?

MERCADET

And the thousand crowns—


VERDELIN

Ah! You still harp upon that!—I have told you that I cannot do it.

MERCADET (*aside*)

It is certain that this fellow will never die of heart failure. (*Aloud*) And so it seems I am to be murdered by my best friend? Alas! It is always thus! You are actually untouched by the memory of Clarissa—and by the despair of a father! (*He cries out towards the chamber of his wife.*) Ah! it is all over!—I am in despair! I am going to blow my brains out!

---

*SCENE THIRTEENTH.*


THE SAME PERSONS, MME. MERCADET AND JULIE.


MME. MERCADET

What on earth is the matter with you, my dear?


JULIE

How your voice frightened us, papa!

### MERCADET

They heard us! See how they come, like two guardian angels! (*He takes them by the hand.*) Ah! you melt my heart! (*To Verdelin*) Verdelin! do you wish to slay a whole family? This proof of their tenderness gives me courage to fall at your feet.

### JULIE

Oh, sir! (*She checks her father.*) It is I who will implore you for him. Whatever may be his demand, do not refuse my father; he must, indeed, be in the most terrible anguish!

### MERCADET

Dear child! (*Aside*) In what accents does she speak! I couldn't speak so naturally as that.

### MME. MERCADET

M. Verdelin, listen to us—

### VERDELIN (*to Julie*)

You don't know what he is asking, do you?

### JULIE

No.

### VERDELIN

He is asking for a thousand crowns, in order to arrange your marriage.

### JULIE

Then, forget, sir, all that I said to you; I do not wish for a marriage which has been purchased by the humiliation of my father.

### MERCADET (*aside*)

She is magnificent!

### VERDELIN

Julie!—I will go at once and get the money for you. (*Exit.*)

## *SCENE FOURTEENTH.*

THE SAME PERSONS, EXCEPT VERDELIN; THEN THE
SERVANTS.

JULIE

Oh, father! Why did you not tell me?

MERCADET (*kissing her*)

You have saved us all! Ah! when shall I be so rich and
powerful that I may make him repent of a favor done so
grudgingly?

MME. MERCADET

Do not be unjust; Verdelin yielded to your request.

MERCADET

He yielded to the cry of Julie, not to my request. Ah! my
dear, he has extorted from me more than a thousand crowns'
worth of humiliation!

JUSTIN (*coming in with Thérèse and Virginie*)

The tradespeople.

VIRGINIE

The milliner and the dressmaker—

THÉRÈSE

And the dry-goods merchants.

MERCADET

That is all right!—I have succeeded in my scheme!—My
daughter shall be Comtesse de la Brive! (*To the servants*)
Show them in!—I am waiting, and the money is ready. (*He
goes proudly towards his study, while the servants look at
him with surprise.*)

*Curtain to the First Act.*

# ACT II.

---

## SCENE FIRST.

*(Mercadet's study, containing book-shelves, a safe, a desk,
an armchair and a sofa.)*

MINARD AND JUSTIN, THEN JULIE.

### MINARD
Did you say that M. Mercadet wished to speak with me?

### JUSTIN
Yes, sir. But mademoiselle has requested that you await
her here.

### MINARD *(aside)*
Her father asks to see me.—She wishes to speak to me
before the interview. Something extraordinary must have
happened.

### JUSTIN
Mademoiselle is here. *(Enter Julie.)*

### MINARD *(going towards her)*
Mlle. Julie!—

### JULIE
Justin, inform my father that the gentleman has arrived.
*(Exit Justin.)* If you wish, Adolphe, that our love should
shine as bright in the sight of all as it does in our hearts, be
as courageous as I have already been.

MINARD

What has taken place?

JULIE

A rich young suitor has presented himself, and my father is acting without any pity for us.

MINARD

A rival!—And you ask me if I have any courage! Tell me his name, Julie, and you will soon know whether I have any courage.

JULIE

Adolphe! You make me shudder! Is this the way in which you are going to act with the hope of bending my father?

MINARD (*seeing Mercadet approach*)

Here he comes.

---

*SCENE SECOND.*

THE SAME PERSONS AND MERCADET.

MERCADET

Sir, are you in love with my daughter?

MINARD

Yes, sir.

MERCADET

That is, at least, what she believes, and you seem to have had the talent to persuade her that it is so.

MINARD

Your manner of expressing yourself implies a doubt on your part, which in any one else would have been offensive to mé. Why should I not love mademoiselle? Abandoned by my parents, it was from your daughter, sir, that I have learned for the first time the happiness of affection. Mlle. Julie is at the same time a sister and a friend to me. She is my whole family. She alone has smiled upon me and has encouraged me; and my love for her is beyond what language can express!

### JULIE
Must I remain here, father?

### MERCADET (*to his daughter*)
Swallow it all! (*To Minard*) Sir, with regard to the love of young people I have those positive ideas which are considered peculiar to old men. My distrust of such love is all the more permissible because I am not a father blinded by paternal affection. I see Julie exactly as she is; without being absolutely plain, she has none of that beauty that makes people cry out, "See!" She is quite mediocre.

### MINARD
You are mistaken, sir; I venture to say that you do not know your daughter.

### MERCADET
Permit me—

### MINARD
You do not know her, sir.

### MERCADET
But I know her perfectly well—as if—in a word, I know her—

### MINARD
No, sir, you do not.

### MERCADET
Do you mean to contradict me again, sir?

### MINARD

You know the Julie that all the world sees; but love has transfigured her! Tenderness and devotion lend to her a transporting beauty that I alone have called up in her.

### JULIE

Father, I feel ashamed—

### MERCADET

You mean you feel happy. And if you, sir, repeat these things—

### MINARD

I shall repeat them a hundred times, a thousand times, and even then I couldn't repeat them often enough. There is no crime in repeating them before a father!

### MERCADET

You flatter me! I did believe myself her father; but you are the father of a Julie whose acquaintance I should very much like to make.

### MINARD

You have never been in love, I suppose?

### MERCADET

I have been very much in love! And felt the galling chain of gold like everybody else.

### MINARD

That was long ago. In these days we love in a better way.

### MERCADET

How do you do that?

### MINARD

We cling to the soul, to the ideal!

**MERCADET**

What we used to call under the Empire, having our eyes bandaged.

**MINARD**

It is love, pure and holy, which can lend a charm to all the hours of life.

**MERCADET**

Yes, all!—except the dinner hour.

**JULIE**

Father, do not ridicule two children who love each other with a passion which is true and pure, because it is founded upon a knowledge of each other's character; on the certitude of their mutual ardor in conquering the difficulties of life; in a word, of two children who will also cherish sincere affection for you.

**MINARD** (*to Mercadet*)

What an angel, sir!

**MERCADET** (*aside*)

I'll angel you! (*Putting an arm around each.*) Happy children!—You are absolutely in love? What a fine romance! (*To Minard*) You desire her for your wife?

**MINARD**

Yes, sir.

**MERCADET**

In spite of all obstacles?

**MINARD**

It is mine to overcome them!

**JULIE**

Father, ought you not to be grateful to me in that by my

choice 1 am giving you a son full of lofty sentiments, endowed with a courageous soul, and—

### MINARD

Mademoiselle—Julie.

### JULIE

Let me finish; I must have my say.

### MERCADET

My daughter, go and see your mother, and let me speak of matters which are a great deal more material than these.

### JULIE

I will go, father—

### MERCADET

Come back presently with your mother, my child. (*He kisses her and leads her to the door.*)

### MINARD (*aside*)

I feel my hopes revive.

### MERCADET (*returning*)

Sir, I am a ruined man.

### MINARD

What does that mean?

### MERCADET

Totally ruined. And if you wish to have my Julie, you are welcome to her. She will be much better off at your house, poor as you are, than in her paternal home. Not only is she without dowry, but she is burdened with poor parents—parents who are more than poor.

### MINARD

More than poor! There is nothing beyond that.

MERCADET

Yes, sir, we are in debt, deeply in debt, and some of these debts clamor for payment.

MINARD

No, no, it is impossible!

MERCADET

Don't you believe it? (*Aside*) He is getting frightened (*Taking up a pile of papers from his desk. Aloud*) Here, my would-be son-in-law, are the family papers which will show you our fortune—

MINARD

Sir—

MERCADET

Or rather our lack of fortune! Read—Here is a writ of attachment on our furniture.

MINARD

Can it be possible?

MERCADET

It is perfectly possible! Here are judgments by the score! Here is a writ of arrest. You see in what straits we are! Here you see all my sales, the protests on my notes and the judgments classed in order—for, young man, understand well in a disordered condition of things, order is above all things necessary. When disorder is well arranged it can be relieved and controlled—What can a debtor say when he sees his debt entered up under his number? I make the government my model. All payments are made in alphabetic order. I have not yet touched the letter A. (*He replaces the papers.*)

MINARD

You haven't yet paid anything?

### MERCADET

Scarcely anything. You know the condition of my expenses. You know, because you are a book-keeper.—See, (*picking up the papers again*) the total debit is three hundred and eighty thousand.

### MINARD

Yes, sir. The balance is entered there.

### MERCADET

You can understand then how you must make me shudder when you come before my daughter with your fine protestations! Since to marry a poor girl with nothing but an income of eighteen hundred francs, is like inviting in wedlock a pro· tested note with a writ of execution.

### MINARD (*lost in thought*)

Ruined, ruined! And without resources!

### MERCADET (*aside*)

I thought that would upset him! (*Aloud*) Come, now, young man, what are you going to do?

### MINARD

First, I thank you, sir, for the frankness of your admissions.

### MERCADET

That is good! And what of the ideal, and your love for my daughter?

### MINARD

You have opened my eyes, sir.

### MERCADET (*aside*)

I am glad to hear it.

## MINARD

I thought that I already loved her with a love that was boundless, and now I love her a hundred times more.

## MERCADET

The deuce you do!

## MINARD

Have you not led me to understand that she will have need of all my courage, of all my devotion! I will render her happy by other means than by my tenderness; she shall feel grateful for all my efforts, she shall love me for my vigils, and for my toils.

## MERCADET

You mean to tell me that you still wish to marry her?

## MINARD

Do I wish! When I believed that you were rich, I would not ask her of you without trembling, without feeling ashamed of my poverty; but now, sir, it is with assurance and with tranquillity of mind that I ask for her.

## MERCADET (*to himself*)

I must admit that this is a love exceedingly true, sincere and noble! And such as I had believed it impossible to find in the whole world! (*To Minard*) Forgive me, young man, for the opinion I had of you—forgive me, above all. for the disappointment I am about to cause you—

## MINARD

What do you mean?

## MERCADET

M. Minard—Julie—cannot be your wife

MINARD

What is this, sir? Not be my wife? In spite of our love, in spite of all you have confided to me?

MERCADET

Yes, and just because of all I have confided to you. I have shown you Mercadet the rich man in his true colors. I am going to show you him as the skeptical man of business. I have frankly opened my books to you. I am now going to open my heart to you as frankly.

MINARD

Speak out, sir, but remember how great my devotion to Mlle. Julie is. Remember that my self-sacrifice and unselfishness are equal to my love for her.

MERCADET

Let it be granted that by means of night-long vigils and toils you will make a living for Julie! But who will make a living for us, her father and mother?

MINARD

Ah! sir—believe in me!

MERCADET

What! Are you going to work for four, instead of working for only two? The task will be too much for you! And the bread which you give to us, you will have to snatch out of the hands of your children—

MINARD

How wildly you talk!

MERCADET

And I, in spite of your generous efforts, shall fall, crushed under the weight of disgraceful ruin. A brilliant marriage for

my daughter is the only means by which I would be enabled
to discharge the enormous sums I owe. It is only thus that
in time I could regain confidence and credit. With the aid of
a rich son-in-law I can reconquer my position, and recuperate
my fortune! Why, the marriage of my daughter is our last
anchor of salvation!—This marriage is our hope, our wealth,
the prop of our honor, sir! And since you love my daughter,
it is to this very love that I make my appeal. My friend, do
not condemn her to poverty; do not condemn her to a life of
regret over the loss and disgrace which she has brought upon
her father!

MINARD (in great distress)

But what do you ask me to do?

MERCADET (taking him by the hand)

I wish that this noble affection which you have for her, may
arm you with more courage than I myself possess.

MINARD

I will show such courage—

MERCADET

Then listen to me.—If I refuse Julie to you, Julie will
refuse the man I destine for her. It will be best, therefore,
that I grant your request for her hand, and that you be the
one—

MINARD

I!—She will not believe it, sir—

MERCADET

She will believe you, if you tell her that you fear poverty
for her.

MINARD

She will accuse me of being a fortune hunter,

MERCADET

She will be indebted to you for having secured her happiness.

MINARD (*despairingly*)

She will despise me, sir!

MERCADET

That is probable! But if I have read your heart aright, your love for her is such that you will sacrifice yourself completely to the happiness of her life. But here she comes, sir, and her mother is with her. It is on their account that I make this request to you, sir; can I count on you?

MINARD

You—can.

MERCADET

Very good—I thank you.

---

## SCENE THIRD.

### THE PRECEDING, JULIE AND MME. MERCADET.

LIE

Come, mother, I am sure that Adolphe has triumphed over all obstacles.

MME. MERCADET

My dear, M. Minard has asked of you the hand of Julie. What answer have you given him?

MERCADET (*going to the desk*)

It is for him to say.

MINARD (*aside*)

How can I tell her?—My heart is breaking!

JULIE

What have you got to say, Adolphe?

MINARD

Mademoiselle—

JULIE

Mademoiselle!—Am I no longer Julie to you? Oh, tell me quickly.—You have settled everything with my father. have you not?

MINARD

Your father has shown great confidence in me.—He has revealed to me his situation; he has told me—

JULIE

Go on, please go on—

MERCADET

I have told him that we are ruined—

JULIE

And this avowal has not changed your plans—your love— has it, Adolphe?

MINARD (*ardently*)

My love!—(*Mercadet, without being noticed, seizes his hand.*) I should be deceiving you—mademoiselle—(*speaking with great effort*)—if I were to say that my intentions are unaltered.

JULIE

Oh! It is impossible! Can it be you who speak to me in this strain?

MME. MERCADET

Julie—

### MINARD (*rousing himself*)

Thero are some men to whom poverty adds energy; men capable of daily self-sacrifice, of hourly toil; men who think themselves sufficiently recompensed by a smile from a companion that they love—(*checking himself*). I, mademoiselle, am not one of these.—The thought of poverty dismays me.— I—I could not endure the sight of your unhappiness.

### JULIE (*bursting into tears and flinging herself into the arms of her mother*)

Oh! mother! mother! mother!

### MME. MERCADET

My daughter—my poor Julie!

### MINARD (*in a low voice to Mercadet*)

Is this sufficient, sir?

### JULIE (*without looking at Minard*)

I should have had courage for both of us.—I should always have greeted you with a smile, I should have toiled without regret, and happiness would always have reigned in our home.—You could never have meant this, Adolphe.—You do not mean it!—

### MINARD (*in a low voice*)

Let me go—let me leave the house, sir!

### MERCADET

Come, then. (*He retires to the back of the stage.*)

### MINARD

Good-bye—Julie.—A love that would have flung you into poverty is a thoughtless love. I have preferred to show the love that sacrifices itself to your happiness—

### JULIE

No,—I trust you no longer. (*In a low voice to her mother*) My only happiness would have been to be his.

### JUSTIN (*announcing visitors*)

M. de la Brive! M. de Mericourt!

### MERCADET

Take your daughter away, madame. M. Minard, follow me. (*To Justin*) Ask them to wait here for awhile. (*To Minard*) I am well satisfied with you. (*Mme. Mercadet and Julie, Mercadet and Minard go out in opposite directions, while Justin admits Mericourt and De la Brive.*)

## SCENE FOURTH.

### DE LA BRIVE AND MERICOURT.

### JUSTIN

M. Mercadet begs that the gentlemen will wait for him here. (*Exit.*)

### MERICOURT

At last, my dear friend, you are on the ground, and you will be very soon officially recognized as Mlle. Mercadet's intended! Steer your bark well, for the father is a deep one.

### DE LA BRIVE

That is what frightens me, for difficulties loom ahead.

### MERICOURT

I do not believe so; Mercadet is a speculator, rich to-day, to-morrow possibly a beggar. With the little I know of his

affairs from his wife, I am led to believe that he is enchanted
with the prospect of depositing a part of his fortune in the
name of his daughter, and of obtaining a son-in-law capable
of assisting him in carrying out his financial schemes.

### DE LA BRIVE

That is a good idea, and suits me exactly; but suppose he
wishes to find out too much about me?

### MERICOURT

I have given M. Mercadet an excellent account of you.

### DE LA BRIVE

I have fallen upon my feet truly.

### MERICOURT

But you are not going to lose the dandy's self-possession?
I quite understand that your position is risky.  A man would
not marry, excepting from utter despair.  Marriage is suicide
for the man of the world.  (*In a low voice*)  Come, tell me—
can you hold out much longer?

### DE LA BRIVE

If I had not two names, one for the bailiffs and one for the
fashionable world, I should be banished from the Boulevard.
Woman and I, as you know, have wrought each the ruin of
the other, and, as fashion now goes, to find a rich English-
woman, an amiable dowager, an amorous gold mine, would
be as impossible as to find an extinct animal.

### MERICOURT

What of the gaming table?

### DE LA BRIVE

Oh!  Gambling is an unreliable resource excepting for certain crooks, and I am not such a fool as to run the risk of disgrace for the sake of winnings which always have their limit. Publicity, my dear friend, has been the abolition of all those shady careers in which fortune once was to be found. So, that for a hundred thousand francs of accepted bills, the usurer gives me but ten thousand. Pierquin sent me to one of his agents, a sort of sub-Pierquin, a little old man called Violette, who said to my broker that he could not give me money on such paper at any rate! Meanwhile my tailor has refused to bank upon my prospects. My horse is living on credit; as to my tiger, the little wretch who wears such fine clothes, I do not know how he lives, or where he feeds. I dare not peer into the mystery. Now, as we are not so advanced in civilization as the Jews, who canceled all debts every half-century, a man must pay by the sacrifice of personal liberty. Horrible things will be said about me. Here is a young man of high esteem in the world of fashion, pretty lucky at cards, of a passable figure, less than twenty-eight years old, and he is going to marry the daughter of a rich speculator!

MERICOURT

What difference does it make?

DE LA BRIVE

It is slightly off color! But I am tired of a sham life. I have learned at last that the only way to amass wealth is to work. But our misfortune is that we find ourselves quick at everything, but not good at anything! A man like me, capable of inspiring a passion and of maintaining it, cannot become either a clerk or a soldier! Society has provided no employment for us. Accordingly, I am going to set up business with Mercadet. He is one of the greatest of schemers. You are sure that he won't give less than a hundred and fifty thousand francs to his daughter?

MERICOURT

Judge yourself, my dear friend, from the style which Mme.

Mercadet puts on; you see her at all the first nights, in her own box, at the opera, and her conspicuous elegance—

### De la Brive

I myself am elegant enough, but—

### Mericourt

Look round you here—everything indicates opulence—Oh! they are well off!

### De la Brive

Yet, it is a sort of middle-class splendor, something substantial which promises well.

### Mericourt

And then the mother is a woman of principle, of irreproachable behavior. Can you possibly conclude matters to-day?

### De la Brive

I have taken steps to do so. I won at the club yesterday sufficient to go on with; I shall pay something on the wedding presents, and let the balance stand.

### Mericourt

Without reckoning my account, what is the amount of your debts?

### De la Brive

A mere trifle! A hundred and fifty thousand francs, which my father-in-law will cut down to fifty thousand. I shall have a hundred thousand francs left to begin life on. I always said that I should never become rich until I hadn't a sou left.

### Mericourt

Mercadet is an astute man; he will question you about your fortune; are you prepared?

### DE LA BRIVE

Am I not the landed proprietor of La Brive?—Three
thousand acres in the Landes, which are worth thirty thousand
francs, mortgaged for forty-five thousand and capable of being
floated by a stock jobbing company for some commercial purpose or other, say, as representing a capital of a hundred thousand crowns! You cannot imagine how much this property
has brought me in.

### MERICOURT

Your name, your horse, and your lands seem to me to be on
their last legs.

### DE LA BRIVE

Not so loud!

### MERICOURT

So you have quite made up your mind?

### DE LA BRIVE

Yes, and all the more decidedly in that I am going into
politics.

### MERICOURT

Really—but you are too clever for that!

### DE LA BRIVE

As a preparation I shall take to journalism.

### MERICOURT

And you have never written two lines in your life!

### DE LA BRIVE

There are journalists who write and journalists who do not
write. The former are editors—the horses that drag the cart;
the latter, the proprietors, who furnish the funds; these give
oats to their horses and keep the capital for themselves. I
shall be a proprietor. You merely have to put on a lofty air

and exclaim: "The Eastern question is a question of great importance and of wide influence, one about which there cannot be two opinions!" You sum up a discussion by declaiming: "England, sir, will always get the better of us!" or you make an answer to some one whom you have heard speak for a long time without paying attention to him: "We are advancing towards an abyss, we have not yet passed through all the evolutions of the evolutionary phase!" You say to a representative of labor: "Sir, I think there is something to be done in this matter." A proprietor of a journal speaks very little, rushes about and makes himself useful by doing for a man in power what the latter cannot do himself. He is supposed to inspire the articles, those I mean, which attract any notice! And then, if it is absolutely necessary, he undertakes to publish a yellow-backed volume on some Utopian topic, so well written, so strong, that no one opens it, although every one declares that he has read it! Then he is looked upon as an earnest man, and ends by finding himself acknowledged as somebody, instead of something.

### MERICOURT

Alas! What you say is too true, in these times!

### DE LA BRIVE

And we ourselves are a startling proof of this! In order to claim a part in political power you must not show what good, but what harm you can do. You must not alone possess talents, you must be able also to inspire fear. Accordingly, the very day after my marriage, I shall assume an air of seriousness, of profundity, of high principles! I can take my choice, for we have in France a list of principles which is as varied as a bill of fare. I elect to be a socialist! The word pleases me! At every epoch, my dear friend, there are adjectives which form the pass-words of ambition! Before 1789 a man called himself an economist; in 1815 he was a liberal; the next party will call itself the social party—perhaps because it is so unsocial. For in France you must always take the opposite sense of a word to understand its meaning.

### MERICOURT

Let me tell you privately, that you are now talking nothing but the nonsense of masked ball chatter, which passes for wit among those who do not indulge in it. What are you going to do when a certain definite knowledge becomes necessary?

### DE LA BRIVE

My dear friend! In every profession, whether of art, science or literature, a man needs intellectual capital, special knowledge and capacity. But in politics, my dear fellow, a man wins everything and attains to everything by means of a single phrase—

### MERICOURT

What is that?

### DE LA BRIVE

"The principles of my friends; the party for which I stand, look for—"

### MERICOURT

Hush! Here comes the father-in-law!

---

## SCENE FIFTH.

### THE SAME PERSONS AND MERCADET.

### MERCADET

Good-day, my dear Mericourt! (*To De la Brive*) The ladies have kept you waiting, sir. Ah! They are putting on their finery. For myself, I was just on the point of dismissing—whom do you think?—an aspirant to the hand of Mlle. Julie. Poor young man!—I was perhaps hard on him, and

yet I felt for him.  He worships my daughter; but what could
I do?  He has only ten thousand francs' income

### DE LA BRIVE
That wouldn't go very far!

### MERCADET
A mere subsistence!

### DE LA BRIVE
You're not the man to give a rich and clever girl to the first
comer—

### MERICOURT
Certainly not.

### MERCADET
Before the ladies come in, gentlemen, we must talk a little
serious business.

### DE LA BRIVE (*to Mericourt*)
Now comes the tug of war!  (*They all sit down.*)

### MERCADET (*on the sofa*)
Are you seriously in love with my daughter?

### DE LA BRIVE
I love her passionately!

### MERCADET
Passionately?—

### MERICOURT (*to his friend*)
You are over-doing it.

### DE LA BRIVE (*to Mericourt*)
Wait a moment.  (*Aloud*) Sir, I am ambitious—and I

saw in Mlle. Julie a lady at once distinguished, full of intellect, possessed of charming manners, who would never be out of place in the position in which my fortune puts me; and such a wife is essential to the success of a politician.

### MERCADET

I understand! It is easy to find a woman, but it is very rare that a man who wishes to be a minister or ambassador finds a wife. You are a man of wit, sir. May I ask your political leaning?

### DE LA BRIVE

Sir, I am a socialist.

### MERCADET

That is a new move! But now let us talk of money matters.

### MERICOURT

It seems to me that the notary might attend to that.

### DE LA BRIVE

No! M. Mercadet is right; it is best that we should attend to these things ourselves.

### MERCADET

True, sir.

### DE LA BRIVE

Sir, my whole fortune consists in the estate which bears my name; it has been in my family for a hundred and fifty years, and I hope will never pass from us.

### MERCADET

The possession of capital is perhaps more valuable in these days. Capital is in your own hand. If a revolution breaks out, and we have had many revolutions lately, capital follows us everywhere. Landed property, on the contrary, must fur-

nish funds for every one. There it stands stock still like a
fool to pay the taxes, while capital dodges out of the way.
But this is no real obstacle. What is the amount of your land?

### DE LA BRIVE

Three thousand acres, without a break.

### MERCADET

Without a break?

### MERICOURT

Did not I tell you as much?

### MERCADET

I never doubted it.

### DE LA BRIVE

A château—

### MERCADET

Good—

### DE LA BRIVE

And salt marshes, which can be worked as soon as the
administration gives permission. They would yield enormous
returns!

### MERCADET

Ah, sir, why have we been so late in becoming acquainted!
Your land, then, must be on the seashore.

### DE LA BRIVE

Within half a league of it.

### MERCADET

And it is situated?

### DE LA BRIVE

Near Bordeaux.

### MERCADET

You have vineyards, then?

### DE LA BRIVE

No! fortunately not, for the disposal of wines is a trouble-some matter, and, moreover, the cultivation of the vine is exceedingly expensive. My estate was planted with pine trees by my grandfather, a man of genius, who was wise enough to sacrifice himself to the welfare of his descendants. Besides, I have furniture, which you know—

### MERCADET

Sir, one moment, a man of business is always careful to dot his i's.

### DE LA BRIVE *(under his voice)*

Now we're in for it!

### MERCADET

With regard to your estate and your marshes,—I see all that can be got out of these marshes. The best way of utilizing them would be to form a company for the exploitation of the marshes of the Brive! There is more than a million in it!

### DE LA BRIVE

I quite understand that, sir. They need only to be thrown upon the market.

### MERCADET *(aside)*

These words indicate a certain intelligence in this young man. *(Aloud)* Have you any debts? Is your estate mortgaged?

### MERICOURT

You would not think much of my friend if he had no debts.

### De la Brive

I will be frank, sir, there is a mortgage of forty-five thousand francs on my estate.

### Mercadet (*aside*)

An innocent young man! he might easily— (*Rising from his seat. Aloud*) You have my consent; you shall be my son-in-law, and are the very man I would choose for my daughter's husband. You do not realize what a fortune you possess.

### De la Brive (*to Mericourt*)

This is almost too good to be true.

### Mericourt (*to De la Brive*)

He is dazzled by the good speculation which he sees ahead.

### Mercadet (*aside*)

With government protection, which can be purchased, salt pits may be established. I am saved! (*Aloud*) Allow me to shake hands with you, after the English fashion. You fulfill all that I expected in a son-in-law. I plainly see you have none of the narrowness of provincial land-holders; we shall understand each other thoroughly.

### De la Brive

You must not take it in bad part, sir, if I, on my part, ask you—

### Mercadet

The amount of my daughter's fortune? I should have distrusted you if you hadn't asked! My daughter has independent means; her mother settles on her her own fortune, consisting of a small property—a farm of two hundred acres, but in the very heart of Brie, and provided with good buildings. Besides this, I shall give her two hundred thousand francs, the interest of which will be for your use, until you find a suitable investment for it. So you see, young man, we do not wish to deceive you, we wish to keep the money moving; I like you, you please me, for I see you have ambition.

### De la Brive

Yes, sir.

### Mercadet

You love luxury, extravagance; you wish to shine at Paris—

### De la Brive

Yes, sir.

### Mercadet

You see that I am already an old man, obliged to lay the load of my ambition upon some congenial co-operator, and you shall be the one to play the brilliant part.

### De la Brive

Sir, had I been obliged to take my choice of all the fathers-in-law in Paris, I should have given the preference to you. You are a man after my own heart! Allow me to shake hands, after the English fashion! (*They shake hands for the second time.*)

### Mercadet (*aside*)

It seems too good to be true.

### De la Brive (*aside*)

He fell head-first into my salt marshes!

### Mercadet (*aside*)

He accepts an income from me! (*He retires towards the door on the left side.*)

### Mericourt (*to De la Brive*)

Are you satisfied?

DE LA BRIVE (*to Mericourt*)

I don't see the money for my debts.

MERICOURT (*to De la Brive*)

Wait a moment. (*To Mercadet*) My friend does not dare to tell you of it, but he is too honest for concealment. He has a few debts.

MERCADET

Oh, please tell me. I understand perfectly—I suppose it is about fifty thousand you owe?

MERICOURT

Very nearly—

DE LA BRIVE

Very nearly—

MERCADET

A mere trifle.

DE LA BRIVE (*laughing*)

Yes, a mere trifle!

MERCADET

They will serve as a subject of discussion between your wife and you; yes, let her have the pleasure of— But, we will pay them all. (*Aside*) In shares of the La Brive salt pits. (*Aloud*) It is so small an amount. (*Aside*) We will put up the capital of the salt marsh a hundred thousand francs more. (*Aloud*) That matter is settled, son-in-law.

DE LA BRIVE

We will consider it settled, father-in-law.

MERCADET (*aside*)

I am saved!

DE LA BRIVE (*aside*)

I am saved!

## SCENE SIXTH.

THE SAME PERSONS, MME. MERCADET AND JULIE.

MERCADET

Here are my wife and daughter.

MERICOURT

Madame, allow me to present to you my friend, M de la Brive, who regards your daughter with—

DE LA BRIVE

With passionate admiration.

MERCADET

My daughter is exactly the woman to suit a politician.

DE LA BRIVE (*to Mericourt. Gazing at Julie through his eyeglass*)

A fine girl. (*To Madame Mercadet*) Like mother, like daughter. Madame, I place my hopes under your protection.

MME. MERCADET

Anyone introduced by M. Mericourt would be welcome here.

JULIE (*to her father*)

What a coxcomb!

MERCADET (*to his daughter*)

He is enormously rich.—We shall all be millionaires!—He is an excessively clever fellow. Now, do try and be amiable, as you ought to be.

JULIE (*answering him*)

What would you wish me to say to a dandy whom I have

just seen for the first time, and whom you destine for my husband?—

### DE LA BRIVE

May I be permitted to hope, mademoiselle, that you will look favorably upon me?

### JULIE

My duty is to obey my father.

### DE LA BRIVE

Young people are not always aware of the feelings which they inspire. For two months I have been longing for the happiness of paying my respects to you.

### JULIE

Who can be more flattered than I am, sir, to find that I have attracted your attention?

### MME. MERCADET (*to Mericourt*)

He is a fine fellow. (*Aloud*) We hope that you and your friend M. de la Brive will do us the pleasure of accepting our invitation to dine without ceremony.

### MERCADET

To take pot-luck with us. (*To De la Brive*) You must excuse our simplicity.

### JUSTIN (*entering, in a low voice to Mercadet*)

M. Pierquin wishes to speak to you, monsieur.

### MERCADET (*low*)

Pierquin?

### JUSTIN

He says it is concerning an important and urgent matter.

MERCADET

What can he want with me? Let him come in. (*Justin goes out. Aloud*) My dear, these gentlemen must be tired. Won't you take them into the drawing-room? M. de la Brive, give my daughter your arm.

DE LA BRIVE

Mademoiselle—(*offers her his arm.*)

JULIE (*aside*)

He is handsome, he is rich—why does he choose me?

MME. MERCADET

M. de Mericourt, will you come and see the picture which we are going to raffle off for the benefit of the poor orphans?

MERICOURT

With pleasure, madame.

MERCADET

Go on. I shall be with you in a moment.

---

*SCENE SEVENTH.*

MERCADET AND PIERQUIN.

MERCADET (*alone*)

Well, after all, this time I have really secured fortune and the happiness of Julie and the rest of us. For a son-in-law like this is a veritable gold mine! Three thousand acres! A château! Salt marshes! (*He sits down at his desk.*)

PIERQUIN (*entering*)

Good-day, Mercadet. I have come—

### MERCADET

Rather inopportunely.  But what do you wish?

### PIERQUIN

I sha'n't detain you long.  The bills of exchange I gave you this morning, signed by a man called Michonnin, are absolutely valueless.  I told you this beforehand.

### MERCADET

I know that.

### PIERQUIN

I now offer you a thousand crowns for them.

### MERCADET

That is either too much or too little!  Anything for which you will give that sum must be worth infinitely more.  Some one is waiting for me in the other room.  I will bid you good-evening.

### PIERQUIN

I will give you four thousand francs.

### MERCADET

No!

### PIERQUIN

Five—six thousand.

### MERCADET.

If you wish to play cards, keep to the gambling table.  Why do you wish to recover this paper?

### PIERQUIN

Michonnin has insulted me.  I wish to take vengeance on him; to send him to jail.

### MERCADET (*rising*)

Six thousand francs worth of vengeance!  You are not a man to indulge in luxuries of that kind.

PIERQUIN

I assure you—

MERCADET.

Come now, my friend, consider that for a satisfactory
defamation of character the code won't charge you more than
five or six hundred francs, and the tax on a blow is only fifty
francs—

PIERQUIN

I swear to you—

MERCADET.

Has this Michonnin come into a legacy? And are the
forty-seven thousand francs of these vouchers actually worth
forty-seven thousand francs? You should post me on this
subject and then we'll cry halves!

PIERQUIN

Very well, I agree. The fact of it is, Michonnin is to be
married.

MERCADET

What next! And with whom, pray?

PIERQUIN

With the daughter of some nabob—an idiot who is giving
her an enormous dowry!

MERCADET

Where does Michonnin live?

PIERQUIN

Do you want to issue a writ? He is without a fixed abode
in Paris. His furniture is held under the name of a friend;
but his legal domicile must be in the neighborhood of Bordeaux, in the village of Ermont.

MERCADET

Stay a while. I have some one here from that region. I
can get exact information in a moment—and then we can
begin proceedings.

PIERQUIN

Send me the paper, and leave the business to me—

MERCADET

I shall be very glad to do so. They shall be put into your
hands in return for a signed agreement as to the sharing of
the money. I am at present altogether taken up with the
marriage of my daughter.

PIERQUIN

I hope everything is going on well.

MERCADET

Wonderfully well. My son-in-law is a gentleman and, in
spite of that, he is rich. And, although both rich and a gentleman, he is clever into the bargain.

PIERQUIN

I congratulate you.

MERCADET.

One word with you before you go. You said, Michonnin,
of Ermont, in the neighborhood of Bordeaux?—

PIERQUIN

Yes, he has an old aunt somewhere about there! A good
woman called Bourdillac, who scrapes along on some six
hundred francs a year, but to whom he gives the title of
Marchioness of Bourdillac. He pretends that her health is
delicate and that she has a yearly income of forty thousand
francs.

MERCADET.

Thank you.  Good-evening—

PIERQUIN

Good-evening (*goes out*).

MERCADET (*ringing*)

Justin!

JUSTIN

Did you call, sir?

MERCADET.

Ask M. de la Brive to speak with me for a moment.  (*Justin goes out.*)

MERCADET.

Here is a windfall of twenty-three thousand francs!  We shall be able to arrange things famously for Julie's marriage.

---

## SCENE EIGHTH.

MERCADET, DE LA BRIVE AND JUSTIN.

DE LA BRIVE (*to Justin, handing him a letter*)

Here, deliver this letter.—And this is for yourself.

JUSTIN (*aside*)

A louis!  Mademoiselle will be sure to have a happy home. (*Exit.*)

DE LA BRIVE

You wish to speak with me, my dear father-in-law?

MERCADET

Yes.  You see I already treat you without ceremony.  Please to take a seat.

DE LA BRIVE (*sitting on a sofa*)

I am grateful for your confidence.

MERCADET

I am seeking information with regard to a debtor, who, like you, lives in the neighborhood or Bordeaux.

DE LA BRIVE

I know every one in that district.

MERCADET

I am seeking information with regard to a debtor, who, like you, lives in the neighborhood of Bordeaux.

DE LA BRIVE

Relations! I have none but an old aunt.

MERCADET (*pricking up his ears*)

An—old aunt—?

DE LA BRIVE

Whose health—

MERCADET (*trembling*)

Is—is—delicate?

DE LA BRIVE

And her income is forty thousand francs—

MERCADET (*quite overcome*)

Good Lord! the very figure!

DE LA BRIVE

The Marchioness, you see, will be a good woman to have on hand. I mean the Marchioness—

MERCADET (*vehemently rushing at him*)

Of Bourdillac, sir!

DE LA BRIVE

How is this? Do you know her name?

MERCADET

Yes, and yours too!

DE LA BRIVE

The devil you do!

MERCADET

You are head over ears in debt; your furniture is held in another man's name; your old aunt has a pittance of six hundred francs; Pierquin, who is one of your smallest creditors, has forty-seven thousand francs in notes of hand from you. You are Michonnin, and I am the idiotic nabob!

DE LA BRIVE (*stretching himself at full length on the sofa*)

By heavens! You know just as much about it as I do!

MERCADET

Well—I see that once more the devil has taken a hand in my game.

DE LA BRIVE (*aside, rising to his feet*)

The marriage is over! I am no longer a socialist; I shall become a communist.

MERCADET

And I have been just as easily deceived, as if I had been on the Exchange.

DE LA BRIVE

Show yourself worthy of your reputation.

MERCADET

M. Michonnin, your conduct is more than blameworthy!

DE LA BRIVE

In what particular? Did I not say that I had debts?

### MERCADET

We'll let that pass, for any one may have debts; but where is your estate situated?

### DE LA BRIVE

In the Landes.

### MERCADET

And of what does it consist?

### DE LA BRIVE

Of sand wastes, planted with firs.

### MERCADET

Good to make toothpicks.

### DE LA BRIVE

That's about it.

### MERCADET

And it is worth.

### DE LA BRIVE

Thirty thousand francs.

### MERCADET

And mortgaged for—

### DE LA BRIVE

Forty-five thousand!

### MERCADET

And you had the skill to effect that?

### DE LA BRIVE

Why, yes—

### MERCADET

Damnation! But that was pretty clever! And your marshes, sir?

### DE LA BRIVE

They border on the sea—

### MERCADET

They are part of the ocean!—

### DE LA BRIVE

The people of that country are evil-minded enough to say
so. That is what hinders my loans!

### MERCADET

It would be very difficult to issue ocean shares!—Sir—I
may tell you, between ourselves, that your morality seems
to me—

### DE LA BRIVE

Somewhat—

### MERCADET

Risky.

### DE LA BRIVE (*in anger*)

Sir!—(*calming himself*). Let this be merely between
ourselves!

### MERCADET

You give a friend a bill of sale of your furniture, you sign
your notes of hand with the name of Michonnin, and you call
yourself merely De la Brive—

### DE LA BRIVE

Well, sir, what are you going to do about it?

### MERCADET

Do about it? I am going to lead you a pretty dance—

### DE LA BRIVE

Sir, I am your guest! Moreover, I may deny everything—
What proofs have you?

MERCADET

What proofs! I have in my hands forty-seven thousand francs' worth of your notes.

DE LA BRIVE

Are they signed to the order of Pierquin?

MERCADET

Precisely so.

DE LA BRIVE

And you have had them since this morning?

MERCADET

Since this morning.

DE LA BRIVE

I see. You have given worthless stock in exchange for valueless notes.

MERCADET

Sir!

DE LA BRIVE

And, in order to seal the bargain, Pierquin, one of the least important of your creditors, has given you a delay of three months.

MERCADET

Who told you that?

DE LA BRIVE

Who? Who? Pierquin himself, of course, as soon as he learned I was going to make an arrangement—

MERCADET

The devil he did!

DE LA BRIVE

Ah! You were going to give two hundred thousand francs

as a dowry to your daughter, and you had debts to the amount of three hundred and fifty thousand! Between ourselves it looks like you who had been trying to swindle the son-in-law, sir—

MERCADET (*angrily*)

Sir!—(*calming himself*). This is merely between ourselves, sir.

DE LA BRIVE

You took advantage of my inexperience!

MERCADET

Of course I did! The inexperience of a man who raises a loan on his sand wastes fifty per cent above their value.

DE LA BRIVE

Glass can be made out of sand!

MERCADET

That's a good idea!

DE LA BRIVE

Therefore, sir—

MERCADET

Silence! Promise me that this broken marriage-contract shall be kept secret.

DE LA BRIVE

I swear it shall— Ah! excepting to Pierquin. I have just written to him to set his mind at rest.

MERCADET

Is that the letter you sent by Justin?

DE LA BRIVE

The very one.

MERCADET

And what have you told him?

DE LA BRIVE

The name of my father-in-law.   Confound it!—I thought
you were rich.

MERCADET (*despairingly*)

And you have written that to Pierquin?  It's all up!  This
fresh defeat will be known on the Exchange!  But, any way,
I am ruined!  Suppose I write to him—Suppose I ask him—
(*He goes to the table to write.*)

---

## SCENE NINTH.

THE SAME PERSONS, MME. MERCADET, JULIE AND VERDELIN.

MME. MERCADET

My friend, M. Verdelin.

JULIE (*to Verdelin*)

Here is my father, sir.

MERCADET

Ah!  It is you, is it Verdelin—and you are come to dinner?

VERDELIN

No, I am not come to dinner.

MERCADET (*aside*)

He knows all.  He is furious!

VERDELIN

And this gentleman is your son-in-law?—(*Verdelin bows*

*to De la Brive.*)    This is a fine marriage you are going to make!

### MERCADET

The marriage, my dear sir, is not going to take place.

### JULIE

How happy I feel!    (*De la Brive bows to her.    She casts down her eyes.*)

### MME. MERCADET (*seizing her hand*)

My dear daughter!

### MERCADET

I have been deceived by Mericourt.

### VERDELIN

And you have played on me one of your tricks this morning, for the purpose of getting a thousand crowns; but the whole incident has been made public on the Exchange, and they think it a huge joke!

### MERCADET

They have been informed, I suppose—

### VERDELIN

That your pocket-book is full of the notes of hand signed by your son-in-law.    And Pierquin tells me that your creditors are exasperated, and are to meet to-night at the house of Goulard to conclude measures for united action against you to-morrow!

### MERCADET

To-night!    To-morrow!    Ah! I hear the knell of bankruptcy sound!

### VERDELIN

Yes, to-morrow they are going to send a prison cab for you.

### MME MERCADET AND JULIE.

God help us!

### MERCADET

I see the carriage, the hearse of the speculator, carrying me to Clichy!

### VERDELIN

They wish, as far as possible, to rid the Exchange of all sharpers!

### MERCADET

They are fools, for in that case they will turn it into a desert! And so I am ruined! Expelled from the Exchange with all the sequelæ of bankruptcy,—shame, beggary! I cannot believe it,—it is impossible!

### DE LA BRIVE

Believe me, sir, that I regret having been in some degree—

### MERCADET (*looking him in the face*)

You! (*In a low voice to him*) Listen to me: you have hurried on my destruction, but you have it in your power to help me to escape.

### DE LA BRIVE

On what conditions?

### MERCADET

I will make you a good offer! (*Aloud, as they start toward opposite doors*) True, the idea is a bold one!—But to-morrow, the 'Change will recognize in me one of its master spirits.

### VERDELIN

What is he talking about?

### MERCADET

To-morrow, all my debts will be paid, and the house of Mercadet will be turning over millions—I shall be acknowledged as the Napoleon of finance.

### VERDELIN

What a man he is!

### MERCADET

And a Napoleon who meets no Waterloo!

### VERDELIN

But where are your troops?

### MERCADET

My army is cash in hand! What answer can be made to a business man who says, "Take your money!" Come let us dine now.

### VERDELIN

Certainly. I shall be delighted to dine with you.

MERCADET (*while they all move towards the dining-room, aside*)

They are all glad of it! To-morrow I will either command millions, or rest in the damp winding-sheet of the Seine!

*Curtain to the Second Act.*

# ACT III.

## *SCENE FIRST.*

*(Another apartment in Mercadet's house, well furnished. At the back and in the centre is a mantel-piece, having instead of a mirror a clear plate of glass; side doors; a large table, surrounded by chairs, in the middle of the stage; sofa and armchairs.)*

JUSTIN, THÉRÈSE AND VIRGINIE, THEN MERCADET.

*(Justin enters first and beckons to Thérèse. Virginie, carrying papers, sits insolently on the sofa. Justin looks through the keyhole of the door on the left side and listens.)*

#### THÉRÈSE
Is it possible that they could pretend to conceal from us the condition of their affairs?

#### VIRGINIE
Old Gruneau tells me that the master is soon to be arrested; I hope that what I have spent will be taken account of, for he owes me the money for these bills, besides my wages!

#### THÉRÈSE
Oh! set your mind at rest. We are likely to lose everything, for the master is bankrupt.

#### JUSTIN
I can't hear anything. They speak too low! They don't trust us.

VIRGINIE

It is frightful!

JUSTIN (*with his ear to the half-open door*)

Wait, I think I hear something. (*The door bursts open and Mercadet appears.*)

MERCADET (*to Justin*)

Don't let me disturb you.

JUSTIN

Sir. I—I—was just putting—

MERCADET

Really! (*To Virginie, who jumps up suddenly from the sofa*) Keep your seat, Mlle. Virginie, and you, M. Justin. Why didn't you come in? We were talking about my business

JUSTIN

You amuse me, sir.

MERCADET

I am heartily glad of it.

JUSTIN

You take trouble easy, sir.

MERCADET (*severely*)

That will do, all of you. And remember that from this time forth I see all who call. Treat no one either with insolence or too much humility, for you will meet here no creditors, but such as have been paid.

JUSTIN

Oh, bosh!

MERCADET

Go!—(*The central door opens. Mme. Mercadet, Julie and Minard appear. The servants leave the room.*)

---

## SCENE SECOND.

MERCADET, MME. MERCADET, JULIE AND MINARD.

MERCADET (*aside*)

I am annoyed to see my wife and daughter here. In my present circumstances, women are likely to spoil everything, for they have nerves. (*Aloud*) What is it, Mme. Mercadet?

MME. MERCADET

Sir, you were counting on the marriage of Julie to establish your credit and reassure your creditors, but the event of yesterday has put you at their mercy—

MERCADET

Do you think so? Well, you are quite mistaken. I beg your pardon, M. Minard, but what brings you here?

MINARD

Sir—I—

JULIE

Father—it is—

MERCADET

Are you come to ask again for my daughter?

MINARD

Yes, sir.

MERCADET

But everybody says that I am going to fail—

MINARD

I know it, sir.

MERCADET

And would you marry the daughter of a bankrupt?

MINARD

Yes, for I would work to re-establish him.

JULIE

That's good, Adolphe.

MERCADET (*aside*)

A fine young fellow.   I will give him an interest in the first big business I do.

MINARD

I have made known my attachment to the man I look upon as a father.   He has informed me—that I am the possessor of a small fortune—

MERCADET

A fortune!

MINARD

When I was confided to his care, a sum of money was entrusted to him, which has increased by interest, and I now possess thirty thousand francs.

MERCADET

Thirty thousand francs!

MINARD

On learning of the disaster that had befallen you, I realized this sum, and I bring it to you, sir; for sometimes in these cases an arrangement can be made by paying something on account—

### MME. MERCADET

He has an excellent heart!

### JULIE (*with pride*)

Yes, indeed, papa!—

### MERCADET

Thirty thousand francs. (*Aside*) They might be tripled by buying some of Verdelin's stock and then doubled with— No, no. (*To Minard*) My boy, you are at the age of self-sacrifice. If I could pay two hundred thousand francs with thirty thousand, the fortune of France, of myself and of most people would be made.—No, keep your money!

### MINARD

What! You refuse it?

### MERCADET (*aside*)

If with this I could keep them quiet for a month, if by some bold stroke I could revive the depression in my property, it might be all right.—But the money of these poor children, it cut me to the heart to think of it, for when they are in tears people calculate amiss; it is not well to risk the money of any but fellow-brokers—no—no—(*Aloud*) Adolphe, you may marry my daughter!

### MINARD

Oh! sir!—Julie—my own Julie—

### MERCADET

That is, of course, as soon as she has three hundred thousand francs as dowry.

### MME. MERCADET

My dear!

### JULIE

Papa!

### MINARD

Ah, sir!—How long are you going to put me off?

### MERCADET

Put you off?—She will have it in a month!     Perhaps sooner—

### ALL

How is that?

### MERCADET

Yes, by the use of my brains—and a little money. (*Minard holds out his pocketbook.*) But lock up those bills! And come take away my wife and daughter. I want to be alone.

### MME. MERCADET (*aside*)

Is he going to hatch some plot against his creditors? I must find out.—Come, Julie.

### JULIE

Papa, how good you are!

### MERCADET

Nonsense!

### JULIE

I love you so much.

### MERCADET

Nonsense!

### JULIE

Adolphe, I do not thank you, I shall have all my life for that.

### MINARD

Dearest Julie!

### MERCADET (*leading them out*)

Come, now, you had better breathe out your idyls in some more retired spot. (*They go out.*)

## *SCENE THIRD.*

#### MERCADET, THEN DE LA BRIVE.

#### MERCADET

I have resisted—it was a good impulse! But I was wrong to obey it. If I finally yield to the temptation, I can make their little capital worth very much more. I shall manage this fortune for them. My poor daughter has indeed a good lover. What hearts of gold are theirs! Dear children! (*Goes towards the door at the right.*) I must make their fortune. De la Brive is here awaiting me. (*Looking through the open door*) I believe he is asleep. I gave him a little too much wine, so as to handle him more easily. (*Shouting*) Michonnin! The constable! The constable!

DE LA BRIVE (*coming out, rubbing his eyes*)
Hello! What are you saying?

#### MERCADET

Don't be frightened, I only wanted to wake you up. (*Takes his seat at the table.*)

DE LA BRIVE (*sitting at the other side of the table*)
Sir, an orgie acts on the mind like a storm on the country. It brings refreshment, it clothes with verdure! And ideas spring forth and bloom! *In vino varietas!*

#### MERCADET

Yesterday, our conversation on business matters was interrupted.

#### DE LA BRIVE

Father-in-law, I recall it distinctly—we recognized the fact that our houses could not keep their engagements. We were on the point of bankruptcy, and you are unfortunate enough to be

my creditor, while I am fortunate enough to be your debtor
to the amount of forty-seven thousand, two hundred and thirty-three francs and some centimes.

### MERCADET

Your head is level enough.

### DE LA BRIVE

But my pocket and my conscience are a little out. Yet who'
can reproach me? By squandering my fortune I have brought
profit to every trade in Paris, and even to those who do not
know me. We, the useless ones! We, the idlers!—Upon my
soul! It is we who keep up the circulation of money—

### MERCADET

By means of the money in circulation—Ah! you have all
your wits about you!

### DE LA BRIVE

But I have nothing else.

### MERCADET

Our wits are our mint. Is it not so?—But, considering
your present situation, I shall be brief.

### DE LA BRIVE

That is why I take a seat.

### MERCADET

Listen to me. I see that you are going down the steep
way which leads to that daring cleverness for which fools
blame successful operators. You have tested the piquant
intoxicating fruits of Parisian pleasure. You have made
luxury the inseparable companion of your life. Paris begins
at the Place de l'Étoile, and ends at the Jockey Club. That

is your Paris, which is the world of women who are talked about too much, or not at all.

### DE LA BRIVE

That is true.

### MERCADET

You breathe the cynical atmosphere of wits and journalists, the atmosphere of the theatre and of the ministry. It is a vast sea in which thousands are casting their nets! You must either continue this existence, or blow your brains out!

### DE LA BRIVE

No! For it is impossible to think that it can continue without me.

### MERCADET

Do you feel that you have the genius to maintain yourself in style at the height to which you aspire?—To dominate men of mind by the power of capital and superiority of intellect? Do you think that you will always have skill enough to keep afloat between the two capes, which have seen the life of elegance so often founder between the cheap restaurant and the debtors' prison?

### DE LA BRIVE

Why! You are breaking into my conscience like a burglar—you echo my very thought! What do you want with me?

### MERCADET

I wish to rescue you, by launching you into the world of business.

### DE LA BRIVE

By what entrance?

### MERCADET

Let me choose the door.

DE LA BRIVE

The devil!

MERCADET

Show yourself a man who will compromise himself for me—

DE LA BRIVE

But men of straw may be burnt.

MERCADET

You must be incombustible.

DE LA BRIVE

What are the terms of our copartnership?

MERCADET

You try to serve me in the desperate circumstances in which I am at present, and I will make you a present of your forty-seven thousand, two hundred and thirty-three francs, to say nothing of the centimes. Between ourselves, I may say that only address is needed.

DE LA BRIVE

In the use of the pistol or the sword?

MERCADET

No one is to be killed; on the contrary—

DE LA BRIVE

That will suit me.

MERCADET

A man is to be brought to life again.

DE LA BRIVE

That doesn't suit me at all, my dear fellow. The legacy,

the chest of Harpagon, the little mule of Scapin and, indeed, all the farces which have made us laugh on the ancient stage are not well received nowadays in real life. The police have a way of getting mixed up with them, and since the abolition of privileges, no one can administer a drubbing with impunity.

### MERCADET

Well, what do you think of five years in debtors' prison? Eh? What a fate!—

### DE LA BRIVE

As a matter of fact, my decision must depend upon what you want me to do to any one, for my honor so far is intact and is worth—

### MERCADET

You must invest it well, for we shall have dire need of all that it is worth. I want you to assist me in sitting at the table which the Exchange always keeps spread, and we will gorge ourselves with the good things there offered us, for you must admit that while those who seek for millions have great difficulty in finding them, they are never found by those who do not seek.

### DE LA BRIVE

I think I can co-operate with you in this matter. You will return to me my forty-seven thousand francs—

### MERCADET

Yes, sir.

### DE LA BRIVE

I am not required to be anything but be—very clever?

### MERCADET

Nimble, but this nimbleness will be exercised, as the English say, on the right side of the law.

DE LA BRIVE

What is it you propose?

MERCADET (*giving him a paper*)

Here are your written instructions. You are to represent something like an uncle from America—in fact, my partner, who has just come back from the West Indies.

DE LA BRIVE

I understand.

MERCADET

Go to the Champs-Elysées, secure a post-chaise that has been much battered, have horses harnessed to it, and make your arrival here wrapped in a great pelisse, your head enveloped in a huge cap, while you shiver like a man who finds our summer icy cold. I will receive you; I will conduct you in; you will speak to my creditors; not one of them knows Godeau; you will make them give me more time.

DE LA BRIVE

How much time?

MERCADET

I need only two days—two days, in order that Pierquin may complete certain purchases which we have ordered. Two days in order that the stock which I know how to inflate may have time to rise. You will be my backer, my security. And as no one will recognize you—

DE LA BRIVE

I shall cease to be this personage as soon as I have paid you forty-seven thousand, two hundred and thirty-three francs and some centimes.

MERCADET

That is so. But I hear some one—my wife—

MME. MERCADET (*enters*)

My dear, there are some letters for you, and the bearer requires an answer. (*She withdraws to the fireplace.*)

MERCADET

I suppose I must go. Good-day, my dear De la Brive (*In a low voice*) Not a word to my wife; she would not understand the operation, and would misconstrue it. (*Aloud*) Go quickly, and forget nothing.

DE LA BRIVE

You need have no fear. (*Mercadet goes out by the left; De la Brive starts to go out by the centre, but Mme. Mercadet intercepts him.*)

---

*SCENE FOURTH.*

MME. MERCADET AND DE LA BRIVE.

DE LA BRIVE

Madame?

MME. MERCADET

Forgive me, sir!

DE LA BRIVE

Kindly excuse me, madame, I must be going—

MME. MERCADET

You must not go.

DE LA BRIVE

But you are not aware—

MME. MERCADET

I know all.

### DE LA BRIVE

How is that?

### MME. MERCADET

You and my husband are bent upon resorting to some very ancient expedients proper to the comic drama, and I have employed one which is more ancient still. And as I told you, I know all—

### DE LA BRIVE (*aside*)

She must have been listening.

### MME. MERCADET

Sir, the part which you have been induced to undertake is blameworthy and shameful, and you must give it up—

### DE LA BRIVE

But after all, madame—

### MME. MERCADET

Oh! I know to whom I am speaking, sir; it was only a few hours ago that I saw you for the first time, and yet—I think I know you.

### DE LA BRIVE

Really? I am sure I do not know what opinion you have of me.

### MME. MERCADET

One day has given me time to form a correct judgment of you—and at the very time that my husband was trying to discover some foible in you he might make use of, or what evil passions he might rouse in you, I looked in your heart and discerned that it still contained good feelings which eventually may prove your salvation.

### DE LA BRIVE

Prove my salvation? Excuse me, madame.

## MME. MERCADET

Yes, sir, prove your salvation and that of my husband; for both of you are on the way to ruin. For you must understand that debts are no disgrace to any one who admits them and toils for their payment. You have your whole life before you, and you have too much good sense to wish that it should be blighted through engaging in a business which justice is sure to punish.

## DE LA BRIVE

Justice! Ah! You are right, madame, and I certainly would not lend myself to this dangerous comedy, unless your husband had some notes of hand of mine—

## MME. MERCADET

Which he will surrender to you, sir, I'll promise you that.

## DE LA BRIVE

But, madame, I cannot pay them—

## MME. MERCADET

We will be satisfied with your word, and you will discharge your obligation as soon as you have honestly made your fortune.

## DE LA BRIVE

Honestly!—That will be perhaps a long time to wait.

## MME. MERCADET

We will be patient. And now, sir, go and inform my husband that he must give up this attempt because he will not have your co-operation. (*She goes towards the door on the left.*)

## DE LA BRIVE

I should be rather afraid to face him—I should prefer to write to him.

MME. MERCADET (*pointing out to him the door by which he entered*)

You will find the necessary writing materials in that room. Remain there until I come for your letter. I will hand it to him myself.

#### DE LA BRIVE

I will do so, madame. After all I am not so worthless as I thought I was. It is you who have taught me this; you have a right to the whole credit of it. (*He respectfully kisses her hand.*) Thank you, madame, thank you! (*He goes out.*)

#### MME. MERCADET

I have succeeded—if only I could now persuade Mercadet.

JUSTIN (*entering from the centre*)

Madame—madame—here they are—all of them.

#### MME. MERCADET

Who?

#### JUSTIN

The creditors.

#### MME. MERCADET

Already?—

#### JUSTIN

There are a great many of them, madame.

#### MME. MERCADET

Let them come in here. I will go and inform my husband. (*She goes out by one door. Justin opens the other.*)

## SCENE FIFTH.

PIERQUIN, GOULARD, VIOLETTE AND SEVERAL OTHER CREDITORS.

### GOULARD

Gentlemen, we have quite made up our minds, have we not?

### ALL

We have, we have—

### PIERQUIN

No more deluding promises.

### GOULARD

No more prayers and expostulations.

### VIOLETTE

No more pretended payments on account, thrown out as a bait to get deeper into our pockets.

---

## SCENE SIXTH.

THE SAME PERSONS AND MERCADET.

### MERCADET

And do you mean to tell me that you gentlemen are come to force me into bankruptcy?

### GOULARD

We shall do so, unless you find means to pay us in full this very day.

### MERCADET

To-day!

PIERQUIN

This very day.

MERCADET (*standing before the fireplace*)

Do you think that I possess the plates for striking off Bank of France notes?

VIOLETTE

You mean that you have no offer to make?

MERCADET

Absolutely none! And you are going to lock me up?—I warn him who is going to pay for the cab that he won't be reimbursed from any assets of mine.                    •

GOULARD

I shall add that along with all that you owe me to the debit of your account—

MERCADET

Thank you. You've all made up your mind, I suppose?

THE CREDITORS

We have.

MERCADET

I am touched by your unanimity!—(*Pulling out his watch*) Two o'clock. (*Aside*) De la Brive has had quite time enough —he ought to be on his way here.—(*Aloud*) Gentlemen, you compel me to admit that you are men of inspiration and have chosen your time well!

PIERQUIN

What does he mean?

MERCADET

For months, for years, you have allowed yourselves to be humbugged by fine promises, and deceived—yes, deceived by preposterous stories; and to-day is the day you choose for showing yourselves inexorable! Upon my word and honor, it is positively amusing! By all means let us start for Clichy.

GOULARD

But, sir—

PIERQUIN

He is laughing.

VIOLETTE (*rising from his chair*)

There is something in the wind. Gentlemen, there is something in the wind!—

PIERQUIN

Please explain to us—

GOULARD

We desire to know—

VIOLETTE (*rising to his feet*)

M. Mercadet, if there is anything—tell us about it.

MERCADET (*coming to the table*)

Nothing! I shall say nothing, not I—I wish to be put behind the bars!—I would like to see the figure you all will cut to-morrow or this evening, when you find he has returned.

GOULARD (*rising to his feet*)

He has returned?

PIERQUIN

Returned from where?

VIOLETTE

Who has returned?

MERCADET (*coming forward*)

Nobody has returned. Let us start for Clichy, gentlemen.

GOULARD

But listen, if you are expecting any assistance—.

PIERQUIN

If you have any hope that—

VIOLETTE

Or if even some considerable legacy—

GOULARD

Come, now!

PIERQUIN

Answer—

VIOLETTE

Tell us—

MERCADET

Now, take care, I beg you. You are giving way, you are giving way, gentlemen, and if I wished to take the trouble, I could win you over again. Come now, act like genuine creditors! Ridicule the past, forget the brilliant strokes of business I put within the power of each of you before the sudden departure of my faithful Godeau—

GOULARD

His faithful Godeau!

PIERQUIN

Ah! If there were only—

MERCADET

Forget all that prosperous past, take no account of what might induce him to return—after being waited for so long—and—let us start for Clichy, gentlemen, let us start for Clichy!—

VIOLETTE

Mercadet, you are expecting Godeau, aren't you?

MERCADET

No!

VIOLETTE (*as with a sudden inspiration*)
Gentlemen, he is expecting Godeau!

GOULARD

Can it be true?

PIERQUIN

Speak.

ALL

Speak! Speak!

MERCADET (*with feeble deprecations*)

Why no, no—yet I do not know—I—Certainly, it is possible that some day or other he may return from the Indies with some—considerable fortune—. (*In a decided tone*) But I give you my word of honor that I don't expect Godeau here to-day.

VIOLETTE (*excitedly*)

Then it must be to-morrow!—Gentlemen, he expects him to-morrow!

GOULARD (*in a low voice to the others*)

Unless this is some fresh trick to gain time and ridicule us—

PIERQUIN (*aloud*)

Do you think it might be?

GOULARD

It is quite possible.

VIOLETTE (*in a loud tone*)

Gentlemen, he is fooling us.

MERCADET (*aside*)

The devil he is! (*Aloud*) Come, gentlemen, we had better
be starting.

GOULARD

I swear that—(*The rumbling of carriage wheels is heard.*)

MERCADET (*aside*)

At last! (*Aloud*) Oh, heavens! (*He lays his hand upon,
his heart.*)

A POSTILLION (*outside*)

A carriage at the door.

MERCADET

Ah! (*Falls back on a chair near the table.*)

GOULARD (*looking through the pane of glass above the
mantel*)

A carriage!

PIERQUIN (*doing the same*)

A post-chaise!

VIOLETTE (*doing the same*)

Gentlemen, a post-chaise is at the door.

MERCADET (*aside*)

My dear De la Brive could not have arrived at a better
moment!

GOULARD

See how dusty it is!

VIOLETTE

And battered to the very hood! It must have come from
the heart of the Indies, to be as battered as that.

MERCADET (*mildly*)

You don't know what you are talking about, Violette!
Why, my good fellow, people don't arrive from the Indies
by land.

GOULARD

But come and see for yourself, Mercadet; a man has stepped
out—

PIERQUIN

Enveloped in a large pelisse—do come—·

MERCADET

No—pardon me.  The joy—the excitement—I—

VIOLETTE

He carries a chest.  Oh! what a huge chest!  Gentlemen,
it is Godeau!  I recognize him by the chest.

MERCADET

Yes—I was expecting Godeau.

GOULARD

He has come back from Calcutta.

PIERQUIN

With a fortune.

MERCADET

Of incalculable extent!

VIOLETTE

What have I been saying?  (*He goes in silence to Mercadet
and grasps his hand.  The two others follow his example, and
then all the creditors form a ring round Mercadet.*)

MERCADET (*with seeming emotion*)

Oh!—gentlemen—my friends—my dear comrades—my
children!—

## SCENE SEVENTH.

THE SAME PERSONS AND MME. MERCADET.

MME. MERCADET (*entering from the left*)
Mercadet! my dear!

#### MERCADET

It is my wife. I thought that she had gone out. She is going to ruin everything!

#### MME. MERCADET

My dear!—I see that you don't know what has happened?

#### MERCADET

I? No, I don't—if I—

#### MME. MERCADET

Godeau is returned.

#### MERCADET

Ah! You say? (*Aside*) I wonder if she suspects—

#### MME. MERCADET

I have seen him—I have spoken to him.—It was I who saw him first.

#### MERCADET (*aside*)

De la Brive has won her over!—What a man he is! (*To Mme. Mercadet, low*) Good, my dear wife, good! You will be our salvation.

#### MME. MERCADET

But you don't understand me, it is really he, it is—

MERCADET (*in a low voice*)

Hush! (*Aloud*) I must—gentlemen—I must go and welcome him.

MME. MERCADET

No—wait, wait a little, my dear; poor Godeau has overtaxed his strength—scarcely had he reached my apartment when fatigue, excitement and a nervous attack overcame him—

MERCADET

Really! (*Aside*) How well she does it!—

VIOLETTE

Poor Godeau!

MME. MERCADET

"Madame," he said to me, "go and see your husband. Bring me back his pardon; I do not wish to see him face to face, until I have repaired the past."

GOULARD

That was fine.

PIERQUIN

It was sublime.

VIOLETTE

It melts me to tears, gentlemen, it melts me to tears.

MERCADET (*aside*)

Look at that! Well! There's a woman worth calling a wife! (*Taking her by the hand*) My darling—Excuse me, gentlemen.—(*He kisses her on both cheeks. In a low voice*) Things are going on finely.

MME. MERCADET (*in a low voice*)

How lucky this is, my dear! Better than anything you could have fancied.

MERCADET

I should think so. (*Aside*) It is very much better. (*Aloud*)
Go and look after him, my dear. And you, gentlemen, be
good enough to pass into my office. (*He points to the left.*)
Wait there till we settle our accounts. (*Mme. Mercadet goes
out.*)

GOULARD

I am at your service, my friend—

PIERQUIN

Our excellent friend.

VIOLETTE

Friend, we are at your service.

MERCADET (*supporting himself half-dazed against the table*)

What do you think?—and people said that I was nothing
but a sharper!

GOULARD

You? You are one of the most capable men in Paris.

PIERQUIN

Who is bound to make a million—as soon as he has a—

VIOLETTE

Dear M. Mercadet, we will give you as much time as you
want.

ALL

Certainly.

MERCADET

That is a little late—but gentlemen, I thank you as heartily
as if you had said it yesterday morning. Good-day. (*In a
low voice to Goulard*) Within an hour your stock shall be
sold—

GOULARD

Good !

MERCADET (*in a low voice to Pierquin*)

Stay where you are.   (*All the others enter the office.*)


PIERQUIN

What can I do for you?

---

## SCENE EIGHTH.

MERCADET AND PIERQUIN.


MERCADET

We are now alone.   There is no time to lose.   The stock of
Basse-Indre went down yesterday.   Go to the Exchange, buy
up two hundred, three hundred, four hundred—Goulard will
deliver them to you—

PIERQUIN

And for what date, and on what collateral?

MERCADET

Collateral?   Nonsense!   This is a cash deal; bring them to
me to-day, and I will pay to-morrow.

PIERQUIN

To-morrow?

MERCADET

To-morrow the stock will have risen.

PIERQUIN

I suppose, considering your situation, that you are buying
for Godeau.

MERCADET

Do you think so?

PIERQUIN

I presume he gave his orders in the letter which announced his return.

MERCADET

Possibly so.—Ah! Master Pierquin, we are going to take a hand in business again, and I guess that you will gain from this to the end of the year something like a hundred thousand francs in brokerage from us.

PIERQUIN

A hundred thousand francs!

MERCADET

Let the stock be depressed below par, and then buy it in, and—(*handing him a letter*) see that this letter appears in the evening paper.—This evening, at Tortoni's, you will see an immediate rise in the quotations. Now be quick about this.

PIERQUIN

I will fly. Good-bye. (*Exit.*)

---

## SCENE NINTH.

MERCADET, THEN JUSTIN.

MERCADET

How well everything is going on, when we consider our recent complications! When Mahomet had three reliable friends (and it was hard to find them) the whole world was his! I have now won over as my allies all my creditors, thanks to the pretended arrival of Godeau. And I gain eight days, which means fifteen, with regard to actual payment. I shall buy three hundred thousand francs' worth of Basse-Indre before Verdelin. And when Verdelin asks for some of that stock, he will find it has risen, for a demand will have raised it above the current quotation, and I shall make at one stroke six hundred thousand francs. With three hundred thousand I will pay my creditors and show myself a Napoleon of finance. (*He struts up and down.*)

#### JUSTIN (*from the back of the stage*)

Sir—

#### MERCADET

What is it—what do you want, Justin?

#### JUSTIN

Sir—

#### MERCADET

Go on! Tell me.

#### JUSTIN

M. Violette has offered me sixty francs if I will let him speak with M. Godeau.

#### MERCADET

Sixty francs. (*Aside*) He fleeced me out of them.

#### JUSTIN

I am sure, sir, that you wouldn't like me to lose such a present.

#### MERCADET

Let him have his way with you.

#### JUSTIN

Ah! sir, but—M. Goulard also—and the others—

#### MERCADET

Do as you like—I give them over into your hands. Fleece them well!

JUSTIN

I'll do my best. Thank you, sir.

MERCADET

Let them all see Godeau. (*Aside*)  De la Brive is well able
to look after himself. (*Aloud*)  But, between ourselves, keep
Pierquin away. (*Aside*)  He would recognize his dear friend,
Michonnin.

JUSTIN

I understand, sir. Ah! here is M. **Minard.** (*Exit.*)

---

## SCENE TENTH.

### MERCADET AND MINARD.

MINARD (*coming forward*)

Ah, sir!—

MERCADET

Well, M. Minard, and what brings you here?

MINARD

Despair.

MERCADET

Despair?

MINARD

M. Godeau has come back; and they say that you are now a
millionaire!—

MERCADET

Is that the cause of your despair?

MINARD

Yes, sir.

### MERCADET

Well, you are a strange fellow!—I disclose to you the fact of my ruin and you are delighted. You learn that good fortune has returned to me and you are overwhelmed with despair! And all the while you wish to enter into my family!—Yet you act like my enemy—

### MINARD

It is just my love that makes your good fortune so alarming to me; I fear all the while that you will now refuse me the hand—

### MERCADET

Of Julie? My dear Adolphe, all men of business have not put their heart in their money-bags. Our sentiments are not always to be reckoned by debit and credit. You offered me the thirty thousand francs that you possessed—I certainly have no right to reject you on account of certain millions. (*Aside*) Which I do not possess!

### MINARD

You bring back life to me.

### MERCADET

Well, I suppose that is true, but so much the better, for I am very fond of you. You are simple, honorable. I am touched, I am delighted. I am even charmed. Ah! Let me once get hold of my six hundred thousand francs and—(*Sees Pierquin enter*) Here they come—

*SCENE ELEVENTH.*

THE SAME PERSONS, PIERQUIN AND VERDELIN.

MERCADET (*leading Pierquin to the front of the stage without perceiving Verdelin*)

Is it all right?

PIERQUIN (*in some embarrassment*)
It is all right. The stock is ours.

MERCADET (*joyfully*)
Bravo!

VERDELIN (*approaching Mercadet*)
Good-day!

MERCADET
What! Verdelin—

VERDELIN
I find out that you have bought the stock before me, and that now I shall have to pay very much higher than I expected; but it is all right, it was well managed, and I am compelled to cry, "Hail to the King of the Exchange, Hail to the Napoleon of Finance!" (*He laughs derisively.*)

MERCADET (*somewhat abashed*)
What does he mean?

VERDELIN
I'm only repeating what you said yesterday—

MERCADET
What I said?—

PIERQUIN
The fact of it is, Verdelin does not believe in the return of Godeau—

MINARD
Ah, sir!

MERCADET
Is there any doubt about it?

VERDELIN (*ironically*)
Doubt about it! There is more than doubt about it. I at

once concluded that this so-called return was the bold stroke
that you spoke of yesterday.

### MERCADET

I—(*Aside*) Stupid of me!

### VERDELIN

I concluded that, relying upon the presence of this fictitious
Godeau, you made purchases with the idea of paying on the
rise, which would follow to-morrow, and that to-day you have
actually not a single sou—

### MERCADET

You had imagined all that?

### VERDELIN (*approaching the fireplace*)

Yes, but when I saw outside that triumphal post-chaise—
that model of Indian manufacture,—and I realized that it was
impossible to find such a vehicle in the Champs-Elysées, all
my doubts disappeared and—But hand him over the bonds,
M. Pierquin!

### PIERQUIN

The—bonds—it happens that—

### MERCADET (*aside*)

I must bluff, or I am lost!— (*Aloud*) Certainly, produce
the bonds.

### PIERQUIN

One moment—if what this gentleman has said is true—

### MERCADET (*haughtily*)

M. Pierquin!

### MINARD

But, gentlemen—M. Godeau is here—I have seen him—I
have talked with him.

MERCADET (*to Pierquin*)

He has talked with him, sir—

PIERQUIN (*to Verdelin*)

The fact of it is, I have seen him myself.

VERDELIN

I don't doubt it!—By the bye, on what vessel did our friend Godeau say he arrived?

MERCADET

By what vessel?—It was by the—by the *Triton*—

VERDELIN

How careless the English newspapers are. They have published the arrival of no other English mail packet but the *Halcyon*.

PIERQUIN

Really!

MERCADET

Let us end this discussion. M. Pierquin—those bonds—

PIERQUIN

Pardon me, but as you have offered no collateral, I would wish—I do wish to speak with Godeau.

MERCADET

You shall not speak with him, sir. I cannot permit you to doubt my word.

VERDELIN

This is superb.

MERCADET

M. Minard, go to Godeau—Tell him that I have obtained an option on three hundred thousand francs' worth of stock, and ask him to send me—(*with emphasis*)—thirty thousand francs for use as a margin.  A man in his position always has such a sum about him.  (*In a low voice*) Do not fail to bring me the thirty thousand.

### MINARD

Yes, sir.  (*Goes out, through the right.*)

### MERCADET (*haughtily*)

Will that satisfy you, M. Pierquin?

### PIERQUIN

Certainly, certainly.  (*To Verdelin*)  It will be all right when he comes back.

### VERDELIN (*rising from his seat*)

And you expect that he will bring thirty thousand francs?

### MERCADET

I have a perfect right to be offended by your insulting doubt; but I am still your debtor—

### VERDELIN

Bosh!  You have enough in Godeau's pocket-book wherewith to liquidate; besides, to-morrow the Basse-Indre will rise above par.  It will go up, up, till you don't know how far it will go.  Your letter worked wonders, and we were obliged to publish on the Exchange the results of our explorations by boring.—The mines will become as valuable as those of Mons—and—your fortune is made—when I thought I was going to make mine.

### MERCADET

I now understand your rage.  (*To Pierquin*)  And this is the origin of all the doubtful rumors.

VERDELIN

Rumors which can only vanish before the appearance of
Godeau's cash

---

## SCENE TWELFTH.

THE SAME PERSONS, VIOLETTE AND GOULARD.

GOULARD

Ah! my friend!

VIOLETTE (*following him*)

My dear Mercadet!

GOULARD

What a man this Godeau is!

MERCADET (*aside*)

Fine!

VIOLETTE

What high sense of honor he has!

MERCADET (*aside*)

That's pretty good!

GOULARD

What magnanimity!

MERCADET (*aside*)

Prodigious!

VERDELIN

Have you seen him?

VIOLETTE

Of course, I have!

PIERQUIN

Have you spoken to him?

GOULARD

Just as I speak to you. And I have been paid.

ALL

Paid!

MERCADET

Paid? How—how have you been paid?

GOULARD

In full. Fifty thousand in drafts.

MERCADET (*aside*)

That I can understand.

GOULARD

And eight thousand francs net, in notes.

MERCADET

In bank-notes?

GOULARD

Bank-notes.

MERCADET (*aside*)

It is past my understanding. Ah! Eight thousand!—
Minard might have given them, so that now he'll bring me
only twenty-two thousand.

VIOLETTE

And I—I, who would have been willing to make some reduc-
tion—I have been paid in full!

MERCADET

All! (*In a low voice to him*) I suppose in drafts?

VIOLETTE

In first-class drafts to the amount of eighteen thousand francs.

MERCADET (*aside*)

What a fellow this De la Brive is!

VIOLETTE

And the balance, the other twelve thousand—

VERDELIN

Yes—the balance?

VIOLETTE

In cash. Here it is. (*He shows the bank-notes.*)

MERCADET (*aside*)

Minard won't bring me more than ten.

GOULARD (*taking a seat at the table*)

And this very moment he is paying in the same way all your creditors.

MERCADET

In the same way?

VIOLETTE (*taking a seat at the table*)

Yes, in drafts, in specie, and in bank-notes.

MERCADET (*forgetting himself*)

Lord, have mercy upon me! (*Aside*) Minard will bring me nothing at all.

VERDELIN

What is the matter with you?

MERCADET

Me?—Nothing—I—

## *SCENE THIRTEENTH.*

THE SAME PERSONS AND MINARD, FOLLOWED BY CREDITORS.

MINARD

I have done your errand.

MERCADET (*trembling*)

And you—have brought me—a few—bank-notes?

MINARD

A few bank-notes?—Of course. M. Godeau wouldn't let me even mention the thirty thousand francs. (*Goulard and Violette rise. Minard stands before the table, surrounded by creditors.*)

MERCADET

I can quite understand that.

MINARD

"You mean," he said, "a hundred thousand crowns; here are a hundred thousand crowns, with my compliments!" (*He pulls out a large roll of bank-notes, which he places on the table.*)

MERCADET (*rushing to the table*)

What the devil! (*Looking at the notes*) What is all this about?

MINARD

The three hundred thousand francs.

PIERQUIN

My three hundred thousand francs!

VERDELIN

The truth for once!

MERCADET (*astounded*)

Three hundred thousand francs!—I see them!—I touch them!—I grasp them!—Three hundred thousand—where did you get them?

MINARD

I told you he gave them to me.

MERCADET (*with vehemence*)

He!—He—! Who is he?

MINARD

Did not I say, M. Godeau?

MERCADET

What Godeau? Which Godeau?

MINARD

Why the Godeau who has come back from the Indies.

MERCADET

From the Indies?

VIOLETTE

And who is paying all your debts.

MERCADET

What is this? I never expected to strike a Godeau of this kind.

PIERQUIN

He has gone crazy! (*All the other creditors gather at the back of the stage. Verdelin approaches them, and speaks in a low voice.*)

VERDELIN (*returning to Mercadet*)

It's true enough! All are paid in full!

## MERCADET

Paid?—Every one of them?—(*Goes from one to the other and looks at the bank-notes and the drafts they have.*)  Yes, all settled with—settled in full!—Ah!  I see blue, red, violet! A rainbow seems to surround me.

## SCENE FOURTEENTH.

THE SAME PERSONS, MME. MERCADET, JULIE (*entering at one side*) AND DE LA BRIVE (*entering at the other.*)

## MME. MERCADET

My friend, M. Godeau, feels himself strong enough to see you all.

## MERCADET

Come, daughter, wife, Adolphe, and my other friends, gather round me, look at me.  I know you would not deceive me.

## JULIE

What is the matter, father?

## MERCADET

Tell me (*seeing De la Brive come in*) Michonnin, tell me frankly—

## DE LA BRIVE

Luckily for me, sir, I followed the advice of madame—otherwise you would have had two Godeaus at a time, for heaven has brought back to you the genuine man.

## MERCADET

You mean to say then—that he has really returned!

## VERDELIN

Do you mean to say that you didn't know it after all?

MERCADET (*recovering himself, standing before the table touching the notes*)

I,—of course I did. Oh, fortune, all hail to thee, queen of monarchs, archduchess of loans, princess of stocks and mother of credit! All hail! Thou long sought for, and now for the thousandth time come home to us from the Indies!—Oh! I've always said that Godeau had a mind of tireless energy and an honest heart! (*Going up to his wife and daughter*) Kiss me!

### MME. MERCADET (*in tears*)

Ah! dear, dear husband!

### MERCADET (*supporting her*)

And you, what courage you have shown in adversity!

### MME. MERCADET

But I am overcome by the happiness of seeing you saved—wealthy!—

### MERCADET

But honest!—And yet I must tell you my wife, my children—I could not have held out much longer—I was about to succumb—my mind always on the rack—always on the defensive—a giant might have yielded. There were moments when I longed to flee away—Oh! For some place of repose! Henceforth let us live in the country.

### MME. MERCADET

But you will soon grow weary of it.

### MERCADET

No, for I shall be a witness in their happiness. (*Pointing to Minard and Julie.*) And after all this financial traffic I shall devote myself to agriculture; the study of agriculture will never prove tedious. (*To the creditors*) Gentlemen, we will continue to be good friends, but will have no more business transactions. (*To De la Brive*)  M. de la Brive, let me pay back to you your forty-eight thousand francs.

### DE LA BRIVE
Ah! sir—

### MERCADET
And I will lend you ten thousand more.

### DE LA BRIVE
Ten thousand francs?  But I don't know when I shall be able—

### MERCADET
You need have no scruples; take •them—for I have a scheme—

### DE LA BRIVE
I accept them.

### MERCADET
Ah!  It is one of my dreams.  Gentlemen (*to the creditors who are standing in a row*)  I am a—creditor!

### MME. MERCADET (*pointing to the door*)
My dear, he is waiting for us.

### MERCADET
Yes, let us go in.  I have so many times drawn your attention to Godeau, that I certainly have the right to see him. Let us go in and see Godeau!

### *Final Curtain.*

# INDEX

# THE COMÉDIE HUMAINE

## INDEX

THE COMÉDIE HUMAINE as arranged by Balzac is a curious ex-
ample of subdivision and inter-subdivision. It is composed of some
eighty-eight separate stories which, however, are connected—nearly
all of them—with the general scheme of the Comédie. This scheme
embraces six Scenes and two Studies, as follows:
Scenes from Private Life.
Scenes from Provincial Life.
Scenes from Parisian Life.
Scenes from Political Life.
Scenes from Military Life
Scenes from Country Life.
Philosophical Studies
Analytical Studies.
The above Scenes or Studies, in turn, are divided into groups includ-
ing stories which the author desired to connect as intimately as
possible. The stories themselves are liable to subdivision, being
made up possibly of two or more narratives strung together on the
slightest thread under some general title. As an example of this
may be cited "The Thirteen," a book composed of three distinct tales,
—"Ferragus," "The Duchesse de l angeais," and "The Girl With the
Golden Eyes."
Granted that a story were entirely coherent in plot, it was not
always or often suffered to lie undisturbed by its restless author. It
was wrought upon, both internally and externally. Internally it
met with the frequent decapitation or addition of chapter heads.
Perchance all the chapters might be merged in one. Perchance some
incident lightly dwelt upon might reveal another situation for the

same actors; a budding process would begin, and thus a new story of the Comédie would be born.   Externally a story might be changed in title, in grouping, or even in its position in the Comédie; it might lose its identity entirely (in a reverse process to one described above) by being incorporated into another story, in the form of a chapter. All these operations might and did happen in the evolution of the Comédie, which fact explains the difficulty oftentimes experienced in locating tales by the titles given in the earlier French editions; also for the varying number of stories accredited to the Comédie.

The present edition does not give the original grouping in absolute order; this was not possible in a given number of volumes of uniform size.   The original grouping has never been considered vital—the author himself was constantly changing it, up to the very day of his death.   Nevertheless, the arrangement as finally left by him has been maintained in so far as mechanical convenience would permit. And for those who desire to follow the Balzacian scheme, or to consider a story in relation to its group-mates and the general plan, these Indices have been prepared, showing:   (1) Alphabetical Index of stories and their position in the accompanying edition; (2) Titles of Volumes; (3) Original Balzac Scheme.—J. WALKER McSPADDEN, Publisher's Editor.

# ALPHABETICAL INDEX

THE STORIES CONSTITUTING THE COMEDIE HUMAINE, AND
THEIR POSITION IN THE ACCOMPANYING
EDITION

·

# TITLES OF VOLUMES

# THE BALZAC PLAN

## OF THE COMÉDIE HUMAINE

The form in which the Comédie Humaine was left by its author, with the exceptions of *Le Député d'Arcis* (incomplete) and *Les Petits Bourgeois*, both of which were added, some years later, by the Édition Définitive.

[On the right hand side is given the original French titles; on the left, their English equivalents. Literal translations have been followed, excepting a few instances where preference is shown for a clearer or more comprehensive English title.]

## COMÉDIE HUMAINE

### SCENES FROM PRIVATE LIFE

#### (*Scènes de la Vie Privée*)

##### BOOK 1.

| | |
|---|---|
| AT THE SIGN OF THE CAT AND RACKET, | *La Maison du Chat-qui-Pelote.* |
| The Ball at Sçeaux, | *Le Bal de Sçeaux.* |
| The Purse, | *La Bourse.* |
| The Vendetta, | *La Vendetta.* |
| Madame Firmiani, | *Mme. Firmiani.* |
| A Second Home, | *Une Double Famille.* |

##### BOOK 2.

| | |
|---|---|
| DOMESTIC PEACE, | *La Paix du Ménage.* |
| The Imaginary Mistress, | *La Fausse Maîtresse.* |
| A Study of Woman, | *Étude de femme.* |

Another Study of Woman,       *Autre étude de femme.*
La Grande Bretêche,        *La Grande Bretêche.*
Albert Savarus,         *Albert Savarus.*

## BOOK 3.

LETTERS OF TWO BRIDES,     *Mémoires de deux Jeunes Mariées.*
A Daughter of Eve,       *Une Fille d'Ève.*

## BOOK 4.

A WOMAN OF THIRTY,     *La Femme de Trente Ans.*
The Deserted Woman,     *La Femme abandonnée.*
La Grenadière,        *La Grenadière.*
The Message,         *Le Message.*
Gobseck,         *Gobseck.*

## BOOK 5.

A MARRIAGE SETTLEMENT.     *Le Contrat de Mariage.*
A Start in Life,        *Un Début dans la vie.*

## BOOK 6.

MODESTE MIGNON,      *Modeste Mignon.*

## BOOK 7.

BÉATRIX,        *Béatrix.*

## BOOK 8.

HONORINE,        *Honorine.*
Colonel Chabert,       *Le Colonel Chabert.*
The Atheist's Mass,      *La Messe de l'Athée.*
The Commission in Lunacy,   *L'Interdiction.*
Pierre Grassou,       *Pierre Grassou.*

## Book 16.

| | |
|---|---|
| Lost Illusions:—I., | *Illusions Perdues:—I.,* |
| The Two Poets, | *Les Deux Poêtes,* |
| A Distinguished Provincial at Paris. Part 1, | *Un Grand homme de province à Paris*, 1re *partie.* |

## Book 17.

| | |
|---|---|
| Lost Illusions:—II., | *Illusions Perdues:—II.,* |
| A Distinguished Provincial at Paris. Part 2, | *Un Grand homme de province,* 2e *p.* |
| Eve and David, | *Ève et David.* |

## SCENES FROM PARISIAN LIFE

### (*Scènes de la Vie Parisienne*)

## Book 18.

| | |
|---|---|
| Scenes from a Courtesan's Life: | *Splendeurs et Misères des Courtisanes:* |
| Esther Happy, | *Esther heureuse,* |
| What Love Costs an Old Man, | *A combien l'amour revient aux vieillards,* |
| The End of Evil Ways, | *Ou mènent les mauvais Chemins.* |

## Book 19.

| | |
|---|---|
| Vautrin's Last Avatar,* | *La dernière Incarnation de Vautrin.* |
| A Prince of Bohemia, | *Un Prince de la Bohème.* |
| A Man of Business, | *Un Homme d'affaires.* |
| Gaudissart II., | *Gaudissart II.* |
| The Unconscious Humorists, | *Les Comédiens sans le savoir.* |

* The fourth and final part of " Scenes from a Courtesan's Life."

*This book is not numbered, inasmuch as it was included after Balzac's death.

COMÉDIE HUMAINE

### SCENES FROM POLITICAL LIFE

(*Scènes de la Vie Politique*)

#### BOOK 26.

| | |
|---|---|
| THE GONDREVILLE MYSTERY, | *Une Ténébreuse Affaire.* |
| An Episode Under the Terror, | *Un Episode sous la Terreur.* |

#### BOOK 27.

| | |
|---|---|
| THE SEAMY SIDE OF HISTORY: | *L'Envers de l'Histoire Contemporaine:* |
| Madame de la Chanterie, | *Mme. de la Chanterie,* |
| Initiated, | *L'Initié.* |
| Z. Marcas, | *Z. Marcas.* |

#### BOOK 28.

| | |
|---|---|
| THE MEMBER FOR ARCIS,* | *Le Député d'Arcis.* |

### SCENES FROM MILITARY LIFE

(*Scènes de la Vie Militaire*)

#### BOOK 29.

| | |
|---|---|
| THE CHOUANS, | *Les Chouans.* |
| A Passion in the Desert, | *Une Passion dans le désert.* |

### SCENES FROM COUNTRY LIFE

(*Scènes de la Vie de Campagne*)

#### BOOK 30.

| | |
|---|---|
| THE COUNTRY DOCTOR, | *Le Médecin de Campagne.* |

#### BOOK 31.

| | |
|---|---|
| THE COUNTRY PARSON, | *Le Curé de Village.* |

*Though not included until after the author's death, its exact position had been previously indicated.

The Ruggieri's Secret,          *La Confidence des Ruggieri*
The Two Dreams,                 *Les Deux Rêves.*

### Book 38.

LOUIS LAMBERT,                  *Louis Lambert.*
The Exiles,                     *Les Proscrits.*
Seraphita,                      *Séraphita.*

### ANALYTICAL STUDIES.

### Book 39.

THE PHYSIOLOGY OF MARRIAGE,     *Physiologie du Mariage.*

### Book 40.

PETTY TROUBLES OF MARRIED       *Petite Misères de la Vie*
    LIFE,                           *Conjugale.*

The above list comprises the entire *Human Comedy*, but in addition to the same there are included in this New Saintsbury Balzac:

### I.  THE DRAMAS (2 volumes).

VAUTRIN,                        *Vautrin.*
QUINOLA'S RESOURCES,            *Les Ressources de Quinola.*
THE STEP-MOTHER,                *La Maratre.*
MERCADET,                       *Mercadet.*
PAMELA GIRAUD,                  *Pamela Giraud.*

### II.  A REPERTORY OF THE HUMAN COMEDY (1 volume).

In which the various appearances of the personages in the novels are reduced to a biographical dictionary.